Macunaíma
The Hero Without Any Character

By Mário de Andrade

Translated from the Portuguese
by Carl L. Engel

KING TIDE
PRESS

Philadelphia, Pennsylvania

Macunaíma

Translation and additional text
copyright © 2023 by Carl L. Engel

First published by King Tide Press, 2023
King Tide Press is a registered trade name of
King Tide LLC, Philadelphia, Pennsylvania

ISBN 979-8-9851497-3-9 ebook
ISBN 979-8-9851497-2-2 pbk.

Cover designed by Alejandro B.

CONTENTS

Introduction		v
Macunaíma: The Hero Without Any Character		1
I.	Macunaíma	1
II.	Maturity	11
III.	Ci, Mother of the Forest	25
IV.	Boiúna Moon	35
V.	Piaimã	49
VI.	The Francesa and the Giant	67
VII.	Macumba	83
VIII.	Vei, the Sun	99
IX.	Letter to the Icamiabas	111
X.	Pauí-Pódole	131
XI.	Old Ceiuci	143
XII.	The Tico-Tico, the Chupim, and the Injustice Of Men	167
XIII.	Jiguê Gets Lice	179
XIV.	The Muiraquitã	191
XV.	Oibê's Guts	207
XVI.	Uraricoera	223
XVII.	Ursa Major	243
	Epilogue	259
About the Authors		263
About the Translator		269
Acknowledgments		271
References		273

INTRODUCTION

In 1898, Theodor Koch-Grünberg, a twenty-nine-year-old anthropologist from the small town of Grünberg, Germany, made his first trip to South America, where he participated in an expedition to find the source of the Rio Xingú, a tributary to the Amazon River that winds from the south through densely forested lowlands. In 1903, he went on a second expedition to the Rio Japurá and Rio Negro, which are northern tributaries that flow into the Amazon from Colombia and Venezuela. For some of this time, he lived among the Baniwa tribe, and he wrote about his experience in the book *Zwei Jahre unter den Indianern. Reisen in Nord West Brasilien, 1903-1905* ("Two Years among the Indians: Travels in Northwest Brazil, 1903-1905"), which he published in 1910, after his return to Germany.

In 1911, he returned to Brazil to begin what would become his most important expedition. From the city of Manaus on the Amazon River, he traveled up the Rio

Branco to Mount Roraima, where he lived among the Pemón people and documented their myths and legends. Then, he continued his journey up the Rio Negro until he crossed through the natural Casiquiare canal system to the Rio Orinoco in Venezuela. In 1923, he published the Pemón people's myths and legends in the book *Vom Roraima zum Orinoco: Ergebnisse einer Reise in Nordbrasilien und Venezuela in den Jahren 1911-1913* ("From Roraima to Orinoco: Findings from a Journey in North Brazil and Venezuela in the Years 1911-1913").

In *Vom Roraima zum Orinoco*, Koch-Grünberg described a character named Makunaima, the "Stammeshero" ("tribal hero"), who is credited with creating all of the animals and fish that the Pemón people hunt and catch. Depending on the tribe, the legend of Makunaima also featured his brothers, Zigé and Ma'nape. In the Pemón language, "Makunaima" means "the big villain" and, consistent with this name, the stories of Makunaima concern his mischievous antics and the consequent trouble from which he must escape. Makunaima also had a supernatural ability to turn people and animals into rocks, which he sometimes did in anger, but usually just as a prank. In contrast with his attitude towards other people, he had a fondness for birds, which always kept him company.

Not only did Koch-Grünberg describe the myths and legends of Makunaima in general terms, but he also recorded many of them in substantial detail. The stories tend to draw inspiration from Makunaima's ability to transform himself and others. For example, Koch-Grünberg recounts a tale in which Makunaima tries to make a fishing hook out of wax, but it isn't strong enough for catching fish. So, he transforms himself into a fish and steals a hook from a fisherman. When the fisherman announces that he is going across the mountains to "the land of the English" (*i.e.*, British Guyana) to buy a new hook, Makunaima and his brother Zigé turn themselves into crickets and hide in the fisherman's basket to join him for the trip.

Most of the stories aren't so lighthearted, however, and feature Makunaima's impulsive and reckless sexuality, as well as his disregard for others. Even as a boy, we're told, Makunaima cajoled his mother into ordering his sister-in-law to take him for walks in the woods, where, on every one of their excursions, he would turn into a man and have sex with her. In another tale, Makunaima sleeps with Zigé's wife and casts a spell to move Zigé's hut and garden to the top of a high mountain. When Zigé nearly dies of starvation, Makunaima takes pity on him and returns the hut to its rightful place. He continues to ridicule Zigé for growing thin, however, and continues his affair with his sister-in-law. This rivalry is the foundation of another tale in which Makunaima turns a leaf into a stingray, and Zigé turns a vine into a poisonous snake, in an escalation of revenge pranks.

Makunaima's main antagonist in these adventures is a man-eating giant named Piai'ma. In one story, the giant traps the hero in a hunting snare and seals him inside a box, and the hero frees himself by repeating a magic spell which he'd overheard the giant recite. In another, Makunaima imitates the call of the giant, who arrives, shoots the hero with a blowgun, drags him away, and chops him up into pieces for soup. Ma'nape follows the trail to Piai'ma's house, where there is a deep hole in which the giant drops his victims to eat them with his wife at the bottom. There, Ma'nape kills Piai'ma and his wife with their own magic potion. He then reassembles the body parts of his brother and revives him.

Mário de Andrade was a thirty-year-old journalist and piano instructor living in São Paulo when, in 1923, he began studying German under the tutelage of Frau Else Schöler Eggbert and Fräulein Käthe Meiche-Blosen. In 1926, he read *Vom Roraima zum Orinoco*, which he discussed in letters to friends in the months and years immediately thereafter. In 1928, he published *Macunaíma*, in which he retold the Makunaima myths and legends, adding characters and events from Brazilian history and culture, and some fictional episodes of his own.

That Andrade was able to take these Pemón folk tales and transform them into something new and quintessentially Brazilian is certainly an accomplishment which merits recognition. Except that's not what Andrade claimed to have done. Rather, he published *Macunaíma* as an entirely original work, without giving credit to the Pemón people for creating the stories or to Koch-Grünberg for recording them. Instead, he simply copied the stories, changed the spellings of the characters' names, and called them his own. (References are made in footnotes throughout this translation to these instances of copying.) Perhaps to account for the structural difficulty of creating a cohesive work from a collection of plagiarized short stories, he characterized the book as a "rhapsody," rather than a novel. For this, maybe the most brazen theft in the history of modern literature, he was immediately catapulted to literary stardom in Brazil. It wasn't until 1931, when he was confronted publicly by Amazonian folklorist Raymundo de Moraes, that he admitted to copying from *Vom Roraima zum Orinoco*. But by then it was too late; Andrade had already become a literary giant. Since his death in 1945, he has appeared on Brazil's currency and gives his name to São Paulo's central library.

This is not to say that Andrade's version is entirely unoriginal, or unworthy of its place in the canon of Brazilian literature. Indeed, the language that he used to tell the stories was itself a substantial contribution to Portuguese letters. Andrade wrote *Macunaíma* in colloquial Brazilian Portuguese, which was a revolutionary departure from the scholarly and formal style that was popular at the time. Although this work seeks faithfully to preserve the colloquial style of Andrade, this contribution to Portuguese is largely lost in translation because English and Portuguese have evolved on separate timelines and from different origins. The contribution of Mark Twain's *Adventures of Huckleberry Finn* to English letters is a close analogue.

Apparent to all readers, however, will be Andrade's contributions to the Modernist movement. Perhaps foremost, he reconstructs Makunaima into a character who is representative of modern Brazil, by subverting the features of the prototypical hero of European literature: a privileged or noble birthright, a superior moral character, and an inclination to defend the community. Although Andrade's version, *i.e.*, "Macunaíma" (respelled in Portuguese), has a privileged birth position and possesses magical qualities, he is a "hero without any character," and acts only in his own self-interest. Andrade changes Macunaíma's race to a combination of the three races of colonial Brazil, giving him black skin, an Amerindian mother, and transforming him into a white man later in the story.

Andrade also includes several original episodes scattered among the Pemón legends. Indeed, the second half of the book includes a journey by Macunaíma to São Paulo, which is entirely the creation of the author. There, he participates in a Candomblé religious ceremony, a blend of Roman Catholic and African rites which is thoroughly Brazilian, and rails against the mechanization of the big city. Ultimately, the depravity of the residents and the commotion of industrialization become too much for Macunaíma to bear, and he flees. His cynical rejection of modernity was, in 1928, still somewhat novel, and was brought to the story entirely from the imagination of Andrade.

But perhaps most importantly, Andrade introduced a universe of Pemón gods and legends to the Brazilian people, and invited them to incorporate these myths into their own culture by blending them with familiar folktales, historical figures, and traditions. Like the titular protagonist, Andrade thereby performed an almost supernatural transformation, turning something uniquely Pemón into a story that is quintessentially Brazilian. And similar is the intent of this translation: to introduce these Brazilian stories of Macunaíma to a new audience, but with credit to the Pemón for creating them and to Theodor Koch-Grünberg for first recording them for publication.

Carl L. Engel
Philadelphia
January, 2023

I
MACUNAÍMA

Deep in the virgin forest, Macunaíma, the hero of our people, was born. At a moment when a hush had fallen so profound that one could hear the murmur of the Uraricoera, a Tapanhuman woman gave birth to the ugly child.[1] Although born of an indigenous woman, he was black with dark skin, and was the son of the god who brings fear in the night. This is the child whom they called Macunaíma.

Even as a small boy, he did outrageous things. For the

---

[1] The Uraricoera River is a small, remote river in the north of Brazil, near its borders with Guyana and Venezuela. Tapanhumas are a fictional tribe of Andrade's creation with a name reminiscent of tribes of the Tupi people, such as the Tupinambás and Temiminós, who are indigenous to Brazil. The Tupi are considered distinct from the Caribe nation, to which the Pemón creators of the original Makunaima folktales belong, but there is genetic and linguistic evidence of at least some ancient contacts between the groups.

first six years of his life, he barely spoke a word. If he were prodded to speak, he would shout "Ai, what a drag!" and wouldn't say anything else. He used to sit in the corner of his hut atop a paxiuba table and survey the work of the others, usually his two brothers: Maanape, already an old man, and Jiguê, in the prime of life.[2] To entertain himself, Macunaíma chopped the heads off saúvas.[3] He spent his days lying around, but if he saw a coin on the ground, he would toddle over to pick it up. He also would get up whenever his family went to bathe naked in the river together. There, he dove under the water, and the women let out cheerful cries at the guaiamums they said must be living at the bottom.[4] In the village, if a girl approached Macunaíma to cuddle, he would put his hands on her goods, and she would run away. As for the men, he spat in their faces. He respected the elders, however, and frequently participated in the murua, the poracê, the torê, the bacorocô, the cucuicogue, and all of the other religious dances of the tribe.

Whenever he went to bed, he would forget to pee

---

[2] A paxiúba is a species of palm tree with long, thin branches. Koch-Grünberg spelled the brothers' names Ma'nápe and Žigé. (Please refer to the Introduction for background on German anthropologist Theodor Koch-Grünberg and his ethnographies about the Pemón people which inspired Andrade to write this novel.)

[3] Saúvas, also known as leaf-cutter ants, feed on leaves and grass and thrive in areas with few trees, making them a formidable agricultural pest.

[4] Guaiamums are land crabs that do not live underwater, but rather in deep burrows dug in the ground that extend to the groundwater. The reader can decide if the women are making a joke.

before climbing into his little hanging bassinet. As his mother's hammock hung directly below him, the hero released a stream of hot piss onto the old woman every night, which kept the mosquitoes far away. Then he fell asleep and kicked his legs in the air as he dreamed of obscenities and extreme debauchery.

When the women met to chat in the middle of the day, the topic was always the hero's antics. They laughed in approval, saying, "The boy's thorns are already sharp." At a religious ceremony, King Nagô gave a speech in which he warned the tribe that the hero was intelligent.[5]

When Macumaima turned six, they gave him a rattle that was filled with water, and after he drank from it, he began to talk like everyone else. He begged his mother to drop the cassava root she was grinding on her grater, and to take him for a walk in the forest.[6] His mother didn't want to go, however, because she couldn't put down the cassava. So, Macunaíma threw a tantrum for the entire day and continued crying into the night. The next day, he fixed his left eye on his mother and waited for her to start working. Once she did, he begged her to drop the basket she was weaving out of soft guarumá branches, and to take him for a walk in the forest.[7] His mother didn't want to go, however, because she couldn't put down the basket.

---

[5] "Nagô" is a name for Yoruba people.

[6] Cassava (also known as "manioc" or "yuca") is a starchy tuber that is a staple source of carbohydrates for the people of the Amazon, who have been farming the plant for thousands of years.

[7] Guarumá is plant with long thin branches, the fibers of which are commonly used by indigenous peoples to weave baskets and other items.

She asked her daughter-in-law, Jiguê's wife, to take the boy instead.

Jiguê's wife was a nice, young woman named Sofará. She approached reluctantly. But this time, Macunaíma behaved himself and didn't put his hands on her goods. Sofará carried the little toddler on her back until they found themselves at the foot of an aninga growing at the edge of a river.[8] The current was stilled by fronds of javari that had fallen onto the surface as the water paused to consider a harmonious channel between them.[9] In the distance was the beauty of biguás and biguatingas soaring across a gap between the trees.[10] The young woman laid Macunaíma on the riverbank, but he immediately threw a tantrum because of all of the ants there! He begged her to take him to the top of a hill nearby in the forest, and she did. As soon as she sat the little boy among the dried tiririca, tajá, and trapoeraba that had fallen to the forest floor, he transformed instantly into a handsome prince.[11] They lay together for a long time.

When they returned to the village, Sofará acted like she was exhausted from having carried the boy on her back over such a long distance. It was really because she and the hero had fooled around for hours. As soon as she laid Macunaíma in a hammock, Jiguê came back from fishing and saw that his wife hadn't done any work. Jiguê was annoyed, and after he checked himself for ticks, he let her

---

[8] An aninga is a leafy plant that grows in the shallow waters of riverbanks.

[9] Javari is a species of palm.

[10] Biguás and biguatingas are aquatic birds related to pelicans.

[11] Tiririca, tajá, and trapoeraba are common ground-covering plants.

have it. Sofará endured the beating without saying a word.

Jiguê didn't suspect anything, however, and after attacking his wife, he sat and braided rope out of fibers from curauá fronds.[12] He hadn't paid attention to what his wife and brother were doing, because he'd found fresh tapir tracks and was focused on setting a snare to trap the animal.[13] Macunaíma asked his brother for some threads of curauá fiber, but Jiguê replied that they weren't a child's toy. Macunaíma wailed through the night, making it impossible for anyone to sleep.

The next day, Jiguê woke up early to set his snare and, sensing that the boy was sad, said, "Good morning to everyone's favorite."

But Macunaíma shut himself in a pantry and sulked.

"Don't you want to talk to me?" asked Jiguê.

"I'm upset."

"Why?"

Macunaíma asked for curauá threads again. Jiguê looked at him with hate burning in his eyes and ordered his wife to find some threads for the boy, which she did. Macunaíma thanked her and left to ask the tribal mystic to braid a rope for him, and to blow a big plume of tobacco smoke onto it.

When everything was ready, Macunaíma asked his mother to put aside her fermenting cachiri and to take him for a walk in the forest.[14] The old woman couldn't leave her work, but Jiguê's wife cunningly told her mother-in-

---

[12] A curauá is a shrub similar to a pineapple plant.

[13] A tapir is an herbivorous mammal with a body similar to that of a pig, and a short prehensile nose trunk.

[14] Cachiri is an alcoholic drink made from fermented cassava juice.

law that she was "at her service." Before long, she was in the forest with the boy on her back.

When he was laid among the dried carurus and sororocas that lined the forest floor, the little boy grew into a handsome prince.[15] He told Sofará to wait a moment and he would come back to fool around with her. Then, he went to the tapir's watering hole to set a snare. When they returned from their tryst, it was late in the evening, and Jiguê had already returned from setting a trap of his own where he'd seen the tapir tracks. His wife had done no work. Jiguê was furious and, before he checked himself for ticks, beat her severely. Sofará endured the thrashing with patience.

The next morning, as the dawning sun was still cresting the forest canopy, Macunaíma woke everyone up with a terrible wail, crying that they all needed to – they just had to! - check the watering hole for the animal that Jiguê was hunting! Nobody believed him, however, and everyone started their work for the day.

Macunaíma was annoyed and asked Sofará to take him on a quick trip to the watering hole to check the trap. The young woman did so, and when she returned, she told everyone that there was a massive tapir caught in the snare and it was already dead. As the whole tribe went to look for the beast, they pondered the little boy's intelligence. When Jiguê showed up with his empty curauá snare, he found everyone dragging the tapir and joined to help them. But when it was time to butcher the kill, he didn't give even a single piece of meat to Macunaíma, only tripe. The hero swore revenge.

The next day, Macunaíma asked Sofará to take him for

---

[15] Carurus and sororocas are common leafy ground-cover plants.

a walk, and they stayed in the forest until nightfall. As soon as the boy had touched the dried leaves of the forest floor, he turned into a seductive prince. They fooled around. After they'd finished three times, they ran to the edge of the forest, teasing each other along the way. There, after they poked each other, they tickled each other, and after they rolled in the sand, they burned like a fire fueled by straw. They could barely stop fooling around.

Macunaíma picked up a copaíba branch and hid behind a piranheira.[16] When Sofará came running past, he hit her on the head. The blow struck with so much force that she fell at his feet and convulsed with laughter. She grabbed one of his legs. Macunaíma moaned with pleasure and tightened his grip on the thick branch. The young woman bit the big toe off his foot and swallowed it. Macunaíma cried with joy and painted tattoos on her body with the blood that sprayed from his foot. He flexed his muscles, lifted himself onto a trapeze of vines, and scurried to the tallest branch of the piranheira. Sofará clambered after him. The branch was thin and bent and swayed under the prince's weight. When Sofará met him at the top, they fooled around again, balancing high in the air. After they finished, Macunaíma wanted to do even more vulgar things with her. He moved to bend her over but was unable to do so because the branch broke and they both plummeted for what felt like an eternity, until they crashed to the forest floor.

After the hero collected his wits, he searched all around

---

[16] Copaíbas and piranheiras are species of large tree. Piranheiras grow next to rivers and have branches that extend down into the water. Their fruit and seeds are eaten by piranhas and other fish, which is the origin of their name.

for the young woman, but she was nowhere to be seen. He was looking up in the trees when, from a branch hanging low overhead, the silence was broken by a terrifying roar that sounded like a puma. The hero crumpled in fear and closed his eyes so he wouldn't have to watch himself become cat food. He heard a giggle and felt a gob of spit drop onto his chest. It was Sofará. He threw rocks at her. When she was wounded, she cried out and painted tattoos on him in a frenzy with the blood that sprayed from the cuts on her body. A stone struck the corner of her mouth and smashed three of her teeth. She jumped from the branch and – wham! – landed with a thud astride the belly of the hero. She wrapped him with her whole body and howled with pleasure. They fooled around again for hours.

The star Papacéia was already shimmering in the sky when the young woman returned to the village, pretending to be exhausted from carrying the boy on her back for so long.[17] Jiguê had grown suspicious, however, so he'd followed the pair into the forest, and had witnessed Macunaíma's transformation and everything that had happened afterward. Jiguê felt as though he'd been made a fool and was furious. He grabbed a rabo-de-tatu and confronted Macunaíma with the intention of beating the hero's ass.[18] The screaming was so loud that it shortened the length of the night, and entire flocks of

---

[17] Papacéia is a creation of Andrade, possibly named by combining "zilike-pupaí," which Koch-Grünberg reports is a Pemón name that means "star head," with "Guaraci" and "Jaci," who are the Tupi-Guarini sun and moon gods, respectively.

[18] A rabo-de-tatu (literally, an "armadillo tail") is a flat, leather whip shaped like its namesake.

birds were so struck with fear that they fell to the forest floor and turned to stone.

When Jiguê was too tired to pummel his brother any further, Macunaíma ran out to the pasture, chewed a cardeiro root, and came back.[19] Jiguê took Sofará to her father, then slept comfortably in his hammock alone.[20]

---

[19] A cardeiro is a kind of cactus that is used in traditional indigenous medicine.

[20] This story about Macunaíma turning into a grown man to sleep with Jiguê's wife in the forest, and Jiguê beating Macunaíma and stealing his tapir meat, is taken almost verbatim from a story that Koch-Grünberg called "Streiche des Makunaima" ("Antics of Macunaíma").

Macunaíma

II
MATURITY

Jiguê was considered a fool, so nobody was surprised when he grabbed a village girl by the hand one day and just made her his new wife. Her name was Iriqui. She always kept a live rat hidden in the curls of her hair and dressed elegantly. Each morning, she would paint her face with aruraúba and jenipapo, and brush half of an açaí across her lips to make them a vivid purple.[1] After that, she would rub her lips with juice from a limão-de-caiena to turn them bright red.[2] Then, Iriqui would drape herself in a cotton cloak on which were stripes of black and green

---

[1] Aruraúba is a shrub that produces bark used to make crimson dye. Jenipapo is a kind of tree that produces a fruit from which dark-blue dye is extracted.

[2] Limão-de-caiena ("Cayenne lemon") is a tree that produces a very acidic fruit used in the production of vinegar. It was introduced to South America from Asia at the port of Cayenne, French Guiana, in the early 1800s, which is the origin of its name.

painted with an aruraúba and some tatajubas, and would dab scented umiri oil on her head.[3] She was beautiful.

A while later, after everyone had eaten Macunaíma's tapir, famine struck the village. No one was able to catch any game. Not even a tatu-galinha![4] And when Maanape killed a boto for them to eat, the cunauru frog called Maraguigana, who was the father of all botos, glared in anger and summoned a flood that destroyed the cornfields.[5] The villagers ate everything they had, even the hardened black crusts from their cooking pots, and the bonfires no longer burned night and day, but only as needed to protect against the cold. There wasn't anything for the people to grill on them, not even one of the tiny pieces of dried meat that they used to bait fish.

Even so, Macunaíma wanted to have a little fun. He told his brothers that there were still plenty of fish to be caught – piabas, jujus, matrinxãs and jatuaranas, all of

---

[3] Tatajubas are trees that bear large oblong fruit with a green-orange color. An umiri is a kind of tree that produces seeds from which oil, which smells like olive oil, can be extracted.

[4] A tatu-galinha, literally a "chicken armadillo," and also known as a "nine-banded armadillo," is common to North and South America.

[5] Cunauru is a common name for the tree frog *Hyla venulosa*, which can eject a caustic and odorless secretion that causes blisters and removes the top layer of skin from a yard away. In the Pemón legends, "Kone'wo" is a mythical tree frog who hunts by sneaking next to his prey and shooting an arrow vertically into the air, thereby placing him in as much danger as his target and merging the roles of prey and predator. "Maraguigana" is a Tupi expression that means a spirit separated from its body. Botos are dolphins that are indigenous to the rivers and coastal waters of Brazil.

these fish from the river – and advised them to go beat timbó.[6]

"But I don't see any timbó around here," replied Maanape.

Macunaíma responded with a fib: "I saw a bunch of timbó in the grotto where the buried money is."

"Then come with us and show us where."

They all went to the grotto by the river. The banks there were treacherous, and the brothers couldn't quite tell where the land ended and the water began among all of the fallen mamoranas.[7] Maanape and Jiguê searched far and wide, until they were covered up to their teeth in mud, sinking – slurp! – into the clay hidden under the floodwaters. They finally jumped free from their holes, screaming with their hands on their butts, the instant some pesky candirus tried to swim between their cheeks.[8] Macunaíma laughed as he watched the idiocy of his two brothers looking for timbó. He pretended to search along with them but didn't take a single step and kept dry on higher ground. When his brothers passed nearby, he put his hands on his knees and let out a tired groan.

"Quit screwing around, boy!" one of them shouted.

---

[6] Piabas, jujus, matrinxãs, and jatuaranas are species of river fish which are commonly eaten by people along the Amazon River. Beating timbó is a method of fishing in which the fisher slaps the surface of the water with timbó vines, thereby releasing a toxin from the plant that numbs fish nearby and causes them to float to the surface of the water.

[7] Mamoranas are a kind of tree that grows in tidewaters.

[8] Candirus are little fish infamous for entering the urethras of people urinating in the river and releasing spikes to prevent removal. There are also tales of the fish entering rectums and vaginas.

Macunaíma sat on the riverbank and kicked the water to drive away a swarm of many different mosquitos: piuns, maruins, arurus, tatuquiras, muriçocas, meruanhas, mariguis, borrachudos, and even varejas, all of these mosquitos.[9]

In the evening, the brothers came to fetch Macunaíma. They were annoyed because they hadn't found even a single timbó vine. The hero filled with dread and, pretending not to know what had happened, asked them, "Did you find any timbó?"

"We didn't find anything!"

"Because I saw some timbó right here," said Macunaíma. "The timbó used to be human like us a long time ago. It saw that you were looking for it and disappeared, because the timbó used to be human like us."

The brothers were satisfied with the boy's intelligent explanation, and the three of them returned to their hut.

The next day, Macunaíma was irritated from being so hungry. He said to his old mother, "Ma, who could lift our house and put it on the hill on the other side of the river? Who could carry it? Close your eyes for a minute, old woman, and ask yourself this."

The old woman did so. Macunaíma asked her to keep her eyes closed for a while longer, and he moved their hut, marombas, arrows, picuás, sapicuás, casks, urupemas, and hammocks, everything they owned, from the forest onto the hill on the opposite side of the river.[10] When the old

---

[9] These are all species of mosquito found in the Amazon.

[10] A maromba is an elevated wooden platform built for livestock to climb during seasonal floods to keep dry. Picuás and sapicuás are large baskets that are carried by burros for transporting goods. An urupema is a sieve woven from plant fibers that is used for sifting cassava flour.

woman opened her eyes, everything was there, and there were also game animals, fish, fruitful banana trees, and more food than they could eat. After they were both full, she cut a banana from a tree.

"Forgive me for asking, Ma, but why'd you take a banana like that?"

"To give to your brother Jiguê and his beautiful wife Iriqui, and to Maanape, who are all suffering from hunger."

Macunaíma grew annoyed. He stewed for a minute before asking the old woman, "Ma, who could carry our house onto the hill on the other side of the river? Who could even lift it? Ask yourself that."

The old woman did so. Macunaíma asked her to close her eyes again and, when she did, he transported all of their possessions – everything – back to their original places in the dirty swamp. When the old woman opened her eyes, everything was back in its place near the huts of Maanape, Jiguê, and beautiful Iriqui, who were all were moaning from hunger.[11]

The old woman flew into a devilish rage. She grabbed the hero around the waist and carried him through the forest until they arrived at a clearing called the Wilderness of Judas, where they walked a league and a half inward, until they could no longer see the forest.[12] It was a vast plain, its flatness interrupted only by little bumps of distant cashew trees. Not even a guaxe interrupted the

---

[11] This episode in which Macunaíma moves his family's hut across the river and back is taken from the story "Streiche des Makunaima" ("Antics of Macunaíma") in *Vom Roroima zum Orinoco*.

[12] "The wilderness of Judas" is a Brazilian expression that means "the middle of nowhere."

solitude.[13] The old woman put the boy on the ground, where he wouldn't be able to grow any bigger. She said, "Your mother is going away now. Go get lost in the bushes over there. You can't grow anymore."

She disappeared in an instant. Macunaíma surveyed the vast expanse before him and felt as though he were about to cry. But there was nobody around to hear him, so he didn't. He mustered some courage and started down a trail, his bowed legs trembling along the way. He wandered around for a week, until he encountered Curupira, who was grilling meat with his dog, Papamel.[14] Curupira lived among the tucunzeiros and was known for asking passing travelers for a cigarette.[15]

Macunaíma said to him, "Grandfather, can you give me some of that meat?"

"Sure," Curupira said.

He cut some meat from the roasted leg and gave it to the boy, asking, "What are you doing on the plain, boy?"

"Just passing through."

"You don't say!?"

"It's true. I'm just passing through."

---

[13] A guaxe is a species of bird known for building bag-shaped nests that dangle from branches on trees with smooth trunks that are difficult for predators to climb.

[14] Curupira is a mythological demon, originating in Tupi folklore, who attacks forest travelers or torments them until they lose their way. Tupi people sometimes blazed trails over mountains to avoid forests where Curupira was believed to live. A papa-mel, also known as an irara or tayra, is a badger-like mammal that lives throughout South and Central America.

[15] A tucunzeiro is a species of palm that grows up to fifty feet and yields a fruit known as tucum which is a common food staple in Amazon communities.

He told Curupira about his mother's punishment for having been so mean to his brothers, and when he got to the part where he carried the house back to the swamp where there wasn't any game, he burst into laughter. Curupira watched him and grumbled, "You're no longer a little kid, boy. You're not a little kid. Grown-ups who do that kind of thing…"

Macunaíma thanked Curupira and asked him the way back to the Tapanhumas' village. Curupira wanted to eat the hero, so he gave misleading directions: "You go over there, young man, walk around that fat stick, break left, and then come back under my big coconuts."

Macunaíma went as directed, but when he arrived at the fat stick, he scratched his leg, mumbled, "Ai! What a drag!" and continued walking forward.

Curupira waited for a long time, but the boy never returned. So, the monster mounted the stag that he rode like a horse and, kicking it violently in the haunches to spur it onward, chased after him, screaming, "Flesh of my leg! Flesh of my leg!"

From inside the hero's belly, the meat responded, "What is it?"

Macunaíma quickened his pace and started running toward a caatinga, but Curupira was still gaining on him.[16] So, the boy looked for a place to hide.

"Flesh of my leg! Flesh of my leg!" shouted Curupira.

The meat answered again, "What is it?"

The boy was desperate. It was a fox's wedding day and the old woman Vei, who was the Sun, glistened on the droplets of rain, reflecting light as though it were a shower

---

[16] The caatinga is an arid brush forest in the northeast of Brazil that covers just over ten percent of the country's territory.

of golden corn.[17] Macunaíma crouched at a puddle, drank the muddy water, and vomited up the meat.

"Flesh of my leg! Flesh of my leg!" Curupira shouted again as he drew nearer.

"What is it?" responded the meat for the third time, now from the puddle. Macunaíma leapt into some bredos and escaped.[18]

When he was a league and a half ahead, he heard a voice singing slowly from behind an anthill: "The agouti's smoking can-na-bis..."[19]

He walked toward the voice and found an agouti sifting cassava flour through a tipiti.[20]

"Grandmother, can you give me some of that cassava to eat?" asked Macunaíma.

"Sure," the agouti said. She gave some cassava to the boy and asked, "What are you doing out here on the caatinga, my grandson?"

"Just passing through."

"Ah, is that so!?"

"It's true! I'm just passing through!"

Macunaíma laughed as he told the agouti about how he tricked Curupira. The agouti watched him and muttered, "A boy mustn't do that, my grandson. A boy mustn't do that. I'll beat your body until it matches your mushy

---

[17] A "fox's wedding day" is a Brazilian idiom for a sun shower. Vei is name of the Sun in the original Makunaima legends, as well.

[18] Bredos are a kind of flowering shrub.

[19] An agouti is a small, forest-dwelling rodent that is native to Central and South America.

[20] A tipiti is a long tubular basket in which cassava is squeezed by pulling both ends, like a finger trap.

brains."

The agouti grabbed a bowl of poisonous cassava juice and flung it at the boy, splashing him.[21] Macunaíma backed away, stunned, but was only able to keep his head free from the liquid; the rest of his body was soaked. The hero sneezed and collapsed to the ground. He felt himself growing stronger, until he became the size of his muscular brother. However, his head, which he'd kept dry, still bore the dopey and nauseating little face of a boy.

Macunaíma thanked the agouti for what she'd done and darted off to his tribe's village, singing all of the way. The night came like a beetle swarm, driving the ants into the ground and plucking the mosquitoes from the water. The warmth of home hung in the air. The old Tapanhuman woman heard the voice of her son in the hazy distance and was shocked. Macunaíma wore a sour expression and said to her, "Ma, I dreamed that my tooth fell out."

"This foretells the death of a parent," remarked the old woman.

"I know it well," responded Macunaíma. "The woman will live through only one more cycle of the sun, simply because she gave birth to me."

The next day, the brothers went fishing and hunting, the old woman worked in the field, and Macunaíma stayed with Jiguê's wife. He turned into a quenquém ant and nibbled on Iriqui to arouse her.[22] But the young woman

---

[21] Cassava contains hydrocyanic acid, which makes it poisonous to consume in its natural state. To be suitable for human consumption, its toxic juice must be squeezed out before it is cooked.

[22] Quenquém is a genus of ants that are abundant throughout South America, several species of which are considered

threw the quenquém far away. So, Macunaíma turned into a little urucum![23] The beautiful Iriqui collected the seeds and gave herself a complete make-over, painting her face and drawing symbols on her body. She became even more beautiful. Macunaíma turned back into a person so he could charm her, and soon moved into her hut.

When the brothers returned from the hunt, Jiguê noticed the switch in places. Maanape said to him that Macunaíma was now a man once and for all and had grown quite strong. Maanape was a sorcerer. Jiguê saw that the hut was full of food. There were pacovas, corn, cassavas, aluá, and cachiri; there were maparás and camorim fish, passionfruit, atas, abios, sapotes, and sapotilhas; there were venison paçocas, and fresh agouti meat; all of these delicious treats.[24] Jiguê decided that he wouldn't gain anything by fighting with his brother and

---

agricultural pests.

[23] Urucum is a species of tree known for producing yellow and orange seed pods that are used by indigenous peoples to make body paint, both as ornamentation and for protection against the sun and insects.

[24] A pacova is a kind of large banana. Aluá is a drink made by fermenting a mixture of corn flower, fruit peels, sugar, lemon juice, and water. A mapará is a kind of catfish. Camorim are a fish native to the coastal waters of Brazil and a common food staple. An ata is a species of tree that grows leaves and roots which are known to possess therapeutic properties, and which produces a fruit known for its laxative effect. An abio is an edible fruit with yellow skin and sweet pulp. A sapote is a soft, plum-like fruit. A sapotilha is an edible fruit with pulp that can be either yellow or the color of chocolate. Paçoca is grilled meat that is shredded, mixed with cassava flour, and cooked into cakes.

left beautiful Iriqui with him. Then, Jiguê sighed, checked himself for ticks, and slept comfortably in his new hammock.

The next day, after an early morning spent fooling around with the beautiful Iriqui, Macunaíma went out for a stroll. He passed through the enchanted kingdom of Pedra Bonita in Pernambuco.[25] Then, as he was arriving in the town of Santarém, he came across a doe that had just given birth.[26]

"I'll hunt it!" he said. Then, he chased the doe. She slipped away easily, but the hero managed to catch her little fawn as it couldn't quite walk yet. He hid behind a carapanaú and, poking the little fawn, made it bleat.[27] The doe went berserk. Her eyes bugged, and she froze where

---

[25] Pernambuco is a state on the east coast of Brazil. Between 1836 and 1838, a group of people gathered at a place called Pedro Bonita ("Beautiful Stone"), named after two towering boulders there, to await the second coming of a deity called Dom Sebastião. The group was forced by police to disperse after its leader, João Antonio dos Santos, upset the authorities by preaching that Dom Sebastião had revealed to him alone where his treasure was hidden. However, his brother-in-law, João Ferreira, reformed the group into a polygamous sect and declared himself king. In 1838, Ferreira proclaimed that it was necessary to carry out ritual human sacrifices to ensure the return of Dom Sebastião and his enchanted kingdom. Several members of the group volunteered themselves and their families for sacrifice and were killed. When news of the sacrifice reached the government, police were dispatched to quash the movement for good, killing Ferreira in the process.

[26] Santarém is a city on the Amazon River in the north of Brazil.

[27] A carapanaúba is a kind of tree with tall, thick trunks that are commonly harvested for timber.

she stood and snorted loudly. She came charging, stopped right in front of the tree, and called lovingly for her fawn. The hero shot an arrow through her breast. She fell and kicked for a bit, then splayed stiffly on the ground. The hero announced his victory. He approached the doe, looked her over, screamed, and fainted. It was the work of Anhanga.[28] It wasn't a doe at all; it was his own Tapanhuman mother whom Macunaíma had slain with the arrow and who lay dead, her entire body covered in scratches from the jacitaras and mandacarus of the forest.[29]

When the hero recovered from having fainted, he called for his brothers. The three of them cried for the entirety of the night watch, drinking oloniti and eating fish with cassava flour.[30] Early in the morning, they laid the body of the old woman in a hammock and went to bury her under a rock at a place called Father of Tocandeiras.[31]

---

[28] Anhangá is a Tupi deity known as the protector of the jungle and animals, who tormented human beings and had the ability to change form. In the mid-16th century, Jesuit missionaries ascribed devilish powers to Anhangá and used him as an antagonist character in plays written and performed to teach Tupi people Roman Catholic morality.

[29] A jacitara is a kind of palm shrub, and a mandacaru is a kind of cactus.

[30] Oloniti is an alcoholic beverage made from fermented cassava flour.

[31] In *Vom Roroima zum Orinoco*, Koch-Grünberg explains that, in the legends of Makunaima, the Pemón people considered the animal characters to represent their species and named them "father," or "pódole" in the Pemón language. Andrade borrows that naming convention throughout *Macunaíma*. A tocandeira is a species of stinging ant used by Caribe tribes in

Maanape, who was a sorcerer of the highest rank, engraved the epitaph. It looked like this:[32]

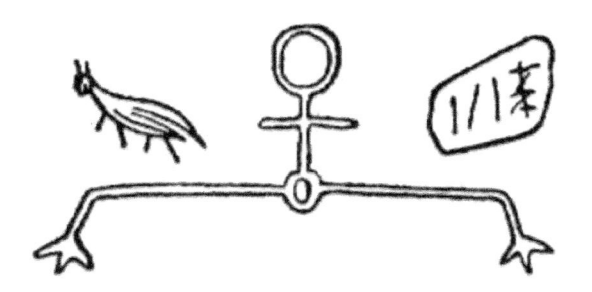

They fasted for the customary length of time, and Macunaíma spent the duration of the fast grieving heroically. The belly of the corpse continued to swell, and by the end of the seasonal rains, the grave site had grown into a gentle hill. When the rains were over, Macunaíma gave a hand to Iriqui, Iriqui gave a hand to Maanape, Maanape gave a hand to Jiguê, and the four of them went out into the world.

---

initiation rituals whereby participants endure the stinging of hundreds of ants held against their bodies in mesh baskets.

[32] This drawing is similar to Pemón symbols that Koch-Grünberg copied in Volume III of *Vom Roroima zum Orinoco*.

Macunaíma

III
CI, MOTHER OF THE FOREST

As the foursome followed a path through the forest far from any igapós or ponds, they found themselves suffering horribly from thirst.[1] There was not even an imbu plum to be seen anywhere nearby, and Vei, the Sun, burned between the branches that relentlessly lashed the travelers' backs.[2] As they marched, they sweated as though they were under a spell that had smeared their entire bodies with piquiá oil. Suddenly, Macunaíma stopped and broke the stillness of the night by waving his arms in alarm. The others froze. They didn't hear anything, but Macunaíma whispered, "Something is there."

The brothers left beautiful Iriqui between the giant roots of a samaúma, where she sat grooming herself, then they cautiously continued onward.[3] Their backs had been

---

[1] An igapó is a portion of forest that has been flooded by a river that has overflowed its banks.

[2] An imbu is one of few fruits that grows in the arid caatinga.

[3] A samaúma is a kind of large tree known for the enormous

lashed to Vei's satisfaction by the time Macunaíma, scouting a league and a half ahead, came upon a sleeping young woman. It was Ci, Mother of the Forest.[4] He saw that her right breast was small and shriveled up, and that she was a member of that tribe of isolated women who'd settled on the beaches of a lake called the Mirror of the Moon, which is fed from Nhamundá.[5] The woman was beautiful, with a body worn by a lifetime of sin and colored with jenipapo.

The hero threw himself on top of her so they could fool around. However, Ci didn't want to. She speared Macunaíma with her trident as he drew his pajeú.[6] They brawled intensely, and their screams echoed beneath the forest canopy, causing the little birds there to shrink in fear. The hero was taking a beating. A punch had already bloodied his nose, and Ci's trident had cut a deep wound on his rear end. The Icamiaban, however, didn't have a scratch, and every move she made painted the hero in more blood, as his dreadful screams caused the little birds

---

roots which buttress its massive trunk.

[4] The name "Ci" is likely derived from "Guaraci" and "Jaci," who are the sun and moon gods, respectively, in Tupi-Guarani mythology.

[5] Nhamundá is an area of northern Brazil where the mythological tribe of warrior women called the Icamiabas lived atop a sacred mountain. After defeating men in battle, they would purify themselves in a river called the Yaci Uara, which means "Mirror of the Moon" in the Tupi language.

[6] A pajeú is a long knife with a handle made of animal horn, and is named for the region of Pernambuco where it was first created.

to shrink even smaller with fear.[7] Finally, seeing yellow spots and unable to match the Icambian, the hero ran away and called for his brothers: "Help! Help! If you don't help me, I'm going to kill her!"

The brothers came and grabbed Ci. Maanape tied her arms behind her back, and Jiguê whacked her on the head with a mucuru.[8] The Icamiaban fell face-first into some ferns on the forest floor. After the Mother of the Forest was immobilized, Macunaíma approached and fooled around with her. There came a flock of jandayas, red macaws, tuins, curicas, parakeets, and parrots to salute Macunaíma, the new Emperor of the Virgin Forest.[9]

The three brothers continued onward with their new

---

[7] The Tupi word "icamiaba" means a woman without a husband, and was used in reference to tribes of bellicose, independent women living in villages with no men. During the exploration of the Amazon River by Francisco de Orellana in 1542, the group was attacked by these indigenous female warriors. The voyage chronicler, a Dominican friar named Fr. Gaspar de Carvajal, compared them to the Amazon warriors of Greek legend, thereby giving the river its colonial name.

[8] A mucuru is a redwood spear that was wielded by the chiefs of several indigenous Amazon tribes.

[9] "Jandaya" is a Tupi word that means "noisy caller," and has been used by Brazilian authors since the mid-19th century to refer generally to birds with "tropical" characteristics. "Tuin" is a Tupi word for a several species of parakeet. Curicas are small, green parrots with black heads and yellow collars. Koch-Grünberg describes in *Vom Roroima zum Orinoco* how Makunaima was fond of birds and kept them as company. This literary technique of listing different native birds (or animals, fish, plants, *etc.*) within the story is also borrowed from Koch-Grünberg's version of the legends.

companion. They crossed through the City of Flowers, bypassed the River of Bitterness, passed under the Waterfall of Happiness, walked the Road of Pleasures, and arrived at the Woods of My Dear, which was in the rocky hills of Venezuela. It was from there that Macunaíma ruled over the mysterious forests, while Ci commanded the raids of the women who wielded tridents.

The hero lived in tranquility. He spent his days laying in a hammock, killing tanoca ants, and sucking down frothy sips of pajuari.[10] Whenever he sang along to the plinking sounds of his cocho, the forest would resound with sweetness, lulling the snakes, ticks, mosquitos, ants, and evil spirits to sleep.[11]

In the night, Ci, bleeding from the melee and smelling of wood resin, came back and climbed into a hammock that she'd woven with strands of her own hair. The two fooled around and laughed with each other. They flirted together for a long time, enjoying each other's company. Ci smelled so strongly that Macunaíma grew light-headed.

"Wow! You sure smell, baby!" he cried with pleasure. He flared his nostrils and felt a vertigo so strong that sleep started to drip from his eyelids. The Mother of the Forest still wasn't satisfied, however, and taking advantage of the way that the hammock wrapped them together, she urged her companion to fool around some more. Dying of exhaustion and feeling like hell, Macunaíma fooled around only to build his reputation. But when Ci wanted to cuddle with him after she'd been satisfied, the hero sighed, "Ai,

---

[10] Pajuari is a beverage made from fermented açaí and is drank as a stimulant.

[11] A cocho is a Brazilian folk instrument that is in essence a viola with five strings.

what a drag!" and fretted. Then, he turned his back to her and fell right to sleep. But Ci wanted to fool around even more. She asked repeatedly, but the hero was fast asleep. So, the Mother of the Forest picked up her trident and poked him. Macunaíma woke up, laughing loudly and contorting away from the weapon's tickle.

"Don't do it! I beg you!"

"I'm doing it!"

"Let a man sleep, my dear."

"We're going to fool around."

"Ai, what a drag!"

They fooled around again.

One day, Ci found the Emperor of the Virgin Forest laying in a drunken mess after a days-long pajuari binge. She started fooling around with him, but in the middle of it, the hero forgot what he was doing.

"What is it, hero?"

"What is what!?"

"Can't you continue?"

"Continue what!?"

"Why, my little pet, we were just fooling around and you stopped right in the middle of it!"

"Ai! What a drag."

Macunaíma was so drunk that he could barely move. As he groped his companion's soft hair, he fell asleep happy.

To rouse him, Ci employed a sublime stratagem. She searched the forest for stinging nettles, and tingled the hero's chuí, as well as her own nalachítchi.[12] This made Macunaíma as ravenous as a hungry lion. Ci felt the same way. The two fooled around together for a long time in a

---

[12] Chuí and nalachítchi are slang words for penis and vagina, respectively.

binge of extraordinary passion.

The sleepless nights were even more joyful. When the burning stars poured an intolerably hot oil onto the earth, fire seemed to flow through the forest. Not even his flock of birds remained in their nests. Craning their necks uneasily, they flew out to a branch high above and, in the greatest miracle of this world, formed a black choir and sang to no end. The noise was tremendous, the powerful aroma and the heat even more so.

Macunaíma pushed the hammock, pitching Ci to the ground. She grew furious and climbed on top of him. They fooled around like this; then, as joy awakened within them, they invented new positions.

Not even six months passed before the Mother of the Forest gave birth to a crimson son. To mark the occasion, famous mixed-race people came from Bahia, Recife, Rio Grande do Norte, and Paraíba to give the Mother of the Forest a red bow, the color of evil, because now she was the master of the crimson chorus in all of the Christmas pageants.[13] Afterward, they left with pleasure and joy, dancing wildly, and followed by a motley band of soccer players, hustlers, schoolchildren, lovers, and troubadours, all of these golden boys. Macunaíma was resting for the customary month, but he refused to fast.[14] The little baby

---

[13] In Northeast Brazil, women performed Pastorais de Natal (what Americans call "Christmas pageants") in which the shepherdesses were divided into a crimson chorus led by a master ("mestra") and a blue chorus led by an anti-master ("contramestra").

[14] New fathers in many Amazonian tribes traditionally fasted after the birth of a child, keeping a diet free of certain prohibited foods, such as big fish and large game, because of a superstition that the consumption of these foods would harm

had a flat head, and Macunaíma flattened it even more by drumming on it every day as he told the infant, "Grow up quickly, my son, so you can go to São Paulo and make a lot of money."[15]

All of the Icamiabans were fond of the crimson boy, and they put all of the tribe's jewels into his first bath so he would always be rich. They sent someone to Bolivia to search for scissors, and slipped them, open, under his pillow, because otherwise Tutu Marambá would come and suck the baby's navel and Ci's toe.[16] Tutu Marambá arrived, saw the scissors, and was tricked by them: He sucked on the pivot pin of the scissors and left satisfied. Everyone directed their attention toward the infant. They sent someone to São Paulo to fetch those famous little shoes knitted by Dona Francisca de Almeida Leite Morais, and to Pernambuco for lace with patterns known as "Rose

---

the newborn's soul.

[15] When *Macunaíma* was published, in 1928, the city of São Paulo was in the midst of explosive growth, with the population quadrupling between 1890 and 1930 to nearly 900,000 people. During the 19th century, the city had become the point of convergence of several railroads built to facilitate the export of coffee. These railroads allowed immigrants to travel to the city with ease, and made it the natural location for industrial growth after the collapse of the coffee economy in the early 20th century. Although Rio de Janeiro was still Brazil's largest city and capital at the time, it was not undergoing the same rapid growth and industrialization as São Paulo.

[16] A tutu is a sort of bogeyman who appears in children's stories and lullabies. Tutu Marambá, also known as Tutu Marambaia, is one iteration. "Marambaia" is a nautical slang word for a sailor who prefers to live on land, *i.e.*, a "landlubber."

Macunaíma

of the Alps," "Flower of Guabiroba," and "For-you-I-suffer," woven by the hands of Dona Joaquina Leitão, better known as Quinquina Cancuda.[17] They filtered the best tamarind juice from the Sisters of Louro Vieira de Óbidos for the boy to swallow, to mask the taste of his roundworm medicine.[18] It was a happy life, and it was good!

But one day, a jucurutu landed on the emperor's hut and let out an ominous screech.[19] Macunaíma trembled with fear, which drove away the mosquitos, and he dipped into the pajuari to see if he could drive away his fear as well. He drank until he fell asleep and slept through the night. The Black Snake came and sucked all of the milk from Ci's healthy breast. Because none of the Icamiabans would sleep with Jiguê, the infant was without a wet nurse. So, the next day he continued to suck the breast of his mother until he exhaled a poisoned gasp and died.

They put the little angel in a funerary urn in the shape of a tortoise, to keep the boitatás from eating the corpse's eyes, and buried him in the very center of the village,

---

[17] Dona Francisca de Almeida Leite Morais is the aunt of the author, Mário de Andrade. Dona Joaquina Leitão, also known as Quinquina Cancuda, was a famous Brazilian lacemaker from the small coastal town of Maragogi. Lacemakers were a common subject of Brazilian poets and authors, and, like riverboat pilots and tribal shamans, have become archetypal characters in Brazilian literature.

[18] The Sisters of Louro Vieira were an order of Roman Catholic nuns who owned a pharmacy in the town of Óbidos on the Amazon River that was famous for selling sweets in the shape of flowers and fruits.

[19] A jucurutu is an amerindian word for several species of small tropical birds which some tribes regard as a bad omen.

accompanied by singing, dancing, and jugs of pajuari.[20]

At the end of the ceremony, Macunaíma's lover, still finely dressed, took from her necklace a famous muiraquitã, gave it to him, and climbed a vine up to the sky.[21] There, Ci turned into a star and, spending her time at leisure, now lives free from ants and dressed radiantly in light. She is Beta Centauri.[22]

The next day, when Macunaíma went to visit his son's grave, he saw that a little plant was growing from the burial plot. The villagers tended it with great care, and it grew into a guaraná.[23] With the crushed fruit of this plant, people cure a multitude of illnesses and refresh themselves in the heat of Vei, the Sun.

---

[20] A boitatá is a fiery snake of Brazilian folklore that has many eyes and protects fields from arsonists.

[21] A muiraquitã is a pendant of green jade carved in the shape of an animal that is usually worn as a necklace. Muiraquitãs are found among many of the tribes dwelling along the Amazon River. Jade is so rare in Brazil that ethnographers in the 19th century believed that muiraquitãs had been brought there by prehistoric immigrants from Asia, until a native source was eventually found.

[22] In the original Pemón legends, a frog named Kunawa climbs to the sky and becomes Beta Centauri.

[23] Guaraná is a vine which produces seeds that are a stimulant used in food and medicine.

Macunaíma

IV
BOIÚNA MOON

Early the next morning, as the hero pined for his eternally unforgettable companion, Ci, he pierced his lower lip and made the muiraquitã into a tembetá.[1] He felt as though he were going to cry. He immediately called for his brothers, said goodbye to the Icamiabas, and left.

They wandered through all of the forests over which Macunaíma now reigned. He received tributes in each one and was always accompanied by a flock of red macaws and jandayas. During the harsh nights, he climbed into an açaí palm with fruit as purple as his soul and imagined Ci's elegant figure in the sky. "Marvada!" he groaned.[2] He was suffering enormously – tremendously! – and for a long

---

[1] "Tembetá" is the Tupi word for an ornament worn in a lower-lip piercing.

[2] Marvada, also known as cachaça, is a liquor made from fermented sugarcane juice. Here, it is used as a term of endearment.

time he tried to summon the good spirits by singing canticles.

"Rudá, Rudá![3]
You who dry the rains,
who make the ocean winds
gust across my land.
Make the clouds drift away,
as my marvada glimmers
clear and steady in the sky!
And render into tranquility
all of the waters of the rivers,
so I can bathe in them,
and so I can fool around with my marvada,
reflected in the mirror of the water!"

After he finished the last song, he climbed down from the tree and cried, leaning on Manaape's shoulder. Jiguê, sobbing out of pity, billowed the fire in the hearth so the hero wouldn't feel cold. Maanape swallowed his tears and summoned Acutipuru, Murucututu, and Ducucu, all of these lords of sleep, with lullabies like this:[4]

"Acutipuru,
to sleep submit
Macunaíma
who's throwing a fit!"

He picked ticks off the hero's body and rocked him in

---

[3] Rudá is the Tupi god of love.

[4] Acutipuru, Murucututu, and Ducucu are creations of Andrade.

Macunaíma

his arms to calm him down until he fell fast asleep.

The next day, the three travelers continued their hike through the mysterious forests. Macunaíma was always followed by his retinue of red araras and jandayas.

After walking for a long time, when the dawn began to chase away the darkness of the night, they heard a girl crying far in the distance. They went to look for the source of the sound and walked a league and a half until they found a waterfall weeping endlessly. Macunaíma asked the waterfall, "What's going on!?"

"Go away!"

"Tell me what's going on."

The waterfall told him what had happened to her:

"Can't you see that I'm Naipi, Chief Mexô-Mexoitiqui's daughter?[5] My name means 'Little Flirt' in my language. I used to be a beautiful young woman, and all of the neighboring chiefs wanted to sleep in my hammock and to find out if my body was softer than an embirossu.[6] But whenever one of them came over, I would bite and kick him because I loved feeling his strength. None of them could keep up, and they all left in dour moods.

"My tribe was enslaved by the boiúna, Capei, who lived in a deep pit with a colony of sauvas.[7] When the ipês on

---

[5] Naipi and Chief Mexô-Mexoitiqui are creations of Andrade.

[6] An embirossu, also known as an embiruçu, is a deciduous tree that grows to a height of around eighty feet and is commonly found in southeastern Brazil.

[7] In the original Makunaima legends, Kapei is the name of an evil sorcerer who is also the moon. The Boiúna is a large mythological snake from Tupi legend which lives in rivers and capsizes boats. Its name means "black snake" in Tupi. "Capar"

the riverbank turned yellow with flowers each year, the boiúna would come to the village to choose a virgin girl to sleep with her in her cave full of skeletons.[8]

"Early one morning, as my body wept blood, yearning to feel a man's strength, an owl in the jarinas by my hut sang that Capei was coming to choose me.[9] The ipês on the riverbank shimmered yellow, and their flowers fell onto the trembling shoulders of a boy named Titçatê, one of my father's warriors.[10] A sadness descended like a horde of army ants upon the village and devoured everything until there was silence.

"As the old shaman was coaxing the night from its burrow once again, Titçatê gathered the flower petals around him and brought them to my hammock on my last night of freedom. Then, I bit Titçatê's wrist.

"Blood splashed from the bite, but Titçatê didn't run away. He groaned with lovesick rage and stuffed my mouth with flowers so I couldn't bite him anymore. Then, he jumped into the hammock, and I slept with him.

"After we fooled around like crazy among the spattering blood and ipê flowers, my victor hoisted me onto his shoulders, threw me into an igara that had been pulled ashore in a thicket of aningas, and darted toward

---

is a vulgar Brazilian term for castrate, and "capei" means "I castrated." The reader can decide whether Andrade's respelling of the character's name is meant to be a pun.

[8] Ipês are flowering trees that are widely distributed between Mexico and northern Argentina.

[9] Jarinas are a kind of palm that grows close to the rainforest floor.

[10] Titçatê is a creation of Andrade.

the wide Rio Zangado, fleeing the boiúna.[11]

"The next day, after the old shaman had put the night back in its hole again, Capei was searching for me and found the bloody hammock empty. She howled and darted after us. She was faster than us, and everyone nearby heard her howls. She kept drawing closer and closer until finally the boiúna's body began churning the waters of the Zangado.

"Faint and still bleeding from the bite on his wrist, Titçatê couldn't paddle any further and we couldn't escape. Capei caught me, spun me around, and put me to the test of the egg.[12] It worked and the boiúna saw that I'd already been with Titçatê.

"I was so angry; I wanted to die and take the world with me. I didn't know yet that she'd seen me on this rock, had thrown Titçatê onto the riverbank, and had transformed him into a plant. He's that one over there at the bottom! He's that beautiful mururê out there in the distance, with his limbs waving across the water at me.[13] His purple flowers are drops of blood from the bite that have curdled in the cold of my waterfall.

"Capei lives beneath me, forever wondering if I really fooled around with the boy. Well, I did. Since then, I've passed the time crying on this rock, and I'll continue grieving that I can no longer make love to my warrior, Titçatê, until the end of that which has no end."

---

[11] An igara is a canoe made from tree bark. The Rio Zangado is not a real river. "Zangado" means "angry" in Portuguese.

[12] The "test of the egg" was a virginity test promoted by the popular Brazilian physician and writer, Júlio Afrânio Peixoto, in the 1920s.

[13] A mururê is a kind of flowering tree.

Naipi stopped. Her tears dripped onto Macunaíma's knees and he sobbed and trembled. "If- if- if I'd been there when the boiúna appeared," he said, "I- I would've killed it!"

He heard a resounding howl and Capei, the boiúna, emerged from the water. Macunaíma rose to his feet, like a glistening statue of heroism, and advanced on the monster. Capei opened her throat wide and released a cloud of apiacás.[14] Macunaíma swatted wildly at the overwhelming swarm of wasps. The monster cracked a whip with tinkling little bells tied at the tail. But at that exact same moment, a tracuá ant bit the heel of the hero's foot.[15] He crouched down, distracted by the pain, and the whip's tail passed over him and lashed Capei's face. She howled again and charged at the thigh of Macunaíma, but he dodged her attack, grabbed a rock, and – clunk! – knocked off the beast's head.

Her body writhed in the current, as her head, with her doe eyes, rolled toward the avenger to kiss his feet in defeat. The hero was terrified and scampered into the thick forest with his brothers.

"Come here, siriri!" shouted the head.[16]

This spurred the brothers further along. They ran a league and a half before they looked back. Capei's head was still rolling after them. They ran until they were too fatigued to run any further, then climbed a bacupari along

---

[14] Apiacás are a kind of wasp infamous for their painful sting.

[15] A tracuá is a species of ant known for inhabiting abandoned termite nests.

[16] A siriri means a small-winged termite in some parts of Brazil, and a small bird in others.

the river to see if the head was still following them.[17] The head stopped at the base of the trunk and asked for bacuparis. Macunaíma shook the tree, and the head gathered the fruit from the ground, ate it all, then asked for more. Jiguê shook bacuparis into the water, but the head refused to enter. So, Maanape threw a piece of fruit with all of his strength, and while the head went after it, the brothers slid down the trunk, scraping their bellies along the way down. They sprinted away until, a league and a half ahead, they came across the house where the Bachelor of Cananéia lived.[18] The old geezer was seated in the doorway, reading profound manuscripts. Macunaíma asked him, "How's it going, Bachelor?"

"Not so bad, strange traveler."

"Catching some fresh air, no?"

"C'est vrai, as the French say."

"Well, so long, Bachelor. I'd stay and chat, but I'm a bit distracted."

Then, they scrambled onward again. They crossed the shell middens of Caputera and Morrete in one breath.[19]

---

[17] A bacupari is a kind of tree known for its orange fruit.

[18] Cananéia is a coastal town in the state of São Paulo. The Spanish explorer Diego Garcia mentioned in his memoirs that, in 1527, he encountered a Portuguese settler there living with "many sons-in-law." Garcia referred to him as the "Bachelor of Cananéia," likely because he was talkative. In the colloquial Castilian of Garcia's time, the word "bachelor" was used in the sense of "scholar" as a slang term for someone who talks too much. Modern historians believe that the "bachelor" likely was a member of Portuguese explorer Gonçalo Coelho's 1502 expedition, and was left behind purposely after having been convicted of a crime.

[19] Shell middens are mounds of fossilized shells left by

There was a Theatine shack just ahead.[20] They entered and shut the door tight. Then, Macunaíma realized that he'd lost the tembetá. He became desperate because it was the only thing that he had which held his memories of Ci. He wanted to leave to search for the stone, but his brothers didn't let him. It wasn't long before the head arrived and - wham! - slammed into the door.

"What was that?" asked one of the brothers.

"Open the door and let me in!"

But could an alligator open it? Neither would they! And the head wasn't allowed to enter. Macunaíma didn't know that the head was his servant and hadn't come to do him harm. The head waited for a long time, but after seeing that they still wouldn't open the door, she carefully considered what to do next. If she turned into water, the others would drink her; if she turned into a mosquito, they would swat her; if she turned into a train, she would be derailed; and if she turned into a river, they would put her on a map. She decided, "I'm going to become the Moon," and shouted, "Open the door, people! I want to grab some things!"

---

prehistoric people. Some shell middens grew over a period of a thousand years, having been built upon by multiple tribes over the centuries. Scholars are divided as to whether these mounds served a secondary purpose, such as to mark territory or fishing waters, or if they were simply the dumping grounds of nearby villages. Caputera and Morrete are towns in the south of Brazil, near São Paulo.

[20] The Theatines are an order of Roman Catholic priests who, like members of the Jesuit, Augustinian, and Dominican orders, have had an evangelical mission in Brazil throughout its history. Unlike these other orders, however, the Theatines focused their ministry on remote rural areas, rather than cities.

Macunaíma peaked through the crack and warned Jiguê, who was already opening the door, "She's loose!" This is where the expression "they're loose!" comes from, which means that a person isn't doing what's been asked of them. Jiguê closed the door again.

When Capei realized that they weren't going to open the door, she fell into deep despair and asked a tarantula if he would help her ascend to the sky.

"The Sun melts my thread," replied the giant spider.

So, the head asked the japims to help her, and they blocked the sun to make the area as dark as night.[21]

"Nobody can see my thread at night," said the giant spider.

The head fetched a calabash from the cold air of the Andes and said, "I'll pour a drop every league and a half, and the thread will whiten from the frost.[22] Let's go."

"So, off we go."

The spider started spinning thread on the ground. With the first breeze that blew, the light thread was lifted to the sky. The giant spider climbed up, and when he reached the end, he poured a bit of frost onto the riverbank below. And as the tarantula continued spinning thread that extended to the riverbank, everything below him turned white. The head shouted, "Goodbye, my people, because I'm going up to the sky!"

She began eating the thread to climb up to the vast expanse of the sky. The brothers opened the door and watched. Capei was ascending steadily.

---

[21] Japims are birds that are known for living in woven nests that hang from tree branches, and for singing imitations of other birds and animals.

[22] A calabash is a kind of gourd.

"Are you really going to the sky, head?"

"Umm." She couldn't open her mouth any further. An hour before dawn, Capei the boiúna arrived in the sky, fat from eating so much thread and blanched from the exertion. All of her sweat fell to Earth in droplets of fresh dew. Because the thread had been frosted, Capei was quite cold. Capei used to be the boiúna, but now her head is the Moon up there in the vast field of the sky.[23] Ever since that happened, tarantulas have preferred to spin their webs at night.

The next day, the brothers searched along the riverbank, but they still couldn't find the muiraquitã. They asked every living thing there: aperemas, marmosets, armadillos, teiús, and muçuãs from the land; tapiucabas, chabós, matinta pereras, woodpeckers, and aracuãs from the trees; and the japim bird and his companion, the marimbondo, in the air.[24] They asked the cockroaches in their camp, and the bird that cries "Taam!" and its mate that responds "Taim!" They asked the lizard that wanders wildly with the rat; the tambaquis, tucunarés, pirarucus, and curimatás in the river; and the pecaís, tapicurus, and

---

[23] In the Pemón legend, Kapei climbs a vine to the sky with his two daughters.

[24] Aperemas and muçuãs are kinds of turtle, teiús are a kind of lizard, tapiocabas and marimbondos are kinds of wasp, and chabós and aracuãs are kinds of bird. Matinta Perera is a figure from Brazilian folklore. She is an old woman who transforms into a bird, perches over the doorway of someone's house, and sings shrilly until the occupant promises a gift of coffee, tobacco, or fish. The next day, Matinta Perera returns to the house in the form of the old woman to collect the gift. If the occupant refuses to deliver the promised gift, a terrible misfortune will befall his household.

iererês on the beach.[25] They asked all of these creatures, but none of them had seen anything, and none of them knew anything. So, the brothers plodded along the road again, searching throughout the imperial domains. Their silence and desperation were ugly.

Occasionally, Macunaíma stopped to think about his marvada. Oh, how he longed for her! On one such occasion, time froze and he began to weep. Tears slid down the hero's baby-fat cheeks and anointed his hairy chest. He sighed and shook his little head, "What now, brothers?!" he cried. "My first love has no equal!"

They continued walking, and everywhere they went, the hero received tributes and was always followed by the motley flock of jandayas and red macaws.

One day, as Macunaíma was laying in the shade to wait while his brothers were fishing, the Negrinho do Pastoreio, to whom Macunaíma prayed daily, took pity on the cursed boy and decided to help him.[26] He dispatched

---

[25] Tambaquis, tucunarés, pirarucus, and curimatás are all species of fish found in the Amazon River. Tapicurus are a kind of bird related to pelicans, and irerês are aquatic birds related to ducks. The birds called "pecaís" seem to exist only in this novel, as there is no other mention of such a bird.

[26] The Negrinho do Pastoreio is a legendary figure popular in southern Brazil. The legend was first recorded in 1857 by Antonio Maria do Amaral Ribeiro, and several versions were published thereafter. In that version, the Negrinho do Pastoreio was the slave boy of a rancher who, by making the boy supply his own flour to feed himself each day and forcing him to sleep on anthills and dung heaps, treated him so poorly that the animals in the nearby stables provided him with tallow candles out of pity. In memory of the boy's suffering, a tallow candle would be lit and left near a dung heap or anthill. In a subsequent version of the legend, a rancher discovered that

a little uirapuru bird.²⁷ The hero soon heard a restless flutter, and the uirapuru landed on his knee. Macunaíma was annoyed and shooed the bird away. Not even a minute passed before he heard the noise again, and the little bird landed on his belly. Macunaíma didn't disturb it this time. The uirapuru clung to him, singing sweetly, and the hero could understand everything that it sang. It sang that Macunaíma was unhappy because he'd lost the muiraquitã on the riverbank when he was climbing the bacupari. But then it sang the lament of the uirapuru: that Macunaíma would never have any luck because a tortoise had already swallowed the muiraquitã, and the clam digger who picked up the tortoise had sold the green stone to a Peruvian merchant named Venceslau Pietro Pietra.²⁸ The new owner of the talisman had made a fortune, and had become a wealthy landowner in São Paulo, the grand city

---

one of his lambs was missing, and ordered one of his slaves, a little black boy ("negrinho" in Portuguese) to find it. When the boy was unable to do so even after searching all night, the rancher grew enraged and whipped the boy to death. To hide his crime, the rancher disposed of the body behind a giant anthill. The next day, the rancher was shocked to see the boy standing next to the anthill with the lost lamb. The boy dusted the ants and dirt from his body, ran away, and disappeared forever. From then on, people who'd lost something would leave a wad of tobacco and a lit candle stump in a pasture ("pastoreio") as an offering to the Negrinho do Pastoreio with the hope that he would assist in their search. Later versions were sanitized for schoolchildren, and feature the Virgin Mary, as the boy's godmother, assuring the reader that the boy went to heaven.

²⁷ An uirapuru is a kind of wren.

²⁸ Venceslau Pietro Pietra is a creation of Andrade.

licked by the Tietê Igarapé.[29]

The little uirapuru bird flew the figure of a letter in the air, and then disappeared. When the brothers returned from fishing, Macunaíma told them, "I was walking on the path, luring a brocket with bait, and I felt a chill run down my spine.[30] I reached behind me, and a gentle centipede crawled onto my hand and told me the whole truth."

Macunaíma recounted the whereabouts of the muiraquitã and told his brothers that he was inclined to go to São Paulo to find Venceslau Pietro Pietra, to recover the stolen tembetá.

"And may a rattlesnake build a bird nest if I don't find the muiraquitã! It would be great if you came with me, men. But if not, no company is better than bad company! I, however, have the mind of a toad, and when something gets in my head it stays there, as firm as a tree trunk. So off I go, if only to confirm the story of the little uirapuru bird – I mean the centipede!"

After the conversation, Macunaíma laughed out loud as he considered his fib about the little bird. Maanape and Jiguê decided to accompany the hero because he needed protection.

---

[29] An igarapé is a natural narrow channel between two river islands, or between a river island and the mainland. The Tietê is not actually an igarapé, but is a river. Nevertheless, Andrade calls it the "igarapé Tietê" throughout *Macunaíma*.

[30] A brocket is a kind of small deer.

Macunaíma

V
PIAIMÃ

Early the next morning, Macunaíma hopped into an ubá and soon arrived at the mouth of the Rio Negro, where he wanted to leave his conscience on the Isle of Marapatá.[1] He placed it at the very top of a mandacaru that was ten-meters high so it wouldn't become food for the saúvas. Then, he returned to the place where his brothers were waiting and, at the height of the day, the three headed toward the leftward edge of the Sun.

They suffered through countless obstacles on their journey: river rapids, gyres, currents, canyons walled with clay, virgin forests, and other marvels of the wilderness. Macunaíma and his two brothers were going to São Paulo, and the Araguaia facilitated their journey.[2] For all of his

---

[1] An ubá is a dugout canoe. The Rio Negro is a river that begins in Colombia and flows into the Amazon River near the city of Manaus. Marapatá is a small island at the confluence of the two rivers.

[2] The Rio Araguaia is a major river that flows from central

conquests and labors, the hero hadn't collected a single vintém, but he'd inherited the Icamiaban star's treasures hidden in the caves of Roraima.[3] Of these treasures, Macunaíma had set aside for the trip no less than forty-times-forty million bags of cocoa, the traditional currency. He calculated that he would need a fleet of boats to carry them. A force of igaras, two hundred lashed together, floated perfectly on the surface of the Araguaia in the shape of a broad arrow. Macunaíma stood at the point and scowled as he surveyed the city from afar. He ruminated on what he saw, gnawing the nails of his fingers, which were now covered in warts because he'd been pointing at Ci's star so often. The brothers paddled, and the mosquitos were driven away with every stroke that resounded in the dozens of connected igaras. He dumped a bunch of bags onto the surface of the river, leaving a wake of chocolate where camuatás, pirapitingas, dourados, piracanjubas, uarus-uarás, and bacus treated themselves.[4]

One day, the sun covered the three brothers in slick sweat, and Macunaíma decided to take a bath. It was impossible to do so in the river, however, because the piranhas were so voracious that, when pitched in battle over a piece of an injured comrade, they leapt in a frenzy more than a meter out of the water. Macunaíma saw

---

Brazil north toward the Atlantic Ocean.

[3] A vintém is an old coin worth twenty réis. Mt. Roraima is a large flat-topped mountain at the border of Brazil, Venezuela, and Guyana, which is known for containing a vast system of caves.

[4] Camuatás, pirapitingas, dourados, piracanjubas, uarus-uarás, and bacus are all species of fish.

Macunaíma

clearly, on a rock in the very middle of the river, a puddle in the shape of a giant's footprint. They pulled their boats onto the rock. The hero, after some hysterics on account of the cold water, got into the puddle and washed himself thoroughly. The water was enchanted, however, because the impression in the rock was an imprint of Sumé's big foot from when he walked around evangelizing about Jesus to the Brazilian Indians.[5] When the hero got out of his bath, his hair was light blond, his eyes were light blue, and the water had washed the black from his skin. Nothing remained that could identify him as a son of the black tribe of Tapanhumas.

Not quite understanding the miracle, Jiguê threw himself into Sumé's big footprint. The water was already opaque from the hero's blackness, however, so when Jiguê scrubbed himself like crazy, splashing water all over his body, he managed only to become the color of new bronze. Macunaíma took pity and consoled him: "Look, brother Jiguê, you didn't become white because there was already blackness in the water. But it's better to have a nasal voice than to be without a nose."

---

[5] Sumé is a legendary Tupi figure who dates back to at least the 16th century. According to legend, Sumé, a white man, appeared mysteriously and taught the natives agricultural techniques and methods for preparing cassava. He was killed after he raised the ire of the chiefs, then pulled the arrows from his body, and walked backward toward the sea. As he went, he left footprints in rocks along the way. Upon hearing the legend, early Jesuit missionaries propagated the idea that Sumé was St. Thomas the Apostle, who is believed to have traveled to India to spread the gospel. Subsequently, other Roman Catholic missionaries cast Sumé as a moralistic character in versions of the legend written to spread Christianity.

Maanape went to wash himself next, but Jiguê had splashed all of the enchanted water out of the footprint. There was only a little bit left at the bottom, so Maanape got wet only on the soles of his feet and the palms of his hands, and he remained a black son of the Tapanhumas. Only the palms of his hands and the soles of his feet were bronze from having washed in the holy water. Macunaíma took pity and consoled him: "Don't be upset, brother Maanape. Our Uncle Judas suffered worse!"[6]

There was the most beautiful view of the Sun from the rock, and the three brothers – one blond, one bronze, and the other black – were on their feet, naked together. All of the creatures of the forest stared in amazement. The jacarèuna, jacarètinga, jacaré-açu, and jacaré-ururau with yellow claws, all of these alligators fixed their eyes on the footprint from where the water had splashed out.[7] In the branches of the ingàzeiras, aningas, mamoranas, embaúbas, and riverside catauaris, all of the forty monkeys of Brazil, including capuchin monkeys, squirrel monkeys, howler monkeys, bugio monkeys, spider monkeys, wooly monkeys, and bearded sakis, watched and drooled with envy.[8] And the sabiás: The sabiàcia, sabiàpoca, sabiàúna, sabiàpiranga, and sabiàgonga, which refuses to share while eating, as well as the sabiá-barranco, sabiá-tropeiro, sabiá-

---

[6] According to the book Acts of the Apostles, Judas Iscariot bought a field with the silver he'd received for betraying Jesus to the authorities, where "fallen prone in the middle of it, he burst apart and all of his entrails were poured out."

[7] Jacarés are a category of reptiles that includes alligators and caimans, but not crocodiles.

[8] Ingàzeiras, mamoranas, and embaúbas are kinds of leafy trees, and catauaris are a kind of palm.

laranjeira, and sabiá-gute, all of these birds were astonished and forgot to end their trills, singing endlessly and in harmony.[9] Macunaíma hated it. He put his hands on his hips and shouted at the creatures, "What are you looking at!?" They all immediately dispersed back to their lives, and the three brothers continued along the trail.

When they entered the lands of the Tietê Igarapé, the bourbon coffee bean was in vogue and the traditional currency was no longer cacao, but was instead called arame, contos, contecos, milreis, borós, tostão, duzentorréis, quinhentorreis, cinqüenta paus, noventa bagarotes, pelegas cobres, xenxéns, caraminguás, selos, bicos-de-coruja, massuni, bolada, calcáreo, gimbra, siridó, bicha, and pataracos.[10] They therefore walked for an entire league and a half where nobody could buy anything for even twenty-thousand bags of cocoa. Macunaíma was very annoyed. To have to work, him, a hero… Dejected, he mumbled, "Ai! What a drag!"

He decided to abandon the enterprise and to return to their homeland where he was the emperor. But Maanape said, "Stop being such an aruá, brother![11] When a crab dies, the mangrove doesn't mourn its death! Don't get discouraged, damnit! I'll arrange everything."

When they arrived in São Paulo, Manaape put some treasure in a bag for buying food and, trading the rest at the São Paulo Commodities Exchange, earned about eighty reals. Maanape was a sorcerer.

---

[9] Sabiás are a category of several species of small passerine songbirds that includes robins.

[10] These are all slang words for money, like "bucks," "Benjamins," and "dough" in the United States.

[11] An aruá is a species of freshwater snail.

Eighty reals wasn't worth much, but the hero reflected intently and said to his brothers, "Be patient. This is definitely enough to get us started. He who wants a horse free of dirt travels on foot." The coins would be enough for Macunaíma to continue.

In the cold pit of night, the brothers came upon the grand city of São Paulo, strewn along the banks of the Tietê Igarapé. The imperial parrots shouted farewell to the hero, and the multi-colored flock returned to the forests up north. The brothers entered a cerrado full of inajás, ouricuris, ubussus, bacabas, mucajás, miritis, and tucumãs, all of which issued plumes of smoke instead of palms and coconuts.[12] All of the stars had descended from the white sky, and shimmered wet with drizzle throughout the city. Macunaíma remembered to look for Ci. Oh, he could never forget such a thing! The triple-mesh hammock that she'd arranged for their lovemaking was woven with her own hair and, as a result, she'd become known as a legendary weaver. Macunaíma roamed the city for a long time, but the streets and plazas were crowded with young women who were so white and radiant! Macunaíma moaned. As he brushed against the women, he murmured with delight, "My God! These little cassava daughters," lacking taste but so beautiful. Finally, he chose three of them. He fooled around with them in a strange hammock planted in the floor, in a longhouse taller than the Paranaguá.[13] Afterwards, because the hammock was so hard, he slept spread across the bodies of the women. The

---

[12] These are all varieties of palm tree.

[13] The Palácio do Paranaguá is a large government building that was constructed in 1907.

Macunaíma

night cost him four hundred bagarotes.[14]

What the hero saw there made him question everything that he'd known before he'd arrived in the city. He woke up to the shouts of the throngs in the streets below, scurrying between the horrid longhouses. And that devilish tamarin that carried him to the top of the hut where he slept...[15] What a world of beasts! What an absurd spectacle of snoring papões, mauaris, juruparis, sacis, and boitatás, in alleyways, in underground caves, on terraces carved into hillsides pocked with grottos where the people were the whitest shade of white, the cassava children![16] The hero questioned everything that he'd known.

The women, laughing, told him that the tamarin was not a monkey, but was a machine called an "elevator." They taught him that all of the chirps, roars, cries, snorts, grumbles, and rustlings were none of those things, but were klaxons, bells, whistles, and horns, and all of them were machines. The cougars were not cougars, but were called Fords, Hupmobiles, Chevrolets, Dodges, and Marmons, and were also machines. The anteaters,

---

[14] A bagarote is slang for a milréis note. A milreis is a unit of a thousand Brazilian reals ("réis" in Portuguese) that was common in periods of high inflation.

[15] A tamarin is a kind of small monkey.

[16] A papão is a generic monster or bogeyman invented to frighten children. Mauaris are invisible beasts who, according to Amazonian legend, steal people's souls. The jurupari is a Tupi god who treated the Tupis wickedly and was associated by Roman Catholic missionaries with the devil. Saci is a Brazilian mythical figure who is traditionally depicted as a mischievous black boy with one leg, a red cap on his head, and a pipe in his mouth. He is a master of deception and is known for playing tricks on people.

boitatás, inajás, and palm fronds of smoke were trucks, trams, trolleys, light-up billboards, clocks, headlights, radios, motorcycles, telephones, lampposts, smokestacks... They were all machinery and everything in the city was one big machine. The hero quietly studied it all. Occasionally, he shuddered, but would always go back to laying still, listening, focusing, and scheming in his haunted dreams. He felt a respect colored with envy for this goddess of robust strength, this magnificent Tupã, whom the cassava daughters called Machine, and who was a more impressive singer of amazing tones than even the Mãe D'água.[17]

He decided to go and fool around with the Machine so he could extend his empire over the cassava children. But the three women laughed heartily and said that this goddess was a big old lie, that there was no goddess, and that nobody fooled around with the Machine because it would kill them. The Machine wasn't a goddess. It didn't even possess the feminine qualities that the hero liked so much. It was made by men. By combing it with electricity, fire, water, wind, and smoke, these men had harnessed the forces of nature. But would an alligator believe it? Neither did the hero! He got out of bed, made a gesture - that one, yes! – of extreme disdain, slapping his left elbow under his right forearm and twirling his wrist for the three women, then left. In that instant, they say, he invented a

---

[17] "Tupã" is a Tupi word for thunder and lightning, which Jesuit missionaries understood to be a god. Owing to this confusion, legends of a god named "Tupã" began to circulate throughout Brazil. In Tupi mythology, the "Mother of Water" ("Mãe D'água" in Portuguese) is another name for the Boiúna. However, in colonial retellings of the legend, the "Mãe D'água" was changed to a mermaid and siren.

magnificent offensive gesture: the banana.

He went to live in a boarding house with his brothers. His mouth was full of thrush from that first night of São Paulan lovemaking. He groaned with pain, and there was no way to heal him until Maanape stole a tabernacle key and gave it to Macunaíma to suck. The hero sucked on it for a long time until he became fully healed. Maanape was a sorcerer.

Macunaíma spent the next week without eating or fooling around, and meditated on the cassava children's futile fight against the Machine. The Machine killed the men, but the men controlled the Machine... He was shocked that the cassava children were its owners, as they lacked the Machine's mystique, ambition, temperance, and strength, and he couldn't explain their misfortunes. This made him homesick, which lasted until, sitting on the balcony of a high-rise apartment with his brothers one night, he concluded, "The cassava children aren't winning against the Machine in this struggle, but it's not winning against them either. It's a draw."

He didn't offer any further insight because he still wasn't used to making speeches. However, he was entirely consumed by anguish – completely! – because the Machine ought to be a god. And the men weren't truly masters over it, because they hadn't created an Iara to explain it, but rather viewed it simply as a reality of the world.[18] Out of all of this grief, he arrived at a clear conclusion: The men were machines, and the Machine was mankind. Macunaíma chuckled. He felt free again,

---

[18] An Iara is a mythical creature invented by European colonists, and is the same as a mermaid and siren. She frequently has been given the designation "Mãe D'água" by Brazilian writers of European descent.

Macunaíma

and immense satisfaction. He turned Jiguê into a telephone machine and called some cabarets to order lobster and French delicacies.

The next day, he was so exhausted from his binge that he felt consumed with grief. He remembered the muiraquitã and decided to act quickly, because one must strike first to kill a snake.

Venceslau Pietro Pietra lived in a marvelous hut that was surrounded by a forest at the end of Rua Maranhão and overlooked the shaded, wet hillsides of Pacaembu.[19] Macunaíma told Maanape that he was going to pay Venceslau Pietro Pietra a little visit because he wanted to get to know him. Maanape lectured him, describing the danger of going there, as the merchant walked with his heels facing forward, and if God marked someone, the merchant found them. He was certainly a formidable brawler. Perhaps he was the giant Piaimã, eater of people![20] Who knew? "You don't want to find out," said Maanape.

"I'm still going," said Macunaíma. "Where they know me, I'm treated with honor. Where they don't know me, I don't care!"

Maanape accompanied his brother.

Behind the merchant's hut lived the Dzalaúra-Iegue

---

[19] Rua Maranhão is a street in São Paulo which, in the first half of the twentieth century, was the location of the homes of some of the wealthiest families in the city. Pacaembu is the neighborhood in which Rua Maranhão is located, and which was rapidly being developed as an upper-class enclave at the time *Macunaíma* was published.

[20] "Piai'ma" is the name of the man-eating giant who is the hero's main antagonist in the original Makunaima legends.

tree, which yielded every kind of fruit:[21] cashews, cajás, cajà-mangas, mangos, pineapples, avocados, jabuticabas, graviolas, sapotas, pupunhas, pitangas, and guajarus smelling of armpits, all of these fruits.[22] And it was very tall. The two brothers were hungry. They made a zaiacúti with leaves cut by saúvas and, hiding on the lowest branch of the tree, shot arrows at the animals devouring the fruit.[23] Maanape said to Macunaíma, "Listen. If you hear a bird singing, don't respond, brother. Otherwise, you can kiss my ass goodbye."

The hero nodded. Maanape shot a blowgun and Macunaíma collected the falling animals from behind the zaiacúti. They fell with a crash, and Macunaíma gathered the macucos, monkeys, micos, curassows, penelopes, jaós, and toucans, all of this game.[24] The clamor disturbed Venceslau Pietro Pietra's rest, and he came out to see what it was. Venceslau Pietro Pietra was the giant Piaimã, eater of people. He arrived at the door of the house and sang like a bird – "Ogoró! Ogoró! Ogoró!" – for what seemed like a long time.

Macunaíma immediately responded: "Ogoró! Ogoró!

---

[21] This magical tree, spelled "Zalaura-yeg" by Koch-Grünberg, is from the original Pemón legends.

[22] Cajás, cajà-mangas, jabuticabas, graviolas, sapotas, pupunhas, and pitangas are all tree fruits. Guajarus are a kind of almond.

[23] A zaiacúti is a screen of branches and leaves made by hunters to hide from animals.

[24] Macucos and jaós are kinds of flightless bird. Micos is a classification of several species of small, long-tailed monkeys. Curassows and penelopes are forest birds that resemble chickens.

Macunaíma

Ogoró!"

Maanape recognized the danger, and urged, "Hide, brother!"

The hero hid behind the zaiacúti among the dead game and ants, but the giant had seen him.

"Who answered me?"

Maanape responded, "I don't know."

"Who answered me?"

"I don't know."

This happened thirteen times, until the giant said, "It was people. Show me who it was."

Maanape tossed out a dead macaque.

Piaimã swallowed the macaque and repeated, "It was people. Show me who it was."

Maanape threw him another dead macaque.

Piaimã swallowed it and repeated again, "It was people. Show me who it was."

Then, he spotted the pinky finger of the hiding hero and shot an arrow in his direction. He heard a long wail – "Whaaaa!" – as Macunaíma squatted with the arrow lodged in his heart. The giant said to Maanape, "Throw me the person that I just hunted!"

Maanape threw howler monkeys, jaós, curassows, alagoas curassows, wattled curassows, black curassows, urus, and nocturnal curassows, all of these game birds.[25] But Piaimã swallowed them and asked again for the person whom he'd shot with his arrow. Maanape hadn't wanted to give away the hero and had thrown the game birds instead. But this had taken a long time, and Macunaíma died. At last, Piaimã bellowed with rage, "Maanape, my grandson, cut the chatter! Throw me the person that I hunted or I'll kill you, wicked old man!"

---

[25] Urus are another type of chicken-like bird.

Macunaíma

Maanape still didn't want to give up his brother, so he picked up six different game animals at once – a macaque, a monkey, a jacu, a jacutinga, a picota, and a jacana – and threw them onto the ground, shouting, "Take six!"[26]

Piaimã was irate. He grabbed branches from four different trees in the woods – an açacurana, an angelim, an apiós, and a carará – then brought them back and stood over Maanape.[27]

"Get out of the way however you can, thrower of false animals," he said. "The alligator doesn't have a neck, and the ant doesn't have balls. As for me, I can balance four branches on the tip of my finger!"

Maanape grew much more afraid and threw – a trick! – the hero onto the ground. This is how Maanape and Piaimã invented the sublime game known as Truco.[28]

Piaimã calmed down. "This is the one," he said.

He grabbed the corpse by the leg and dragged it into his house. Maanape climbed down from the tree in despair. When he went to follow his dead brother, he came across a little sarara named Cambgique.[29] The ant asked, "What brings you here, partner?"

"I'm going after the giant who killed my brother."

"I'll come with."

---

[26] Jacus, jacutingas, picotas, and jacanas are all more birds similar to chickens.

[27] These are all large trees. The angelim is the tallest species of tree in the region where it grows.

[28] Truco is a popular card game in Brazil in which players each cast a card to try to collect tricks, similar to the games of Hearts and Spades.

[29] A sarara is a kind of ant. In the original legends, "Kambezike" is a wasp.

Then, Cambgique sucked up all of the hero's blood, which was spread across the ground and in branches, and led Maanape by slurping the drops along the way back to Piaimã's house.

They entered the house, crossed the hallway and the dining room, passed through the pantry, exited onto the side terrace, and stopped in front of the basement. Maanape lit a torch of jutaí so he could see well enough to descend the little black stairwell.[30] Right in front of the door to the cellar was the last drop of blood. The door was closed. Maanape scratched his nose and asked Cambgique, "Now what!?"

At that, Zlezlegue the tick crawled from under the door and asked Maanape, "What now, partner?"

"I'm going after the giant that killed my brother."

Zlezlegue said, "Alright, then close your eyes, partner."

Maanape closed them.

"Open your eyes, partner."

Maanape opened them and Zlezlegue the tick had turned into a Yale key.[31] Maanape picked the key off the floor and opened the door. Zlezlegue turned back into a tick and instructed, "With the bottles at the very top, you will convince Piaimã." Then, he disappeared.

Maanape took ten bottles and opened them, and a perfect aroma filled the air. It was the famous cassava whiskey called chianti. Maanape entered another room of

---

[30] Jutaí is a category of trees that grow big seed pods.

[31] In the original Makunaima legends, "Seléseleg" is a lizard who turns into a canoe to transport Ma'nape across a river to Piai'ma's house. The Yale Lock Shop was founded in 1840 by Linus Yale, Sr., in Newport, New York, and specialized in expensive, handmade bank locks. In the early 20th century, the company expanded worldwide.

the cellar and saw the giant there with his lover, an old rustic woman named Ceiuci, who was very fat and always smoking something.[32] Maanape gave the bottles to Venceslau Pietro Pietra, a lump of Acarán tobacco to the woman, and the couple forgot the world.[33]

The hero had been chopped into twenty-times-thirty morsels and was floating atop a cauldron of boiling polenta. Maanape picked out the little chunks and bones, and spread them out on the cement to cool. After they had cooled, Cambgique the sarara spit all of the blood he'd sucked on top. Maanape wrapped all of the bloody morsels in banana leaves, threw the packet in a basket, and took it back to the boarding house.

When he arrived, he put the basket on the floor and blew some smoke into it. Macunaíma emerged, still very wobbly and halfway like polenta, from the leaves. Maanape gave guaraná berries to his brother, and he became sturdy again. He swatted away some mosquitos

---

[32] Ceiuci is a fairy from Tupi legends who suffered from eternal hunger. She was impregnated by the Sun, Guaraci, via fruit juice that trickled into her vagina, and gave birth to the demigod Jurupari. Jurupari set out to rid the world of the evils that plagued it, particularly the dominion of women over men. He established cults and sacred festivals forbidden to women, who would drop dead immediately upon hearing the men's chants and cheers. Even though she knew the risk, Ceiuci attempted to attend one of these festivals and died instantly. Unable to restore her to life, Jurupari took her to the sky where she became the constellation Pleiades, which Tupi people called "Ceiuci." In the original legend, Piai'ma's wife is named Kamaliua.

[33] Acará is a town and region near the mouth of the Amazon River.

and asked, "What happened to me?"

"You ignored my warnings! I told you not to respond to the little bird's song. I said that if you did..."[34]

The next day, Macunaíma woke up with scarlet fever and lay in his hammock imagining what kind of gun machine he needed to kill Venceslau Pietro Pietra. After he recovered, he went to the house of the Englishmen to ask for a Smith & Wesson.[35] One of the Englishmen said, "The revolvers are still very green, but we'll check to see if there's an early harvest."

---

[34] This story, in which Macunaíma and Manaape hunt at the Dzalaúra-Iegue tree, Macunaíma ignores Manaape's warning not to answer his bird call and is hunted and killed by Piaimã, and Maanape rescues his pieces from the giant's soup and used them to resurrect his brother, is taken almost verbatim from a story that Koch-Grünberg called "Makunaima's Tod und Wiederbelebung" ("Macunaíma's Death and Revival").

[35] Horace Smith and D.B. Wesson met in 1850 while working together as gunsmiths at the Robbins & Lawrence Company in Windsor, Vermont. Together, the men designed a "repeating" pistol (a firearm that could fire multiple self-contained cartridges before reloading) and started production in 1852 as Smith & Wesson Company. The venture soon failed, however, and the partners sold their business to Oliver Winchester in 1854. That same year, while assisting Winchester to operate the factory, D.B. Wesson designed the first revolver, which he and Smith soon patented. The pair then reformed Smith & Wesson to manufacture and sell revolvers. On account of their patents, Smith & Wesson had monopolies not only on revolvers, but also on the only cartridges that were fully waterproof and could be carried around in one's pocket. A few years later, the American Civil War broke out and the partners grew rich selling handguns. By 1870, they were the largest supplier of military revolvers in the world.

Macunaíma

They crouched under the gun tree. The Englishman said, "You wait here. If a revolver falls, then catch it. But don't let it fall to the ground!"

"Okay."

The Englishmen shook the tree until a barely ripe revolver fell out.

"This one is good."

Macunaíma thanked them and left. He wanted the others to believe that he spoke English, but he couldn't even say "sweetheart." The Englishman had done the talking. Maanape wanted a revolver, too, as well as bullets and whiskey. Macunaíma advised, "You don't speak English well, brother Maanape. It would be cruel for you to go. It's possible that when you ask for a gun, they'll give you a pickle. Let me go."

So, Macunaíma went back to speak with the Englishmen. Under the gun tree, the Englishmen shook the branches vigorously, but no gun fell out. Next, they went to the bullet tree. The Englishmen shook it, and a cache of bullets dropped out that Macunaíma let fall to the ground before he picked them up.

"Now, the whiskey," he said.

They went to the whiskey tree, and the Englishmen shook it. It dropped two boxes that Macunaíma caught in the air. He thanked the Englishmen and returned to the boarding house.[36] When he arrived there, he hid the boxes

---

[36] In the story "Kalawunseg der Lügner" ("Kalawunseg the Liar"), Koch-Grünberg tells of a young man named Kalawunseg, who goes to the land of the English to purchase a gun. An Englishman tells him that the guns are not yet ripe, but takes him to the gun tree anyway. He warns Kalawunseg not to let the gun hit the ground, then shakes one loose. Kalawunseg catches it, then says that he wants gunpowder and bullets, too. The Englishman shakes these items from the

under the bed and went to speak with his brother. "I spoke English with them, brother. But they didn't have guns or whiskey because there was a swarm of leopard ants that ate everything. I brought some bullets, though. I'm giving you my revolver, too. If anyone messes with me, shoot."

Then, he turned Jiguê into a telephone machine, called the giant, and cursed his mother.

---

powder tree and the bullet tree, and Kalawunseg takes them home and tells everyone the story. In Pemón legends, and in *Macunaíma*, the "land of the English" is not England, but is instead Guyana, which was a British colony until 1966.

VI
THE FRANCESA AND THE GIANT[1]

Maanape loved coffee and Jiguê loved to sleep. Macunaíma wanted to build a lean-to for the three to live in, but they couldn't get it done. The guys were always idling, as Jiguê spent the day sleeping and Maanape sat around drinking coffee. This enraged the hero. He grabbed a spoon, turned it into a bug, and said, "Now bury yourself in the ground coffee beans. When brother Maanape comes for more, bite his tongue!"

Next, he picked up a boll of cotton, turned it into a white taturana, and said, "I'm going to tuck you into the hammock. When brother Jiguê comes to sleep, suck his blood."[2]

---

[1] "Francesa" literally means "woman from France," but was used as a slang term for any wealthy Brazilian woman with European style and taste.

[2] A taturana is a fuzzy caterpillar that is painful to touch and a pest to fruit orchards.

Maanape came and entered the boarding house to drink more coffee. The little bug stung his tongue. "Ai!" Maanape yelped.

Macunaíma said smugly, "Are you hurt, brother? When a bug stings me, it doesn't hurt."

Maanape was enraged. He flung the bug across the room and said, "Be gone, pest!"

Then, Jiguê entered the shelter to take a nap. The little white taturana sucked so much of his blood that it turned pink.

"Ai!" shouted Jiguê. Macunaíma said, "Are you hurt, brother? When a taturana bites me, I like it."

Jiguê was irate. He flung the taturana across the room and said, "Be gone, pest!"

The three brothers then went to continue the construction of the lean-to. Maanape and Jiguê worked on the pent roof, while Macunaíma gathered some bricks that the brothers had strewn about. Maanape and Jiguê were furious and wanted to get revenge on their brother. The hero didn't suspect a thing. Jiguê picked up a brick but, to make it hurt less, he turned it into a ball of very hard leather. He passed the ball to Maanape who was further ahead, and Maanape, with a kick, sent it careening into Macunaíma. It smashed the hero's nose completely.

"Ow!" the hero cried.

The brothers shouted sarcastically, "Hey! Are you hurt, brother!? Because when a ball hits us, it doesn't hurt!"

Macunaíma filled with rage. He kicked the ball over the horizon and said, "Be gone, pest!"

He came to where the brothers were. "Stop working on the lean-to!" he ordered, before turning the bricks, rocks, tiles, and tools into a cloud of içás that overtook

São Paulo for three days.[3]

The bug fell into Campinas, as did the taturana, and the ball fell onto a field nearby.[4] And it was in this way that Maanape discovered the coffee bug, Jiguê created the pink caterpillar, and Macunaíma invented the soccer ball: three pests.[5]

The next day, during one of his frequent ruminations about his marvada, the hero realized that he'd failed horribly, and that he couldn't ever appear on Maranhão Street again because Venceslau Pietro Pietra now knew exactly who he was. He used his imagination and, at around three o'clock, he came up with an idea. He decided to trick the giant. He tucked a membi into his throat, turned Jiguê into a telephone machine, and called Venceslau Pietro Pietra to tell him that a francesa wanted to speak with him about the machine business.[6] Pietra was interested and said to come over right away because his old woman, Ceiuci, had left with their two daughters, and they could negotiate freely.

So, Macunaíma borrowed a few beauty products from the landlady of the boarding house: something called "rouge," stockings made of silk, a substance that covered body odors, a belt scented with aromatic grasses,

---

[3] Içás are winged female saúvas.

[4] Campinas is a large city that is approximately fifty miles from São Paulo.

[5] In a story that Koch-Grünberg called "Wie der Stachelrochen und die Giftschlange in die Welt Kamen" ("How the Stingray and the Venomous Snake Came into the World"), Makunaima creates stingrays and venomous snakes in a similar prank on his brothers, and brags that the pests don't hurt him.

[6] A membi is a little whistle made of bone.

something to make the neckline moist and scented of patchouli, and something called "mittens," all of these beauty items. He hung two mangoes over his chest. To complete the outfit, he rubbed his eyes, which had become languid, with blue from a campeche stick.[7] He was wearing so much make-up and so many accessories that they felt heavy on his body, but he'd turned into a beautiful francesa who bathed herself in jurema smoke and pinned a sprig of Paraguayan pine on her breast to ward off spells.[8] Then, she went to the palace of Venceslau Pietro Pietra, who was the giant, Piaimã, eater of people.

As he was leaving the boarding house, Macunaíma saw a hummingbird with a scissored tail. He didn't like this bad omen and thought about abandoning the meeting, but he'd made a promise to Pietra, so he performed an exorcism on it and continued onward.

Upon arrival, he found the giant at the gate, waiting for him. After paying the francesa many gratuitous compliments, Piaimã plucked the ticks from her body and carried her into the most beautiful bedroom in the house, with pillars of acaricuara and cross-beams of itaúba.[9] The floor was set in a chessboard pattern of muirapiranga and satinwood planks, and the space was furnished with those

---

[7] Campeche is a tree known for producing wood used in making dye.

[8] The bark from the jurema plant's root is smoked as a psychedelic by jurema cults in northern Brazil.

[9] An acaricuara is a species of tree known for producing hard wood used in construction, and itaúbas are a kind of flowering laurel tree.

famous white hammocks from Maranhão.[10] Right in the center of the room, there was a table of carved rosewood with blinding white tableware from Breves and ceramics from Belém set atop a lace tablecloth woven from banana-palm fibres.[11] In enormous basins taken from the caves at the Rio Cunani, tacacá was being cooked with tucupi, as well as soup made with a Paulistan pulled from a Continental-brand refrigerator, jacarezada, and polenta.[12] The wines were a superior Puro de Ica coming from Iquitos, an imitation Port from Minas, a caiçuma aged eighty years, ice-cold champagne from São Paulo, and an infamous jenipapo liqueur that was as terrible as three days of rain.[13] And there were hand-made centerpieces with decorative paper cuttings, as well as splendid Falchi confections, cookies from the Rio Grande, and piles of gourds painted in the brilliant black of cumati-tree dye and carved with designs in a style originating in Monte

---

[10] Muirapiranga is another name for brazilwood. Maranhão is a state in the northeast of Brazil.

[11] Breves and Belém are both cities situated in northeast Brazil near the mouth of the Amazon River.

[12] The caves at the Rio Cunani are an archeological site discovered in 1895 which were full of prehistoric ceramics and pottery. They are located in the far north of Brazil, near the border of French Guiana. Tacacá is a thick spicy soup of cassava broth, and tucupi is a sauce made by simmering fresh cassava juice. A Paulistan is a person from São Paulo. Jacarezada is an alligator stew.

[13] Puro de Ica is a kind of pisco brandy. Iquitos is a city on the Amazon River in Peru. Minas is short for Minas Gerais, a state in southeastern Brazil. Caiçuma is an alcoholic drink made from fermented cassava.

Alegre.[14]

The francesa reclined in a hammock and, moving with grace, started snacking. She was famished and ate until she was full. After that, she drank a cup of Puro to assist digestion and decided to get straight to the point. She was soon asking the giant if it was true that he owned a muiraquitã in the shape of an alligator. The giant went inside and returned with a snail in his hand. As Macunaíma watched, he pulled a green stone from inside of it. It was the muiraquitã! Macunaíma felt a chill from all of the excitement and thought that he might cry. But he disguised it well, asking if the giant wanted to sell the rock. Venceslau Pietro Pietra winked cheekily, declaring that he would neither sell the stone nor give it away. So, the francesa begged him to let her borrow the rock and take it home. Venceslau Pietro Pietra cutely winked a second time and said that he wouldn't lend the stone either. "You think that I'll just give it away like that for a couple of giggles, francesa? Really!?"

"But I want the rock so badly!"

"Keep wanting it!"

"Well, you're giving me no less than what you've given me already, two-bit trader!"

"Trader my foot, frenchie! Bite your tongue! I'm a

---

[14] In 1880, the Falchi brothers, Emidio, Bernardino, and Panfilio, constructed a factory for the production of chocolate and candy in São Paulo. A cumati is a tree known for its fruit which is used to make paint for pottery and other objects. Monte Alegre is a town on the Amazon River where an archeological site called the Caverna da Pedra Pintada (the "Cave of Painted Rock") is located, where there are painted designs and animal icons that are believed to be between five hundred and two thousand years old.

collector!"

He went inside and emerged carrying a large basket woven from embira fibres and full of rocks.[15] There were turquoises, emeralds, beryls, polished pebbles, iron shaped into needles, crystals like drops of water, tin plates, emery stones, dove eggs, horse bones, axes, machetes, arrowheads of chipped stone, grigris made of petrified elephant bones, Greek columns, Egyptian gods, Javanese Buddhas, obelisks, Mexican altars, Guyanese gold, carved stones from Iguape, opals from the Alegre Igarapé, rubies and garnets from the Rio Gurupi, white stones from the Rio das Garças, itacolumite, tourmalines from Vupabuçu, blocks of titanium from the Rio Piriá, bauxite from Macaco Creek, limestone fossils from Pirabas, pearls from Cametá, the large boulder that Oaque, the Father of Toucans, shot with a blowgun from the top of a mountain, and a lithoglyph from Calamare. All of these rocks were there in the basket.[16]

---

[15] Embira is a category of plants identified by their strong fibers used to make cord.

[16] A grigri is a kind of talisman from the west coast of Africa. Iguape is a town on the Atlantic coast in the state of São Paulo. The Rio Gurupi is a river at the eastern end of the Amazon Rainforest which flows to the Atlantic Ocean, and the Rio das Garças is a small river in the Amazon Rainforest near the border with Bolivia. Itacolumite is a kind of sandstone that is known as a source of diamonds. Tourmalines are semi-precious stones that appear in various colors. Vupabuçu, also called the Pond of Black Water, was famous for its proximity to a quarry of emeralds and sapphires. Rio Piriá is a river in the north of Brazil near the mouth of the Amazon River. Macaco Creek is in the south of Brazil, near São Paulo. The Pirabas Formation is an archeological site discovered in the late 19th century on Brazil's northern Atlantic coast, and is famous for

Macunaíma

Piaimã told the francesa that he was a famous collector of rocks. But the francesa was Macunaíma, the hero. Piaimã divulged that the jewel of the collection was the muiraquitã in the shape of an alligator, purchased for a thousand contos from the Empress of the Icamiabas on the beaches of Lake Jaciuruá.[17] But it was all a lie. Then, he sat in the hammock very close to the francesa – right next to her! – and murmured that whether it was eight or eighty, he would neither sell nor lend the rock, but he could give it away, "if you comply." The giant wanted to fool around with the francesa.

When the hero realized, because of how Piaimã was acting, what "comply" meant, he was terrified. He thought, "The giant thinks I'm a francesa!"

"Back off, shameless Peruvian!" he shouted, before running away through the garden. The giant ran after him. The francesa jumped into a thicket to hide, but a little

---

its trove of fossilized marine and amphibian fauna. Cametá is a town on the Rio Tocantins near the mouth of the Amazon River. The Oaque were an ethnic group within the Tupi-Guarini people who were encountered by early European explorers of Brazil. There is no indication that this name was given to a god before this reference. A series of lithoglyphs depicting various animals were discovered carved into a rock called Calamare deep in the Brazilian Amazon near Guyana in the early 20th century.

[17] A conto is a unit of 1,000,000 Brazilian reals (or 1,000 milréis) that was used only in times of inflationary crisis. Lake Jaciuruá, also known as Jaci-uaruá, is the location of a mythical temple to Diana where a tribe of woman warriors worshipped the moon. Jaci-uaruá was called the "mirror of the moon" and the women would sacrifice muiraquitãs there as part of a religious ritual to attract men from other tribes.

Macunaíma

black girl was already there. Macunaíma, not paying attention to who she was, said, "Leave me alone, Caterina."[18]

The girl didn't move an inch. Macunaíma, already halfway fed-up with her, whispered, "Caterina, get out of here or I'll smack you!"

But the girl didn't budge. So, Macunaíma gave the pest a brutal slap and his hand stuck to her.

"Caterina, let go of my hand, or I'll get away anyhow and give you another slap! Caterina!"

But Caterina was a doll made of carnaúba wax and had been put there by the giant.[19] It became very quiet. He gave Caterina another slap with his free hand and became even more stuck.

"Caterina! Caterina! Let go of my hands and get lost, curlyhead! Or else I'll kick you!"

He kicked the doll and his leg stuck to it, and the hero was firmly adhered to the wax dummy.

Piaimã approached with a basket. He took the francesa from the trap and yelled at the basket, "Open your mouth, basket! Open your big mouth!" The basket opened its mouth, and the giant dumped the hero inside. The basket closed its mouth, and Piaimã picked it up and returned to his house.

The francesa, instead of a purse, carried a quiver that held little darts for a blowgun. The giant leaned the basket against the front door and entered the house to put the quiver among the rocks of his collection. But the quiver was made of cloth that stank of rotting meat.

---

[18] "Caterina" is a slang term for "prostitute."

[19] Carnaúba is a kind of palm known for producing wax used in a variety of commercial and industrial applications.

This made the giant suspicious. "Is your mother as smelly and fat as you, creature?" he asked, before rolling his eyes with pleasure. He thought that the quiver was the francesa's baby son. But the francesa was Macunaíma, the hero, who'd just listened to the question from the basket and was growing even more afraid. "Perhaps it's really true that Venceslau believes that I passed underneath some kind of rainbow and changed my nature. Curse you, damnit!"[20]

He blew on some cumacaá root that had been ground into a powder that could loosen chords, loosened the binding on the basket, and jumped out.[21] As he was escaping, he encountered the giant's jaguar, which was named Xaréu, like the fish, so it wouldn't be hydrophobic.[22] The hero was terrified and scrambled wildly around the garden. The beast chased after him, and they ran past the Ponta do Calabouço, took a route from Guajará Mirim, and turned to the east.[23] In Itamaracá,

---

[20] This episode about Makunaima becoming caught in a trap and captured by Piai'ma, who steals his blowgun quiver, is taken from a story that Koch-Grünberg called "Makunaima in der Schlinge des Piai'ma" ("Macunaíma in the Snare of Piaimã"). In the original version, Makinaima becomes entangled in a snare, rather than stuck to a wax dummy. The doll of wax (or "tar baby") is a feature of many North and Latin American folktales. The version familiar to American readers, featuring Br'er Rabbit and Br'er Fox, was published in 1881 by Joel Chandler Harris under the pseudonym Uncle Remus.

[21] A cumacaá is a kind of flowering plant with roots known for their medicinal use as a relaxant.

[22] A xaréu is a kind of Atlantic migratory fish.

[23] The Ponta do Calabouço was a fort constructed by the Portuguese in Rio de Janeiro in 1603. As of the publication of

Macunaíma took some time to eat a dozen jasmine mangos that were said to have been born from the body of Dona Sancha.[24] They headed southwest and, in the heights of Barbacena, the fugitive spotted a cow at the top of a sloped path that was cobbled with pointed stones.[25] He remembered drinking milk and developed a craving. He walked slowly up the pathway so as not to grow tired. The cow was of the ill-tempered Guzerá breed and stashed her milk greedily.[26] So, Macunaíma said a prayer like this:

"Show mercy, Our Lady,
And St. Anthony of Nazaré,
A gentle cow gives milk,
An angry one gives what it wants!"[27]

The cow showed kindness and gave the hero some milk. Then, he ran to the south. As he crossed Paraná, already well on his way back from the pampas, he wanted

---

this translation, the building is home to the National History Museum. Guajará Mirim is a town in the far west of Brazil on the border with Bolivia.

[24] Itamaracá is an island on the Atlantic coast near the city of Recife. Dona Sancha is a character from a popular Brazilian nursery rhyme.

[25] Barbacena is a town in the south of Brazil near Rio de Janeiro.

[26] A Guzerá is a breed cow that was imported from Gujarat, India ("Guzerate" in Portuguese), to Brazil, where it proliferated.

[27] This verse is a popular folk poem of the people of the town of Rio Pardo in the far south of Brazil.

to climb one of the trees there.[28] He heard snarling at his tail, however, and soon found himself being hounded by the jaguar. He screamed, "Leave me alone, you prick!"

He ran past every chestnut, ipê, and cambuí suitable for climbing and, before arriving at the city of Serra in Espírito Santo, he almost smashed his head on a rock covered with carved pictures that he didn't understand.[29] Surely there was money buried there... Macunaíma was in a hurry, however, and darted for the banks of Bananal Island.[30] Finally, he saw a thirty-meter-tall anthill with an entrance right on the ground in front of him. He used all of his strength to crawl through the hole and climb up to the top. The jaguar had him trapped there.

The giant arrived and saw the jaguar stalking the anthill. Right inside the entrance, the francesa had lost a little silver chain. "My treasure must be here," mumbled the giant. The jaguar disappeared. Piaimã ripped a maripa palm from the ground, including the roots. He cut the branches from the trunk and stuck it through the hole to flush out the francesa. But would an alligator leave? Nor did she! The hero opened his legs and was, as they say, impaled by the maripa.[31] Seeing that the francesa still wouldn't leave, Piaimã went to fetch some pepper. He

---

[28] Paraná is a Brazilian state between the border with Argentina and the cities of São Paulo and Rio de Janeiro.

[29] A cambuí is a species of small, flowering tree. Serra is a town in Espírito Santo, a state on the Atlantic coast.

[30] Bananal Island is the largest river island in the world. It is located in central Brazil in the state of Tocantins and is formed by a split of the Araguaia River. It is approximately two hundred miles long and thirty-five miles wide.

[31] A maripa is a kind of palm tree.

brought a swarm of fire ants, which is what the giant used for pepper, put them in the hole, and they bit the hero. But even then, the francesa still didn't leave. Piaimã was stung by some fire ants and swore revenge. He shouted at Macunaíma, "Now I'll really get you, because I'm going to fetch the elite jararaca!"[32]

When the hero heard this, he froze. Nobody could survive being trapped with a jararaca. He screamed at the giant, "Wait a second, giant! I was just leaving!" But to buy time, he took the mangoes from his chest and stuck them in the opening of the hole, saying, "First, put these outside for me, please."

Piaimã was so furious that he threw the mangoes far away. Macunaíma witnessed the giant's rage. He took the low-cut dress and put it in the opening of the hole, saying again, "Put this outside, please."

Piaimã threw the dress far away, too. Macunaíma stuck his belt in the opening, then his shoes, and did this with all of his clothes. Steam rose from the giant's ears; he was so angry. He threw all of the items far away without even looking at what they were. Finally, the hero timidly stuck his butt in the opening of the hole and said, "Now, I'm tossing out this smelly gourd."

Piaimã, blind with rage, grabbed the buttocks without looking and threw them, with the hero attached, a league and a half away. Then, he continued to wait while the hero picked mororó where he'd landed.[33]

---

[32] A jararaca is a kind of pit viper native to tropical regions of North and South America.

[33] Mororó is a flowering plant known for its medicinal uses. This tale of Piai'ma using ants as pepper to flush Makunaima from a hole is taken from a story that Koch-Grünberg called "Makunaima und Piai'ma" ("Makunaima and Piai'ma").

Macunaíma later returned to the boarding house, accepting a blessing from the dog and calling his uncle's cat – just to say hi! He was sweating, and all scratched up with fire in his eyes, and he strained his lungs to catch a breath. He rested for a while and, as if attacked by hunger, inhaled a dish of fried mussels from Maceió, a dried duck from Marajó, and washed it all down with mocororó.[34] Then, he lay in a hammock.

Macunaíma was extremely frustrated. Venceslau Pietro Pietra was a famous collector, and he wasn't. He bristled with envy and decided to imitate the giant. However, he didn't find joy in collecting rocks because he already had an abundance of them on his land: on the sharp crags, in the mountain springs, in the rapids, in the broad valleys, and on high gravel beds. And all of these rocks had once been wasps, ants, mosquitos, ticks, animals, little birds, people, young women, girls, and even the delicate parts of young women and girls. Why gather even more stone when it's so heavy to carry!? He stretched his tired arms and mumbled, "Ai! What a drag!"

He thought about all of this and came to a decision: He would gather a collection of all of the swear words that he loved.

He dedicated himself to the task. In an instant, he recalled an abundance of them in all of the living languages, and even some in Greek and Latin, which he'd studied a bit. The Italian collection was complete, with words for all of hours of the day, every day of the year, all of the circumstances of life, and every conceivable human

---

[34] Maceió is a small city on the Atlantic coast near Recife, and Marajó is a large island on the coast of Brazil near the mouth of the Amazon River. Mocororó is an alcoholic beverage made from fermented cassava.

emotion. And each one of them was obscene! But the jewel of the collection was an Indian phrase that not even he would ever say.

VII
MACUMBA

Macunaíma was extremely frustrated. He hadn't been able to recover the muiraquitã, and this made him hateful. The situation would improve, however, if he killed Piaimã. So, he left the city and went into a nearby forest to test his strength. He ran through the trees for a league and a half before he finally saw a peroba that seemed to grow forever.[1] He grabbed its sapopema root and pulled to break it from the trunk, but the leaves at the top were shaken only by the wind.[2] "I'm still not strong enough," Macunaíma concluded. He grabbed a tooth from the little rat called "crô," made a crude incision in his leg, as is often prescribed to cowards, and, bleeding, returned to the boarding house.[3] He felt dejected from not yet having

---

[1] Peroba is a kind of tall, hardwood tree.

[2] A sapopema is a kind tree root that grows up the base of the trunk and buttresses it.

[3] A crô is a species of rat.

Macunaíma

enough strength, and was so distracted that he tripped over the threshold.

The hero saw stars because of all of the pain, and among them was Capei, waning and surrounded by a mist. "You don't start something new after the Moon is waning," he sighed. This consoled him.

The weather was cold the next day and, to warm up, the hero decided to get revenge against Venceslau Pietro Pietra by giving him a beating. However, because he still wasn't strong enough, he was terrified of the giant. So, he decided to take a train to Rio de Janeiro to seek help from the devil Exu, in whose honor a macumba would be performed the next day.[4]

It was June and the weather was quite cold. The macumba would be prayed in Mangue in the zungu of Aunt Ciata, a sorceress like no other, a noble mãe-de-santo who sang to the guitar.[5] At eight o'clock,

---

[4] Exu is a deity who was introduced to Brazil by Yoruba people from West Africa. Exu has a violent, capricious, cunning, rude, vain, and indecent character, such that early Christian missionaries in Brazil analogized him to the Devil and made him a symbol of evil and hatred. A "macumba" is a religious ceremony celebrated by practitioners of several Afro-Brazilian religions. The ceremony described in this chapter is based on a trance ritual celebrated by practitioners of the Afro-Brazilian Candomblé religion, which combines religious traditions of West African peoples such as the Yoruba, Fon, and Bantu, with Roman Catholic rituals and saints.

[5] Aunt Ciata, also known as "Tia Ciata," was a famous mãe-de-santo, or priestess of the Candomblé religion, and a prominent member of Rio de Janiero's African community until her death in 1924. She is best known for hosting parties, ceremonies, and concerts at her house that are credited with giving rise to samba music. In fact, the first samba record was recorded there. A

Macunaíma arrived carrying an obligatory bottle of wine under his arm. There were already many people there – conservatives, poor people, lawyers, waiters, stonemasons, dandies, bureaucrats, and thieves, all of these people – and the event was beginning. Macunaíma took off his shoes and socks like the others. Among the throng stood the milonga, which was made from a cabatatu-wasp nest and dried açacu root.[6] He entered the crowded room and, after swatting away a swarm of mosquitoes, went down on his hands and knees to greet the candomblèzeira who was sitting on a stool and not saying a word.[7] Aunt Ciata was an old black woman who'd experienced a century of suffering. She wore a dour expression, was very thin, and had white hair that spread out like light cast upon her tiny head. Nobody could see her eyes anymore. She was just an ever-sleepy set of bones, dangling to the earthen floor.

Vai, a boy who they said was a son of Oxum and Our Lady of Conception, whose macumba was in December, delivered a lit candle for each of the sailors, carpenters,

---

zungu was a bunkhouse used to house slaves or black laborers. Mangue ("Mangrove") is a neighborhood in Rio de Janeiro that was created by infilling a mangrove swamp.

[6] The term "milonga" (literally, "mixture") has various meanings within Candomblé and other Afro-Brazilian religions, but generally refers to the mixture of African cultures in Brazil. The term has been used to describe different arts that combine elements of these various cultures, including theatrical performances, dances, musical styles, rhetorical devices, and, in this instance, statuary. Cabatatu wasps build nests in the shape of an armadillo shell. Açacu is a species of flowering tree known for its caustic sap.

[7] A candomblèzeira is a Candomblé priestess.

journalists, rich men, construction foremen, women, and government employees – so many government employees! – all of these people, and extinguished the gas flame that illuminated the parlor.[8]

Then, the macumba began in earnest, with a xirê to salute the saints.[9] At the start came the ogã, player of the atabaque drum.[10] He was a black son of Ogum named Olelê Rui Barbosa, a professional fado artist with a face covered in pockmarks.[11] The atabaque was slapped in a tight rhythm that guided the whole procession. The candles cast florets onto the paper walls, and the smoothly dancing shadows appeared ghostly. After the ogã, Aunt Ciata arrived almost without a stir, as only the people's lips moved, carrying a monotone prayer. Then followed lawyers, stewards, healers, poets, the hero, muggers,

---

[8] Oxum is a Candomblé goddess, responsible for female fertility and was analogized by Roman Catholic missionaries to Our Lady of Conception. She is the wife of the god Xangô.

[9] "Xirê" is a Yoruba word that means wheel and dance. In Candomblé rituals, a xirê is sung and performed at the beginning to summon the gods to the gathering.

[10] An ogã is an honorary position bestowed upon esteemed and public members of Candomblé who show themselves to be protectors of the community. Some ogãs, called alabês, are assigned to play the atabaque drum during the trance ritual.

[11] Ogum is the Candomblé god of metallurgy and war. Rui Barbosa was an abolitionist Brazilian politician. In 1890, as the Minister of Finance, he caused a scandal by ordering the destruction of records of slave ownership, to prevent slave owners from recovering their slaves or from receiving compensation for them. "Olelê" is an ideophone commonly sung in Brazilian music to express joy. "Joyful Rui Barbosa" is an approximate translation.

Portuguese immigrants, and senators, all of these people dancing and singing the response to the prayer: "Let us be saved!"

Aunt Ciata sang the name of the saint that they had to salute: "Oh, Olorum!"[12]

And the people responded, "Let us be saved!"

Aunt Ciata continued, "Oh, Tucuxi Boto!"[13]

And the people responded, "Let us be saved!"

There was a little sweetness in the quiet, monotonous prayer.

"Oh, Yemaya! Nana Buruku! And Oxum! The three Mothers of Water!"[14]

"Let us be saved!"

And so it continued. When Aunt Ciata stopped singing,

---

[12] Olorum is the supreme creator of the Candomblé gods, but keeps distant from mankind and does not interfere in their world. He does not receive sacrifices, nor is he directly worshiped; rather, it is the gods and saints who receive this attention from practitioners. Olorum has been analogized to God by Christian missionaries.

[13] John Luccock was an English merchant who worked in Brazil and who, between 1808 and 1818, kept extensive diaries which became a valuable and well-known source for Brazilian historians. In his records, he tells of a situation where several African sailors refused to re-embark on the company's ship after he had brought aboard the skull of a tucuxi boto, a species of river dolphin, because they viewed the tucuxi as the manifestation of a spirit that was capable of doing harm as well as good.

[14] Yemaya is the Candomblé goddess who lords over the sea. Nana Buruku is the oldest of the Candomblé water gods, and lords over the mud at the bottom of lakes, from which human beings were created.

Macunaíma

she raised her hands to the ceiling and shouted, "Come out, Exu!" Exu was the peg-legged devil, a demon as wicked as he was adept at making mischief. There was a commotion, and everyone was howling, "Uuum! Uuum! Exu! Our Father, Exu!"

The devil's name resounded with a rumble, shortening the length of the night.

The xirê continued, "Oh, King Nagô!"

"Let us be saved!" sweetly in the monotone prayer.

"Oh, Baru!"[15]

"Let us be saved!"

When Aunt Cianta stopped singing, she waved her arms and shouted, "Come out, Exu!" Exu was the pé-de-pato, a malicious spirit.[16] There was again a commotion with everyone howling, "Uuuum! Exu! Our Father, Exu!"

And the devil's name resounded with a rumble, shortening the length of the night.

"Oh, Oxalá!"[17]

"Let us be saved!"

And so it continued. They hailed all of the saints of witchcraft – the Boto Branco who seduces lovers, Xangô, Omulu, Iroco, Oxóssi, the fierce Boiúna Mother, and

---

[15] Baru is a name for the god Xangô that refers to his position as king.

[16] Pé-de-pato, or "duck foot," is one of many names used for the Devil to emphasize his animalistic qualities. Others include Cão Miúdo, which means "tiny dog," and Bode Preto, meaning "black goat."

[17] Oxalá is the creator of humankind and occupies the highest rank in the pantheon of Candomblé gods. He is worshiped by the other gods and, unlike Olorum, by practitioners. He has been analogized to Jesus Christ by Roman Catholic missionaries.

Obatalá who grants believers strength to fool around all night, all of these saints – and the xirê ended.[18] Aunt Ciata sat on her stool in a corner, and all of these sweating people – doctors, bakers, engineers, lawyers, police officers, maids, fat people, murderers, and Macunaíma, all of them – came to put candles on the floor around her. The candles cast the motionless mãe-de-santo's shadow onto the ceiling. Almost everyone had already removed some clothes, and their breathing became heavy because of the smell of body odor, perfume, musk, and sweat. It was time to drink, and Macunaíma tried for the first time the fearsome cachiri called cachaça.[19] After he took a sip, he clicked his happy tongue and laughed.

After the drink, and between more drinks, came the prayers of invocation. Everyone was restless and fiery, hoping that a saint would appear at the macumba that night. It was already past the time when more saints would appear, however, no matter how ardently the people begged. Aunt Ciata's macumba was not like those false macumbas, in which the pai-de-terreiro always pretended to turn into Xangô, Oxóssi, or whomever, to satisfy the

---

[18] The Boto Branco ("White Dolphin") is a Candomblé spirit who transforms from a dolphin into a white man and seduces young women. Xangô is the Candomblé god of thunder, government, and justice. Omulu is the god who protects believers against smallpox and other diseases. He is associated with St. Roch and Lazarus, whose resurrection is described in the Gospel of John, on account of their shared association with illness and healing. Iroco is a rare god and is associated with the gameleira tree. Oxóssi is the god of hunting and abundance. Obatalá is another name for Oxalá.

[19] Cachaça is a spirit distilled from molasses.

macumba celebrants.[20] It was a serious macumba, and when a saint appeared, it was truly without any deception. Aunt Ciata didn't allow these corruptions in her zungu, and it had been more than twelve months since either Ogum or Exu had appeared in Mangue. Everyone hoped that Ogum would come. Macunaíma only wanted Exu, the one who could avenge him upon Venceslau Pietro Pietra.

Between sips of brandy, all of these half-naked people, some on their knees and others on all fours, prayed around the sorceress for the apparition of a saint. In the middle of the night, they went inside to eat a goat, the head and legs of which were already displayed on the peji in front of an image of Exu that was an anthill with three shells for his eyes and mouth.[21] The goat had been killed in honor of the devil, and was seasoned with a powder made from goat horn and the spur of a fighting cock. The mãe-de-santo took the abundance of food with respect and made the sign of the cross three times. All of the people – merchants, booklovers, hobos, academics, and bankers – all of these people dancing around the table sang:

"Bamba querê
Come out, Aruê
Mongi gongo
Come out, Orobô!
Oh!

---

[20] A pai-de-terreiro is a Candomblé priest; a terreiro is a Candomblé temple.

[21] "Peji" is the name of the altar in several Afro-Brazilian religions.

Oh mungunzá
Good acaçá
Vancê nhamanja
Father Guenguê,
Oh!"[22]

As they talked and joked, they devoured the consecrated goat. Each of them grabbed their own bottle of booze, as nobody could share because everyone was drinking so much brandy! Macunaíma laughed loudly and knocked over a bottle of wine on the table. He viewed it as a sign of joy, and everyone thought for a moment that the hero was the one predestined to arrive on that sacred night. He was not.

The chanting had just restarted when he saw a woman jump into the middle of the room, compelling everyone to silence with a wail. She began a new chant. Everyone trembled and the candles cast the young woman's shadow, twisting like a monster, in the corner of the ceiling. It was Exu! The ogã frantically beat the atabaque to realize the

---

[22] Bambaquerê is an old style of dance that originated in the state of Rio Grande do Sul and borrows heavily from fandango. Aruê is the spirit of the dead in the tradition of the Bororós people. An orobô is a fruit originally from West Africa which has become a symbolic item within Candomblé ceremonies as offerings to Xangô. Mungunzá is a corn-based dish similar to grits, and is traditionally served at Candomblé celebrations. Acaçá is a corn-based dish cooked in banana leaf, like a tamale. It is the most important dish of Candomblé, and its preparation and use in rituals involve strict rules and ceremony. "Mongi gongo," "vancê nhamanja" and "guenguê" are attempts by Andrade to render African speech into Portuguese.

Macunaíma

crazy rhythms of the new chant, a free chant, of flustered notes full of difficult jumps, crazy bursts of ecstasy, and bass trembling with fury. The woman shook in the middle of the room, a polaca with too much make-up on her face, a broken strap on her slip, and her fat body already almost entirely naked.[23] Her breasts swung, beating her shoulders, face, and belly – whap! – with a slap. This red-haired woman kept on chanting until froth rolled from her parting lips, and she gave a howl that shortened the length of the night even further. Then, she fell in front of the mãe-de-santo and went still.

There passed a time of sacred silence, which lasted until Aunt Ciata rose from the stool. A little mazomba switched it in an instant with a new bench that had never been sat upon and had belonged to someone else.[24] The mãe-de-terreiro made her way forward, accompanied by the ogã. All of the others were on their feet, flattening themselves against the walls. Only Aunt Ciata approached and arrived close to the frozen body of the polaca in the center of the parlor. The sorceress took off her clothes and was naked, wearing only necklaces, a bracelet, and dangling earrings of silver beads. She took the curdled blood of the eaten goat from a bowl that the ogã was holding, and rubbed the paste onto the head of the babalaó.[25] When she

---

[23] "Polaca" literally means "Polish woman," but was used a term for prostitute.

[24] A mazomba is girl with Portuguese-Brazilian parents.

[25] A babalaô is a priest of the Cult of Ifá, a Yoruba religion. Babalaôs never found a role within Candomblé, but are considered priests in Santeria, Candomblé's Cuban analog. This has created tension between Brazilian babalaôs and the mães- and pais-de-santo of Candomblé.

Macunaíma

poured the green mixture onto the frozen woman, she writhed and moaned, and an iodine smell intoxicated the atmosphere. The mãe-de-santo intoned the sacred prayer of Exu, a monotone incantation.

When it ended, the woman opened her eyes and started moving quite differently than before the ceremony. She was no longer a woman, but was the cavalo-do-santo, Exu.[26] Exu, the romãozinho, had come to join everyone at the macumba.[27]

The naked duo danced an improvised jongo, moving to the rhythm of Aunt Ciata's crackling bones, the slaps of Exu's breasts, and the ogã's steady drumming.[28] Everyone else stripped naked, too, and waited for the great beast in their presence to select the Son of Exu. The jongo ended. Macunaíma trembled as he fought the urge to ask the cariapemba for Venceslau Pietro Pietra to be beaten.[29] He didn't know what gave him this impulse, but he stumbled into the middle of the room, tackled Exu, and fell on top of him. Macunaíma felt victorious. Then, the consecration of the new Son of Exu was celebrated to excess, and everyone ululated in honor of the new son of Icá.[30]

---

[26] "Cavalo-do-santo" ("sacred horse") is an honorific in Afro-Brazilian religions, used to refer to someone who puts themselves in service of the gods.

[27] "Romãozinho" ("little Romeo") is a name for the Devil.

[28] A jongo is a kind of samba dance associated with rural areas, with different choreography depending on the region.

[29] Cariapemba is a god from Angola and the Congo who corresponds with Exu in Candomblé.

[30] Icá is the name of the devil in the legends and myths of the Caxinaua people, a tribe that lives in the Amazon.

After the ceremony, the devil was led to the stool to begin the adoration. Thieves, senators, bumpkins, black people, ladies, soccer players, and everyone else began crawling under the dust that was turning the room orange, and after they beat the left sides of their heads on the ground, they kissed the knees and the entire body of the uamoti.[31] The red-haired woman, stiff and trembling, with foam dripping from her mouth in which everyone wetted their thumbs before crossing themselves, groaned some gurgling mumbles, half-mournful and half-joyous. She was no longer a polaca; she was Exu, the most magnificent jurupari of their religion.[32]

Everyone kissed, worshipped, and blessed themselves even more, and the hour of requests and promises arrived. A butcher asked that everyone buy his rancid meat and Exu agreed. A farmer asked him to eradicate saúvas and disease in his crops, and Exu laughed, saying that he didn't agree to that. A coquette asked for a position as a public-school teacher so she could get married, and Exu agreed. A doctor made a speech in which he asked to write the Portuguese language with elegance, and Exu didn't agree. So it went. Finally, Macunaíma, the new son of the devil, had a turn. He said, "I come to ask for my father because I'm very frustrated."

"What is your name?" asked Exu.

"Macunaíma, the hero."

"Uhm," the man grumbled. "A name starting with 'Ma' is a malignant omen." But he received the hero with

---

[31] An uamoti is an evil spirit in Tupi culture.

[32] Jurupari was a Tupi god who dwelled in the forest and kidnapped disobedient women and children. In colonial Brazil, Jesuit missionaries analogized him to the Devil.

affection and promised to do everything within his power because Macunaíma was his son. So, the hero asked Exu to inflict suffering on Venceslau Pietro Pietra, who was the giant Piaimã, eater of people.

What happened next was horrible. Exu picked up three sprigs of lemon balm blessed by an apostate priest and threw them into the air. They intersected to form a cross, commanding the ego of Venceslau Pietro Pietra to come and receive a beating from Exu. He waited for a moment, until the ego of the giant came and entered the polaca's body. Exu then ordered his son to attack the ego that had just incarnated. The hero picked up a heavy stick and coldly walked up to Exu. He delivered a beating and then some more. Exu shouted:

"Beat me slowly.
How it hurts, hurts, hurts!
I have a family.
And it hurts, hurts, hurts!"

At last, purple from the blows and bleeding through his nose, mouth, and ears, Exu fainted and fell to the ground. It was horrible. Macunaíma ordered the giant's ego to take a hot, salty bath, and afterward the body of Exu steamed and wetted the ground. Then, Macunaíma ordered the giant's ego to tread on glass strewn about a field of nettles and brambles in the mountain ridges of the Andes at the height of winter. Afterward, Exu's body bled with cuts from glass, scratches from the thorns, and scrapes from the nettles, and he was gasping from fatigue and trembling from the cold. It was horrible. Macunaíma next ordered Venceslau Pietro Pietra's ego to endure a horn from a bull, a kick from a bronco, a bite from an alligator, and the stings of forty-times-forty thousand fire ants. Exu's body, bleeding and blistering, writhed on the ground. It was marred by a row of bite marks on one leg, forty-times-forty thousand ant stings that were still invisible on its skin, a forehead cracked by a bronco's hoof, and a puncture from a sharp horn in its stomach. The room filled with an intolerable stench. Then, Exu groaned:

"Bludgeon me slowly.
It hurts, hurts, hurts!
I have a family.
And it hurts, hurts, hurts!"

Macunaíma ordered many-times-many similar afflictions, and Venceslau Pietro Pietra's ego suffered everything through Exu's body. At last, the hero's lust for revenge couldn't inspire any further punishment and he stopped. The woman that remained on the dirt floor was breathing slowly. There was an exhausted silence. It was horrible.

In the palace of Rua Maranhão in São Paulo, there was endless commotion. All of the doctors who'd come to assist were in despair. Venceslau Pietro Pietra howled as he bled from all over his body. He had a horn in his stomach, a crack in his forehead that looked like a kick from a bronco, and was burnt, cold, bitten, and completely covered in bruises and bumps from the fierce beating with the stick.

At the macumba, the spectators continued to watch in silence. Aunt Ciata came in her fashion and began praying the great prayer of the devil. It was an entirely sacrilegious prayer and uttering even a single incorrect word brought death. It was the prayer of Our Father Exu, and it went like this:

"Our Father Exu, who is found in the thirteenth

chamber of the bottom left sector of hell, we desire you greatly, all of us!"

"We desire! We desire!"

"Oh, Father Exu, each day give us a new day, your will be done that way, for the terreiro in the zungu belongs to Our Father Exu forever and always. Amen!"

"Glory to the Gêge fatherland of Exu!"[33]

"Glory to the Son of Exu!"

Macunaíma thanked them.

Aunt Ciata concluded the prayer: "Boy who was a Gêge prince, who turned into Our Father Exu of the age of ages, forever let him be so. Amen."

"Forever let him be so, amen!"

Exu gradually healed, and an enchantment was causing everything to disappear as the brandy circulated. Soon, the polaca's body was healthy again. A great noise sounded, and the room filled with the odor of burning tar as the woman put her lips on an onyx ring. Then, she awoke, still red and fat, only more tired, and was once again just a polaca. Exu had gone away.

For the finale, everyone threw a party together, eating mounds of ham, celebrating, and dancing a wild samba. Then, everything ended and real life returned. The macumba celebrants – Macunaíma, Jaime Ovalle, Dodô, Manu Bandeira, Blaise Cendrars, Ascenso Ferreira, Raul Bopp, and Antônio Bento, all of these macumbeiros – emerged into the dawn.[34]

---

[33] The Gêge people are a West African ethnic group related to the Yoruba people.

[34] These are Brazilian public intellectuals who were contemporaries of Andrade. Jaime Ovalle was a poet and popular musician. Manu Bandeira, Blaise Cendrars, and Ascenso Ferreira were famous poets and magazine editors.

Macunaíma

Raul Bopp was a journalist, writer, and diplomat, and Antônio Bento was an art critic. Not much is known about Dodô (real name Geraldo Barrozo do Amaral), other than that he was an engineering student during the 1920s and retired as an engineer in central Brazil. A macumbeiro is a macumba celebrant.

VIII
VEI, THE SUN

Macunaíma was wandering along a path when he came upon a tall Volomã tree.[1] On one of its branches sat a pitiguari which, immediately upon seeing the hero, shrieked, "Look who's coming up the path! Look who's coming up the path!"[2]

Macunaíma looked up with the intention of thanking the bird, but the Volomã was full of fruit. The hero had arrived after being hungry for hours, and his stomach rumbled as he eyed the sapotas, sapotilhas, sapotis, bacuris, abricôs, mucajás, miritis, guabijus, melancias, and ariticums, all of these fruits.[3]

"Volomã, give me a piece of fruit," Macunaíma

---

[1] In the original Makunaima legends, "Walo'mã" is the Father of Frogs.

[2] A pitiguari is a small songbird.

[3] Sapotis, bacuris, abricôs, guabijus, and ariticums are tree fruits. Melancias are a kind of watermelon.

demanded.

The tree didn't want to give him any, however. So, the hero shouted, "Boiôiô, boiôiô! Quizama quizu!"[4]

All of the fruit fell from the tree, and he ate his fill. Volomã hated him. She picked the hero up by his feet and threw him from Guanabara Bay all the way onto a desert island that historically had been inhabited by the nymph Alamoa, who'd arrived with the Dutch.[5] Macunaíma was so exhausted that he fell asleep in midair. He landed, without waking, underneath a fragrant little guariroba palm where a vulture was perched.[6]

At that moment, the bird needed to heed nature's call, and the hero was soon dripping in the vulture's excrement. It was still dawn and the air was extremely cold. Macunaíma woke up trembling and covered in filth. He immediately searched every inch of the little island for a pit with buried money, but there wasn't one. Nor was

---

[4] In a story that Koch-Grünberg called "Die Weltbaum und die Grosse Flut" ("The World Tree and the Great Flood"), Makunaima shouts the magic words "Elupa-yeg makupa-yeg palulu-yeg," as he knocks over the Wazaka Tree to take its fruit. The stump of the tree then turns into the base of Mt. Roraima.

[5] Guanabara Bay is the bay on which Rio de Janeiro is situated. The desert island is Ilha de Fernando de Noronha, which sits in the Atlantic Ocean about two-hundred miles off the coast of northeastern Brazil. According to legend, a beautiful nymph lived there who would entice fishermen and travelers to the island, only to drive them mad by transforming into a bright light and leaving behind only her skeleton. She lives on the rocky summit of Morro do Pico, the highest point. The island was a part of New Holland during the mid-17th century, until the expulsion of the Dutch from Brazil in 1654.

[6] A guariroba is a species of palm known for its bitter taste.

there the enchanted little silver chain that locates the treasure of the Dutch for its wearer. There were only red jiquitaia ants.[7]

Caiuanogue, the morning star, passed overhead.[8] Macunaíma, feeling nauseous from living in filth, asked her to carry him to the sky. Caiuanogue approached, but the hero stank.

"Go take a shower!" she said, before turning away and moving on. Just like that, the expression "Go take a shower!" was born, which Brazilians use in reference to certain European immigrants.

Capei, the Moon, sailed along next. Macunaíma shouted a demand at her: "Your blessing, godmother Moon!"

"Umm…" she responded.

Then, he asked the Moon to carry him to the island of Marajó. Capei approached, but Macunaíma's stench was still too sour.

"Go take a shower!" she said, then turned around and left. The expression became fixed forever. Macunaíma shouted for Capei to give him at least a little fire to warm himself.

"Ask my neighbor!" she said, pointing at the Sun, who'd already arrived in the distance and was rowing across the Paraná Guaçu. Then, she went away.[9]

---

[7] "Jiquitaia" is a Tupi term that includes several species of red biting ants, similar to the American term "fire ants."

[8] The morning star is named "Kaiuanog" in the Pemón legends.

[9] The Paraná Guaçu, also known as the Rio Paraná, is a major river that flows from central Brazil south to Buenos Aires, Argentina. "Guaçu" means "large river" in Tupi.

Macunaíma was still trembling, and the vulture kept relieving itself onto him because the little island was no more than a rock with no space to escape. Vei approached, red and covered in sweat. Vei was the Sun. This was fortuitous for Macunaíma because, back at the house, he'd always given the Sun little gifts of cassava cake to lick dry.

Vei put Macunaíma on a raft with a rust-colored sail that had been painted with murici and told her three daughters to clean the hero up.[10] They picked the ticks from his body and groomed his fingernails. Afterward, Macunaíma was once again in order. However, because she was a red old woman, and so sweaty, the hero didn't suspect that she was really the good Sun, poncho of the poor. Therefore, he asked the person named Vei where he could get some heat, because, although he was clean at last, he was shivering from the cold. Vei was, in fact, the Sun and had woken up early to make Macunaíma her son-in-law. But she couldn't warm anyone yet, because it was still too early for her to gather enough strength. To amuse herself while she waited, she whistled a signal, and her three daughters fondled and tickled the hero all over his body.

He giggled quietly, letting them tickle as they pleased and really enjoying it. When they stopped, he asked for more, writhing in anticipation. Vei noticed the shamelessness of the hero and became angry. She was losing her will to use fire from her body to heat anyone up. The girls grabbed their mother and tied her up, and Macunaíma slapped the old woman's belly until there was a bonfire where everyone could warm themselves.

---

[10] "Murici" means "small tree" in Tupi and is a kind of tree which produces berries used to make dye.

Heat enveloped the raft, spread across the waters, and gilded the air. Macunaíma lay on his stomach as they glided atop a blue breaker. The silence was infinite.

"Ai… what a drag…"

The hero sighed. The only other sound was the murmur of the wave. A happy tingle crawled over Macunaíma, and it felt good. The youngest girl strummed an urucungo that her mother had brought from Africa.[11] The Paraná was wide and there wasn't a cloud in the diamond field in the sky. Macunaíma laid his head back in his hands, and while the older daughter of light swatted away a swarm of mosquitoes and black flies, the third girl, with box braids, was tickling the hero's belly which fluttered with joy. He laughed happily, stopping to indulge in verse after verse, which he sang like this:

"When I die, don't cry for me,
I quit life without regret;
An idiot survives.

For my father there was exile,
For my mother, unhappiness;
An idiot survives.

Papa came and said to me:
'You shall not have love!'
An idiot survives.

Momma came and put on me,
A necklace made of pain;
An idiot survives.

---

[11] An urucungo is an instrument comprised of a hunting bow with a hollow gourd affixed to one end to project sound.

Let the armadillo prepare the grave
With its fangless teeth;
An idiot survives.

For the most unhappy,
Of all of the disgraced,
An idiot survives."

It felt good. His body shimmered as gold dusted the salt crystals on his skin. And the smell of the briny air, the lazy oar of Vei, and the woman tickling his stomach like that… ah! Macunaíma relished the pleasure. Ah! "You're pulling my-! What kind of daughter-? A delightful one, people!" he cried. Then, closing his mischievous eyes, laughing impishly, and worn out from the good life, the hero enjoyed himself until he fell asleep.

As soon as Vei's steering oar stopped lulling him, Macunaíma woke up. In the distance, he noticed a pink skyscraper towering over everything.[12] They pulled the raft ashore at the edge of the magnificent village of Rio de Janeiro.

Before them was a vast cerrado full of brazilwood trees, with colorful palaces on either side. The cerrado was Avenida Rio Branco, where Vei, the Sun, lived with her three daughters of light.[13] Vei wanted Macunaíma to be her son-in-law because he was a hero by all accounts and

---

[12] The "towering pink skyscraper" is likely the twenty-two-story Joseph Gire Building, which was the tallest building in Latin America when it was completed in 1927.

[13] Avenida Rio Branco was a major traffic artery in Rio de Janeiro's central business district and was the location of many grand public buildings.

had given her all of those cassava cakes to suck dry. She said, "My son-in-law, you must marry one of my daughters. For a dowry I'll give you Europe, France, and Bahia.[14] However, you must be faithful and can't go fooling around with other girls around here."

Macunaíma thanked her and promised that he'd do as she asked, swearing upon the memory of his mother. Vei left with her three daughters to break the day over the great cerrado and repeated her command that Macunaíma not fool around with other girls.[15] Macunaíma again promised and swore upon his mother.

Vei and her three daughters hadn't even entered the vast cerrado before Macunaíma was overwhelmed by the urge to fool around with a girl. He lit a cigar and the urge strengthened. An array of young women strolled under the trees, radiating talent and beauty.

"I'm being held to a flame that consumes everything!" Macunaíma cried. "But there's no way that I'm free right now to let a woman do bad things to me!"

A bright light suddenly shined in his brain. He lifted himself onto the raft and, sweeping his arms across the fatherland, solemnly declared, "POOR IN HEALTH AND RICH IN SAÚVAS, THESE ARE THE EVILS OF BRAZIL!"

He jumped from the raft and ran to salute the icon of Saint Anthony, who was captain of the regiment, then made advances at all of the young women along the avenue.[16] He soon ran into one who was selling fish

---

[14] Bahia is a state along the Atlantic coast of Brazil.

[15] A cerrado is a savanna covered with dry, stunted shrubs and trees.

[16] St. Anthony of Padua (1195-1231) was a Franciscan friar and is recognized by Roman Catholics as a Doctor of the Church.

Macunaíma

outside in the little yard of his close friend, and she smelled even more acrid than him! A nice fishy stench. Macunaíma winked at her and the two climbed onto the raft, fooled around for a long time, then lay laughing with one another.

When Vei came back from the day with her three daughters at twilight, the girls arrived to find Macunaíma and the portuguesa fooling around again.[17] The three daughters of light were angered by what they saw. "This is what you do, hero!?" the eldest shouted. "After our mother, Vei, told you not to leave the raft and not to go to fool around with other girls?!"

"I was very sad!" the hero said.

"You weren't sad! There wasn't an ounce of sadness, hero! Now you'll be punished by our mother, Vei!"

Outraged, they went to the old woman. "Mother Vei, look what your son-in-law did! We hadn't even stepped foot on the cerrado before he scampered off, found a good one, brought her onto your raft, and fooled around with her endlessly! Now they're laughing with each other!"

The Sun heated up and scolded him: "But but but, my warnings! Didn't I tell you not to lie on top of any girls!?

In Brazil, where he is called St. Anthony of Lisbon on account of his birth there, he is known for a miraculous battlefield apparition. At the time of the War of Spanish Succession in the 17th century, St. Anthony was the patron saint of the Portuguese military. In 1668, Dom Pedro II, King of Portugal, enlisted St. Anthony to serve as a private in the army, and the saint was seen fighting bravely against the Spaniards in several battles. For his bravery, St. Anthony was promoted to the rank of captain, and his annual salary was paid to the Franciscan friars.

[17] A portuguesa is a woman from Portugal.

Macunaíma

I did! And still you were on top of her, fooling around in my raft. And now you're laughing with each other!"

"I'd been feeling a bit sad!" Macunaíma repeated.

"If you'd obeyed me and married one of my daughters, you would've always been young and handsome. Now you'll stay young for a short time just like all of the other men, before becoming used up and decrepit."

Macunaíma wanted to cry. He sighed. "If I'd known…"

"Oh, 'if I'd known' is a prayer of no value to anyone. You ignored my warnings! You are what you are, but you're very naughty. You really are! I'm not giving you my daughters anymore!"

Macunaíma stepped on her toes right back: "Well, I don't want any of them either, you know! Three's a crowd!"

Vei went with her three daughters to a hotel for some rest, and they left Macunaíma to sleep with the portuguesa on the raft.[18]

---

[18] This episode comes from a story that Koch-Grünberg called "Akalapizeima und die Sonne" ("Akalapizeima and the Sun"), in which Walo'ma the frog climbs to the top of a very tall tree to evade capture by a man named Akalapizoima. When the man grabs Walo'ma, the frog kicks him into the sea and swims him to a tiny island. The frog leaves him there under a tree where vultures defecate onto him, because the island is too small for him to avoid it. He asks Kaiuanog and Kapei to take him to the sky, but they both refuse because he'd given the sun cassava cakes to lick but hadn't given them any. Kapei also refuses to give him fire to warm himself. Then, Vei the sun comes with her daughters. At first, the man doesn't know that she's the sun, because she hasn't warmed up yet. When he asks her to call the sun, she takes him onto her boat and her daughters tend to him. She wants him to be her son-in-law, so

After a few hours, the Sun rose with her three girls to make their pass over the bay, and they found Macunaíma and the portuguesa still fast asleep. Vei woke the couple up and gave the Vató Stone to Macunaíma as a present.[19] The Vató Stone sparked fire at the will of whoever possessed it. Then, the Sun disappeared with her three daughters of light.

Macunaíma spent the day traipsing through town with the fishmonger and fooling around with her. After night fell, they were asleep on the shore of Flamengo when a hideous ghost appeared.[20] It was Mianiquê-Teibê, which had come to swallow the hero.[21] It breathed through its fingers, listened through its navel, and had eyes in the place of breasts. Its mouth was two mouths, and they were hidden in the inner folds of its toes. Macunaíma woke up from the stench of the ghost and sprinted like a deer away

---

she offers him her daughter's hand in marriage, as long as he doesn't fool around with other women. The man, however, is soon caught fooling around with a vulture's daughter. Vei tells him that, had he married her daughter, he would've remained young and handsome forever, but now he's doomed to grow old and ugly. Akalapizoima accepts his fate, marries the vulture's daughter, and becomes the father of all people.

[19] In a story that Koch-Grünberg called "Wie die Menschen das Feuer Erhielten" ("How People Obtained Fire"), he tells a story in which an old woman named Pelenosamo shits vató stones, which create fire when struck.

[20] Flamengo is a neighborhood on the bay in Rio de Janeiro.

[21] Mianiquê-Teibê is a creation of Andrade, but the description is similar to the headless men called "Ewaipanomas" whom Sir Walter Raleigh depicted in *The Discovery of Guyana*, published in 1599, and who thereafter became regular characters in Latin American folklore.

from Flamengo. Mianiquê-Teibê ate the fishmonger and left.

Macunaíma couldn't find any more fun in the capital of the Republic after that. He traded the Vató Stone for the publication of his portrait in a newspaper and returned to the village along the Tietê Igarapé.

Macunaíma

IX
LETTER TO THE ICAMIABAS

To Our very dear subjects, the Lady Amazons.

The Thirtieth of May in the year One Thousand Nine Hundred and Twenty Six, São Paulo

Ladies,

You will be more than a little surprised, I'm certain, by the return address and literature of this epistle. We are obliged, however, to begin these lines of longing and boundless love with some disagreeable news. It is quite true that in the good city of São Paulo – the greatest in the universe, in the words of its prolix inhabitants – you are not known as "Icamiabas," but rather by a spurious term, the appellative "Amazons." It is supposed that you voyage astride bellicose destriers and emanate from classical Hellas, so that is what you are called. This weighs heavily on Us, your Emperor, so superfluous in erudition; but you must agree with Us that, as a result, you are more heroic and more illustrious, having been plated in this respectable platinum of tradition and ancient purity.

But We shall not squander your unfettered time, much less perturb your perception, with news of bad caliber. So, We move on immediately to the report of Our accomplishments here.

Not even five suns after Our departure from you, the most terrible misfortune weighed on Us: On the beautiful night of the Ides of May of the current year, We lost the muiraquitã, which is also spelled muraquitã, or, by some scholars who are cognizant of esoteric etymologies, spelled muyrakitan, or even muraquéitã. Don't smile! You should know that this vocabulary, so familiar to your Eustachian tubes, is almost unknown here. In these most civilized locales, the warriors call themselves policemen, watchmen, civic guards, boxers, lawyers, political agitators, *et cetera*. Some of these terms are absurd neologisms, execrable bagasse with which the derelict and *petit maîtres* defile the good Lusitan language. But there is insufficient time for Us to discuss "*sub tegmine fagi*" the Portuguese language, also called Lusitan. What will interest you more, without a doubt, is to know that the warriors from here do not seek militant ladies for the epithalamic bond. They instead prefer ones who are docile and easily exchanged for tiny and volatile sheets of paper that the vulgar call money, the "*curriculum vitae*" of Civilization, and which today We place in a position of honor among Our appurtenances. In this way, the word muiraquitã, which still pains the Latin ears of your Emperor, is unknown to the warriors, and generally to everyone else who breathes in these parts. Only some "subjects of importance in virtue and letters," as it is said about the good, old, and classic Brother Luís de Sousa, who was referenced by Dr. Rui Barbosa, still project their

Macunaíma

jewelers' lamps onto the muiraquitãs and appraise them at a mediocre value, assessing that they originated from Asia and not from your violently polished fingers.[1]

We were still discouraged as a result of having lost Our muiraquitã in the shape of a sauria, when, perhaps by some metaphysical influence or, who knows, provoked by some anguished libido, as explained by the wise Teuton, Dr. Sigmund Freud (pronounced "Froyd"), a marvelous archangel appeared to Us in a dream.[2] We learned from him that the lost talisman was in the esteemed hands of Dr. Venceslau Pietro Pietra, subject of the Viceroyalty of Peru, who, candidly, is Florentine in origin, like the Cavalcantis of Pernambuco.[3] And as the Doctor lingered in the illustrious city of Anchieta, We left without delay to come here in search of the stolen golden fleece.[4]

---

[1] Fr. Luís de Sousa (1555-1632) was a Dominican Friar who lived in Portugal for most of his life, and who is famous for his histories of St. Bartholomew of Braga and St. Dominic.

[2] Sauria is a category of many different species of tropical lizard. Sigmund Freud was a contemporary of Andrade. Influential papers, such as *The Ego and the Id* (1923) and *The Dissolution of the Oedipus Complex* (1924), were published in the years preceding the publication of *Macunaíma* in 1928.

[3] The Viceroyalty of Peru was the body that governed the Spanish colonial empire from its formation in 1542 until the South American wars of independence in the early 19th century. The Cavalcantis were a noble Florentine family who relocated to Pernambuco, Brazil, in the 16th century. Their number and political power grew gradually until they owned one-third of the sugar plantations in the province. The family dynasty was the target of the failed Praieira Revolution of 1848, which was quashed by the Brazilian military.

[4] St. José de Anchieta (1534-1597) was a Jesuit priest and

Our relations with Doctor Venceslau are as favorable as possible, and without a doubt you will very soon receive the welcome news that We have recovered the talisman. And We will ask you for a reward for it.

Because, esteemed subjects, it is incontestable that We, your Emperor, find Ourselves in a precarious situation. It was Our task to convert the treasure which We had taken into the current coinage of the country, and such conversion has been very difficult for Us to execute, due to oscillations in the exchange rate and a drop in the price of cacao.

You would know better than Us that the ladies from here do not succumb to a heavy hand, nor fool around gratuitously for the sake of fooling around, but yield only to showers of cheap metal, emblazoned flutes of champagne, and comestible monsters which are commonly given the name "lobsters." And what enchanted monsters, Amazon women!!! Prepared from a carapace, polished, and presented like a ship's hull, their floppy legs, tentacles, and tails are removed with great effort. By way of a method of intense ingenuity, the entire crustacean is laid upon a plate of porcelain from Sèvres, which appeared to Us like a sailing trireme, tacking across the waters of the Nile and carrying in its bilge the priceless body of Cleopatra.[5]

---

missionary, and one of the co-founders of São Paulo. He was a prolific writer of plays and stories, through which he sought to teach the indigenous people about Christianity using characters and themes from their folklore. He was canonized a saint in 2014 by Pope Francis.

[5] Sèvres, a suburb of Paris, was the location of the Manufacture Nationale de Sèvres, a porcelain factory established in 1740 and owned by the French crown, that was famous for

Placing care on the accentuation of the word "Cleopatra," Ladies Amazon, it weighs on Us greatly that you would not prefer together with Us the pronunciation which accords with the lessons of the classics, to the more modern pronunciation of "Cleopatra" to which some vocabulists carelessly subscribe, without realizing that it is a despicable gangue that they bring to Us like a flood from France, a patois of evil death.

So, it is for this particular monster, conqueror of even the most refined palates, that the ladies here tumble on their nuptial beds. Therefore, you must understand the reward that We referenced earlier. Lobsters are very precious here, Our very precious subjects, and some of them We acquired for sixty contos or more, which, when converted into Our traditional money, reached the enormous sum of eighty-million bags of cacao. It is quite possible for you to conceive, then, how much We have spent, and We already had a paucity of the cheap metal as a result of fooling around with difficult women. We would quite like to impose an abstinence on Our burning flame, though painful, so We can spare you the expense. However, Our mighty spirit will not yield to the enchantments and gallantries of such delightful shepherdesses!

They walk around in dresses of shimmering jewels and the finest cloth that accentuate their elegant postures and barely cover their physiques which, as is their manner, they expose to evoke the beauty of shape and skin tone. The women from here are always extremely white, and they demonstrate so many great aptitudes in making love that to enumerate them all would be perhaps tedious, and

---

producing the finest porcelain in Europe. A trireme is a war galley with three decks of oarsmen, one on top of the other.

it certainly would break the mandates of discretion that the relationship between Emperor and subjects requires. What belles! What elegance! What cachet! What libertine, inflammatory, and ignoble lushes!! We think about them constantly, although We are neither neglectful nor derelict with respect to Our muiraquitã.

It seems to Us, illustrious Amazons, that you would benefit greatly from learning the indulgences, merriments, and tricks of Love from them. You would be leaving your proud and solitary beliefs for more congenial teachers, in whom the Kiss exalts, the Lusts incandesce, and, "*urbi et orbe*," the subtle force of the *Odor di Femina*, as the Italians write, demonstrates its glory.

As long as We have not restrained Ourselves on this delicate subject, We will not abandon it without some additional reports which may be useful to you. The ladies of São Paulo, who tend to be very beautiful and wise, are not content with the gifts and excellence that Nature has conceded them. They are quite preoccupied with themselves, and whatever they cannot create themselves, they order to be transported from all over the world, the most sublime and elegant products known, and assimilate this fescennine – I mean, feminine – wisdom from the ancestral civilizations. It is for this reason that they are called mistresses of Old Europe, and especially of France, and from them they have learned to pass the time in a manner quite divergent from you. Now, they preen themselves and spend hours on this delicate occupation; now, they enchant the convivial theaters of society; now, they don't do anything; and in these tasks they spend the day so frenzied and strenuous that, after coming home at night, there is barely energy left for fooling around and they immediately deliver themselves into the arms of

Orpheus, as they say.[6] But you must know, my women, that here, day and night diverge singularly from your combat schedule; the day begins when for you it is noon, and night begins when you're enjoying your most restorative hours of sleep in your quarters.

The Paulistan women learned all of this from the madams of France, and more than only the polishing and grooming of fingernails, but also, *"horresco referens,"* about the stiffest appendage of their lawful companions. Let Us move on from this vivid imagery!

There is still much to tell you about the way they cut their hair, in such a gracious and strong manner that more resembles the ephebes and Antinous of perverse memory, than the matrons of their direct Latin ancestry.[7] Nevertheless, you will agree with Us on the absurdity of long tresses around here, if you consider what was said above. As the doctors of São Paulo do not forcefully reject their requests, but instead address them in exchange for gold and fees, they regard the aforementioned hairstyles as being of little concern, observing that in this way they abate the maladies that arise in longer hair, which is the habitual pasture and abode of pernicious insects, as is the case among yourselves.

Not content with what they have learned from the madams of France, these subtleties and badges of gallantry *à Luís XV*, Paulistan women import products to enhance their essences from the most inhospitable regions of the world, such as little Japanese slippers, rubies

---

[6] The Greek god of sleep is Morphius. The reader can decide whether the error is Macunaíma's or Andrade's.

[7] Antinous was the young and beautiful Greek lover of the Roman emperor Hadrian.

from India, inventions from North America, and many other international creations and treasures.

Next, We will speak to you in a general manner about an illustrious flock of women, originally from Poland, who linger here and reign generously. They are greatly endowed in their proportions and are more numerous than the sands of the ocean. Like you, Amazonian women, these ladies form a gynaeceum, as the men who inhabit their houses are reduced to slaves and condemned to a vile office of service. Indeed, they are not called men, respond to the diminutive "*garçon*," are very polite and silent, and always wear the same gloomy outfit.

These ladies live chambered in the same locale, which here they call a "quarter," or sometimes "the tenements" or "the zone of ruin." It is worth noting that the last of these expressions would not even be included in this commentary on the things of São Paulo if it weren't for Our urge to be exact and knowledgeable. But if these dear ladies, like you, form a tribe of women, you are much different in physique, lifestyle, and ideals. Indeed, We report that they live at night, and they don't dedicate themselves the labors of Mars, nor burn their right breasts. Rather, they court only Mercury.[8] As for their chests, they allow them to be covered by gigantic, sagging breasts, which, even if they do not contribute to gracefulness, serve numerous, ardent purposes of utmost virtue and prodigious excitement.

They further differ physically, somewhat monstrously, although it is a benign monstrosity, as their brains are in their pudenda, similar to the notion from the language of madrigals that "the heart is in the hands." They speak

---

[8] Mars is the Roman god of war, and Mercury is the Roman god of commerce, communication, merchants, and thieves.

Macunaíma

numerous and very rapid dialects; they are well-travelled and highly educated; they are all always obedient; they are rich in variety, as some are blondes, some are brunettes, some are thin, and some are rotund; and they are so abundant in number and diversity that it is a mystery to Us how they could all be originally from the same country. Furthermore, they are all given the exciting, albeit unfair, epithet of "francesas." Our suspicion is that not all of these ladies are originally from Poland, that they conceal the truth, and they are Iberians, Italians, Germans, Turks, Argentines, and Peruvians, and are from all of the other fertile parts of both hemispheres.

We would greatly appreciate if you shared in Our suspicion, Amazon women, as well as if you invited some of these ladies to stay in your lands in Our Empire, so you learn from them a modern and profitable way of life, which will greatly increase the treasury of your Emperor. And even if you do not want to let your solitary beliefs go, the constant presence of several hundred of these ladies among you will greatly facilitate for Us the "*modus in rebus*" upon Our return to the Empire of the Virgin Forest, which, by the way, We would propose to rename the Empire of the Virgin Silva, more consistent with the lessons of the classics.

However, to conclude the principal matter, We would like to warn you about a danger that will result from this immigration if you do not attract some powerful doctors from beyond the limits of the State while We are away. With these women being very fiery and free, it is quite possible that the inconsequential sequestration in which you live will weigh too heavily on them and, so they do not lose the skills and secrets that earn their daily bread, it really is possible that they go to the extreme of using wild beasts, howler monkeys, tapirs, and wily candirus for practice. And it weighs ever more on Our conscience and noble sentiment of duty that you, Our subjects, may learn certain depravities from them, as did the companions of the gentle declaimer Sappho on the pink island of Lesbos, vices which hardly withstand scrutiny under the light of human possibility, much less the scalpel of rigid and sound morals.

As you see, We have taken full advantage of Our stay in the illustrious land of the Bandeirantes, and even though We care about Our talisman, We certainly have neither effort nor vile metal to spare, for We have gained valuable intelligence from this eternal Latin civilization, based on which We will commence a series of improvements upon Our return to the Virgin Forest, which will greatly facilitate Our existence and further display Our showcase of national culture to the most erudite minds in the universe.[9] Therefore, We will now tell you something about this noble city, as We intend to build an equal within your dominions in Our Empire.

São Paulo was built atop seven hills, conforming to the traditional feature of Rome, the Cesarean city and *"capita"* of the Latinity from which We derive. The graceful and restless clear waters of the Tietê kiss her feet. The waters are magnificent, the winds as mild as that of Aquisgrana or Antwerp, and the surrounding woodlands so equal to them in vitality and abundance that it could well be asserted, in the fine manner of the chroniclers, that the urban fauna generated spontaneously from three Ws.[10]

---

[9] The Bandeirantes were slave catchers, fortune seekers, and explorers, who were descendants of the first two generations of Portuguese immigrants in São Paulo and were responsible for Brazil's expansion inland beginning in the 16th century.

[10] Aquisgrana, now Aachen, Germany, was developed at the

The city is beautiful, and I am grateful for its conviviality. It is carved artfully throughout by narrow streets and apertures for the most exquisite statues, lamps, and rare sculptures, diminishing the space with such finesse that the population does not fit in these arteries. In this way, the effect of a large accumulation of people is obtained, the estimate of which can be increased at will, which is instrumental in the elections that are an invention of the inimitable Mineiros.[11] At the same time, the aediles have a wide range of materials at their disposal, with which they earn days of honor and everyone's admiration, with bursts of eloquence of the purest style and sublime craftsmanship.

The aforementioned arteries are all covered with tumbling little papers and sailing fruit peels, and most of all a very fine dust, which dances in the air and in which a thousand and one specimens of voracious microbes, which decimate the population, are scattered each day. In this way, Our superiors have solved the problem of disease transmission, as such insects devour the measly lives of the rabble, and stem the accumulation of both workers and the unemployed, thereby constantly keeping the populations in proportion and at manageable levels. And not content for this dust to be raised by the footsteps of pedestrians and by roaring machines that they call "automobiles" and "trams" (they sometimes use the word "bond," an inauthentic term certainly coming from the English), they engage diligent aediles, some kind of anthropoid riding atop monstrous centaurs of bluish

---

site of a Roman spa city.

[11] Mineiros are people from the State of Minas Gerais in southeastern Brazil.

monochrome, which collectively are given the name Public Sanitation.[12] During that *"per amica silencia lunae,"* when movement ceases and the dust settles innocuously, they leave from their mansions, and, with gyrating cylindrical brooms for tails, kick up dust from the asphalt as they are pulled along by mules, and roust insects from their slumber and incite them to activity with wild gestures and dreadful screams. These nocturnal operations are conducted discreetly under tiny lights that are distributed far and wide, in such a way that it remains almost totally dark and they do not disturb the work of malefactors and thieves.

To imitate this seems to Us like it would be excessive, and We maintain that this is the Paulistans' only custom that does not accord with Our temperament, so orderly and peaceful in nature. However, far be it from Us to reproach the administrators of São Paulo, because We know very well that malefactors and their arts are pleasing to the valiant Paulistans. The Paulistans are ardent and bold, and are greatly accustomed to the hardships of war. They live in a constant state of combat, both personal and collective, with everyone armed from head to toe. Around the city, therefore, there are a great number of disturbances in which it is common that hundreds of thousands of heroes called Bandeirantes enter the fracas. For this reason, São Paulo is endowed with a formidable and considerable Police, who inhabit expensively engineered white palaces. The Police also serve to mitigate the excess of public wealth, so the countless gold of the Nation does not depreciate. They work at this endeavor,

---

[12] The Portuguese word for a streetcar is a "bonde," which derives from the English word "bond" and is said to refer to the tickets required to ride.

Macunaíma

devouring the national treasury, with diligence and by every available means: Through parades and shimmering clothing; through the spectacles of the commendable Eugênia, who We still do not have the pleasure of knowing; or, finally, by attacking the naïve bourgeoisie as they return from their theater or cinema, venturing home by automobile through the pleasant orchards that circle the capital.[13] The Police serve also to amuse the Paulistan housemaids; and, for all of its luster, it is said that its officers attend to the task like dutiful newsboys in parks built *"ad hoc,"* such as the Parque Dom Pedro Segundo and the Jardim da Luz.[14] When the number of these Police increases, its men are sent to distant and less fertile reaches of the homeland to be devoured by swarms of giant anthropophagites, which infest Our geography and perform the inglorious task of collapsing honest Governments to the ground with the full enjoyment and general assent of the population, who acquit them at the ballot boxes and at governmental galas. The mazorqueiros catch the policemen, roast them, and eat them in the German style, and the bones that they drop on the barren land become excellent fertilizer for future coffee plantations.[15]

---

[13] Eugênia Álvaro Moreyra (1898-1948) was a Brazilian actress, journalist, and theater director based in Rio de Janeiro.

[14] The Parque Dom Pedro Segundo in São Paulo was cleared of trees in 1922 as a place for ballfields and recreation. The Jardim da Luz opened in 1825 and is the oldest park in São Paulo. In the early 20th century, both parks were known as crime hotspots.

[15] The mazorqueiros were the members of the secret police force, called the Mazorca, of Juan Manuel de Rosas, who was dictator of Argentina from 1835 until his defeat in 1852 in the

In this way, so well organized, the Paulistans live and prosper in a state of perfect order and progress. They have no shortage of time to build generous hospitals, attracting all of the lepers of South America: Mineiros, Paraibanos, Peruvians, Bolivians, Chileans, and Paraguayans, who, before going to live in these beautiful leprosaria to be served by women – always women! – of strange and decadent beauty, enliven the roads of the State and the streets of the capital in garish equestrian entourages, or in magnificent marathons that are the pride of Our sporty race, in whose countenance pulses the blood of the heroic Latin bigas and quadrigas![16]

But, my women, there are still so many diseases and insects left throughout this great country for Us to take care of! Everything is heading toward a catastrophe without moderation, and We are being corroded by disease and myriapods! Before long, We will be a new colony of England or North America! For this reason and for the eternal legacy of these Paulistans, who are the only useful people in the country and are therefore called Locomotivas, We put Ourselves to the task of metrifying a distich, which contains the secrets of so much misfortune:

"POOR IN HEALTH AND RICH IN SAÚVAS, THESE ARE THE EVILS OF BRAZIL."

This distich is what We wrote for posterity in the book

Platine War with Brazil. The term "mazorqueiro" is used in Brazil to mean any violent political agitator.

[16] Paraibanos are people from the state of Paraíba. Bigas are chariots drawn by two horses, and quadrigas are drawn by four.

Illustrious Visitors of the Instituto Butantan during Our visit to this establishment, which is famous in Europe.[17]

The Paulistans live in towering Palaces of fifty, a hundred, or even more floors. During the breeding season, clouds of mosquitoes of various species, much to the delight of the natives, bite the men and women and leave marks of such quality that the people do not need caustic nettles for stimulating massages, such as those used among the forest-dwellers. The mosquitoes dedicate themselves to this task and work such miracles that a countless multitude of boisterous boys and girls, whom We call "Italians," emerges in the squalid neighborhoods. They are destined to feed the factories of the golden potentates, and to serve, as slaves, the aromatic leisure of the Croesans.[18]

These and other multimillionaires are who erected the twelve-thousand silk factories around the city, and the famous cafes in its recesses, the world's finest, where all of the fretwork is made of carved rosewood that has been covered with gold leaf and inlaid with tortoiseshell.

The Palácio do Governo is entirely gold, in the fashion of the Queen of the Adriatic.[19] And, in silver carriages

---

[17] The Instituto Butantan is a biologic research center based in São Paulo that was founded in 1901 to combat an outbreak of bubonic plague there. It soon became world-renowned for its collection of tropical plants and venomous reptiles, spiders, and insects, which were used in the creation of medicines.

[18] Croesus was the king of Lydia (in present-day Turkey) from 561 to 546 B.C., and became legendary for his extraordinary wealth.

[19] The Palácio do Governo was constructed in 1881 at the site of the Pátio do Colégio, incorporating its existing buildings. The Pátio do Colégio was the Jesuit school and church, where,

lined with the finest fur, the President, who keeps many wives, cruises in the late afternoons, smiling serenely.

We could illustrate for you the Paulistans' many other magnificent qualities, lady Amazons, if this epistle were not already so protracted. However, by affirming for you that this is, without a doubt, the most beautiful earthly city, We have already done much to bestow favor on these men of profit. But We would feel ashamed if We concealed in silence a unique curiosity of these people. We inform you that their wealth of intellectual expression is so prodigious that they speak in one language and write in another. Having arrived in these hospitable lands, We put Ourselves to the task of studying the local ethnology, and of all of the surprising and amazing linguistic originalities that We have discovered, this certainly was not the least. In conversation, the Paulistans use a barbaric and multifarious language which is crass in nature and vulgar in vocabulary, and which does not cease to express flavor and force in apostrophes and in the voices of lovers in the night. We are aware, solicitous even, of these qualities, and We will be grateful for the opportunity to teach them to you upon arrival. But even though they use disgraceful language in the natural conversation of this land, as soon as they take up the pen, they are stripped of all of that vulgarity, and the Latin Man of Linnaeus emerges, expressing himself in another language (very close to Virgilian, in the words of one panegyrist), a lovely

---

on January 25, 1554, the city of São Paulo was founded at its inaugural mass. It was siezed by the government for use as an administrative building upon the expulsion of the Jesuits from the Portuguese Empire in 1759. In 1953, the site was returned to the Jesuits, and the school and church were restored to their original appearance. The Queen of the Adriatic is Venice, Italy.

language which, with eternal reverence, is called "The Language of Camões!"[20] You will be grateful to learn of such originality and sophistication, and you will be even more amazed that, to the great and almost total majority, not even these two languages suffice and, for additional music and grace, they are further enriched by genuine Italian, which is well versed throughout all of the corners of the city. We learned extensively about all of that, thank the gods, and We have spent many hours in conversation about the letter z in the word "Brazil" and the issue of the pronoun "se." Moreover, We have acquired many bilingual books, called "burros," as well as the *Pequeno Larousse* dictionary, and We are already in a position to recite many famous passages from the philosophers and the testicles of the Bible in original Latin.[21]

With all of that said, Amazon women, you need to know that this great city has been elevated to these advancements and bright civilization by your superiors, who are called politicians. This appellative designates a very refined race of doctors, so unfamiliar to you that you would consider them monsters. They are unparalleled in

---

[20] Carl Linnaeus (1707-1778) was a Swedish scientist who is considered the father of biological taxonomy for his invention of the binomial Latin nomenclature for naming organisms. Virgil (70-19 B.C.) is a Roman poet who is most famous for writing the epic poem *The Aeneid*. Luís de Camões (1525-1580) is considered the greatest poet of the Portuguese language, and his importance to its development is analogous to Shakespeare's influence on English. He is most famous for the epic poem *The Lusiads*, about Vasco de Gama's discovery of a sea route to India.

[21] The *Pequeno Larousse* dictionary was a Spanish-language dictionary published in 1912 in Paris.

grandeur, audacity, wisdom, honesty, and morality, but are in fact monsters; although they appear something like men, they really originate from uirauaçus and have little in common with humans.[22] They all obey an emperor, called "Big Papa" in the familiar argot, who lives in the oceanic city of Rio de Janeiro, the most beautiful city in the world in the opinion of every foreigner, which We have verified with Our own eyes.

Finally, Amazon women and much beloved subjects, We have suffered greatly and have endured arduous and constant burdens beyond the duties of Our position, which have kept Us separated from the Empire of the Virgin Forest. Here, everything is delight and bliss, but nevertheless We do not have satisfaction or rest, because We still have not recovered the talisman. We would like to repeat, however, that Our relations with Doctor Venceslau are as amicable as possible, that negotiations are underway and perfectly on track, and you are quite welcome to send in advance the reward that We mentioned above. Your abstemious Emperor is content with little; if you cannot send two hundred igaras packed with bags of cacao, send only one hundred, or even fifty!

Receive the blessing of your Emperor for more health and fraternity. Observe with respect and obedience these poorly scribbled lines and, above all, do not forget to send the reward and the polonesas that We require desperately.[23]

---

[22] "Uirauaçu" is a Tupi word for certain large birds of prey.

[23] "Polonesa" is a word for "Polish woman" without the negative connotations of "polaca."

Macunaíma

May Ci protect Your Excellencies,

Macunaíma
Emperor

X
PAUÍ-PÓDOLE

Venceslau Pietro Pietra had been wounded extensively in the beating and his whole body was wrapped in cotton gauze. He spent months in his hammock, during which time Macunaíma couldn't take even a single step toward recapturing the muiraquitã, as it was tucked inside a snail hidden under the giant's body. He imagined putting termites in his adversary's slipper, because they say that it causes death, but Piaimã had backwards feet and didn't wear slippers. Macunaíma was frustrated and spent the day in his hammock munching on tender tapioca crepes between long sips of liquor. As he was doing so, Antonio the Indian, a famous saint, along with his companion, the Mother of God, came seeking a bunk at the boarding house.[1] He visited Macunaíma, made a speech, and

---

[1] Antônio Tamandaré was a Tupinambá native who fled the Jesuit-founded village where he lived and started a religious movement called Santidade ("Sanctity"), which blended symbols and rites from Roman Catholic and Tupi traditions.

baptized the hero on behalf of a god who had a form that was a combination of fish and tapir and who was expected to arrive any day. That was how Macunaíma joined the Caraimonhagan religion which was causing a furor in the countryside of Bahia.[2]

Macunaíma took advantage of the delay by perfecting the two languages of the land, spoken Brazilian and written Portuguese. He soon knew the names for everything. On Dia da Flor, a holiday invented so Brazilians would be charitable, there were so many mosquitos that Macunaíma stopped studying and went into the city to clear his thoughts.[3] What he saw there was absurd. He stopped at every store window and observed a pack of monsters inside each one, so many that it looked like the Serra do Ererê, where everyone had taken refuge while the great flood inundated the world.[4] Macunaíma was walking along when he encountered a girl with a

---

He was accused by the Portuguese authorities of declaring himself Pope and was sentenced to death. At his execution, his tongue was torn from his mouth and he was strangled by indigenous people from other Jesuit-led villages. During the inquisitions that followed, Roman Catholic authorities discovered that many native converts believed that the "Mother of God" was not the mother of Jesus, but was instead the Pope's wife.

[2] "Caraimonhaga" is the Tupi name for the Santidade religion.

[3] Dia da Flor ("Flower Day") was a civic holiday in the early 20th century, on which day people were encouraged to purchase paper flowers sold for the benefit of charitable institutions.

[4] The Serra do Ererê is a mountain along the Amazon River. In 1895, caves containing pre-Columbian wall paintings were discovered high in the cliffs.

basket full of roses. The girl stopped him and put a flower in his lapel, saying, "It costs a milréis."

Macunaíma was very upset because he didn't know the name of the hole in the clothing machine where the girl had stuck the flower. The hole was called a "buttonhole." He rummaged thoroughly through his memory, but he'd never actually heard that name before. He wanted to refer to the hole, but he was overwhelmed by all of the other holes he'd heard of in this new world and felt embarrassed in front of the girl. "Orifice" was a word that people wrote, but no one ever said "orifice." After thinking for a while, he had no clue of the name of it, and he noticed that he'd arrived in front of São Bernardo, having walked all the way from the Rua Direita, where he had come across the girl, and past the home of Master Cosme.[5] So, he went back, paid the girl, and said in a huff, "This woman swindled me! Never again put a flower in my… in my puíto, lady!"

Macunaíma was speaking with a foul mouth once again. He had uttered an extremely filthy obscenity! The girl didn't know that "puíto" was a swear word, and as the

---

[5] São Bernardo is a suburb of São Paulo, and the Rua Direita is a main thoroughfare through central São Paulo. Master Cosme Fernandes is another person (in addition to the criminal described in ch. IV, n. 18) who's been identified as the "Bachelor of Cananéia." Cosme Fernandes was a successful settler and merchant on the coast of Brazil who amassed a fortune by selling supplies to sailors from other countries. His dealings with rival empires drew the ire of the Portuguese crown, who launched an expedition to turn his settlement, Cananéia, into a colonial town. In opposition, he launched a raid on São Vicente (present-day São Paulo), which was successful. He then returned to Cananéia and disappeared from history.

hero was returning to the boarding house in a daze from the interaction, she laughed to herself, finding humor in the word. She said it herself: "Puíto." Then, she repeated it with joy: "Puíto. Puíto." She thought that it was fashionable, so she began telling everyone that, if they wanted, she would stick a rose in their puíto. Some wanted to and others didn't. Other girls heard the word, used it, and "puíto" caught on. Nobody said "en boutonnière" anymore, for example; only "puíto" was ever heard.[6]

It was as though Macunaíma had been mired in olive oil for a week, not eating, fooling around, or sleeping, because he wanted only to study the languages of the land. He knew that he could ask someone what the name of that hole was, but he was ashamed that they would think that he was ignorant and dumb.

At last, the pipe-smoking Sunday that was Cross Day had arrived, a new holiday invented so Brazilians could get more rest. In the morning, there was a parade in Mooca; at noon, there was an outdoor mass in Coração de Jesus; at five o'clock, there was a car parade and confetti war on Avenida Rangel Pestana; and in the evening, after the deputies and vagrants marched down the Rua Quinze,

---

[6] In a story that Koch-Grünberg calls "Pu'yito. Wie Tiere und Menschen Ihren After Bekamen" ("Pu'yito. How Animals and People Got Their Anuses"), he tells about Pu'yito, a living anus. In ancient times, humans and animals didn't have anuses, and instead defecated from their mouths. Pu'yito would sneak around, fart in their faces, and run away. One day, he exhausted everyone's patience, so they captured him and tore him apart. Then, each one took a piece of Pu'yito and stuck it to their behind. Ever since that day, people and animals have defecated from anuses instead of their mouths.

Macunaíma

they went to set off fireworks in Iparanga.[7] So, to relax, Macunaíma went to the park to watch the fireworks.

As soon as he left the boarding house, he encountered a girl who was pale and light blonde, completely white, a good little cassava daughter wearing a hat of red tucumã covered in daisies.[8] Her name was "Fraulein" and she required constant protection. They went to the park together, and it was beautiful. There were elaborate combinations of fountain machines and electric-light machines, where people stood and leaned against each other in the dark, holding hands to steady themselves in the face of such amazement. Fraulein did the same and Macunaíma whispered sweetly, "Mani. Little cassava daughter."[9]

The German girl was moved to tears, and she turned and asked him if he'd let her stick a daisy in his puíto. At first, the hero was very startled – shocked! – and even

---

[7] Mooca is a district near the center of São Paulo. The Coração de Jesus, or the Santuário do Sagrado Coração de Jesus ("Sanctuary of the Sacred Heart of Jesus") is a church in São Paulo built in 1881 by St. John Bosco (popularly known as "Don Bosco") and his disciples. In front of the church used to be a large grassy plaza where outdoor masses were held. Avenida Rangel Pestana is a main thoroughfare in central São Paulo. Rua Quinze is a pedestrian street in the center of the city that was one of the most fashionable and wealthy streets in the city at the time of *Macunaíma*'s publication. Iparanga is a neighborhood in São Paulo where Dom Pedro I, the first emperor of Brazil, is said to have made the decision in 1822 to declare Brazil's independence from Portugal.

[8] Tucumã is a kind of palm.

[9] In some Tupi-Guarani myths, cassava grows from the corpse of a white girl named Mani.

started to grow angry. But then he put the pieces together and realized that he'd done something clever. He burst into laughter.

Unbeknownst to Macunaíma, "puíto" had already entered the journals that scientifically study the spoken and written languages of Brazil, and it was more than settled by the laws of catalexis, ellipsis, syncope, metonymy, metaphony, metathesis, proclisis, prothesis, apheresis, apocope, haplology, and etymology, all of these popular laws, that "puíto" was derived from the word "botoeira" by way of an intermediary word, the Latin word "rabanitius" (botoeira-rabanitius-puíto). Although the word "rabanitius" was not found in medieval documents, the doctors claimed that it certainly existed and was prevalent in Vulgar Latin.[10]

At that moment, a man from the multiracial crowd climbed a statue and began an enthusiastic speech explaining to Macunaíma what Cross Day was. In the clear nighttime sky, there was neither a cloud nor Capei. The people were met with a familiar sight: the fathers of the trees, the fathers of the birds, the fathers of the animals, and their relatives, brothers, fathers, mothers, aunts, sisters-in-law, daughters, and sisters, all of these stars twinkling quite happily in the firmament above this land without evil, which is rich in health and poor in saúvas. Macunaíma listened with appreciation, agreeing with the long speech. It was only after the man had gestured and explained for a while that Macunaíma noticed that the Cross was made up of four stars that he knew quite well were the Father of Curassows, who lived in the field of

---

[10] "Botoeira" was the term used at the time in São Paulo for a lapel buttonhole, and "rabanitius" is a made-up word.

the sky.[11] He was angry at the speaker's lie and shouted, "No, it's not!"

"My good sirs," said the speaker. "What this other guy is talking about is those four stars, 'glistening like impassioned tears,' in the words of the sublime poet. They are the sacrosanct and traditional Cross which-"

"No, they aren't!"
"Psycho!"
"The symbol is more-"
"No, it isn't!"
"Back off!"
"Let's take it outside!"
"Psycho! Psycho!"
"That mysterious shining Cross is our beloved homeland's most sublime and marvelous-"
"No, it isn't!"
"You see, with-"
"Don't cause a riot!"
"With its... four... spangles of bright silver-"
"No, it isn't!"

"No, it isn't!" the others also shouted. With all of that commotion, the speaker was finally quelled, and everyone present, excited by the hero's cries of "no it isn't," was overcome with the urge to cause mayhem. Macunaíma was trembling so furiously, however, that he didn't even notice. He jumped onto the pedestal of the statue and began to tell the story of the Father of Curassows, which went like this:

"No, it isn't! Ladies and gentlemen, those four stars over there are the Father of Curassows! I swear that it's

---

[11] "The Cross" refers to the constellation commonly known as the Southern Cross.

the Father of Curassows, my people, who appears in the vast field of the sky! He ascended from the great Fulano Forest in the age when animals were no longer men.[12] At that time, there were two brothers-in-law who lived quite far from one another. One was named Camã-Pabinque and he was a sorcerer.[13] One day, Camã-Pabinque's brother-in-law went into the forest to enjoy a bit of hunting. As he was doing so, he encountered Pauí-Pódole and his partner, the firefly Camaiuá.[14] Pauí-Pódole was the Father of Curassows and, a long time ago, he and Camaiuá were people like us.[15] He was perched on a high branch of a teak tree, where he was resting. The sorcerer's brother-in-law immediately returned to his hut and told his companion that he'd run into Pauí-Pódole and his partner, Camaiuá. The man said further that he'd wanted to kill Pauí-Pódole with his blowgun, but couldn't reach the Father of Curassows's lofty perch in the teak tree. So, he grabbed a paracuuba spear with a bamboo point and went to fish for carapicu.[16] Camã-Pabinque soon arrived at his brother-in-law's hut and said, 'Sister, what did your companion say to you?'

"The sorcerer's sister told him everything, including that Pauí-Pódole was perched in the teak tree with

---

[12] "Fulano" is a term used to convey uncertainty, so "fulano forest" means something like "some forest."

[13] Camã-Pabinque is a creation of Andrade.

[14] In the Pemón version of the legend, "Kamayua" is a giant wasp.

[15] Pauí-Pódole is the Father of Curassows in the original Pemón version, as well.

[16] A paracuuba is a type of tall, flowering tree. Carapicu is a kind of coastal fish.

Camaiuá the firefly. The next morning, Camã-Pabinque came out of his tent and saw Pauí-Pódole chirping on his branch. The sorcerer turned into a flood of tocandiras and climbed up the trunk, but the Father of Curassows saw the ants and emitted a sharp tweet.[17] He blew so hard that the sorcerer plummeted from the tree and onto the weeds of the forest floor. Camã-Pabinque next turned into the tiny tocandira Opalá, to climb up once again. But Pauí-Pódole turned around, saw the bug, and blew again, creating a gusting wind that sent Opalá tumbling onto the wildflowers of the forest floor. Then, Camã-Pabinque turned into a fire ant named Megue, a tiny little thing, who climbed up the teak tree, bit the Father of Curassows right on the cleft of his nose, skittered around his body, took his unmentionable between his stingers, and – yikes! – sprayed formic acid onto it.[18] Well! You guys! A jet of blood sprayed from Pauí-Pódole's wound and launched Megue far into the distance! The sorcerer couldn't escape from Megue's body anymore, however, because of the shock he'd experienced. So, he created a plague of little fire ants and left it for us, the people!

"Poor in health and rich in saúvas, these are the evils of Brazil.

"So, as I was saying: The next day, Pauí-Pódole wanted to go live in the sky to avoid suffering the ants of this land any longer, and he did. He asked Camaiuá to illuminate the way with his bright green-little lantern. The firefly Cunavá, Camaiuá's nephew, went to the front to light the

---

[17] Tocandiras are a species of ant, sometimes called "bullet ants," which are known for their painful stings and are a feature of religious rituals involving pain and strength.

[18] In the Pemón version of the legend, Megue is simply "Meg."

way for his uncle and asked his brother to come up and help.[19] His brother asked their father to join, and their father asked their mother, and their mother asked the whole swarm. The chief of police, the inspector of the block, and many others formed into a cloud of fireflies that illuminated the way for each other. They made their way up to the sky, enjoyed themselves, and, one after the other, decided not to return. And that path of light can still be seen transiting space. Pauí-Pódole then flew to the sky and stayed there. You guys! Those four stars are not the Cross! That's not the Cross at all! It's the Father of Curassows! It's the Father of Curassows, you guys! It's the Father of Curassows, Pauí-Pódole, who appears in the vast field of the heavens! There's nothing else to say about it."[20]

---

[19] In the Pemón version of the legend, "Kunava" is a magical plant that lights the way with its torch.

[20] In a story that Koch-Grünberg called "Mauai-Pódole, E'moron-Pódole, and Paui-Pódole," a nameless sorcerer's brother-in-law encounters Paui-Pódole, the Father of Curassows, who is with Kamayua. The brother-in-law tries to shoot Paui-Pódole with his blowgun, but the dart can't reach where he's sitting up in his tree. So, the sorcerer goes to the tree, turns into an ant, and starts to climb. Paui-Pódole, however, begins to sing, which blows the sorcerer to the ground. The sorcerer then turns into Opala, who is another kind of ant, and climbs again. But Paui-Pódole again blows him from the tree. Finally, the sorcerer turns into Meg the ant and climbs up Paui-Pódole's nose. Paui-Pódole sneezes him out, and he becomes forever trapped in the body of an ant. Then, Paui-Pódole flies up to the sky and turns into the Southern Cross constellation. Kamayua flies up to join him while Kunava lights the way.

Macunaíma stopped, exhausted by his oration. Then a long joyful murmur arose from the crowd, and the people beamed even brighter as they observed the fathers of the birds, the fathers of the fish, the fathers of the insects, the fathers of the trees, all of these familiar beings that appear in the field of the sky. The Paulistans were comforted by all of these fathers of creation, who shimmered and dwelled in the sky, and filled the people's eyes with wonder. All of these marvels used to be people before they became strange beings who gave birth to all living things. And now they are the little stars in the sky.

The people left moved, happy in heart, satisfied by the explanations, and attentive to the living stars. Nobody bothered anymore with Cross Day, nor with the fountain machines mixed with the electric-light machines. They went home and each one put an animal skin under the bedsheet because they'd played with fire that night and were certain that they were going to wet the bed.[21] Then, they all went to sleep, and darkness fell.

Macunaíma stood alone on the base of the statue. He'd been moved, too. He looked up. The Cross wasn't there! But he could see Pauí-Pódole clearly, admiring Macunaíma and laughing, grateful for what the hero had done. Suddenly, he let out a loud drawn-out chirp, like a train whistle. But it wasn't a train, it was a chirp, and the blast extinguished all of the lights in the park. Then, the Father of Curassows gently waved a wing in farewell to the hero. Macunaíma went to thank him, but the bird stirred up a cloud of dust, set off in a burst, and spread his wings to fly across the vast field of the sky.

---

[21] "A child who plays with fire wets his bed at night" is a popular warning given to Brazilian children.

Macunaíma

XI
OLD CEIUCI

The next day, the hero woke up with a bad cold because, notwithstanding the heat of the night, he'd slept in his clothes because he was afraid of Cruviana, who kidnaps people sleeping naked.[1] He was feeling proud after the success of his speech the day before and, after waiting impatiently for fifteen days of misery, decided to tell the people about more of his escapades. But by the time he felt ready, it was early in the morning, and he who tells stories during the day grows an agouti tail. So, he invited his brothers to go hunting and they accepted.

When they arrived at the woodlands of Bosque da Saúde, the hero said, "Here's good."[2]

---

[1] "Cruviana" is a regional slang term that means "cold drizzle" in the state of Bahia, and "cold wind" in the state of Pará. There is a folktale in which a foreigner is warned to watch for "cruviana" at dawn, so he brings a gun with him because he thinks "cruviana" might be a monster.

[2] Bosque da Saúde is a neighborhood in São Paulo that, at the

He told his brothers to wait while he went to scout for game. When he was out of view, he set fire to some woods, crouched down, and waited for a red brocket to emerge. But there weren't any red brockets there. So, when the fire burned out, did an alligator come out? Neither did any red brockets, nor even a grey brocket; only a pair of scorched rats emerged. The hero slayed the rats, ate them, and returned to the boarding house without calling for his brothers.

When he arrived, he gathered servants, the landlady, girls, typists, students, and bureaucrats – so many bureaucrats! – and told all of these neighbors that that he'd gone hunting by the Arouche market and had killed two "brockets.[3] But not red brockets. Two grey brockets that I ate with my brothers. I wanted to bring you a piece, but I tripped on a curb, fell down, dropped the bundle, and a dog ate everything."

Everyone doubted the story and distrusted the hero. When Maanape and Jiguê returned, the neighbors asked them if it was true that Macunaíma had hunted two grey brockets near the Arouche market. The brothers were furious because they hadn't known about the lie, and one of them shouted, "What grey brockets are you talking about!? The hero didn't kill any deer! There weren't any brockets on the hunt! The cat meows but hunts little, everyone! It was only two charred rats that Macunaíma caught and ate."

The neighbors realized that everything the hero had

---

time of *Macunaíma*'s publication, was known for its extensive parkland.

[3] Largo do Arouche ("Arouche Square") is a public plaza in central São Paulo.

said was a lie, grew enraged, and entered his room to take revenge. Macunaíma was playing a little flute made of hollowed papaya branches. He stopped blowing and began to whittle the mouthpiece of the flute, admiring it quietly. Then, he snapped, "Why is this mob in my room right now!? It's bad for our health, you guys!"

Someone asked him, "What exactly did you hunt, hero?"

"Two red brockets."

The servants, girls, students, and bureaucrats, all of these neighbors, laughed at him. Macunaíma was still whittling the mouthpiece of the flute. The landlady crossed her arms and scolded him: "My dear, why are you telling us that there were two brockets when there were really only two charred rats!?"

Macunaíma looked straight at her and said, "I lied."

All of the neighbors wore the expression of André on their faces, and each one walked out into the still afternoon. André was a neighbor who was always moping around in shame. Maanape and Jiguê looked at each other, each one jealous of their brother's intelligence. Maanape asked him, "Why did you lie, hero!?"

"It wasn't because I wanted to. I wanted to just tell everyone what had happened, but then I noticed that I was lying."

He tossed the little flute aside, grabbed a ganzá, cleared his throat, and sang.[4] For the entire afternoon, he sang so mournfully that he wept with every verse. He stopped only when his sobbing became so heavy that he couldn't continue any longer and dropped the ganzá. Outside, a gloomy twilight filtered through a patch of fog. Macunaíma was sad and longed for the unforgettable Ci.

---

[4] A ganzá is a kind of cylindrical rattle.

He called his brothers so they could console him together. Maanape and Jiguê sat next to him on the bed, and the three spoke for a long time about the Mother of the Forest. Waxing nostalgic, they talked about the Uraricoera's forests, overgrowth, fog, gods, and treacherous ravines. There they had been born and had laughed for the first time in their hammocks. More than five hundred families of guiras sang perched on maquiras outside the clean boarding house.[5] Close to fifteen-times-a-thousand species of animals animated the forest that had so many millions of trees that they couldn't keep count. A white man from the land of the English had brought in his gothic saddlebag a malady which lived in a den of black mumbuca ants, and now made Macunaíma cry with longing for the past. In the darkness, the heat softened as though it had been soaked in water; through the windows, people were heard singing as they did their evening chores; and the hero's mother had been turned into a gentle hill at a place called Father of Tocandeiras. Ai, what a drag… Suddenly, the three brothers heard the murmur of the Uraricoera nearby! Oh, how good life had been there! The hero again broke down weeping as he lay on the bed.

When he no longer felt the urge to cry, Macunaíma swatted at the mosquitoes and tried to relax. He decided to insult the giant's mother with a mouthful of obscenities that had just arrived from Australia. He turned Jiguê into a telephone machine, but the brother was still very upset by the hero's lies, and there was no way to turn him on. The device had a defect. So, Macunaíma smoked some

---

[5] A guira is a species of bird known for its cream-colored plumage and large black tail feathers. A maquira is kind of palm tree.

parica seeds to conjure salacious dreams, and fell fast asleep.[6]

The next day, he decided to get revenge on his brothers and planned to catch them in a snare. He got up with the early dawn and hid in the landlady's room, fooling around with her to pass time. Then, he returned to his brothers and told them with enthusiasm, "Hey, brothers, I found a fresh tapir track right in front of the Commodities Exchange!"

"What'd you say, scrub jay!?"

"It's true! Who else has to say it!?"

Nobody had ever killed a tapir in the city. The brothers were surprised, but went with Macunaíma to hunt the beast. When the hero said that they'd arrived, they began searching for the trail. Seeing the three brothers bent over the asphalt, a world of people, merchants, brokers, hagglers, and dealers, began searching, too. They looked everywhere. Did you find it? Neither did they! So, they asked Macunaíma, "Where'd you see the tapir track? There aren't any tracks around here!"

Macunaíma didn't even lift his head and kept repeating the words "tetápe, dzónanei pemonéite hêhê zeténe netaíte."

The brothers, barterers, deadbeats, street vendors, mourners, and Hungarians started looking for the tapir tracks again. Whenever they got tired and stopped to ask Macunaíma where he'd last seen them, he always responded without interrupting his search, "Tetápe, dzónanei pemonéite hêhê zeténe netaíte."

That entire world of people searched until dusk, when

---

[6] A parica is a kind of tree that produces seeds which are used as a stimulant and narcotic, typically by grinding them into a powder and snorting them through the nose.

they finally stopped, discouraged. Macunaíma excused himself: "Tetápe, dzónanei pemo-"

They didn't even let him finish, as everyone shouted over him, asking what that phrase meant. Macunaíma responded, "I don't know. I learned those words back home when I was little."[7]

Everyone was incensed. Macunaíma acted oblivious, saying, "Calm down, people! Tetápe hêhê! I didn't say there was a tapir trail! That's not what I said! And there's nothing else to say about it."

The situation worsened. One of the merchants was enraged by the truth, and the reporter next to him, seeing that he was angry, became angry, too.

"That's not right! We're out here working to earn our daily bread and some guy had us take a whole day off just to search for a tapir trail!"

"But I didn't ask anyone to look for the trail! Forgive me! My brothers Maanape and Jiguê went around asking everyone for help! Not me! It's their fault!"

The outraged mob turned on Maanape and Jiguê.

---

[7] In a story that Koch-Grünberg called "Kalawunseg der Lügner" ("Kalawunseg the Liar"), Kalawunseg lies to his brothers-in-law about having seen a tapir in the forest. The next morning, the three men go hunting for the tapir, but the brothers-in-law don't see the tapir's tracks, so they ask Kalawunseg where he'd seen it. Kalawunseg speaks the gibberish words "tetápe, dzónanei pemonéite hêhê zeténe netaíte," and says he can't find it, so the brothers-in-law grow angry and leave. Then, Kalawunseg goes deer hunting with his wife. When they burn a field to flush out some deer, only two rats emerge. Kalawunseg kills and eats them, then tells his neighbors that he had killed two deer. When the neighbors ask his wife what happened, she reveals that he only killed two rats and they all find out that he was lying.

Everyone – and there was a pack of them! – was in the mood for a fight. A student climbed onto the roof of a car and made a speech against Maanape and Jiguê: "Gentlemen, life in a great urban center like São Paulo already requires such intense work that not even a moment spent on frivolous activity is permitted by this magnificent system of progress. Let us rise up, each one of you, against the deleterious miasmas that defile our social organism. And as the Government shuts its eyes and squanders the Nation's treasury, let us be the ones who bring justice-"

The people were extremely angry. "Hang them! Hang them!" they shouted.

"You're not hanging anyone!" yelled Macunaíma, directing their rancor away from his brothers.

So, everyone turned against him once again, and now they were furious. The student continued, "And when the people's honest work is interrupted by a stranger-"

"What!? Who's a stranger!?" yelled Macunaíma, offended by the remark.

"You!"

"Am not!"

"Are too!"

"Go feed a jacu some birdseed, boy!" shouted Macunaíma. "Your mother's a stranger, you hear!?" Then, turning to the people, he said, "What are you thinking, huh!? I'm not afraid! Not of one, not of two, not of ten thousand of you. And in a little while, I'm going to demolish everything around here!"

A grieving woman in front of the hero turned to the merchant behind her. She was angry with him: "Don't grope me! Shame on you!"

The hero went blind with rage because he thought that she was talking to him. He said, "What do you mean 'don't

grope'!? I'm not groping anyone, bitch!"
"Hang the groper! Beat him!"
"Come at me, goons!"

He advanced toward the crowd. A lawyer tried to run away, but Macunaíma kicked him in the back, then pushed his way through the multitude, doling out kicks and headbutts. Suddenly, he saw a tall, blond, and handsome man in front of him. He was a policeman. Macunaíma despised such beauty and spit in the policeman's face. The policeman grabbed the hero by the nape of his neck and yelled something in a strange language: "You're under arrest!"

The hero froze. "Why under arrest?"

The policeman responded with a bunch of phrases in the strange language and held him tight.

"I'm not doing anything!" the hero objected with fear in his voice.

The policeman didn't want to discuss it, however, and led him down the steep, narrow alley with everyone following along. Another policeman arrived and the two spoke many words – so many! – in the strange language, and soon they were both pushing the hero down the alley. A witness to everything recounted the events to a gentleman who was standing in the doorway of a fruit shop, and the magnanimous gentleman passed through the crowd and stopped the policemen. By that time, they had reached Rua Libero.[8] The gentleman made a speech to the policemen about how they shouldn't take Macunaíma prisoner because the hero hadn't done anything wrong. A bunch of policemen were gathered there, but none of them understood the speech because none of them understood Brazilian words. The women

---

[8] Rua Libero is a commercial street in the center of São Paulo.

wept with pity for the hero. The policemen continued to speak in their strange language until someone in the crowd shouted, "You can't!"

The people felt the urge to fight once again, and they were now shouting from all sides: "Release him!" "Don't take him!" "You can't!" "You can't!" "Drop him!" It was a commotion. A farmer started making a speech insulting the Police. The policemen didn't understand any of it, however, and were gesticulating in confusion and speaking in their strange language. The people, meanwhile, had formed into a fearsome mob. Macunaíma took advantage of the mayhem, and his legs did exactly what he wanted! A streetcar came clanging down the track, and Macunaíma hopped aboard to go see how the giant was faring.

Venceslau Pietro Pietra had already started to recover from the beating he'd taken at the macumba. It was hot inside the house because they were cooking polenta, but there was a fresh southern breeze outside. So, the giant, the old woman Ceiuci, and her two daughters, along with servants carrying chairs, had come to sit in the front doorway to enjoy the fresh air. The giant still hadn't removed his cotton bandages, which made it difficult to walk. They were still sitting together when Macunaíma arrived.

A young man named Chuvisco was wandering aimlessly through the neighborhood and found Macunaíma on the corner trying to provoke the giant.[9] He stopped to watch the hero. Macunaíma turned around and said, "You didn't see anything!"

"What are you doing, bud?"

"I'm scaring the giant, Piaimã, who's sitting over there

---

[9] "Chuvisco" literally means "drizzle."

with his family."

Chuvisco mocked him: "Come on! Can't you see that the giant's not afraid of you!?"

Macunaíma stared at the fat young boy and became angry. He wanted to beat him up but remembered an old maxim: "When you're angry, count the buttons on your clothes three times." So, he did and calmed back down. He responded, "You want to bet? I'll go walk past them, and I guarantee that Paiamã runs inside because he's so afraid of me. Hide nearby and just listen to what they say."

Chuvisco warned, "Just you try scaring the giant, friend! You already know what he's capable of. Piaimã may appear weak and feeble, but it's the seeds inside the pepper which retain the heat. If you're really not afraid of him, I'll take the bet."

He turned into a vapor droplet and hung close to Venceslau Pietro Pietra and his wife, daughters, and servants. Macunaíma chose the finest swear word of his collection and spat it in Piaimã's face. The expletive hit hard, but Venceslau Pietro Pietra wasn't bothered at all, a veritable elephant. Macunaíma yelled another, even uglier, mouthful at the old shrew. It was a direct hit, but she was no more bothered than her husband. So, Macunaíma shouted his whole collection of insults, which was ten-thousand-times-ten thousand swear words. Venceslau Pietro Pietra said very quietly to the old woman Ceiuci, "Some of those we didn't already know. Remember them for our daughters."

Chuvisco returned to the corner where the hero was doubled over with laughter. "Were they afraid or what!?" asked Macunaíma.

"They weren't afraid at all! The giant even saved your insults for his daughters to play with later. You don't think they're afraid of me? Just go over there and listen."

Macunaíma turned into a caxipara, which is a male saúva, and burrowed into the cotton bandages wrapped around the giant. Chuvisco turned into a cloud of mist, and as he passed in front of the family, he peed in the air and sprayed a lazy shower. As the drops started to fall, the giant looked at one that was clinging to his hand and filled with dread at the idea of all of that water around him.

"Let's go inside, everyone!" They were all very frightened and ran inside.

Chuvisco turned back into a boy and said to Macunaíma, "See?"

And that's how it is to this day: The giant's family is afraid of Chuvisco but not of swear words.

Macunaíma was resentful and asked his rival, "Tell me one thing: Do you know the lang-pang-gauge-page language?"

"I've never heard one more robust!"

"So then, my nemesis, go-po to-poo shit-pit!" said the hero. Then, he returned to the boarding house.

He was still very upset because he'd lost the bet, however, and decided to go fishing. But he couldn't fish with a bow and arrow, a basket-trap, a throw net, a pool trap, a line, a spear, a hook, decoys, a fishing rod, lures, nor a hand net, not with any of these traps, because he didn't have any of them. So, he made a hook out of mandaguari wax, and took it to a place on the riverbank near an Englishman who was fishing for aimará with a real fishing rod.[10] But when Macunaíma dropped the wax hook in the water, a catfish swallowed it and plucked it clean from the line.

Back at the boarding house, he said to Maanape, "What

---

[10] A mandaguari is a kind of bee. An aimará is species of large, predatorial freshwater fish.

do we do!? We need to take the Englishman's hook. I'll turn into a fake aimará to trick that meathead. Then, when he catches me and hits me on the head, I'll go 'guh!' and act like I died. He'll throw me in the basket, and then you'll ask for the biggest fish to eat, and it'll be me."

He did it. He turned into an aimará and jumped into the pond, and the Englishman fished him out and hit him on the head. The hero screamed "guh!" but the Englishman removed the hook from the fish's throat as though he hadn't heard a thing.

Maanape came and asked the Englishman in English, "Give me fish? Yes?"

"Alright." And the Englishman gave him a red-tailed lambari.[11]

"I'm starving, Englishman! Give me the big one, eh!? That little fat one in the basket!"

The Englishman refused. Macunaíma was in a daze and his left eye was swollen shut, but Maanape was a sorcerer and still recognized him. He repeated the process until the Englishman finally gave him the aimará, then said his thanks and left. When he was a league and a half away, the aimará turned back into Macunaíma. In the end, the Englishman pulled the hook from the hero's throat three times. Macunaíma whispered to his brother, "What do we do? We still need the Englishman's hook. I'll try turning into a piranha and yanking the hook from the rod."

He turned into a ferocious piranha, jumped into the pond, and plucked the hook from its line. Then, he turned around, and swam a league and a half downstream to a place called the Well of Umbu, where there were some rocks covered with red inscriptions carved by the

---

[11] "Lambari" is a classification of several species of small freshwater fish.

Phoenicians.[12] Notwithstanding the pain, he was happy to pull the hook from his throat, because now he could fish for corimã, piraíba, aruana, pirara, and piaba, all of these fish.[13] The two brothers were leaving when they heard the Englishman talking to a Uruguayan. "What can I do now!? I don't own any more of the hooks that the piranha swallowed. I guess I'll follow you to your country."

Macunaíma waved at them with both arms, and shouted, "Wait a minute, tapuitinga!"[14]

The Englishman turned around and Macunaíma mocked him by turning into a London Bank machine.[15]

---

[12] The era when prehistoric South Americans in the area of southern Brazil, Uruguay, and northern Argentina first developed stone tools is known as "The Umbu Tradition."

[13] Corimãs, piraíbas, aruanas, piraras, and piabas are all species of freshwater fish.

[14] "Tapuitinga" was a word coined to refer to Jesuit missionaries from Central Europe who were active in the Amazon from 1750 to 1753. In Tupi, it literally means "white barbarian," and came to refer to any non-Portuguese white person.

[15] In a story that Koch-Grünberg called "Weitere Taten des Makunaíma" ("More Acts of Macunaíma"), Macunaíma transforms into a beeswax hook to catch fish, but isn't strong enough. So, he and his brother Zigé decide to steal a rod from a man fishing nearby for aimará. To do so, they plan for Makunaima to turn into an aimará and let the man catch him, then for Zigé to ask for the aimará with the hook still inside. After catching Makunaima, however, the fisherman rips the hook from his mouth. So, Makunaima turns into a piranha and tries to bite the hook from the line. This time the trick works, but Makunaima loses the hook almost immediately while fishing for aimará himself. When the fisherman decides to go

The next day, he told his brothers that he was going to catch fish in the Tietê Igarapé. Maanape warned, "Don't go, hero, because you'll run into old Ceiuci, the giant's wife. She'll eat you!"

"There's no fear of hell for those who've already rowed over the waterfall!" Macunaíma replied.

As soon as he cast a line from his tree stand, the old woman Ceiuci came out to fish with a casting net. The old crone saw Macunaíma's silhouette reflected in the water, quickly tossed the net, and caught only shadow. The hero didn't even find it funny as he was trembling with fear. To ingratiate himself to her, he said, "Good morning, grandmother."

The old woman turned her face and saw Macunaíma sitting on the edge of his tree stand.

"Come here, grandson."

"No, I'm not going down there."

"Then I'll send wasps."

And she did. So, Macunaíma plucked a bunch of guapuruvu fronds and killed the wasps.[16]

"Come down, grandson, because otherwise I'll send novatos!"[17]

And she did. The novato ants darted toward Macunaíma and he fell in the water. The old woman cast

---

to the "land of the English" (meaning Guyana) to buy a new hook, Makunaima and Zigé turn into crickets and hide in his basket to go along for the journey. The brothers remain there to this day.

[16] A guapuruvu is a tree that resembles a tall fern.

[17] Novatos are a kind of ant that live in trees and are known for delivering painful stings. If someone touches a tree in which the ants are living, they will drop down and sting them.

her net over him, wrapped him up, and went home. When she got there, she put the bundle by a red table lamp in the living room. She called her eldest daughter, who was quite skilled around the house, so the two could eat a "duck" that she'd hunted. But the duck was actually Macunaíma, the hero. Her daughter was very busy, however, because she kept the house so dutifully, so the old woman made a fire in preparation.

The old woman had two daughters, and the youngest, who was not skilled at all and seemed to know only how to sit around and sigh, watched the old woman make a fire and thought, "Mother usually tells me what she caught as soon as she comes back from fishing, but not today. I'll go look." She rolled the fishing net open, and a handsome young man jumped out. The hero said, "Hide me!"

The girl was feeling impulsive because she'd been sitting around idly for such a long time, and took Macunaíma to her room to fool around. When they were done, they lay in bed laughing together.

After the fire had burned down to hot coals, old Ceiuci came with the skilled daughter to pluck the duck, but they found only the casting net. The old woman was furious. "This has to be the work of my youngest daughter. She's so impulsive."

She pounded on the door to the girl's room, shouting, "Hand over my duck right now, or I'll kick you out of my house forever!"

The girl was scared and told Macunaíma to toss twenty milréis under the door to see if it would satisfy the glutton. Macunaíma, in fear, tossed a hundred of them, which turned into a bunch of partridges, lobsters, sea bass, vials of perfume, and caviar. The greedy old woman swallowed it all and asked for more. So, Macunaíma tossed another handful of milréis under the door. The coins turned into more lobsters, rabbits, pacas, champagne, lace, mushrooms, and frogs, and the old woman kept eating and asking for more. So, the kind-hearted girl opened a window overlooking deserted Pacaembu and said, "I'll tell you three riddles, and if you solve them, I'll let you run away.[18] What is long, plump, and tubular, enters hard and exits soft, satisfies the people's taste, and isn't an indecent word?"

"Ah! This is obscene!"

"Fool! It's a noodle!"

"Ah... so it is! Isn't that funny."

"Now, where's the place that women have the curliest hair?"

"Oh, that's good! I know this one! It's right there!" he said, pointing.

"You dog! It's Africa!"

"Show me, please! Just to make sure!"

"Here's the last one. Tell me what this is:

Boy, let us do,
what God wants us to:
To join hair with hair,
To let the naked one in there."

Macunaíma said, "Ah! Who doesn't know this one, too!? But don't let anyone hear anything we're saying, because you have no shame, lady!"

"Yeah, everyone knows that one. You meant eyelashes meeting in sleep with the naked eye inside, right? Because if you hadn't gotten at least one of the riddles right, I'd have to serve you to my gluttonous mother. Now, run

---

[18] Pacaembu was a planned "city-garden" neighborhood in São Paulo. The streets and parks were completed in 1925.

along without making a fuss. I'll be sent away. I'll fly to the sky. On the street corner, you'll find some horses. Take the dark-brown one whose footsteps are neither soft nor hard. That's the good one. If you hear a little bird crying 'Baúa! Baúa!' it means that old Ceiuci is coming. Now, run along without making a fuss. I'll be sent away! I'll fly to the sky!"

Macunaíma thanked her and jumped out the window. On the corner were two horses, a dark-brown one and a blue roan. "The dark-brown one was made by God for racing," Macunaíma mumbled. He mounted it and they opened into a canter. They travelled for a long time, and as they approached Manaus at a gallop, his horse stumbled and tore up the ground.[19] At the bottom of the divot, Macunaíma saw something glowing. He dug quickly and discovered pieces of the god Mars, a Greek sculpture found in those areas still in the Monarchy and described by Araripe de Alencar this past April 1st in a newspaper called *Commerce of the Amazons*.[20] He was examining its magnificent torso when he heard "Baúa! Baúa!" Old Ceiuci was coming. Macunaíma spurred his horse and, after passing through nearby Mendoza, in Argentina, where he spotted a galley off the coast that was fleeing from French Guyana, he arrived at a place where some priests were gathering honey. He cried, "Hide me, fathers!"

---

[19] Manaus is the largest city in the Amazon and is situated on the Amazon River at its confluence with the Rio Negro.

[20] This article in *Commerce of the Amazons* is Andrade's creation and references the "nobility archeology" that was in fashion at the time, which sought to link Amazonian tribes to ancient European civilizations to show that they had the capacity to be "civilized."

Just as the priests hid Macunaíma in an empty pot, the old woman arrived mounted on a tapir.

"Did you see my grandson ride through here on his little grass-eating horse?"

"He just passed through."

The old woman dismounted the tapir, mounted a reddish-hazel horse that had never been useful nor of any value, and continued onward. When she turned at the Paranacoara Mountains, the priests took the hero from the pot, gave him a bronze-molasses horse that was as strong as it was beautiful, and sent him on his way.[21] Macunaíma thanked them and rode onward. Just ahead, he encountered a wire fence, which required him to draw on his experience as a horseman. He pulled on the bit, knocked the beast to the ground with a hard shove, bound the fallen animal's hoofs, turned it onto its side, and pulled it under the wire. Then, the hero jumped over the fence and mounted the horse again. He rode at a gallop for a very long time. Passing through Ceará, he deciphered the indigenous inscriptions of Aratanha; in Rio Grande do Norte, coasting along the ridgeline of the Cabelo-não-Tem, he deciphered another.[22] In Paraíba, going from Mamanguape to Bacamarte, he passed Pedra Lavrada,

---

[21] The Paranacoara Mountains are a creation of Andrade. Coara is the name of the eastern region of the state of Paraná, which is flat and suitable for farming. The reader can decide whether Andrade is making a joke.

[22] Ceará and Rio Grande do Norte are states in northeastern Brazil on the Atlantic coast. Aratanha, or Serra da Aratanha, is a mountain in the state of Ceará. The Cabelo-não-Tem is an area of forests and streams in the state of Paraíba, just across the border from Rio Grande do Norte.

Macunaíma

which bore enough inscriptions to compose a novel.[23] He didn't read them because he was in a hurry, nor did he read the inscriptions at Barras and Poti in Piauí, at Pajeú in Pernambuco, nor at the Narrows of Inhamum.[24]

On the fourth day of his journey, he heard a little song floating through the air: "Baúa! Baúa!" Old Ceiuci was coming. Macunaíma pumped his legs as fast as he could toward a eucalyptus forest. But the little bird continued to close in on Macunaíma, and the old woman kept rushing toward him. At last, he encountered a surucucu that was in party with the left-handers.[25]

"Hide me, surucucu!"

Just as the surucucu had hidden the hero in its burrow under a latrine, Old Ceiuci showed up.

"Did you see my grandson pass through here on his little grass-eating horse?"

"He just passed through."

The glutton dismounted from her reddish-hazel horse that had never been useful or of any value, mounted a

---

[23] Paraíba is a state on Brazil's Atlantic coast next to Rio Grande do Norte. Mamanguape and Bacamarte are both small towns in Paraíba. Pedra Lavrada is a town in Paraíba, and home to the Pedra de Retumba ("Retumba Rock"). In 1886, a mining engineer reported having found a large rock formation covered in inscriptions, of which he made a detailed drawing. However, over the centuries, expeditions by scholars to find the rock all have failed, leaving it one of the great archeological mysteries of Brazil.

[24] Barras and Poti are towns in the northeastern state of Piauí. Pajeú is a town in Pernambuco. Inhamum is a region in the northeastern state of Maranhão.

[25] A surucucu is a venomous snake that can grow up to three meters in length.

Macunaíma

lame, white-blazed horse, and continued onward.

After she left, Macunaíma overheard a discussion between the surucucu and an accomplice about making a bar-be-que out of him. The hero hopped from the burrow into the outhouse, and tossed a glimmering ring, which he'd been given as a present to wear on his pinky finger, onto the ground. The brilliant object turned into four carts full of corn, polysulphate fertilizer, and a second-hand Ford. While the surucucu looked at everything with satisfaction, Macunaíma let the bronze-molasses horse rest, mounted a blue-specked horse that could never keep still, and rode at a gallop through floodplains and deltas. He passed in a flash over the sea of sand on the Parecis Plateau and, after tumbling and dangling on his way down, entered a caatinga near Natal and frightened some hens from Camutanga that hatch golden chicks.[26] A league and a half further, having left the banks of the São Francisco which were still littered with debris from the Easter Sunday Flood, he passed through an open gap and into a dell surrounded by high hills.[27] He was riding along when he heard someone hiss at him: "Psst." He stopped dead with fear. From a thicket of catingueira emerged a tall, ugly woman with a braid that hung down to her feet.[28] The lady asked the hero in a whisper, "Did they leave yet?"

---

[26] The Parecis Plateau is near Brazil's border with Bolivia at the southern edge of the Amazon basin. Natal is a large city on the Atlantic coast and is the capital of the state of Rio Grande do Norte. Camutanga is a town in Pernambuco.

[27] The Rio São Francisco experienced a historic flood on Easter Sunday of 1926.

[28] Catingueira is a plant that grows as a thick shrub or a tree, depending on the quality of soil.

"Did who leave!?"

"The Dutchmen!"

"You're going insane! What Dutchmen!? There aren't any Dutchmen, lady!"

She was Maria Pereira, a Portuguese woman who'd lived in that dell in the hills since the war with the Dutch. Macunaíma didn't quite know where in Brazil he was anymore, and decided to ask, "Tell me one thing – although, what one person calls a 'lightning bug' another calls a 'firefly' – what's the name of this place?"

The woman responded proudly, "This is the Hole of Maria Pereira."[29] Macunaíma giggled and scampered away while the woman slid back into hiding. The hero continued onward until he at last made it to the other side of the Rio Chuí, where he came across a jabiru fishing.[30]

"Cousin jabiru, will you take me home?"

"At your service!"

The jabiru immediately transformed into an airplane machine. Macunaíma climbed onto its bare back and they took flight. They flew over the Urucuia Plateau in Minas Gerais, did a circuit around Itapecerica, and headed toward the northeast.[31] Passing over the Mossoró dunes, Macunaíma looked below and spotted Bartolomeu

---

[29] The Hole of Maria Pereira is the name of an area of narrow rapids where the current of the Rio São Francisco runs fastest.

[30] The Rio Chuí is a small river that forms part of Brazil's border with Uruguay. "Jabiru" is a name for several bird species that resemble storks.

[31] The Urucuia Plateau in Minas Gerais is a sandstone formation that is one of the largest plateaus in Brazil. The Rio Itapecerica is a tributary to the Rio São Francisco with its origin at the confluence of two streams near the town of Itapecerica.

Macunaíma

Lourenço de Gusmão with his cassock rolled up, struggling to walk on the sandy expanse.[32] The hero shouted at him, "Come along with us, your eminence!" But the priest replied, "Go away!" and waved him off.

The jabiru-plane and Macunaíma flew over the Tomabador mountain range in Matto Grosso, passed to the left of the rocky hills of Santana do Livramento, climbed up to the Telhado do Mundo, and quenched their thirst in the fresh waters of Vilcanota.[33] On the last leg of their journey, they flew over Amargosa in Bahia, over Gurupá, over Gurupi with its enchanted city, and finally returned to the illustrious settlement upon the Tietê Igarapé.[34] After just a short while, they were at the door of the boarding house. Macunaíma was grateful and wanted to pay for the help, but he remembered that he

---

[32] Mossoró is a town on the Atlantic coast in Brazil's north and is near the vast dunes at the estuary of the Rio Apodi-Mossoró. Fr. Bartolomeu Lourenço de Gusmão (1685-1724) was a Brazilian Jesuit priest who studied philology and mathematics, and is best remembered for his early designs of lighter-than-air airships.

[33] Santana do Livramento is a Brazilian town on the border with Uraguay. The Telhado do Mundo ("Roof of the World") is a term, which European ethnographers in the 19th century attributed to Brazilian Yorubans, that refers to the sky and stars. Vilcanota is the name of both a mountain range in the Peruvian Andes and a river fed by the glacial runoff of these mountains that crosses into Brazil and connects with the Amazon River.

[34] Amargosa is a town in Bahia, the name of which translates literally to "Bitter." Gurupá is a small town on the Amazon River in the state of Pará, and Gurupi is a larger town in the center of Brazil in the state of Tocantins.

was trying to save money. He turned to the jabiru and said, "Look, cousin, I can't pay, but I'll give you some advice that's worth more than gold. In this world, there are three things that are the downfall of man: Beaches, gold, and short skirts. Don't fall down!"

But he was so used to spending that he immediately forgot about saving. He gave ten coins to the jabiru, walked up to his room feeling satisfied, and told everything to his brothers, who were annoyed by the delay. The ordeal, in the end, had cost a bundle. Maanape then turned Jiguê into a telephone machine and made a complaint to the Police, who deported the gluttonous old woman. However, Piaimã wielded a lot of influence, and she soon returned to join an opera company.

The daughter who was sent away still runs in the sky, pumping her legs in constant motion. She's a comet.

Macunaíma

XII
THE TICO-TICO, THE CHUPIM, AND THE INJUSTICE OF MEN

The next day, Macunaíma woke up feverish. He'd been delirious for the entire night and had dreamed of a ship.

"That means there's a sea voyage in your future," the boarding-house landlady told him. Macunaíma thanked her and was so giddy that he immediately turned Jiguê into a telephone machine so he could call Venceslau Pietro Pietra and insult his mother. But the mysterious operator told him that there was no response at the other end of the line. Macunaíma found that strange and wanted to investigate. But when he moved to get out of bed, he felt a hot rash all over his body and his limbs felt like water. He groaned, "Ai, what a drag."

He turned his face to the wall and started cursing by the mouthful. When his brothers came to see what was going on, they discovered that he had measles. Maanape soon went to Beberibe to look for the famous healer, Bento, who made cures using an Indian's soul and a pot

Macunaíma

of water.[1] Bento gave him a sip of water and sang a prayer chant. Within a week of receiving the cure, the hero's skin was already peeling, and he was able to get out of bed and investigate what had happened to the giant.

There was nobody at the palace, and the neighbor's maid told him that Piaimã had gone to Europe with his whole family to recover from the beating. Macunaíma stopped trembling with fear and became annoyed instead. He fooled around madly with the maid, then returned to the boarding house in a dour mood. Maanape and Jiguê saw the hero at the front door and one of them asked, "Who killed your dog, brother?"

Macunaíma told them what had happened and started to cry. The brothers were sorry to see the hero like this, so they took him to visit the Guapira Leprosarium.[2] But the outing wasn't any fun because Macunaíma was so upset. It was evening when they got back to the boarding house, and everyone was forlorn. They smoked an enormous wad of tobacco in a goat-horn pipe shaped like a toucan's head, which made them sneeze quite a bit. After that, they could think.

---

[1] In 1912, Bento José da Veiga, also known as "Bento the Miracle-Worker," claimed to have discovered a source of miraculous water in the Rio Beberibe that could cure any ailment. His claims attracted thousands of sick people to the village of Beberibe, which caused panic and protests among the local population, who feared an epidemic. After two weeks of disarray in the village, and the steadfast refusal of Bento (who accepted donations for his healing treatment) to stop, he was arrested by the police.

[2] The Guapira Leprosarium was a hospital constructed in 1904 in the Serra de Cantareira, a large woodland park in the north of São Paulo.

"So, brothers," said Macunaíma. "You've been lazy, wasting your time and cooking the cock.[3] The giant had no reason to wait and has disappeared. Now you have to eat the stew!"

Jiguê slapped his forehead and cried, "I guess so!"

The brothers sat mired in dread, until Jiguê at last suggested that they chase after the muiraquitã in Europe. They still had forty contos remaining from the sale of cocoa to cover expenses. Macunaíma immediately agreed, but Maanape, who was a sorcerer, thought about it and concluded, "I have a better idea."

"Well, spit it out!"

"Macunaíma pretends to be a pianist, gets a pension from the Government, and then goes by himself."

"But why go through so much trouble if we have a bunch of money and you two could help me in Europe!"

"Why only do one when we could do both! We could do it your way. But brother, isn't it better to be on the Government dole? It is. So, let's go!"

Macunaíma thought about it and slapped his forehead. "I've got it!"

The brothers were nervous. "What is it!?"

"I'll pretend to be a fashionable painter!" He went to fetch tortoiseshell-glasses, a little gramophone, golf socks, and gloves, and turned himself into a painter.

The next day, as he waited for his brothers to meet with the Government for him, he killed some time by painting. After that, he grabbed a novel by Eça de Queiroz and went for a walk in Cantareira.[4] As Macunaíma was lying

---

[3] To "cook the cock" is a Brazilian expression that means to waste time.

[4] Eça de Queiroz (1845-1900) was a Portuguese writer who published realist novels about corruption within the

Macunaíma

on his stomach and amusing himself by knocking down tapipitinga-ant hills, a travelling salesman passed by, proudly displaying a woodpecker feather. The salesman greeted him: "Good morning, friend. How are you? I'm good, too, thank you very much. You at work?"

"Don't work, don't eat."

"Very true. Well, see you around."

The salesman continued onward. A league and a half ahead, he saw a fox and decided to conduct some business. He caught the little fox, forced it to swallow ten silver coins worth two milréis, then turned back with the animal under his arm. As he approached Macunaíma, he started hustling: "Good morning, friend. How are you? I'm good, too, thanks. I'll sell you my fox if you'd like."

"What would I do with that grimy creature!" Macunaíma responded, plugging his nose.

"But I'm giving you a great deal! When it does its business, only silver comes out! I'll sell it to you cheap!"

"Quit talking nonsense! Who's ever seen a fox like that!?"

So, the street peddler pressed the stomach of the fox, and the creature expelled the ten silver pieces.

"Are you seeing this!? It shits silver! Get rich with me! I'll sell it to you cheap!"

"How much does it cost?"

"Four hundred contos."

"I can't afford it. I only have thirty."

"Well, so that you continue as a customer, I'll give it to you for thirty contos!"

Macunaíma unbuttoned his pants and took the bag that

---

bourgeoisie and clergy, and whose books were sometimes met with protest and official censure. Cantareira refers to Serra de Cantareira.

held his money from where it was tucked in the band of his underwear. He had only a forty-conto bill and six chips from the Casino de Copacabana. He handed over the bill and, feeling guilty about having received such a good bargain, he gave the chips to the salesman as a tip and thanked him for his kindness.

As soon as the salesman slipped between the sucupiras, guarubas, and parinaris of the forest, the fox had to relieve itself again.[5] The hero held his bag up to its rump to catch the silver, but shit came out instead. Macunaíma immediately discerned the scam and let out a wretched scream before returning to the boarding house.[6]

Turning a corner, he found José Prequeté and shouted at him, "Zé Prequeté, go pick the grubs from your feet and eat them with your coffee!"[7]

José Prequeté was outraged and insulted the hero's mother. But the hero laughed, let it go, and continued onward. He soon remembered that he was going home

---

[5] A sucupira is a tall flowering tree, and parinaris are a variety of tree known for their woody fruit. Guarubas are a kind of bright-yellow parakeet.

[6] In a story that Koch-Grünberg called "Kone'wo," Kone'wo the frog hides silver coins in the branches of a tree and asks an Englishman to trade his gun for this "silver tree" that grows infinite silver coins. When Kone'wo shakes the tree and coins fall out, the Englishman agrees to the deal and gives the frog his gun. The frog then flees as the Englishman shakes the tree and no more coins fall out.

[7] Zé Prequeté was an infamous beggar in 19th-century São Paulo who used to beg on the steps of the cathedral, and whose name became a slang term for a lazy or useless person. Sometimes "Zé" in the slur would be replaced with the Spanish name "José," to make it anti-Hispanic.

angry and started yelling again.

The brothers still hadn't returned from the Government office, so the landlady came into the room to console Macunaíma and they fooled around. Afterward, the hero started crying. When his brothers returned, everyone was startled because they were both five meters tall. They hadn't realized that the Government already had a-thousand-times-a-thousand painters apply for a European pension. They told Macunaíma that he was to be appointed, but not until St. Never's Day, which was a long time away. The plan had failed, and the brothers had grown tall from disappointment. When they saw their brother crying, they were quite concerned and wanted to know what had happened. And as they were distracted from their disappointment, they returned to their original sizes, Maanape already an old man and Jiguê in his prime.

The hero cried, "Wah-wah-wah! The salesman tricked me! Wah-wah-wah! I bought a fox from him for forty contos!"

The brothers were pulling their hair out. It was no longer possible for them to go to Europe because there was only a night and a day until the last ocean liner departed before the seasonal break. They held the hero as he wept. He rubbed andiroba oil on himself to keep the mosquitoes away and fell fast asleep.[8]

Dawn the next day brought a dreadful heat and Macunaíma, enraged by the Government's injustice, was sweating more than ever and from every pore. He wanted to go outside and relax, but his clothing made the heat so much worse. He grew even angrier, until he was so

---

[8] The oil extracted from the andiroba tree has long been used by Amazon natives to make medicinal remedies.

enraged and spiteful that he started to come down with butecaiana, the disease of rage.[9] He cried, "Ah! Walking burns me up, and the heat laughs at me!"

He took off his pants to cool down and stepped on top of them. His rage calmed in an instant, and Macunaíma, feeling satisfied, said to his brothers, "Patience, brothers! I'm not going to Europe. I'm American and my place is in America. European civilization is certain to corrupt the integrity of my character."

For a week, the three wandered throughout Brazil, across shoals of marine sand, sparsely wooded peninsulas, ravines cut by rivers, clearings, rapids, dwarf forests, floodplains, swamps, tidal whirlpools, canyons, water tornadoes, frosty wildernesses, tidal flats, rainforests, boulder fields, sink holes, valleys, mountain lakes, and shallow lagoons, all of these places, searching the ruins of convents and the bases of crosses for pots with money inside. They didn't find any.

"Patience, brothers!" Macunaíma repeated sadly. "We'll play the lottery!"

He went to Praça Antônio Prado to meditate on the injustice of men.[10] He leaned against a plantain tree, brooding over the injustice of men as all of the businessmen and mechanized nonsense passed close by. Macunaíma was ready to change the motto to "Poor in health and rich in painters, these are the evils of Brazil" when he heard a chirping – "Eeh-eeh-eeh!" – behind him.

---

[9] "Butecaiana" is a disease mentioned to Andrade in a letter from a friend in Recife the year before *Macunaíma* was published and does not appear elsewhere.

[10] Praça Antônio Prado is a square in São Paulo named after its first mayor, Antônio Prado, who died at the age of 88, a year after *Macunaíma*'s publication.

Macunaíma

He turned around and saw two birds on the ground, a tico-tico and a chupim.[11]

The tico-tico was tiny and the chupim was big and strong. The little tico-tico paced the dirt, always accompanied by the chupim crying for something to eat. It caused a fury. The little tico-tico thought that the big chupim was its chick, but it wasn't. It flew off and found a morsel to put in the chupim's beak. The big chupim swallowed it and, in the morning, started crying again in his own language, "Eeh-eeh-eeh! Mama! Bring me a snack! Bring me a snack!" The little tico-tico was flustered because he was hungry, too, and the chupim's pleas from earlier – "Bring me a snack! Bring me a snack!" – bothered him because he was unable to endure his beloved's suffering. He flew off to fetch little bugs and kernels of corn, all of these morsels, and put them in the chupim's beak. The chupim swallowed them and immediately called for the little tico-tico again. Macunaíma was meditating on the injustice of men and felt extremely bitter about the injustice of the chupim. Macunaíma knew that, in the beginning, little birds used to be people like us. So, the hero picked up a club and killed the little tico-tico.

He left the scene. After he'd walked a league and a half, he felt hot and decided to drink a sip to cool off. He always kept a little bottle of booze in his jacket pocket, attached to his puíto by a silver chain. He unscrewed the top and, as he slowly drank, heard something behind him

---

[11] A tico-tico is a kind of sparrow, and a chupim is another species of small bird. The two birds have a parasitic relationship whereby chupims lay their eggs, which have the same speckled pattern as tico-tico eggs, in the tico-tico's nest, and the tico-tico feeds and raises the chupim's chicks as though they were its own.

crying, "Eeh-eeh-eeh!" He was shocked. It was the big chupim.

"Eeh-eeh-eeh! Daddy! Bring me a snack! Bring me a snack!" he said in his language.

Macunaíma felt spiteful. He opened the bag holding the fox's excrement and said, "Here! Eat this!"

The chupim hopped onto the edge of the bag and ate everything without knowing what it was. It grew fatter and fatter, until it turned into a huge black bird and flew into the forest shouting, "Never give up! Never give up!" It had become the Father of Chupims.

Macunaíma followed it. A league and a half ahead, a macaque was eating a baguaçu.[12] The macaque picked up the fruit, put it next to a rock between his legs, squeezed, and – crack! – the fruit broke open. Macunaíma looked at him with doe eyes and his mouth watering. He said, "Good morning, uncle. How are you?"

"I'm alright, nephew."

"How's everything at home? Good?"

"Same as always."

He continued chewing as Macunaíma stood watching. The monkey became furiously annoyed: "Don't look at me squint-eyed. I'm not a greengrocer. And don't look at me side-eyed either, because I'm not delicious!"

"But what are you doing there, uncle!?"

The macaque hid the fruit in a closed fist, and responded, "I'm mashing my balls so I can eat them."

"Go lie on a beach!"

"Wow, nephew, if you're not going to believe what I say, why ask!?"

Macunaíma started to believe him and asked, "Does it taste good?"

---

[12] A baguaçu is kind of coconut that contains large edible seeds.

The monkey smacked his lips. "Oh yeah! Just try it!"

He broke off another fruit and, pretending that it was one of his testicles, gave it to Macunaíma to eat. Macunaíma really liked it.

"It's very good, uncle! Do you have more?"

"They're all gone. But if mine were delicious, yours will be, too! Eat them, nephew!"

The hero was afraid. "It doesn't hurt, does it?"

"What if it feels good!?"

The hero picked up a paving stone. The macaque, laughing silently, managed to say to him, "Do you really have the courage, nephew?"

"For the love of cassava, let's do it!" the hero shouted emphatically. He gripped the cobblestone firmly and slammed it – wham! – onto his testicles. He dropped dead. The macaque teased him: "My boy, I didn't tell you to die! I spoke and you didn't listen! You see what happens to the disobedient? Now, *sic transit!*"[13] Then, he put on a pair of rubber gloves and scurried away.[14]

---

[13] "Sic transit gloria mundi" is a Latin phrase that was used in the coronation ceremonies of Roman Catholic Popes for several hundred years until 1963. During the ceremony, a priest would chant to the new Pope, "Pater Sancte, sic transit gloria mundi," which means "Saint Peter, thus passes the glory of the world," a reference to the new Pope's connection with St. Peter, who was the first Pope of the Roman Catholic Church.

[14] In the story "Kone'wo," Kone'wo is smashing fruit with a rock when a jaguar approaches him and asks what he's doing. Kone'wo responds that he's smashing his testicles and eating them. The jaguar asks if they taste good, and Kone'wo tosses him a piece of fruit to try. He says to the jaguar, "Taste good? Then, try yours." The jaguar picks up a stone, smashes his testicles, and dies. Kone'wo says, "Did I forget to say that you

Macunaíma

A little bit further ahead, a rainstorm came and washed the hero's green flesh, preventing putrefaction. Soon, a force of murupeteca and guajuguaju army ants swarmed throughout the dead body.[15] Some lawyer, attracted by the army ants, came across the corpse. He bent down and took the corpse's wallet, but there was only a business card with the address of the boarding house. So, he decided to take the corpse there. He carried Macunaíma on his back and started walking, but the corpse weighed too much, and the lawyer realized that he couldn't manage the load. So, he urged the corpse onward and gave it a whack with a switch. The corpse lightened and the attorney was able to carry it the rest of the way.

When Maanape saw his brother's body, he burst into tears and threw himself on top. Looking over the corpse, he discovered what had been crushed. Maanape was a sorcerer. He immediately asked the landlady if he could borrow two Bahia coconuts. When she returned, he tied them with a tangled knot where the crushed testicles were and blew pipe smoke onto the dead hero. Macunaíma got up very slowly. They gave him guaraná fruit and left him to sit by himself, killing the ants that were biting him. He was trembling in the cold of a passing rainstorm, so he took the little bottle from his pocket and drank the last drops to warm himself up. Then, he asked Maanape for a hundred milreis and went to a chalet to play the

---

would die?" and abandons the jaguar.

[15] Murupetecas travel in swarms of up to two hundred thousand ants and are known for using their bodies to form bridges and other living structures to help the swarm advance. Guajuguajus emerge after rains to consume small rodents and insects, and are known for traveling in masses with 1,000 ants in each row across the column.

numbers.[16] The brothers soon realized that their last real had been lost. So, they lived with the decision of the older brother, Maanape the sorcerer.

---

[16] "Chalet" was a slang term for illegal gambling parlors.

XIII
JIGUÊ GETS LICE

Macunaíma woke up the next day with an enormous rash in addition to the injuries he'd suffered the day before. The brothers came to examine him and saw that he had erysipelas, a long illness.[1] The brothers took good care of him and every day they brought home all of the remedies for erysipelas that their friends and neighbors, all of these Brazilians, recommended. The hero spent a week in bed. Each night, he dreamed of ships, and when the landlady of the boarding house came to check on him every morning, she would tell him that the ship portended a sea voyage in his future. As she left, she'd lay the Estado de São Paulo newspaper on the patient's bed, and Macunaíma would spend the rest of the day reading advertisements for erysipelas remedies.[2] And there were

---

[1] Erysipelas is a bacterial infection that causes a bright red rash.

[2] The *Estado de São Paulo* newspaper was founded in 1875 in association with liberal and abolitionist groups. In the 1920s, when *Macunaíma* was written, it was the leading newspaper in

so many advertisements!

By the time the weekend had arrived, the hero was peeling all over his body. He went into town to look for more itches to scratch, walking around astonished and amazed until, exhausted by his illness, he stopped by the park at Anhangabaú.[3] He stood in front of the monument to Carlos Gomes, who was a very famous musician but is now a little star in the sky.[4] The sound of a fountain splashing in the evening reminded the hero of the waters of the sea. Macunaíma sat on the fountain's edge and watched bronze aquatic horses weeping tears of gushing water. In the darkness of the grotto behind the statue he saw a light. He looked closer and made out a magnificent ship that was floating toward him on the water. "It's a vigilenga," he mumbled.[5] But the ship kept getting bigger. "It's a gaiola," he said.[6] But the gaiola kept growing so big – so huge! – that the hero jumped in fear and shouted into

---

opposition to the sitting government.

[3] Vale do Anhangabaú ("Anhangabaú Valley") was a park in São Paulo that was turned into an expressway shortly after *Macunaíma*'s publication.

[4] Antônio Carlos Gomes (1836-1896) is considered the most important composer of Brazilian opera. Popular during his lifetime, his funeral service was a national event. In 1922, the Monument to Carlos Gomes was constructed in front of the São Paulo Municipal Theater. The monument is comprised of a statue of a seated Gomes at the top of a staircase overlooking a fountain, in which there is a statue of Glory standing atop three winged horses jumping over the water.

[5] A vigilenga is a small boat with a single sail.

[6] A gaiola is a large, motorized riverboat used to ferry goods and passengers.

the mouth of the night, "It's a vaticano!"[7] The words echoed. The ship emerged clearly visible behind the bronze horses. Its silver hull gave it cutting speed, and the masts strained to hold their sails and were adorned with flags that the rushing wind pressed between gusts of air. The shout drew chauffeurs from the esplanade, and they were all curious about the hero's gesticulations. They followed the line of his gaze until they saw the dark fountain.

"What is it, hero?"

"Look over there! Look at the magnificent vaticano that's sailing across the vast waters of the sea!"

"Where!?"

"Behind the horse on the starboard side!"

Everyone looked at the ship coming from behind the horse on the starboard side. It was already quite close and was about to pass between the horse and the stone wall and out through the mouth of the grotto. The ship was massive.

"No, it's not a vaticano! It's an ocean liner making a voyage across the sea!" shouted a Japanese chauffeur who'd made many voyages across the sea. The ocean liner was enormous. It was lit up all over, covered in shimmering gold and silver, and decorated festively with flags. The sparkling glass in the portholes of the cabins looked like a necklace draped around the hull and, on the five raised decks, music flowed between people dancing to cururu drums.[8] The chauffeur remarked, "It's from Lloyd!"

"No, it's from Hamburg!"

---

[7] A vaticano is an enormous gaiola.

[8] Cururu is a style of drumming meant for dancing.

"No way! I can see what it says! It's the steamboat *Conte Verde*!"[9]

It appeared to be the steamboat *Conte Verde*, but it was actually the Mãe D'água pretending to be a steamboat to prank the hero.

"Goodbye, everyone!" shouted the hero. "I'm going to Europe, where everything's better! I'm in search of Venceslau Pietro Pietra, who is the giant Piaimã, eater of people!"

All of the chauffeurs hugged Macunaíma and bid him farewell. The steamboat *Conte Verde* was stopped and Macunaíma hopped onto the ledge of the fountain to climb the gangplank. The crew members all waved and called to Macunaíma as music played behind them. They were strong sailors, fine Argentinians, and there were also many beautiful ladies with whom the hero could fool around until he got sick from the bouncing of the waves.

"Drop the ladder, captain!" the hero shouted.

The captain took off his feathered headdress and twirled a finger in the air. Everyone, the fine Argentinian sailors and the beautiful girls with whom Macunaíma could fool around, this whole crew, let out boos and curses, mocking the hero while the ship's stern turned toward land and it darted back into the grotto. The whole crew had contracted erysipelas but continued making fun of the hero anyway. When the steamboat crossed the strait between the grotto wall and the horse on the port side, the chimney belched a cloud of mosquitoes – black flies, midges, horse flies, marimbondos, cabas, potós, and

---

[9] Lloyd North Germany and Hamburg-America were German companies that ran ocean liners between Germany and Brazil at the turn of the 20th century. The *Conte Verde* was an Italian ocean liner that was in operation around the same time.

Macunaíma

blowflies, all of these biting and stinging insects — which chased away the chauffeurs.[10]

The hero, seated on the edge of the fountain, suffered bites all over his body, and his erysipela had worsened such that he was now entirely covered in a rash and felt the onset of cold and fever. He swatted away the mosquitoes and walked to the boarding house.

The next day, Jiguê came home with a young woman, made her swallow three pellets of lead so she wouldn't get pregnant, and slept with her in a hammock. Jiguê had become a very valiant womanizer and spent his days cleaning the shotgun and whittling the little lamp. Every morning, Jiguê's companion, whose name was Suzi, would go to buy enough cassava for four people. But Macunaíma, who was her lover, would buy a lobster for her every day, put it in the bottom of a straw basket, and spread cassava on top so nobody would suspect anything. Suzi was a skilled sorceress. When she arrived at home, she'd leave the basket in the parlor and go to lay down to dream. As she was dreaming, she'd mumble to Jiguê, "Jiguê, my dear Jiguê, I'm dreaming that there's a lobster under the cassava."

Jiguê would go to look and there it would be. It was like that every day, and Jiguê, waking up each morning with heartache, eventually grew suspicious. Macunaíma noticed his brother's pain and cast a spell to try to alleviate it. He left a gourd on the terrace one night, praying softly:

"Water of heaven,
enter this guard,
Paticl enter the water,

---

[10] Marimbondos and cabas are kinds of wasp, and a potó is another variety of flying and stinging insect.

Macunaíma

Moposêru enter the water,
Sivuoímo enter the water,
Omaispopo enter the water,
Lords of Water, chase away the cuckhold's pain!
Aracu, Mecumecuri, and Pai, may they enter the water,
 and drive away the cuckhold's pain when the sufferer drinks,
 from the guard of the enchanted Lords of Water!"[11]

The next day, Macunaíma gave Jiguê some of the water to drink, but it didn't have an effect and Jiguê grew even more suspicious.

After Suzi had dressed to go to the market, she whistled a fashionable foxtrot to signal her lover to come along. Her lover was Macunaíma, and he joined her. Jiguê's partner left the boarding house first, followed by Macunaíma. They snuck away and fooled around, but when it was time to go back home, the market had already sold out of cassava. So, Suzi went behind the house in disguise, sat on the basket, and pulled some cassava from her maissó.[12] Everyone ate quite well. Only Maanape grumbled, "Caboclo from Taubaté, horse of pangaré, a woman who stands to pee, Lord, set us free!" and pushed the food aside.[13]

---

[11] According to Tupi-Guarini mythology, the Lords of Water govern the rivers of the Amazon. Before going on a fishing trip, tribesmen would sing a long incantation in which they named the multitude of Lords of Water, and asked them not to hide their fish or act with hostility toward the fishermen. These specific Lords of Water are creations of Andrade.

[12] "Maissó" is a Tupi word for "vagina."

[13] A caboclo is a person whose race is a combination of indigenous Brazilian and white. Taubaté is a small city near São

Macunaíma

Maanape was a sorcerer. He didn't want to know about the cassava, so he didn't eat and chewed coca leaves to sate his hunger. That night, when Jiguê was ready to climb into the hammock, his partner started groaning, saying that she was stuffed after swallowing too many pitomba seeds.[14] Jiguê knew that she'd only said it so he wouldn't fool around with her, and he was outraged.

As she left for the market the next morning, she whistled the fashionable foxtrot. Macunaíma left after her. Jiguê was feeling valiant, and he picked up an enormous mirassanga and walked slowly after them.[15] He searched for a long time until he found Suzi hand-in-hand with Macunaíma in the Jardim da Luz. They were already giggling to each other. Jiguê snuck behind them, swung the mirassanga onto their heads, took his companion to the boarding house, and left his exhausted brother among the swans on the shore of the pond.

From then on, Jiguê did all of the shopping, holding his partner captive in their room. Suzi, without anything to do, passed the time behaving immorally. One day, the holy Anchieta, who arrived in this world long ago, passed by her house and, out of pity, taught her how to catch lice. Suzi had red hair *à la garçonne* which was soon teeming with lice – so many! After that, she no longer dreamed that there were lobsters under the cassava and stopped behaving immorally. When Jiguê left for the market each morning, she would cut off her hair, stick it to her partner's club, and use it to hunt lice. But there was a mess

---

Paulo. Pangaré is a coloring of horses where the fur is dark red, except the nose and belly, which are white.

[14] A pitomba is an edible fruit from a tree of the same name.

[15] A mirassanga is a kind of club.

of lice – so many! So, fearing that her companion would catch her at work, she said, "Jiguê, my dear Jiguê, when you come back from the market every afternoon, first knock on the door for a little while. It'll make me happy and I'll go cook the cassava."

Jiguê agreed. Every day, he went to the market to buy cassava, and when he returned, he would knock on the door for a while. Each time, Suzi would put her hair back on her head and wait for Jiguê to come in.

"Suzi, my dear Suzi, I knocked on the door several times. Are you happy?"

"Very!" she would say, before leaving to cook the cassava.

Every day was like this. But there was a mess of lice – so many! – and she never could figure out how many lice there were because she counted her collection one by one. While Jiguê was at the market one day, he started to wonder what his partner was doing while we was there, and wanted to surprise her; so, he did. He kicked his legs in the air and came home walking on his hands. He opened the door with his feet and scared Suzi. As soon as she saw him, she screamed and quickly slapped her hair back onto her head. But she put the hair from her forehead onto her neck, and the hair from her neck onto her forehead. Jiguê cursed Suzi, called her a pig, and laid into her until he heard someone climbing up the stairs. So, Jiguê stopped and went to sharpen his dagger.

The next morning, Macunaíma wanted to fool around with Jiguê's partner again. He told his brothers that he was going on a long hunt, but he didn't go. He bought two bottles of butiá liquor, a dozen sandwiches, and two pineapples from Pernambuco, and hid himself in a little room.[16] A little while later, he went home and, showing Jiguê his shopping bag, said, "Brother Jiguê, there's a fruit orchard at the end of many of the streets. I saw a herd of game animals in one of them. Go see for yourself!"

His brother looked at him with suspicion, but Macunaíma performed well: "Go look! There were pacas, armadillos, and agoutis.[17] Just kidding. I didn't see any agoutis. There were pacas and armadillos, but no agoutis."

Jiguê was convinced by what he'd heard, immediately picked up a shotgun, and said, "Then, I'll go. But first swear that you won't fool around with my fiancée."

Macunaíma swore on the memory of his mother that he wouldn't even look at Suzi. Jiguê turned to grab his shotgun and knife, said goodbye, and left. Jiguê had barely rounded the corner when Macunaíma helped Suzi by emptying the shopping bags and laying out a tablecloth made of a famous lace called "bee's nest," which a thief had stolen in Muriú do Ceará-Mirim for the damned Geracina in Ponta do Mangue.[18] When everything was ready, the two jumped into the hammock and fooled around. Then, they giggled together, and after they had laughed for a long time, Macunaíma said, "Uncork a bottle

---

[16] A butiá is a variety of palm tree that bears fruit used to make alcohol and vinegar.

[17] A paca is a kind of large rodent.

[18] To make lace, lacemakers used cardboard forms of designs, which were passed down over generations. The lace called "bee's nest" was a famous and valuable design monopolized by the lacemakers of Muriú do Ceará-Mirim, a beach village in the northeastern state of Rio Grande do Norte. Dona Geracina was a famous lacemaker in Ponta do Mangue, a beach town in the eastern state of Pernambuco.

for us to drink."

"Okay," she said, and they drank the first bottle of butiá liquor, which was very tasty. They clicked their tongues and hopped back into the hammock. They fooled around for as long as they wanted, then they giggled to themselves again.

Jiguê walked a league and a half, went to the ends of the streets, and spent a long time searching for fruit orchards. Could an alligator find one? Nor did he! There wasn't a fruit orchard anywhere and Jiguê went home, continuing to search the ends of the roads along the way. When he finally returned to the boarding house, he went up to the room and found his brother Macunaíma and Suzi still laughing together. Jiguê grew enraged and slapped Suzi, and she broke down crying. Then, Jiguê grabbed the hero and whacked him with a club with all of his strength. He beat him for a long time, until Manuel arrived. Manuel was the attendant of the boarding house, and an islander. But by then, the hero had been seriously wounded. Meanwhile, Jiguê was starving, so he ate the sandwiches and pineapples, and drank the butiá liquor.

The two victims spent the night feeling sorry for themselves. Jiguê was bored the next morning, so he picked up a blowgun and went out to search again for a fruit orchard. He was being very silly. Suzi watched him leave, wiped her eyes, and said to her lover, "Let's not cry."

Macunaíma relaxed his sour expression and left to go speak with brother Maanape. Jiguê, upon his return to the boarding house, asked Suzi, "Where's the hero?"

But she was furious and started whistling a song. So, Jiguê grabbed his club, approached his partner, and said very sadly, "Go away, loser!"

At that she smiled happily. She gathered all of the

remaining lice without counting them – and there were a lot of lice – tied them to a rocking chair and sat on it. The lice jumped and Suzi went up to the sky and turned into a star that hops around. She's a shooting star.

The hero could barely see Maanape in the distance, when he picked himself up, feeling sorry for himself, and ran into his brother's arms. He told a sad story about how Jiguê had no reason for beating him so severely. Maanape was angered by what he'd heard and went to speak with Jiguê. But Jiguê was already on his way to speak with Maanape, and they met in the hallway. Maanape gave his version of the events to Jiguê, Jiguê gave his own version to Maanape, and they confirmed that Macunaíma had neither shame nor character. They returned to Maanape's room and found the hero still feeling sorry for himself. To cheer him up, they took him for a ride in an automobile machine.

XIV

THE MUIRAQUITÃ

When Macunaíma opened a window the next morning, he saw a little green bird. This made the hero content, and he was still feeling that way when Maanape entered the room and told him that the newspaper machines had announced Venceslau Pietro Pietra's return. Macunaíma refused to think about the giant any longer and decided just to kill him. He left town and went into a forest to test his strength. After he had travelled a league and a half, he found a peroba with a trunk the size of a streetcar. "This'll do," he said. He stuck his arm in a hole in the trunk and pulled the tree from the earth, roots and all. "I have the strength!" Macunaíma cried, and he felt satisfied with himself. When he tried to return to the city, however, he couldn't even walk because he was so covered in ticks. Macunaíma cried in a weakened voice, "Ah, ticks! Get away, fellas! I don't owe you anything!"

The ticks fell onto the ground as a result of this enchantment and scurried away. Ticks used to be people like us… One day, a tick put up a little shop on the side of

Macunaíma

the road and did brisk business because he didn't mind selling on credit. So much credit was extended to so many Brazilians who didn't pay, that, in the end, the tick went broke and had to close the little store. Now, he bites people to collect his accounts.

When Macunaíma arrived in the city, it was already well into the night. He immediately went to stake out the giant's house. There was a haze over everything, and the house looked empty because all of the windows were dark. Macunaíma wanted to find a housemaid to fool around with, but there was a group of taxis parked on the corner and all of the young women were already flirting and giggling over there. Macunaíma then wanted to set a trap for curiós but didn't have bait.[1] There was nothing to do and he felt sleepy. He didn't want to nap, however, because he was waiting for Venceslau Pietro Pietra. He thought, "I'll keep watch, and if Sleep comes for me, I'll hang him." He didn't have to wait long before he saw a figure approaching. It was Emoron-Pódole, the Father of Sleep.[2] Macunaíma lay very still among some termite nests

---

[1] Curiós are a kind of songbird that are common throughout Brazil.

[2] E'moron-Pódole is regarded as the Father of Sleep in Pemón legends, too, and is a creature of ambiguous nature. Koch-Grünberg speculated that he's a sort of bird or lizard because he guards a nest of eggs. According to legend, some hunters were trying to steal the eggs, but kept falling asleep as they neared the nest. So, the tribal magician went to fetch the eggs. He, like the hunters, fell asleep as he approached the nest, but instead of turning around, continued forward, sleeping at intervals until he was able to grab three eggs. He brought them back to show the tribe, then ate them in front of everyone. As a result, sleeping became a regular habit of all people.

to keep from surprising the Father of Sleep so he could ambush him. Emoron-Pódole kept coming closer, but when he arrived at last, the hero nodded off, slammed his chin onto his chest, bit his tongue, then screamed, "I'm scared!"

Sleep immediately ran away. Macunaíma walked onward, very disappointed. He thought, "Now, maybe I didn't catch it, but I almost did. I'll try a second time and may monkeys lick me if I don't catch the Father of Sleep and hang him!" There was a stream nearby with a fallen tree overtop that served as a bridge. Beyond it was a lagoon, whitened by moonlight after the evening haze had dissipated. The view was quiet and made peaceful by a small fountain singing the lullaby of the poor. He expected the Father of Sleep to be huddled somewhere around there. Macunaíma crossed his arms and, with his left eye closed, kept still between the termite nests. It wasn't very long before he saw Emoron-Pódole walking toward him again. The Father of Sleep kept coming closer until he suddenly stopped. Macunaíma heard what he was saying to himself: "This guy's not dead. Who's ever heard of a dead man who doesn't burp when he's spotted!"

So, the hero belched: "Brrap!"

"Where have you ever seen a dead man burp, you guys!?" joked Sleep, who then immediately ran away.

It is for this reason that the Father of Sleep still prowls at night, and everyone, as a punishment, is unable to sleep while standing up.

Macunaíma was feeling disappointed about what had happened, until he heard a commotion and saw a chauffeur on the other side of the stream waving him over. He was confused and shouted madly, "It's just me, bud! Not a francesa!"

"Go away, you jinx!" replied the young man.

Macunaíma

Macunaíma then noticed a little housemaid in a yellow linen dress painted with tatajuba dye.[3] After she'd crossed the fallen tree over the stream, the hero shouted towards the bridge, "Did you see anything, log?"

"I saw her goods!"

"Ha! Ha! Hahaha!" Macunaíma laughed wildly. He followed after the couple, but by the time he'd caught up to them, they were already done fooling around and were resting on the shore of a lagoon. The girl was sitting on the edge of an igarité which had been pulled onto the beach.[4] Still completely naked after their swim, she was eating raw lambaris and laughing with the young man. He was floating face down on the water by the girl's feet and catching the little fish for her. The crests of waves broke on his back, slid over his wet naked body, and splashed back into the lagoon to the sound of their giggles. The girl kicked the water, splashing gracefully like a fountain stolen from Luna, and blinded the boy.[5] He ducked his head under the surface and filled his mouth with water. When he emerged, the girl squeezed his cheeks with her feet and, just like that, the entire jet of water hit her stomach. The breeze spread the smooth strands of the girl's hair one by one across her face. When the boy saw this, he propped his chin on his companion's knee, lifted his chest out of the water, stretched his arm up high, and pushed aside the hair from the girl's face so she could eat

---

[3] A tatajuba is a species of mulberry tree.

[4] An igarité is a type of canoe with a mast and sail.

[5] Luna is a Roman goddess who is the personification of the moon. The name is sometimes used to refer to Diana, who is the Roman goddess of the moon, and the two are sometimes described as a single goddess.

the lambaris in peace. To thank him, she stuck three of the little fish into his mouth and, laughing giddily, pulled her knee away. The boy's chin no longer had support, and in an instant his face was in the water with the girl pressing his neck into the bottom of the lagoon with her feet. She began slipping without realizing it because of all of the fun that she was having, and continued to slip until the canoe finally overturned and she flipped over along with it! The girl tumbled comically on top of the young man, and he wrapped himself around her like a clinging ficus vine. All of the lambaris fled while the two fooled around again in the water.

Macunaíma approached. He sat on the hull of the overturned igarité and waited. When he saw that they were done fooling around, he said to the chauffeur:

"I haven't eaten in three days,
I haven't spit in a week,
Adam, he was made of clay,
Nephew, a cigar is what I seek."

The chauffeur responded:

"Forgive me, my kinsman,
If I don't give you a smoke;
The leaves, match, and paper,
Would fall in the water and soak."

"Don't worry about it. I have one," replied Macunaíma. He took out a tortoiseshell cigar case made by Antônio do Rosário in Pará, offered tauari-leaf cigars to the young man and the housemaid, and lit a match for the two of them and another for himself.⁶ Then, he swatted away the mosquitoes and began to tell a story. The night passed quickly, and nobody was bothered by the song of the tinamou that marked the hours of darkness.⁷ It went like this:

"In the old days, you guys, the automobile wasn't a machine like it is today. It was a brown puma named Palauá who dwelled in the Fulano Forest.⁸ One day, Palauá said to her eyes, 'Go to the seashore, my green eyes. Hurry, hurry, hurry!'

"The eyes left and the brown puma went blind. But she raised her nose, sniffed the wind, sensed that Aimalá-Pódole, the Father of Traíras, was swimming in the sea nearby, and shouted, 'Come back from the seashore, my green eyes! Hurry, hurry, hurry!'⁹

---

⁶ Fr. Antônio do Rosário (1647-1704) was a Dominican Friar from Lisbon. In 1686, he traveled to Brazil, where he wrote extensively. He is best known for his work *Frutas do Brasil* ("Fruits of Brazil"), in which he imagines a kingdom where Pineapple is king and Sugarcane is queen, and Europe is a foreign land of flowers. Rosário uses the allegory to argue for the superiority of the New World, the fruits of which are edible and useful, as opposed to the flowers of Europe, which are endowed only with ephemeral fragrance. A tauari is a species of tree related to the Brazil-nut tree.

⁷ A tinamou is a kind of mostly flightless bird, of which there are several species.

⁸ In the Pemón legends, "Paluá" is a river otter.

⁹ Aimalá-Pódole is the Father of Traíras in the original Pemón legends, too. A traíra is a species of fish known for its sharp teeth and strong bite. Because the fish is cannibalistic and lurks in the shadows, "traíra" is also a slang term for a deceitful

"The eyes came back and Palauá was able to see again. A ferocious black tiger passed by and yelled at Palauá, 'What are you doing, bud!?'

"'I'm sending my eyes to look at the sea.'

"'Is it nice?'

"'Nice enough for dogs!'

"'Then send mine, too, bud!'

"'I'm not sending them now because Aimalá-Pódole is on the seashore.'

"'Send them now or I'll swallow you whole, bud!'

"So, Palauá said, 'Go to the seashore, yellow eyes of my friend the tiger. Hurry, hurry, hurry!'

"The eyes rolled away and the black tiger was blind. Aimalá-Pódole was there and – gulp! – swallowed the tiger's eyes. Palauá suspected what had happened because he detected the Father of Traíras's bitter stench. She tried to sneak away, but the ferocious black tiger sensed this and yelled to the brown puma, 'Wait a second, bud!'

"'Can't you see that I need to fetch dinner for my children?' responded Palauá. 'Another day.'

"'Send my eyes back first, bud, because I've had enough of the dark.'

"Palauá shouted, 'Come back from the seashore, yellow eyes of my friend the tiger! Hurry, hurry, hurry!'

"But the eyes didn't come back, and the black tiger was furious. 'Now I'm going to swallow you, bud!'

"He darted after the brown puma. It was such a wild chase through the woods that – chii! – the little birds shrank teeny-tiny from terror, and the night was paralyzed by fear. This is why, even when it is daylight over the canopy of the trees, it's always night inside the forest. Before long, poor Palauá couldn't run another step.

---

person.

"After sprinting a league and a half, Palauá was exhausted and turned around. The black tiger was closing in on her. Palauá arrived at a hill called Ibiraçoiaba and came across the giant anvil that had belonged to the foundry of Alfonso Sardinha at the beginning of Brazilian life.[10] Next to the anvil were four discarded wagon wheels. So, Palauá tied them to her feet so she could keep moving without as much effort. Then, as the expression goes, she cut the end of the hammock once again, and made a bold escape! The puma covered a league and a half of ground in an instant, but she drew the tiger along after her. They made so much noise that the little birds shrank even tinier from fear. The night felt more threatening because she couldn't walk, and the atmosphere was further haunted by the groans of a nightjar.[11] The nightjar is the Father of the Night and was crying over his daughter's misery.

"Palauá's stomach panged with hunger. The tiger was on her tail, but Palauá couldn't move any further with her stomach on her back like that. She was at the islet of Boipeda, where a cuisarruim lived.[12] She saw an engine nearby and swallowed it whole. As soon as the engine dropped into the puma's stomach, the poor creature had

---

[10] Alfonso Sardinha is credited with building the first iron furnace in the Americas in 1597. He is believed to have been the son of an Iberian blacksmith, and to have established the furnace outside São Paulo near the magnetite deposits at a hill called Açoiaba, which means "the place where the sun hides" in Tupi.

[11] A nightjar is a kind of nocturnal bird.

[12] Boipeda is a small island on the Atlantic coast of the state of Bahia. "Cuisarruim" is a term derived from "coisa ruim" ("bad thing") and refers to a devil or demon.

renewed energy and sprinted off. She ran a league and a half before looking back. As she did so, the black tiger pounced.

"There was a darkness in which they were guided only by the melancholy of the night. The puma bumped into an ash tree and tumbled wildly down the side of a hill. These were her final moments as Palauá! She snapped up two fireflies in her mouth and continued with them held between her teeth to light the way. She'd barely made it another league before she looked back again. The tiger was close because the brown puma stank and the blind pursuer had a hound dog's sense of smell. So, Palauá ingested a purgative of castor oil, took a can of a substance called gasoline, and poured it into her X. Then, off she went – vroom! vroom! vroom! – like a braying donkey. There was so much noise that not even the spooky crashes of broken plates on the Morro do Assobio could be heard there.[13]

"The black tiger was thoroughly confounded because he was blind and no longer smelled the puma's stench. Palauá ran much further before looking back again. She didn't see the tiger. Her face steamed from the heat and she couldn't run another step. Palauá had arrived in the port of Santos, where there was a vast grove of banana trees nearby and a branch across the road.[14] The exhausted beast poured water onto her snout to cool off. Then, she cut a big leaf from a banana tree and hid, pulling

---

[13] On November 4, 1926, the newspaper *O Estado do Paraná* ("The State of Paraná") reported a ritual at a place called the Morro do Assobio ("Whistling Hill") near the coastal city of Natal, whereby a woman dressed in white led a ceremony in which participants screamed and smashed plates.

[14] Santos is the closest seaport to São Paulo.

it over her like a cape, and went to sleep. The ferocious black tiger passed by, but the puma didn't make a sound and wasn't discovered. Because she was so afraid of being caught, the puma never let go of the things that had helped her escape. She still always moves with wheels on her feet, a motor in her belly, a purgative of oil down her throat, water in her snout, gasoline by her tailbone, and two fireflies in her mouth, and is always covered by a canopy of banana leaf – ai ai! – ready to zoom away. Now, if someone steps into a swarm of ants called taxis, climbs through her shiny exterior, and twists her ear – what! – she zooms off quicker than God! And she's assumed a strange name to disguise herself even further. She's the automobile machine.[15]

"But because she'd drank water, Palauá couldn't move. To own an automobile of your own is to sit miserable at home, you guys.

"They say that the puma later gave birth to an enormous litter. She had sons and daughters, some with masculine names like 'Ford,' and others with feminine

---

[15] According to Pemón legend, the jaguar obtains its beautiful eyes in a similar episode, which Koch-Grünberg titled "Das Augenspiel" ("The Eye Game"): The jaguar sees a crab playing with his eyes on the beach. The jaguar asks the crab to send her eyes down to the water, but the crab resists because he's afraid that Aimalá-Pódole will swallow them. After the jaguar pressures him, however, they both send their eyes to the water. Just as the crab had warned, Aimalá-Pódole swallows the jaguar's eyes. The jaguar starts to starve because she can't hunt without eyes, and a king vulture comes to stalk her. The jaguar offers to kill a tapir for the vulture, if the vulture helps her regain her sight. So, the vulture fetches some milk, pours it into the jaguar's eye sockets, and creates beautiful new eyes. The jaguar keeps her promise and kills a tapir for the vulture.

names like 'Chevrolet.' The end."

By the time Macunaíma had stopped speaking, the couple were sobbing. A breeze blew across the water and through the air. The young man ducked his head under the water to hide his tears and brought up a lambari, impishly holding its tail in his teeth. He shared the food with the young woman. Then, in the doorway of the house, a Fiat puma opened her throat and howled at the moon: "Baah-ooh-ah! Baah-ooh-ah!"

There was a tremendous roar, and a suffocating aroma of fish took over the air. Venceslau Pietro Pietra was coming. The chauffeur and the housemaid immediately got up and offered their hands to Macunaíma, inviting him to come with them. "Your giant has come back from a trip. Aren't we going to see what he's like?"

They did. They found Venceslau Pietro Pietra at the front gate talking to a reporter. The giant laughed at the three of them and said to the chauffeur, "Shall we go inside?"

"Why not!?"

Piaimã had pierced ears. He stuck one of the young man's legs in his right earlobe, and the other leg in his left, then carried him on his back. They crossed the lawn and entered the house. Right in the middle of the acapu-paneled hall, which was furnished with wicker sofas made by a German-Jewish craftsman in Manaus, there was an enormous hole over which a japecanga vine had been hung to make a swing.[16] Piaimã sat the young man on the

---

[16] Acapu is a chocolate-colored wood. Manaus was known for its multicultural immigrant population at the turn of the 20th century, including its Jewish and German populations. A japecanga is a flowering vine related to lilies.

vine and asked him if he wanted to swing for a bit. The young man said yes. Piaimã pushed him for a long time, until suddenly there was a snag. The japecanga had thorns that penetrated the chauffeur's flesh, and blood started to drain into the hole.

"Stop! I've had enough!" the chauffeur cried.

"Swing, I tell you!" Piaimã responded.

Blood was flowing. The giant's woodsy companion was at the bottom of the hole, and the blood was dripping into a pot full of macaroni that she was preparing for him. The young man groaned on the swing: "Ah, if my father and mother were at my side, I wouldn't be suffering at the hands of this devil!"

Piaimã gave a very strong tug on the vine, and the boy fell into the pot of macaroni.

Venceslau Pietro Pietra went to fetch Macunaíma. The hero was already giggling with the little housemaid. The giant said to him, "Are we going inside?"

Macunaíma stretched his arms, mumbling, "Ai... What a drag..."

"Let's go! Are we going?"

"Yeah, sure…"

So, Piaimã did with him as he'd done with the chauffeur and carried the hero upside down on his back with the hero's feet secured in the holes of his earlobes. Macunaíma aimed the blowgun and, hanging upside down like this, looked like an acrobatic rifleman from the circus, shooting at the bullseye on a target. The giant grew very annoyed, and turned around and saw everything. "Don't do that!" he shouted.

He took the blowgun and tossed it aside, and Macunaíma grabbed some branches with his now empty hands.

"What are you doing?" asked the suspicious giant.

"Can't you see that the branches are hitting my face!?"

Piaimã felt the hero on top of his head, and Macunaíma tickled the giant's ears with the branches until Piaimã laughed aloud and jumped for joy. "Stop bothering me!" he shouted.

They entered the atrium. Below the stairs was a golden cage for little singing birds. Except, instead of little birds, the giant kept snakes and lizards. Macunaíma jumped into the cage and covertly started eating snakes. Piaimã invited him to join him on the swing, but Macunaíma was busy swallowing snakes. He counted, "Five down the hatch," and swallowed another one.

Finally, the hero ran out of snakes and, outraged, climbed out of the cage. He looked with ire upon the thief of the muiraquitã and growled, "Hmm... what a drag!"

But Piaimã insisted that the hero swing.

"I don't even know how to swing," Macunaíma snarled. "You'd better go first."

"I'll do no such thing, hero! It's even easier than drinking water! Get on the japecanga right now. I'll push you!"

"Then, I accept. But you go first, giant."

Piaimã continued to insist, but the hero kept on saying that the giant had to swing first. At last, Venceslau Pietro Pietra climbed onto the vine, and Macunaíma pushed him higher with each swing. He sang:

"Don't fall in,
Sir Captain,
Sword in your belt,
Saddle horn in your hand!"

The hero yanked the vine. The thorns hooked into the giant's flesh and his blood spattered everywhere. The woman below didn't know that the blood was from her giant and added it to the macaroni. The sauce was thickening.

"Stop! Stop!" Piaimã screamed.

"I said swing!" responded Macunaíma. He pushed the giant until he was quite dizzy, then gave the japecanga another strong tug. Eating the snakes had filled him with rage. Venceslau Pietro Pietra fell into the pit screaming a song: "Fee-fie-foe... If I escape from this hole, I'll never eat another soul!"

He saw the steaming macaroni below him and shouted at the old woman, "Move it away or I'll swallow you!"

But could an alligator move it away? Not even the dripping pan! The giant fell into the boiling macaroni, and an aroma of cooking flesh rose into the air that was so strong that it killed all of the tico-ticos in the city. The hero fainted. Piaimã struggled wildly but was quickly near death. With great effort, he stood up on the bottom of the pot. He wiped away the noodles that were running down his face, rolled his eyes, and licked his moustache. "It needs more cheese!" he cried. Then, he died.

This was the end of Venceslau Pietro Pietra, who was the giant Piaimã, eater of people.[17]

---

[17] In a story that Koch-Grünberg called "Piai'ma's Tod" ("Piaimã's Death"), Piai'ma takes a man back to his house by sticking the man's legs in his ear piercings and letting the man dangle down his back. In his house is a deep hole with a vine slung across it. He orders the man to swing on the vine and shows him how. Once the man is sitting on the vine, Piai'ma pushes him so hard that the man loses his balance and falls into the hole. As he tries to climb out, Piai'ma hits him on the head with a club, knocking him back into the hole and killing him. Piai'ma and his wife then eat the body. Piai'ma repeats the process with several other men until he encounters a young

When Macunaíma awoke from having fainted, he fetched the muiraquitã and left on a tram machine for the boarding house. The entire way there, he cried and moaned, "Muiraquitã, muiraquitã, my darling's treasure. I can see you, but I don't see her!"

---

fisherman who at first refuses Piai'ma's advances. Nevertheless, Piai'ma forces the fisherman to put his legs in his ear piercings so he can carry him home. When they arrive at the hole, Piai'ma asks the fisherman to swing, but the fisherman asks Piai'ma first to show him how. Piai'ma agrees and, as he's swinging, the fisherman hits him with a trumpet and knocks him into the hole. Waiting at the bottom of the hole is Piai'ma's wife, armed with a club to kill the fisherman. When Piai'ma falls to the bottom, she believes that it's the fisherman and swings her club, killing Piai'ma instantly.

Macunaíma

XV
OIBÊ'S GUTS

The three brothers turned back toward their homeland. They were all content, but the hero was even more so, because he felt something that only a hero could feel: total satisfaction. They started their journey home. When they reached the summit of Pico do Jaraguá, Macunaíma turned around to reflect on the grand city of São Paulo.[1] He meditated somberly for a long time, then shook his head and mumbled, "Poor in health and rich in saúvas, these are the evils of Brazil."

He wiped away a tear and compressed his little lips to stop their quivering. Then, he cast a spell: Waving his arms in the air, he turned the giant village into a sloth made entirely of stone. The brothers continued onward.

After careful consideration, Macunaíma spent all of his remaining coins on what had excited him most about Paulistan civilization: a Smith & Wesson revolver, a Patek

---

[1] Pico do Jaraguá is the tallest mountain in the city of São Paulo.

watch, and a pair of leghorns.[2] Macunaíma made earrings for himself out of the revolver and watch, and carried the rooster and hen in a cage. Not a single coin remained of what he'd won from the giant, but dangling from his pierced lip was the muiraquitã.

And everything was made easier by it. They canoed down the Araguaia River, and while Jiguê paddled, Maanape handled the rudder. They felt like men again. Macunaíma, perched on the bow, took note of the bridges that he'd need to build or repair to make life easier for the people of Goiás.[3] Night fell, and Macunaíma watched the little lights of the revelers gently dancing sambas in the ipueiras of the wide river until he fell fast asleep.[4] He woke up energized the next day and, standing on the bow of the igarité with the cage tucked under his left arm, plucked a violin and sang laments from his homeland to the world, like this:

"The antianti is fair,
Pirá-uauau,
The ariramba gives thanks,
Pirá-uauau,

---

[2] On May 1, 1839, Antoine Norbert de Patek co-founded Patek, Czapek & Co., a manufacturer of high-quality pocket watches, in Geneva, Switzerland. In 1844, he saw a pocket watch of extraordinary thinness that had been manufactured by a Frenchman named Jean Adrien Philippe. The next year, upon the expiration of Patek's contract with Czapek, Patek and Phillipe formed Patek Phillipe & Co., a world-famous manufacturer of luxury timepieces.

[3] Goiás is a rural state in central Brazil.

[4] An ipueira is a marsh or swamp caused by the overflow of a river from its banks.

The village ruins are where,
Upon the Uraricoera's banks?
Pirá-uauau."[5]

He scanned the river's banks in search of the village where he'd grown up. As he floated with the current, every scent of fish and every clump of bromelia filled him with enthusiasm, and the hero howled at the whole world, going crazy and shouting senseless emboladas and pantomimes like this:[6]

"Guided to the ruins,
Caburé,
Paçoca of arapaçu,
Caburé,
Brothers, let's go onward,
to the banks of the Uraricoera!
Caburé!"[7]

The Araguaian waters murmured, calling for the igarité with a little roar. The song of the Iaras could be heard in the distance. Vei, the Sun, lashed the backs of the oarsmen, Maanape and Jiguê, who each glistened with sweat, as well as the standing hero's hairy body. A wet heat

---

[5] An antianti is a kind of small bird, a pirá is a kind of fish, and an ariramba is a waterfowl similar to a kingfisher.

[6] A bromelia is a kind of flowering shrub. Emboladas are a genre of songs in which lyrics are spoken in double time during verses, and choral refrains are sung.

[7] A caburé is a variety of owl. Paçoca is a dish of roasted meat that has been shredded and mixed with cassava flour. An arapaçu is a kind of bird that feeds on tree-dwelling insects.

was stoking a fire of delirium in the three men. Macunaíma remembered that he was the emperor of the Virgin Forest. He shook his fist at the Sun and shouted, "Eropita boiamorebo!"

The sky immediately darkened, and a fiery cloud arose on the horizon which turned the calm of the day into evening. The fiery cloud continued its approach until Macunaíma realized that it was a flock of yellow macaws and parakeets, all of these talking birds.[8] There were trumpet parrots, corral parrots, cutapada parakeets, xarãs, purple-breasted parrots, blue-fronted parrots, mealy parrots, macaws, araricas, little blue parrots, ararais, arara-tauas, severe macaws, pionus parrots, scarlet macaws, monk parakeets, tribas, vultures, red-fan parrots, anapuras, blue-and-yellow macaws, and tuim parakeets, all of these birds that comprised the multicolored entourage of Emperor Macunaíma.[9] And all of these squawking talkers formed a tent of wings that protected the hero from the Sun's bitter spite. There was such a roar of water, gods, and little birds, that nothing else could be heard. The igarité stopped as the oarsmen sat stunned. But Macunaíma, scaring the leghorns, shook his fist at everything and shouted, "There once was a yellow cow, and whoever spoke first had to eat her shit! Ding-a-ling!

---

[8] According to legend, St. José de Anchieta was on a canoe headed toward the town of Santos, suffering with his companions from the blistering sun. A flock of birds appeared overhead, and St. José de Anchieta shouted the words "Eropita boiamorebo!" to their leader. At that, the birds stopped their journey to provide the priest and his companions with shade during the rest of their trip.

[9] Xarãs, araricas, ararais, and arara-tauas are species of macaw ("arara" in Portuguese). A triba is a kind of parakeet.

She's arrived!"

The world went mute, no one saying a thing, and the silence brightened the shadow of languor that loomed over the igarité. And out there in the far-away distance could be heard the roar of the Uraricoera. The hero grew even more enthusiastic, and the violin shrieked vibrantly at his hands. Macunaíma cleared his throat and spat into the river, and while the spit was sinking, it transformed into a repulsive mata-mata.[10] The hero wailed at the world like a madman, without even thinking about what he was singing, like this:

"Butterfly bu-butterfly,
Butterfly bu-butterfly:
A boss on her belly on the bow,
Baby sister,
On the banks of the Uraricoera!"

The mouth of the night swallowed all of the noise, and the world went to sleep. There was only Capei, the enormously fat Moon, her face as plump as that of a polaca after a night – spicy! – of many happy indiscretions, ample flirting, and too much cachiri. Macunaíma started to miss what he'd experienced in the grand Paulistan village. He envisioned all of those white-skinned ladies with whom he'd played husband and wife, and it felt so good! He whispered sweetly, "Mani! Mani! Little daughters of cassava!"

His lips trembled so violently that the muiraquitã fell out and almost dropped into the river. Macunaíma put the tembetá back into his lip and ruminated on its owner, the

---

[10] A mata-mata is a kind of large freshwater turtle with a brown spiked shell.

feisty and sexy devil who'd beaten him so savagely: Ci. Ah! Ci, Mother of the Forest, his marvada who'd been unforgettable ever since she'd made him sleep in the hammock woven with her hair! "Whoever has a long-distance lover undertakes a Trojan effort," he considered. What witchcraft by the marvada! And she was up there in the field of the sky, dazzling with elegance, all dressed-up and fooling around with who knows whom. He felt jealous. He raised his arms in the air, startling the leghorns, and prayed to the Father of Love:

"Rudá, Rudá!
You who are in the sky,
And command the rains.
Rudá! Make it so that my beloved,
No matter how many partners she takes,
Finds that all are flaccid!
Blow into this marvada
Thoughts of her marvado!
Make her remember me tomorrow,
When the Sun sets in the west!"

He scanned overhead. Ci wasn't there, only Capei, fat and filling the sky. The hero laid down on the igarité, used the cage as a headrest, and slept among marions, piuns, and muriçocas.[11] The night was already turning yellow when Macunaíma was awakened by the chirps of chupims in a bamboo thicket. He wanted to investigate and jumped onto the riverbank, telling Jiguê, "Wait a second."

He went deep into the forest, a league and a half inward, to fetch the beautiful Iriqui, his lover who'd been Jiguê's wife. She was dressing herself and picking ticks

---

[11] Marions, piuns, and muriçocas are kinds of mosquito.

from her skin as she reclined against the roots of a samaúma tree, waiting for him. The two were overjoyed to see each other and fooled around for a long time before returning to the igarité.

At midday, the parrots again spread out overhead, shading Macunaíma. They did this for several days in a row. One afternoon, the hero was restless and missed sleeping on firm ground, so he went to do so. As soon as he went to hop onto the riverbank, however, a monster emerged in front of him. It was the beast Ponde, a Jucurutu de Solimões, who capsizes boats in the night and swallows the occupants.[12] Macunaíma shot an arrow which had the flat head of a sacred ant called curupê adhered to its tip.[13] He didn't even aim, certain that the shot would be a beauty. But when the arrow reached Ponde, the beast turned into an owl in a puff of smoke.

Further ahead, after crossing a plateau and climbing a mountain peak covered in rocks, he encountered the Mapinguari Monster, a monkey-man who lurks in the forest doing bad things to young girls.[14] The monster

---

[12] A Jucurutu do Solimões is a mythical bird of Amazon legend whose mournful cries would cause hunting and war expeditions to turn around in fear of its torment. The Solimões is a name for the Amazon River and its tributaries situated above the confluence with the Rio Negro. The name was used by early Portuguese colonists to refer to the native tribes who lived there, and who were known for shooting arrows tipped with venom, called "solimão" in Portuguese.

[13] A curupê is a kind of ant.

[14] The Mapinguari is a monster similar to a yeti or bigfoot. Although it is generally regarded as a mythical creature of folklore, there are some Amazonian tribes who believe that it really exists. Some scholars have suggested that the Mapinguari

Macunaíma

grabbed Macunaíma, but the hero whipped out his toaquiçu and showed it to Mapinguari.[15]

"Make no mistake, partner!"

The monster laughed and let Macunaíma pass. The hero walked a league and a half in search of some ground without ants. He climbed to the top of a forty-meter-high cumaru and, after a long time scanning the fields, finally saw a faraway light.[16] He went toward it and came across a ranch. It was Oibê's ranch.

Macunaíma knocked at the ranch-house door and a sweet voice groaned from inside, "Who goes there!"

"I come in peace!"

The door opened and there appeared a beast so enormous that the hero was terrified. It was the monster Oibê, the fearsome Minhocão.[17] The hero felt a chill, but then remembered the Smith & Wesson, mustered some courage, and asked for lodging.

"Come in. Mi casa, su casa."

Macunaíma entered, sat on a large basket, and just stayed there. After a while, he asked, "Are we going to talk?"

"We are."

"About what?"

Oibê stroked his beard, thinking until his face

---

is based on the folkloric memory of the giant sloths that used to inhabit the area, and which are believed to be extinct.

[15] "Toaquiçu" is a Tupi word for "penis."

[16] A cumaru is a species of tree indigenous to the Amazon.

[17] The Minhocão is a mythical gigantic beast that inhabits the rivers and floodplains of Brazil and resembles a snake or worm. According to some accounts, its head looks like that of a pig. Oibê is a creation of Andrade.

brightened with satisfaction. "We're going to talk dirty."

"Geez! Such horrible taste!" the hero cried.

Then, they talked dirty for an hour.

Oibê was cooking his dinner. Macunaíma was not hungry, but he put his cage on the floor and, in deceit, rubbed his belly and groaned, "Ughh!"

Oibê grumbled, "What is it, man!?"

"I'm hungry! I'm hungry!"

Oibê scooped some yams and beans into a trough, filled a gourd with cassava flour, and offered them to the hero. But he didn't offer him any of the meat roasting on a cinnamon-sassafras spit, which smelled wonderful. Macunaíma swallowed everything without chewing. He wasn't hungry at all, but his mouth had started to water at the roasting meat. He rubbed his belly and groaned, "Ughh!"

Oibê grumbled, "What is it, man!?"

"I'm thirsty! I'm thirsty!"

Oibê picked up the bucket and went to fetch water from the well. While he was gone, Macunaíma took the cinnamon-sassafras spit from the coals, swallowed the entire hunk of meat without chewing, then went back to sitting quietly and waiting for Oibê to return. When the Minhocão came back with a full bucket, Macunaíma filled a coconut with water, and drank. Then, he stretched and sighed, "Ay, yai, yai!"

The monster went crazy. "What now!? What is it, man!?"

"I'm sleepy! I'm sleepy!"

So, Oibê carried Macunaíma to the guest room, said goodnight, and closed the door behind him. Then, he went to eat his dinner. Macunaíma put the cage with the hens in a corner and covered it with some patterned cotton sheets. He looked around the room for the source of an incessant crackling noise that came from all sides. Macunaíma flicked the flint of his lighter and saw that it was cockroaches. He jumped right back into the hammock, but not without first looking back to check on the leghorns. The birds were quite happy eating cockroaches. Macunaíma laughed to himself, burped, and fell asleep. Before long, he was covered in cockroaches licking him.

When Oibê noticed that Macunaíma had eaten the meat, he was enraged. He grabbed a little bell, wrapped himself in a white sheet, and went to haunt the guest. But it was only a joke. He knocked on the door and rang the little bell: Ding-a-ling!

"Hello?"

"I come to fetch my meee-eat!" Ding-a-ling!

He opened the door. When the hero saw the ghost, he was so scared that he froze. He didn't know that it was Oibê. The phantasm charged toward him. "I come to fetch my meee-eat!" Ding-a-ling!

Macunaíma realized that it wasn't a ghost at all, but was the monster Oibê, the terrible Minhocão. He mustered up some courage, pulled out his left earring, which was the revolver machine, and fired a shot at the ghost. Oibê ignored it, however, and continued to approach. The hero was terrified. He jumped from the hammock, grabbed the cage, and escaped through the window, tossing cockroaches aside as he ran. Oibê ran after him. Trying to eat the hero had only been a joke. Macunaíma scrambled wildly outside, but the Minhocão grabbed him. Macunaíma put his finger down his own throat, tickled a bit, and regurgitated the swallowed flour. The flour turned into sand, and while the monster struggled to move across the slippery surface, Macunaíma fled. He took a right, descended Morro do Estrondo,

Macunaíma

which sounds every seven years, then passed through some woods, and, after taking a rough shortcut, crossed Sergipe from one end to the other.[18]

In a rocky crevice there, he finally stopped panting. In front of him was a big cave with a little grotto bored inside where a little altar had been placed. In the mouth of the cave sat a friar.

Macunaíma asked the friar, "What's your name?"

The friar cast his cold eyes upon the hero and responded patiently, "I am Mendonça Mar, the painter. Disgusted by the injustice of men, it has been three centuries since I withdrew from society and struck out for the backwoods. I discovered this cave and built this altar to Bom Jesus da Lapa with my own hands. Now I live here, forgiving people, having become Friar Francisco da Soledade."[19]

---

[18] The Morro do Estrondo ("Thunder Hill") is a nickname given to a sandy hill on the beaches of the coastal city of Natal. According to legend, every seven years there would be a colossal boom of thunder and a tornado of sand. Therefore, the lumberjacks who were harvesting the hills in the area at the turn of the 20th century were afraid to sleep there at night. Sergipe is a small state on Brazil's coast.

[19] Francisco de Mendonça Mar was a stone mason and goldsmith in Bahia, who was imprisoned in the late 17th century in connection with a dispute over the construction of a governor's palace. After his release, he fled to some remote rocky cliffs on the banks of the Rio São Francisco, where he lived in a cave as a hermit. There, he built the Sanctuary of Bom Jesus da Lapa ("Good Jesus of the Rock") and performed acts of charity for visiting pilgrims. When the Archbishop of Bahia learned of Mendonça Mar's activity, he invited the hermit to join the priesthood. In 1705, Mendonça Mar was ordained a Roman Catholic priest and adopted the name Fr.

"That's nice," Macunaíma said. Then, he left in a flash.

The area was riddled with caves, and just ahead he saw another stranger doing something so silly that he stopped in amazement. It was Hercules Florence.[20] He'd put a small pane of glass in the mouth of a tiny cave and was covering and uncovering it with a blue taro leaf. Macunaíma asked, "Woah, woah, woah! Aren't you going to tell me what you're doing there, sir!?"

The stranger turned around, his eyes glimmering with joy, and said, "Gardez cette date: 1927! Je viens d'inventer la photographie."

Macunaíma laughed out loud. "Geez! This was already invented years ago, sir!"

Hercules Florence fell, stunned, onto the blue taro leaf and began jotting down the musical notes of a birdsong that he remembered. The man was crazy. Macunaíma sped away.

After he'd run a league and a half, he looked back and saw that Oibê was already nearby. He put his index finger down his throat, and all of the yams that he'd swallowed fell onto the ground and turned into a turtle squirming on its back. Oibê came to flip over this turtle of filth, and Macunaíma fled. A league and a half ahead, he turned around. Oibê was on his tail. So, he shoved his index finger down his throat again, and this time beans and water spewed out. Everything turned into a swamp full of bullfrogs, and while Oibê struggled his way through it, the

---

Francisco da Soledade.

[20] Hercules Florence was a French-born Brazilian who, in 1832, independently invented a process for photography (three years before Louis Daguerre invented his daguerreotype process). He is credited with coining the term "photographie" for the process of creating images with a camera.

hero gathered some worms for the chickens, then left in a hurry.

He gained a big lead and stopped to rest. He was quite surprised, having run such a long distance, to find himself once again at the gate to Oibê's ranch. He decided to hide in the orchard. There was a starfruit tree, and Macunaíma started pulling branches from the tree to cover himself. The cut branches grabbed him, dripping with tears, and he heard the starfruit tree's lament:

"Gardiner of my father,
Don't cut my hair,
Because the bad man buried me
By the fig tree whose fruit
The little bird plucked bare...
Coo, coo, little bird!"

All of the little birds wept with pity and groaned in their nests as the hero froze with fright. He grabbed the patuá that he wore among his necklaces and cast a spell.[21] The starfruit tree turned into a glamorous princess. The hero had a naughty desire to fool around with her but could already hear Oibê thrashing about. "I come to fetch my meee-eat!" Ding-a-ling!

Macunaíma grabbed the princess by the hand, and they ran away in a hurry. Ahead there was a fig tree with enormous roots at the base of its trunk. Oibê was already at their heels and Macunaíma didn't have time to look for a better hiding place. He tucked himself and the princess into a nook within the tree's roots. The Minhocão stuck

---

[21] A patuá is a little sac on a necklace in which herbs, animal hair, and other similar natural items are kept, and which is worn by practitioners of Candomblé to ward off evil spirits.

his arm inside and grabbed the hero's leg. He tried to pull him out, but Macunaíma laughed and said, "You think that you grabbed my leg, but you didn't! It's a root, bozo!"

The Minhocão let go, and Macunaíma shouted, "Actually, it really was my leg! You dumb clown!"

Oibê stuck his arm back in, but the hero had already pulled in his leg and the Minhocão found only roots. There was a heron nearby. Oibê said to her, "Sister heron, talk some sense into the hero. Don't let him leave. I'm going to fetch a hoe to dig them out."

The heron kept watch. When Oibê was out of earshot, Macunaíma said to her, "So, you fool, this is how you talk sense into a hero!? You have to get up close and bug your eyes!"

The heron did so, and Macunaíma threw a handful of fire ants in her eyes. While the heron was shouting of blindness, the hero climbed from the hole with the princess, and they slipped away once again. Near Santo Antônio in Mato Grosso, they were dying of hunger when they came across a banana tree.[22] Macunaíma said to the princess, "Climb up, eat the good green ones and throw the yellow ones to me."

She did so. The hero gorged himself while the princess danced with the wind for his entertainment. Soon, Oibê was coming, so they cut the end of the hammock once again.

After they ran another league and a half, they finally arrived at a hummock poking out of the Araguaia River. The igarité, however, was beached much farther downriver on the opposite bank with Maanape, Jiguê, and the beautiful Iriqui, all of whom were asleep. Macunaíma

---

[22] Santo Antônio is a town on the Rio Cuiabá in the state Mato Grosso, near Brazil's border with Bolivia.

looked back. Oibê was almost on top of him. So, he put his finger down his throat for the last time, tickled a bit, and expelled the roast into the water. The roast turned into a very bushy floating island of herbs. Macunaíma carefully placed the cage on the island, then tossed the princess alongside. Pushing off the bank with his foot, he launched the floating island for the river to carry away.

By the time Oibê arrived, the fugitives were long gone. So, the Minhocão, who was a famous werewolf, started to tremble, grew a tail, and turned into a wild dog. He stretched open his enchanted throat and a blue butterfly flew out from his belly. It was the soul of a man who'd been trapped inside the body of a wolf via a spell cast by the dreadful Carrapatu, who appears in the cave at Iporanga.[23]

Macunaíma and the princess fooled around and laughed together as they floated with the current down the river. When they passed close to the igarité, the brothers woke up to Macunaíma's squeals and chased after the couple. Iriqui was jealous because the hero didn't want to know her anymore and fooled around only with the princess. To win the hero back, she threw one of her famous tantrums. Jiguê immediately felt sorry for her and told Macunaíma to go fool around with her for a little while. Jiguê was being very silly.

The hero was already tired of Iriqui, however, and responded, "Iriqui is lifeless, brother. But the princess throws it back! Can't give Iriqui credit for that! Oh, that winter Sun, springtime rain, a woman's tears, a thief's word... Ay, yai, yai! Don't fall for these things!"

---

[23] Carrapatu is a monster who prowls the rooftops of houses in the night, and kidnaps little children who scream. Iporanga is a town in the hills southeast of São Paulo.

Macunaíma started fooling around with the princess again. Iriqui was heartbroken, so she called six macaws, ascended with them to the sky, and, weeping rays of light, turned into a star. The blue-and-yellow macaws turned into stars, too. The seven of them became the Setestrêlo.[24]

---

[24] The Setestrêlo ("Seven Stars") is a cluster of stars also known as the Pleiades or Seven Sisters, and forms part of the constellation Taurus.

XVI

URARICOERA

Macunaíma woke up the next morning with a terrible cough and a scorching fever. Maanape didn't believe his brother's complaints and made him a breakfast of avocado sprouts, thinking that the hero was only malnourished. In fact, the hero had malaria, and his cough had been caused by laryngitis, which everyone in São Paulo carries. Macunaíma spent hours laying on his back on the bow of the igarité and wasn't feeling any better. In the afternoon, when the princess couldn't wait any longer to fool around, the hero would even refuse, sighing, "Ai… what a drag…"

After another day of travel, they reached the headwaters of a river and heard the roar of the Uraricoera nearby. They had arrived. A curious little bird was perched in a monguba, and upon seeing the boat, immediately shouted, "Lady of the harbor, take this way past me!"[1]

---

[1] A monguba is a kind of wetland tree.

Macunaíma happily thanked him. He stood and surveyed the passing landscape. They approached the fort of São Joaquim, built by a brother of the great Marquis.[2] Macunaíma shouted a greeting to a corporal and a soldier who had only tattered rags for pants and caps, and who spent their days keeping saúvas out of their shirt cuffs. At long last, everything again felt familiar. He saw the gentle hill that once had been his mother in the place called Father of Tocandeiras, he saw the treacherous marsh dotted with lily pads that hid electric eels and the smell of fish, and he saw that the old cassava clearing by the tapir's watering hole was now stubble and the old longhouse was now in ruins. Macunaíma wept.

It was approaching the middle of the night when they pulled the igarité onto the riverbank and entered the dilapidated longhouse. Maanape and Jiguê decided to make a fishing rod to catch something to eat, and the princess went to gather some rice. The hero rested. He was sleeping when he felt a hand press on his shoulder. He opened his eyes and saw an old man with a beard standing next to him. The old man said, "Who are you, noble stranger?"

"I'm no stranger, friend. I'm Macunaíma, the hero, and I've come to retire here in my homeland. Who are you?"

The old man bitterly swatted away mosquitoes and

---

[2] Forte São Joaquim ("Fort Saint Joseph") was built in 1775 at the confluence of the Uraricoera and Tacutu rivers in the far north of Brazil, and was strategically located to repel invasions by Dutch and Spanish expeditions. The Marquis is Sebastião José de Carvalho e Melo, Marquis of Pombal, who served as the Secretary of the Crown's State under King José I of Portugal from 1750 to 1777.

answered, "I'm João Ramalho."[3] He stuck two fingers between his lips and whistled, and his wife and fifteen children appeared. They left to search for a new settlement where they could live without any people.

The next morning, everyone went to work very early. The princess went to the fields, Maanape went into the forest, and Jiguê went to the river. Macunaíma excused himself, climbed into a montaria, and made a quick trip to the mouth of the Rio Negro to retrieve his conscience, which he'd left on Marapatá Island.[4] Could an alligator find it? Nor could he. So, the hero took a conscience from some Hispanic American, put it in his head, and it was all the same.

A school of jaraquis swam under the montaria.[5] Macunaíma was distracted as he grabbed at the fish and didn't notice when he drifted into Óbidos.[6] The boat was

---

[3] João Ramalho was an early Brazilian colonist who arrived in São Vicente (which soon later was renamed São Paulo) around 1510. He became influential in indigenous society when he married the daughter of a chief, and he was able to form a trade network among the various tribes, including an indigenous slave market. His children are considered the first "mamelucos," or people of mixed Portuguese and Amerindian ancestry. For this reason, he is sometimes regarded as the "Father of the Bandeirantes." In 1562, he led a militia in the defense of the newly formed city of São Paulo against an attack by a coalition of indigenous tribes. He died in 1580 and is buried in the crypt of the Metropolitan Cathedral of São Paulo.

[4] A montaria is a small dug-out canoe.

[5] Jaraquis are a species of freshwater fish common in the lower Amazon.

[6] Óbidos is a town on the Amazon River about halfway between Manaus and the Atlantic Ocean.

already full of fresh fish by then, but the hero, realizing where he was, was obliged to throw everything back, because they say in Óbidos that "whoever eats jaraquis stays here," and he had to get back to the Uraricoera. It was still the middle of the day when he returned, so he lay in the shadow of an inga tree, picked the ticks from his body, and slept. By afternoon, everyone except Macunaíma had returned to the longhouse ruins. They all went outside to wait for him. Jiguê crouched down and put his ear to the ground to check for the hero's little steps, but he didn't hear them. Maanape climbed atop an inajá sapling to see if he could spot the sparkle of the hero's earrings, but he didn't see them. So, they wandered throughout the forest and meadow shouting, "Macunaíma! Brother!"

There was no sign of him anywhere until Jiguê arrived at the inga and shouted, "Brother!"

"What is it!?"

"I bet you were sleeping!"

"I wasn't sleeping at all! I was just trying to lure a tinamou. When you made all that noise, the tinamou ran away!"

They went back to the ruins. Things continued in this way for several days. The brothers grew very suspicious, but Macunaíma noticed and hid it well: "I keep hunting, but I can't find anything. Jiguê neither hunts nor fishes and spends the entire day sleeping."

Jiguê was frustrated because fish were becoming rare and game even more so. He went to the beach on the riverside to see if he could catch fish there, and came across the sorcerer Tzaló, who has only one leg. Tzaló possessed an enchanted bowl that was made from half of a pumpkin. He dipped the bowl in the river, filled it halfway with water, and poured it onto the beach. A pile of fish fell out, and Jiguê realized what the sorcerer had done. When Tzaló dropped the bowl and began killing the fish with a club, Jiguê stole it from the one-legged sorcerer.

When Jiguê was later making fish with the bowl, he lost count of how many he'd created. There were pirandiras, pacus, cascudos, bagres, jundiás, and tucunarés, all of these fish.[7] Jiguê, after hiding the pumpkin bowl at the root of a vine, returned to the ruins laden with fish. Everyone was amazed by this abundance and ate well. Macunaíma was suspicious.

The next day, pretending to sleep with his left eye closed, he waited for Jiguê to go fishing, then got up to follow him. He discovered everything. After Jiguê had left, Macunaíma put the cage with the leghorns on the floor, picked up the hidden bowl, and did the same thing that his brother had done. In the same way, he created a pile of fish. There were acarás, piracanjubas, aviús, gurijubas, cangatis, piramutabas, mandis, and surubims, all of these fish.[8] Macunaíma tossed the bowl aside in a hurry to kill them all, and it fell down an embankment and – plunk! – sank into the river. A pirandira named Padzá swam by. He thought that the bowl was a pumpkin and swallowed it, and it turned into Padzá's bladder. Macunaíma tucked the cage under his arm and went back to the longhouse ruins to report what had happened. Jiguê was outraged.[9]

---

[7] These are all species of fish native to the Amazon River.

[8] Aviús are small river shrimp. The rest are all fish found in freshwater rivers.

[9] In a story that Koch-Grünberg called "Eteto: Wie Kasana-Pódole der Königstier, seinen Zweiten Kopf Erhielt" ("Eteto: How Kasana Pódole, the King Vulture, got its Second Head"), a young man named Eteto encounters Zaló the river otter

"Princess sister-in-law," Jiguê cried to the princess, "It is I who was fishing, while your companion was laying under the ingá tree and bothering everyone else!"

"Liar!" yelled Macunaíma.

"So, what did you do today?" asked Jiguê.

"I hunted a deer."

"Where is it!?"

"Woah! I ate it. I was walking down a path, just wandering along, when I came upon the trail of a… gray brocket. No. It was a red brocket. I squatted down and crept along the trail. I was looking down at the ground, you know, and I hit my head on something soft. It was so funny! You know what it was!? The deer's ass, you guys!" Macunaíma laughed out loud. "The deer asked me, 'What are you doing there, brother!' 'Stalking you!' I responded. And then I killed the gray brocket and ate the guts and everything. I was bringing a piece for you, but I slipped while crossing a mountain stream and fell into the water. The meat drifted far downstream and a swarm of saúvas devoured it."

---

using a gourd to catch fish. Zaló fills the gourd with water, tosses it onto the riverbank, and fish spill onto the shore. As Zaló is clubbing and gathering the fish, Eteto takes the gourd, goes upstream, and catches a bunch of fish in the same way. Before he goes home, he hides the gourd in a tree trunk. His family is suspicious because he has never brought home fish before, but they eat it. The next day, Eteto's brother-in-law follows him and sees him using the gourd to catch fish. Eteto asks him to club the fish on the shore, then hides the gourd. But when they're done fishing, the brother-in-law says that he wants to stay and hunt by himself. Once alone, he takes the gourd and tries to catch fish. As he's clubbing his catch, the gourd rolls into the river, where it is eaten by a fish named Pazá and turns into the fish's bladder.

The lie was such a stretch that Maanape couldn't believe it. He was a sorcerer. He walked right up to his brother and asked, "You went hunting?"

"I mean… I did, yeah."

"What did you hunt?"

"A deer."

"Where is it!?"

Maanape waved his hands over his head, and the hero blinked from fear and confessed that everything was bogus.

The next day, Jiguê was looking for the bowl when he encountered the giant armadillo and sorcerer named Caicãe, who never had a mother.[10] Caicãe, seated at the door of his burrow, took out a violin made from the other half of the enchanted pumpkin and strummed it as he sang like this:

"Damn damn the porcupine!
Damn damn the agouti!
Damn damn the opossum!
Damn damn the peccary!
Damn damn the oncilla!
Eh!…"[11]

A throng of game animals appeared. Jiguê observed everything closely. Caicãe tossed the enchanted violin aside, picked up a club, and killed all of the game that he could. As Caicãe was doing so, Jiguê stole the violin from the sorcerer who never had a mother.

---

[10] Caicãe is a creation of Andrade.

[11] A peccary is a small mammal that closely resembles a pig. An oncilla is a kind of spotted cat that resembles a small jaguar.

After he'd scurried away from Caicãe, Jiguê played something that had never been heard before, and a multitude of animals gathered in front of him. After hiding the violin in the roots of another vine, Jiguê returned to the longhouse ruins laden with meat. Everyone was surprised and ate well. Macunaíma again grew suspicious.

The next day, he pretended to sleep with his left eye closed until Jiguê left, then got up to follow him. He discovered everything. When his brother returned to the longhouse ruins, Macunaíma picked up the violin, did as he'd observed, and an abundance of animals appeared before him: deer, agoutis, anteaters, capybaras, armadillos, spotted turtles, pacas, wood foxes, otters, mud turtles, peccaries, monkeys, tegus, tapirs, striped tapirs, jaguars, jaguarundis, pampas deer, ocelots, cougars, margays, and tinamous.[12] There was so much game! The hero was afraid of the enormous pack of beasts, and left in a scramble, hurling the violin deep into the woods. The cage tucked under his arm was getting whacked by branches, and the rooster's and hen's cackles were deafening. The hero thought that it was the beasts and bolted even faster.

The violin fell into the jaws of a peccary that had a bellybutton on its back and broke into ten-times-ten pieces, which the beasts thought were bits of pumpkin and swallowed. The pieces turned inside the animals' bellies.

The hero burst through the entrance of the ruined longhouse, desperately trying to catch his breath. Unable to do so, he nevertheless recounted everything that had happened. Jiguê felt spiteful and said, "From now on, I'm

---

[12] Tegus are a kind of lizard, jaguarundis are a kind of small wild cat, and margays are a kind of spotted big cat.

not hunting or fishing anymore!"

Then, Jiguê started preparing for bed. Everyone was growing hungry. They asked him to reconsider, but Jiguê hopped in his hammock and closed his eyes. The hero swore revenge. He made a fake hook with the fang of an anaconda, and spoke to the charm: "False hook, if brother Jiguê comes to try and use you, pierce his hand."

Jiguê couldn't sleep because he was so hungry. Seeing the hook, he asked his brother, "Brother, is this hook any good?"

"It's magnificent!" Macunaíma said as he was cleaning the leghorns' cage.

Jiguê decided to go fishing because he was famished. He said, "Let's see if this hook is any good."

As he took the charm and examined it in the palm of his hand, the anaconda tooth pierced his skin and released all of its venom. Jiguê ran through the nearby woods, chewing and swallowing cassava, but this didn't help at all. So, he searched for the head of an anhuma, which is an antidote against snakebite.[13] He found one and rubbed it on his hand, but it didn't help at all. The venom turned into a leprous wound and started consuming Jiguê. First, it devoured an arm, then half of his torso, then his legs, then the other half of his torso, then the other arm, his neck, and his head. Only Jiguê's shadow remained.

The princess hated Macunaíma, which is why she recently had been fooling around with Jiguê. Macunaíma was quite aware of that, but thought, "I planted cassava and it has grown. Nobody is deprived of anything when the thief lives in the same house. Be patient!" He shrugged. The furious princess said to the shadow, "When

---

[13] An anhuma is a species of large wetland bird related to a goose.

Macunaíma

the hero goes out to satisfy his hunger, turn into a cashew tree, a banana tree, and grilled venison." The shadow was poisonous because of his leprosy, and the princess wanted to kill Macunaíma.

The next day, the hero woke up so hungry that he got up immediately and went for a walk to find something to eat. He came across a cashew tree full of fruit. He wanted to eat some cashews, but he saw that it was the leprous shadow and kept walking. A league and a half ahead, he came across a smoking rack of grilled venison. He was purple with hunger, but he noticed that the bar-be-que was the leprous shadow and walked past. A league and a half further, he came across a banana tree laden with ripe bunches. By then, the hero was cross-eyed with hunger, and it appeared to him that the leprous shadow was standing next to the banana tree.

"Alright!" he shouted. "Now I can eat!"

He devoured all of the bananas, which were the leprous shadow of his brother, Jiguê. When Macunaíma's vision returned and he saw what he'd done, he realized that he was going to die. He decided to pass the disease to other people so he wouldn't die alone. He picked up a saúva and rubbed it on a lesion on his nose vigorously. The saúva used to be a person like us and it became leprous, too. Next, the hero grabbed a jaguataci ant and did the same thing.[14] The jaguataci ant also caught leprosy. After that, it was time to turn a seed-eating ant, a guiquém ant, a tracuá ant, and a black mumbuca ant all into lepers, as well.[15] Soon, there were no more ants around where the

---

[14] The jaguataci ant does not appear outside of *Macunaíma* and may be a creation of Andrade.

[15] Like the jaguataci, the guiquém ant does not appear in other texts. A tracuá is a kind of carpenter ant, and a mumbuca is

hero sat. He was too weak to even lift his arm, as he was already approaching death. He waited for his health to recover a bit, mustered up some strength, then picked up the sand fly biting his knee and gave it leprosy, too. This is why whenever this bug bites someone now, it enters the skin, crosses the body, and comes out the other side, and the little entrance hole turns into an ugly sore called a Bauru wound.[16]

Macunaíma spread the leprosy to seven other people and was cured as a result. He returned to the longhouse ruins. Jiguê's shadow conceded that the hero was very intelligent and wanted desperately to return to his family. It was already nighttime, and blending himself with the darkness, the shadow was no longer able to follow the path home. He sat on a rock and shouted, "A little fire, princess sister-in-law!"

The princess, limping severely because she was sick with zamparina, came with a torch and lit the way.[17] The shadow swallowed the torch and his sister-in-law. He yelled again, "A little fire, brother Maanape!"

Maanape soon arrived with another torch to light the

---

actually a kind of bee with dark coloring.

[16] A Bauru wound is an ulcer formed by an infection of leishmaniasis, which is caused by a parasite that is transmitted by sandflies. The disease is endemic to the region around Bauru, a small city near São Paulo.

[17] Zamparina was the name given to a pandemic that afflicted Rio de Janeiro in 1780, which caused a high fever and left survivors paralyzed. The disease was named after a Venetian singer also named Zamparina, who had arrived from Lisbon to perform in Rio de Janeiro around the time that the pandemic had broken out, and who was very popular among the upper classes.

way. He dragged himself along sluggishly, however, because a barbeiro had drained his blood and he had a hookworm infection. The shadow swallowed the torch and brother Maanape. He shouted, "A little fire, brother Macunaíma!"

He wanted to swallow the hero, too. But Macunaíma, having seen what had happened to his brother and his companion, leaned against the door inside the ruined longhouse and kept very quiet. The shadow asked for a little fire, but not receiving an answer, mourned until dawn. Then, Capei appeared, illuminating the land, and the leper was able to find the longhouse. He sat in a canjerana by the doorway and waited for an opportunity to take revenge on his brother.[18]

In the morning, Macunaíma was curled up on the floor by the door. He woke up and listened. He didn't hear anything and concluded, "Damn! He's gone!"

He walked out the door and, as he passed under the threshold, the shadow climbed onto his shoulders. The hero didn't feel any weight. He was starving but the shadow wouldn't let him eat, swallowing everything that Macunaíma picked up: tamarind, mango, yam, sugar apple, cashews, guava, sapota, uxi nuts, guama beans, bacuri, cupuaçu, palm peaches, hog plums, soursop, and grumixama, all of these foods of the forest.[19]

---

[18] Canjeranas are a family of tall, hardwood trees.

[19] Uxi nuts come from the uxi tree and are known for their medicinal properties. Guama beans come from inga trees and are also known as "ice-cream beans" on account of their sweet flavor and smooth texture. A bacuri is the fruit of the bacuri tree, and is a popular ingredient in desserts, liqueurs, and other foods. A cupuaçu is a fruit from a tree of the same name, and is filled with sweet, white pulp. A grumixama is a small fruit

Macunaíma

So, Macunaíma went fishing because he now had no one else to fish for him. But every time a fish tugged the hook and he tossed it into his basket, the shadow jumped from his shoulders, swallowed the fish, then returned to his perch. The hero thought, "I need to make an adjustment!" The next time a fish bit, Macunaíma gave a heroic effort, and tugged on the rod so hard that the fish ended up all the way in Guyana. The shadow ran after the fish, and Macunaíma scrambled to hide in some woods in the opposite direction.

When the shadow returned to find that his brother was no longer there, he hurried to look for him. After running for a little while, he crossed the land of the Tatus-Brancos Indians.[20] He was terrified because he had to pass between the ghosts of Jorge Velho and Zumbi and couldn't ask for permission because they were having an argument.[21] The exhausted hero turned around and saw

---

similar to a cherry.

[20] The Tatus-Brancos Indians ("White Armadillo Indians") are a legendary tribe of people who live underground like armadillos during the day and only come out at night. They have bright white skin as a result of their sunless existence and are feared to cannibalize anyone who has the misfortune of wandering into their territory.

[21] Domingo Jorge Velho was a notorious hunter of slaves and raider of native villages at the end of the 17th century. Zumbi was the famous leader of Quilombo dos Palmares, a community of runaway slaves and their descendants. After he refused to submit the community to the authority of the Portuguese government, the community was raided by troops led by Jorge Velho. Zumbi was gravely wounded in the attack and was later executed. His head was displayed on a pole in a public square in Recife to dispel rumors that he was immortal.

that Jiguê's shadow was drawing near. He was in Paraíba and, unwilling to speed ahead, he stopped. The hero's malaria kept him from taking another step. Nearby were some workers destroying anthills to build a pond. Macunaíma asked them for water. They didn't have even a drop, but they gave him some umbuzeiro root.[22] The hero gave the leghorns a drink, thanked the workers, and shouted, "The devil takes those who work!"

The workers unleashed a pack of dogs on the hero. This was actually what he wanted, because he was afraid of the shadow and the dogs drove him to run faster. A cattle road stretched in front of him. Macunaíma saw that it was covered in shade and took the road without thinking twice. Further ahead, he saw a sleeping Malabar ox named Espácio who came from Piauí.[23] The hero slapped him so furiously that the ox galloped away, blind with fear, toward a spring. Macunaíma pushed through a narrow forest trail and hid under a mucumuco.[24] Jiguê's shadow heard the rumble of the galloping steer, thought that it was Macunaíma, and went after it. He caught up to the ox and hopped on his back. Then, he sang with satisfaction:

"My beautiful ox,

---

[22] Umbuzeiro root has a sweet taste and is used in indigenous medicines.

[23] The "Malabar ox" appears in the Brazilian folk song "O Bumba Meu Boi" ("The Beat of My Ox"). The Malabar Coast is the southwest coast of India, where the Portuguese had colonies in the 16th and 17th centuries, and the term "Malabar" is used to describe things from that region.

[24] A mucumuco is a kind of shrub.

Ox of such glee,
Say goodbye,
To the whole family!

Oh, bumba,
Frolic meu boi!
Eh, bumba,
Frolic meu boi!"[25]

But the ox couldn't eat because the shadow swallowed everything in front of him. So, the bull became even more downcast, skinny, and sluggish. When the ox passed through a wilderness called Água Doce, near Guarapes, he stared in awe at a beautiful view of a shady orange grove in the middle of some sand dunes.[26] A chicken was pecking at the ground below the trees, which is a harbinger of death. The doomed shadow sang:

"My pretty ox,
Ox of doom,
Say goodbye,
Until next afternoon!

Oh, bumba,
Frolic meu boi!
Eh, bumba,
Frolic meu boi!"

The next day, the bull was dead and had already started

---

[25] This is a version of "O Bumba Meu Boi" where Andrade has altered the lyrics but retained the meter.

[26] Guarapes is a town in the south of Brazil near São Paulo.

to turn green. The mournful shadow consoled itself by singing like this:

"My ox has died,
How sad do I seem?
Another shall be supplied,
Tomorrow,
In the Bom Jardim."

The Bom Jardim was a seaside ranch in Rio Grande do Sul.[27] A giantess, who'd liked to fool around with the bull, arrived and saw him dead. She started bawling and said that she wanted to take the corpse with her.

The shadow grew angry and sang:

"Giantess, to your home return,
Because it is dangerous,
When your lover does spurn,
Your offers so generous!"

The giantess thanked him and danced away. As soon as she'd left, an individual named Manuel da Lapa walked past, carrying cashew leaves and cotton bolls.[28] The shadow greeted his acquaintance:

---

[27] Bom Jardim ("Good Garden") was a ranching community outside the southern city of Porto Alegre that was known in the 19th century for its large population of German immigrants.

[28] Manuel da Lapa is a reference to a popular Brazilian toada (a short rhyming song similar to a limerick) about a man named Manué who lives in Lapa. Andrade recites an abbreviated version here.

"Mr. Manuel who comes from Açu,[29]
Mr. Manuel who comes from Açu,
Comes bearing a small sack of cashews!

Mr. Manuel who comes from the grassland,
Mr. Manuel who comes from the grassland,
Comes with a small bale of cotton in hand!"

Manuel da Lapa was quite pleased with the greeting and, to show his thanks, danced a tap dance and covered the dead ox with the cashew leaves and cotton bolls.

The old shaman was already coaxing the night from its hole, and the shadow was thoroughly confounded because he couldn't see the ox under the cotton and leaves. He danced around in search of him. A firefly admired the shadow and sang, asking:

"Beautiful shepherd,
What brings you this way?"

The shadow responded, singing:

"I came to fetch my ox,
Little girl,
That I lost today."

The dancing firefly flew down from her branch and showed the ox to the shadow. He climbed onto the corpse's green stomach and started to cry.

By the next morning, the ox was rotten, and a flock of

---

[29] Açu is a town in the state of Rio Grande near the Atlantic coast. The town is referenced in the original toada and repeated by Andrade here.

vultures had gathered: black vultures, yellow-headed vultures, forest vultures, and red-headed vultures that only eat eyes and tongues, all of these bald creatures. And they were dancing with glee. The biggest one led the dance, singing:

"The vulture step is ugly, ugly, ugly!
The vulture step is clean, clean, clean!"

It was a king vulture, the Father of Vultures. When he was done singing, he sent a young little vulture to go inside the ox to see if it was rotten enough yet. The little vulture entered through one hole and exited out the other, and confirmed that it was. Then, everyone partied together, dancing and singing:

"Ox so beautiful,
Ox Malachi,[30]
A crow flies above,
The ox has died,

Oh, bumba,
Frolic meu boi!
Eh, bumba,
Frolic meu boi!"

And this is how they invented the renowned festival

---

[30] Malachi is a Biblical name chosen to fit the rhyme scheme for this translation. Andrade and the original toada on which he based this poem both used "Zebedee," who was the father of the apostles James and John. The name Zebedee ("Zebedeu" in Portuguese) rhymes with the word for "died" ("morreu").

of Bumba Meu Boi, also known as Boi Bumba.[31]

The shadow was angry that they were eating his ox and leapt onto the king vulture's shoulders. The Father of Vultures was feeling smug and shouted, "I found a decoration for my head, you guys!" Then, it flew high into the air. Ever since that day, the king vulture, who is the Father of Vultures, has had two heads.[32] The leprous shadow is the head on top.

---

[31] Bumba Meu Boi is a festival celebrated throughout Brazil but is embraced particularly by people in the state of Maranhão. The earliest known reference to the festival was in a journal of a resident of Maranhão written in 1829, but it is believed to already have been decades-old by then. During the festival, a folkloric tale is told through song and dance, using a giant puppet of an ox. In the story, a slave and rancher named Father Francisco steals and kills his owner's prized ox and removes its tongue in obedience to the desires of his wife Mother Caterina. The master orders his enslaved natives and cowhands to find the culprit, and they capture Father Francisco. Forced to rectify the situation, he leads a dance to bring the ox back to life. Doctors and shamans are called to assist and, at the culmination of the festival, everyone dancing together resurrects the ox. The festival is traditionally enjoyed by working-class Brazilians as an annual celebration of their triumphs over the ridiculous demands of their employers.

[32] In "Eteto: How Kasana Pódole, the King Vulture, got its Second Head," Eteto makes a fishhook from iron and asks it to pierce his brother-in-law's hand. When the brother-in-law grabs the hook, it penetrates his skin and winds throughout his body until he's eviscerated and dies. The dead brother-in-law's mother tells his shadow to turn into a banana tree or grilled venison to tempt Eteto into eating him, so Eteto will die, too. Eventually, Eteto eats the shadow in the form of bananas, and keeps eating bananas until he turns into Wewe-Pódole, Father of Gluttons. When night falls, Wewe-Pódole demands that his

Originally, the king vulture had only one head.

---

family members bring fire for him to see, then swallows them all. The next morning, Wewe-Pódole leaps onto the shoulders of a man and nearly starves him by swallowing anything that he tries to eat. After the man runs away, Wewe does the same thing to a tapir until it dies of hunger. When a king vulture comes to eat the tapir's corpse, Wewe-Pódole hops onto the bird's shoulders. The vulture says, "Ah, a companion for my head," then flies to the sky with Wewe-Pódole, giving the king vulture two heads.

XVII

URSA MAJOR

Macunaíma dragged himself to the longhouse ruins and saw that no one was there. He was upset because he couldn't understand the silence. He had died without anyone crying, in complete abandonment. His brothers had gone away, having transformed into the second head of the king vulture, and there weren't any women nearby. A silence began to spread along the riverside of the Uraricoera. How tedious! And above all, ai!.. what a drag!

Macunaíma had to abandon the longhouse when the last wall, which had been secured only by fronds of catolé, began to collapse.[1] But malaria had made him so weak that he couldn't even build a papiri.[2] He brought a hammock to the top of a hill where there was a rock with money buried underneath. He tied it to two leafy cashew trees

---

[1] A catolé is a kind of palm tree.

[2] A papiri is a temporary shelter made from leaves and branches.

and laid on it for many days, sleeping, being bored, and eating cashews. How lonely! Even his motley personal entourage of birds had dispersed.

Macunaíma had been too wrought with grief to notice when an orange-winged parrot had passed overhead in a flurry. The other parrots had asked their kinsman where he was going, and he'd answered, "The corn has ripened in the land of the English, so that's where I'm going!"

All of the parrots had joined him on his journey to eat corn in the land of the English. But first, they'd turned into parakeets, so the parakeets would take the blame for ruining the harvest, rather than the parrots. Only a very talkative, white-eyed parrot had stayed behind.

Macunaíma consoled himself, thinking, "When evil wins, the devil takes... his time." He spent his days in boredom and distracted himself by asking the bird to repeat in the tribal language everything that had happened to the hero since infancy. Ahhh... Macunaíma yawned, drooling cashew juice, and lay limply in the hammock with his hands behind his head, the pair of leghorns perched on his feet, and the parrot on his belly.[3] Night fell. Smelling of cashew fruit, the hero fell fast asleep. When dawn came, the parrot took its beak from under its wing and ate breakfast, devouring the spiders that had spun webs in the night between the branches and the hero's body. Then, it shouted, "Macunaíma!"

The sleeper didn't stir.

"Macunaíma! Oh, Macunaíma!"

"Let me sleep, parrot..."

---

[3] The cashew fruit contains two parts: the nut that readers are familiar with, and the juicy pseudofruit to which it is attached. Although the sweet juice is bottled and sold commercially, it is not widely exported outside Brazil.

"Wake up, hero! It's daytime!"

"Ai... What a drag!.."

"Poor in health and rich in saúvas, these are the evils of Brazil!"

Macunaíma laughed and scratched his head which was full of pixilinga from bird lice.[4] Then, the parrot repeated the stories that it had told the night before, and Macunaíma felt proud of all of his past glories. It inspired enthusiasm, and he found himself telling the parrot another tall tale. And this is how it went every day.

Whenever Papaceia, who is the star Vesper, appeared to tell everyone to go to sleep, the parrot would grow outraged because its stories would be interrupted.[5] One night, he even insulted Papaceia. Macunaíma responded like this:

"Don't insult him, parrot! Taína-Cã is good. Taína-Cã is the star Papaceia and takes pity on the Earth and sends Emoron-Pódole to give the peace of sleep to all of these creatures that are able to be at peace because they don't have thoughts like us.[6] Taína-Cã is human, too. He was shining up there in the vast field of the sky when the eldest daughter of Chief Zozoiaça of the Karajá tribe, an older

---

[4] Pixilinga is an infestation of mites caused by contact with birds or mammals, although it is most commonly transmitted to humans through chickens.

[5] Papaceia is a Tupi name for Vesper, which is a name given to the planet Venus during sunset.

[6] According to a legend of the Karajá people, "Tahina-Can" is a star identified by a woman named "Imaherô" as a suitable husband. The Karajá are an indigenous people who live inland along the Rio Araguaia near Bananal Island.

woman named Imaerô who'd never married, said, 'Father, Taína-Cã shines so beautifully that I want to become his wife.'[7]

"Zozoiaça laughed because it wasn't possible to grant Taína-Cã a marriage to his eldest daughter. Suddenly, a silver piroga glided down the river in the night.[8] The oarsman jumped out, slapped the gunnel, and said to Imaerô, 'I'm Taína-Cã. I heard your request and came in my silver canoe. Will you marry me, please?'

"'Yes,' she said, overjoyed. She gave her hammock to her fiancé, and went to sleep with her younger sister, Denaquê.[9]

"When Taína-Cã hopped out of his hammock the next morning, everyone was shocked. He was a very wrinkled old man, trembling like the light of the Papaceia star. Imaerô said, 'Go away, old geezer! Just see if I'm going to marry an old man! I won't settle for anything less than a brave and muscular young man from the Karajá nation!'

"Taína-Cã was crestfallen and dwelled on the injustice of men. But Chief Zozoiaça's youngest daughter felt sorry for the old geezer, and said, 'I'll marry you.'

"Taína-Cã sparkled with joy. The event was arranged. Denaquê, preparing the bridal gown, sang night and day, 'Tomorrow at this hour, furrum-fum-fum…'

"Zozoiaça replied, 'Me too, with your mother, furrum-fum-fum.'

"After fondling each other until their fingers went numb – as all fiancés eagerly anticipate, parrot – the

---

[7] Chief Zozoiaça is a creation of Andrade.

[8] A piroga is a type of long, thin dugout canoe.

[9] The sister's name is "Denakê" in the original Karajá legend, which is repeated here nearly verbatim by Andrade.

hammock woven by Denaquê danced to the rhythm of love, furrum-fum-fum.

"Daylight had barely broken over the horizon when Taína-Cã jumped from their hammock and said to his companion, 'I'm going to clear some brush to make a field. Stay in the hut and don't wander over there to spy on me.'

"'Okay,' she said. And she remained in the hammock, thinking happily about the strange little old man who'd given her the most delicious night of lovemaking that she could ever imagine.

"Taína-Cã cleared the brush, set fire to all of the anthills, and prepared the ground. At that time, the Karajá nation still didn't know which plants were edible, and its people ate only fish and game.

"The next morning, Taína-Cã told his companion that he was going to fetch seeds for planting and repeated his order. Denaquê continued to lay in the hammock for a bit, thinking about the vigorous delights of their nights of lovemaking that the good old geezer had given to her. She formed a plan.

"Taína-Cã arrived in the sky and went to Berô-Can.[10] There he said a prayer, straddled the creek, and watched the water flow between his legs. A little while later, seeds of corn, achiote, tobacco, and cassava, all of these good plants, came floating on the water.[11] Taína-Cã picked up everything that passed under him, then came down from the sky and went to the field to plant the seeds. He was working in the Sun when Denaquê appeared. She longed

---

[10] Berô-Can is the Karajá name for the Rio Araguaia.

[11] An achiote is a plant known for its orange-red seeds which are used as a cooking spice and to make body paint.

to see her partner, who'd given her such vigorous pleasure during their nights of lovemaking. Denaquê shouted for joy. Taína-Cã wasn't an old geezer! Taína-Cã was a brave and muscular young man from the Karajá nation. They made a bed of tobacco and cassava leaves and fooled around, trembling under the Sun.

"As they returned to the hut, they were laughing giddily with one another. Imaerô was furious. She shouted, 'Taína-Cã is mine! I'm the reason he came down from the sky!'

"'Tough luck!' Taína-Cã replied. 'When I wanted you, you didn't want me. So now you can go play with yourself!' Then, he climbed into the hammock with Denaquê.

"Imaerô was dejected and sighed, 'Leave the alligator alone, because the pond will dry up eventually!' Then, she fled into the forest, screaming as she ran. She turned into an araponga which, yellow with envy of the nighttime silence enjoyed in the forest during the day, screams to break it.[12] Since then, on account of Taína-Cã's kindness, the Karajá have been eating cassava and corn, and smoking tobacco to cheer themselves up.

"Whenever the Karajá needed something, Taína-Cã would go up to the sky to get it and then bring it back down. After all, it's not like Denaquê, even with her ambition, would ever date the little stars in the sky while he was away! Well, in fact she did. And Taína-Cã, who is Papaceia, saw everything. He was so saddened by it that he wept and took whatever he was carrying back up to the vast field of the sky. He stayed up there and never brought

---

[12] Araponga is a name given to a group of several species of bird known for their extremely loud calls, which sound like a hammer striking an anvil.

anything down to the Karajá people again. If Papaceia had continued to bring things from the other side of the sky, heaven would be here on earth, because we would have everything. But for now, it remains our wish. And that's the end of the story."

The parrot was asleep.

One day in January, Macunaíma woke up late to the ominous call of a tincuã.[13] Daylight had already broken, and the morning fog had retreated to its burrow. The hero shivered and felt a charm that had been placed on his neck: a little bone from a dead pagan child. He looked for the parrot, but it had disappeared. There were only the rooster and the hen, fighting over the last spider. The terrible heat was so still that he could hear the little glass bells of grasshoppers. Vei, the Sun, slid across Macunaíma's body, having taken the form of a woman's hand, and tickled him. She felt wicked with spite because the hero hadn't made a woman out of one of her daughters of light. The hand caressed his body so tenderly that lust stiffened his muscles for the first time since his long journey! Macunaíma remembered that he hadn't fooled around with anyone in a long time and recalled something about cold water being good for erasing such desires. The hero slipped from his hammock, removed the strands of spiderweb that covered his body, hiked down to the Valley of Tears, and bathed in a nearby dell that repiquetes from the rainy season had turned into a pond.[14]

---

[13] A tincuã is a species of bird named onomatopoetically after its call.

[14] A repiquete is a rise in the level of a river caused by distant

Macunaíma placed the leghorns gently on the shore and approached the water's edge. The pond was covered entirely in gold and silver, and he dipped his face beneath the surface to see what was at the bottom. Macunaíma saw there a beautiful fair-skinned young woman, and he ached even more deeply with desire. It was an Iara.

She approached coyly, gyrating as she did so, and winked at the hero as though she were saying, "Go away, you silly boy!" Then, she left as she came, gyrating coyly. The hero felt so aroused that he arched his back and his mouth watered. "Damn!.."

Macunaíma wanted her. He put his thumb in the water and, in a flash, the pond covered his skin in webs of gold and silver. When he started to feel cold, he pulled it out.

He repeated this several times. It was nearing the height of the day, and Vei was furious. She had hoped that Macunaíma would fall into the treacherous arms of the young woman in the pond, but the hero was afraid of the cold. Vei knew that the woman wasn't actually a woman, but was an Iara. The Iara approached again while gyrating seductively. What a beauty she was! A brunette with a rosy-cheeked daytime face, which was wrapped in short hair feathered like the wings of a chupim, like day surrounded by night. She wore a serious expression and had a little nose so delicate that it wasn't even fit for breathing. And because she only showed her frontside and danced without turning around, Macunaíma couldn't see the hole in the back of her neck from where the treacherous woman breathed. The hero couldn't decide whether to go to her or not. The sun was enraged. She picked up a whip of fire and lashed the hero's back. The Iara opened her arms to show off her goods and shut her

---

rains upriver or over tributaries.

Macunaíma

eyes sleepily. Macunaíma felt his spine catch fire. He shuddered, braced himself, and threw himself on top of her. Splash! Vei cried out in victory and her tears rained onto the pond in a shower of gold. It was the height of the day.

When Macunaíma emerged from the water, he realized that they'd been tussling at the bottom for a long time. He laid on his stomach for a while, his life depending on his exhausted breaths. He was bleeding from bites all over his body, and was missing his right leg, toes, coconuts, ears, and nose, all of his treasures. Gradually, he gathered the strength to get up. As he tallied his losses, his hatred for Vei grew. The hen was clucking and laid an egg on the beach. Macunaíma picked it up and threw it at the happy face of the Sun. The egg splattered right on her cheeks which were stained yellow forever. She dimmed to afternoon.

Macunaíma sat on a rock that used to be a tortoise in ancient times, and counted the treasures that he'd lost in the pond: a leg, fingers and toes, his coconuts, ears, the earrings made from the Patek machine and the Smith & Wesson machine, and his nose, all of these treasures. The hero jumped up with a shout that shortened the length of the day. Piranhas had eaten his lips and the muiraquitã, too! He went crazy.

He gathered a mountain of timbó, assacú, tingui, and canambí, all of these plants, and poisoned the pond forever.[15] All of the fish died and floated to the top with their bellies up: blue bellies, yellow bellies, and pink bellies. All of these bellies painted the surface of the pond. Afterward, it was dusk.

Macunaíma gutted all of these fish, as well as some

---

[15] These are all species of plants known to be toxic to fish.

piranhas and botos, feeling for the muiraquitã in their bellies. The ground was covered in their bloody entrails, and everything was stained with blood. It was evening by then.

Macunaíma combed the area. He found his two arms, fingers and toes, ears, nuquiiri, and nose, all of these treasures, and secured them all in their places with thatch and fish paste.[16] He couldn't find his leg or the muiraquitã, however. They had been swallowed by the Ururau monster which couldn't be killed with just timbó or a stick.[17] The blood covering the beach and pond curdled and turned black. At last, it was nighttime.

Macunaíma continued his search. He wailed in grief so loudly that the nearby beasts shrank from the noise. Nothing. The hero crossed a field, hopping only on one leg and shouting, "My memory! Memory of my marvada! I don't see her or you or anything!"

As he hopped, tears dripped from his little blue eyes onto the little white flowers of the field and dyed them blue, turning them into forget-me-nots. Once the hero ran out of energy, he stopped. He crossed his arms with such heroic despair that space expanded to contain his enormous silent grief. A puny little mosquito made the hero's disgrace even more hellish, buzzing shrilly, "I come

---

[16] "Nuquiiri" is a slang term for testicles.

[17] There is a folktale from the 18th century about a man who turned into a giant ururau, which is an indigenous name for a kind of cayman, and has lived in the Rio Paraíba do Sul ever since, where he flips canoes and eats the occupants. He is said to have overturned a canoe that was delivering a church bell, and now lives inside the bell at the bottom of the river.

from Minas. I come from Minas."[18]

Macunaíma no longer found grace in this land. As Capei, who was still quite young, glowed up there in the diamond field of the sky, the hero brooded, still undecided about whether to live up there or on the island of Marajó. For a moment, he even thought about living in the city of Pedra, with its energy of Delmiro Gouveia, but he didn't have the will to go through with it.[19] It would be impossible to live there as he had lived earlier. This is why he no longer found joy on Earth. Everything that had comprised his existence, even all of the adventures, fooling around, fantasies, suffering, and heroism, in the end had resulted only in his still being alive. To stop in the city of Delmiro or on the island of Marajó, which are of this Earth, wouldn't be any more meaningful. And he didn't have the stomach to join an organization.

---

[18] Minas refers to the state of Minas Gerais.

[19] Delmiro Gouveia was a Brazilian industrial tycoon whose holdings included Brazil's second hydroelectric power plant and its first shopping center. In 1900, after his shopping center was burned down by the Pernambuco state police, Gouveia kidnapped the governor's sixteen-year-old daughter and she became his second wife. In 1913, fearing that they were in danger in the state capital, Recife, he moved with her to the small interior town of Pedra, where he bought a farm and built a fur and leather business. In 1914, he built a sewing-thread factory that soon dominated the Brazilian market and attracted the attention of the British firm J. & P. Coats, which had previously held a monopoly on sewing thread in Latin America. On October 10, 1917, he was murdered on the porch of his house in the middle of the night. The killer was never identified. In 1943, Pedra was renamed "Delmiro Gouveia" in his honor.

"What's going on!?" he asked himself. After thinking some more, he concluded, "When the vulture is on top of the caipora, and the bottom one is shitting on the top one, the world has lost its way.[20] I'm going to the sky."

Macunaíma ascended to the sky to live with his marvada and became the beautiful but useless glow of a constellation. It didn't matter that his glow was useless, because it was the same as that of all of the relatives of all of the fathers of those living in their land: mothers, fathers, brothers, sisters, sisters-in-law, and daughters, all of these kinsmen who now live as the useless glow of the stars.

He planted the seed of a matamatá vine, known as the son of the moon, and while the vine was growing, he grabbed a pointed shell and wrote on the rock that had been a tortoise long ago:

I DIDN'T COME INTO THE WORLD TO BE A STONE

As the plant reached full growth, it grabbed onto one of Capei's points. The wounded hero tucked the cage with the leghorns under his arm and climbed up to the sky, singing sadly:

Let's say goodbye,
To the ruins,
Just like the little bird,
Over the ruins,

---

[20] The caipora is a character from Tupi mythology who is usually depicted as a small native boy who smokes a pipe. He is known as a protector of the forests and animals, and for bringing misfortune or death on those who cross him.

Who beat its wings to fly,
From the ruins,
And left a feather in its nest,
In the ruins...

When he arrived, he knocked on the door of Capei's hut. The Moon descended to the front yard and asked, "What do you want, Saci?"[21]

"Can you please bless me with some bread, godmother?"

Capei noticed that it wasn't Saci, but Macunaíma the hero, and she didn't want to give him a place to stay because she remembered how much he used to stink. Macunaíma was furious and he slapped the Moon's face several times, which is why she still has all of those dark spots to this day.[22]

Macunaíma then went to knock on the door of

---

[21] Saci is a character from Brazilian folklore that is depicted as a young black man who wears a red cap and is missing a leg. Traditionally, the Saci was a malicious and monstrous son of a demon. In 1921, however, Brazilian author José Bento Monteiro Lobato published a popular story called "The Saci," in which he depicted the figure as a kind defender of nature, who sometimes plays fun tricks, and a friend to children. Because many Brazilians were introduced to the Saci by Lobato's story, the oral tradition of the Saci thereafter became confused, with the Saci depicted as having qualities that are a combination of both versions.

[22] According to Pemón legend, Kapei the moon and Vei the sun were once close friends. When Kapei fell in love with one of Vei's daughters, however, Vei objected and ordered the daughter to smear her menstrual blood on Kapei's face. Kapei has had a dirty face ever since, and always avoids Vei.

Caiuanogue, the morning star. Caiuanogue appeared in the little window to see who it was and, confused by the blackness of the night and the hero's hobble, asked, "What do you want, Saci?"

He soon noticed that it was Macunaíma, however, and didn't even wait for an answer, remembering that the hero smelled terrible. "Go take a shower!" he yelled, as he slammed the little window.

Macunaíma was enraged and shouted, "Come outside, jackass!"

Caiuanogue was terrified and trembled as he peaked through the keyhole. This is why the beautiful little star appears so tiny and flickers so much.

So, Macunaíma went to knock on the door of Pauí-Pódole, the Father of Curassows. Pauí-Pódole liked Macunaíma because he had defended him against the speaker from the great mixed-race crowd at the Cruzeiro festival.

Pauí-Pódole opened it and said, "Ah, hero, an afternoon chat! It would be a great honor for me to host a descendant of a tortoise, the oldest race of all, at my bar. In the beginning, the only living creature was the Great Tortoise. It was he who in the silence of the night took from his belly a man and woman. These were the first living people and the first members of your tribe. The others came afterward. You're too late, hero! We already have twelve at the table and you would make thirteen. It makes me want to cry, but I can't!"

"What a shame, Saint Germaine!" the hero cried.[23] Pauí-Pódole felt sorry for Macunaíma, so he cast a spell.

---

[23] "Saint Germaine" was chosen for its near rhyme with "shame." In the Portuguese, "Santa Helena" is used because it rhymes with "pena."

He grabbed three little sticks and threw them into the air, making a cross, then turned Macunaíma, with all of his stuff – the rooster, hen, cage, revolver, and watch – into a new constellation: Ursa Major.

They say that a professor (German, naturally) has been going around saying that, because Ursa Major has only one leg, it is Saci.[24] It's not! Saci still appears in the world, spreading fire and holding onto the mane of a wild horse. Ursa Major is Macunaíma. It really is the wounded hero who, after so much suffering in the land that's poor in health and rich in saúvas, grew fed up with everything and left to brood in solitude in the vast field of the sky.

---

[24] This reference to a German professor is Andrade's only trace of attribution to Koch-Grünberg for his enormous contribution to *Macunaíma*.

Macunaíma

EPILOGUE

The story has ended and its glory has faded away.

There was no longer anyone there. A spell had been cast over the Tapanhuma tribe and her children had died one by one. There was nobody there. The fields, holes, bluffs, footpaths, and ravines, as well as the mysterious forests, everything had become a secluded desert. An immense silence slept on the banks of the Uraricoera.

No known person on earth could speak about the absence of the tribe or recount its folklore. So, who could know about the hero? Now, the brothers who'd turned into the leprous shadow were the second head of the Father of Vultures, and Macunaíma was the constellation Ursa Major. So, nobody could ever learn their beautiful story, and the tribe's language went extinct. An immense silence slept on the banks of the Uraricoera.

One day, a man journeyed there. It was early in the morning, and Vei had sent her daughters to guide the passage of the stars. The vast, dreadful desert had killed the fish and the little birds, and nature itself had collapsed and fallen into abandon there. The silence was so intense that it gave any man in the area an erection. Suddenly, a voice fell from some branches onto the man's aching chest: "Currr-pac, papac! Currr-pac, papac!"

The man froze with fear, like a child. A hummingbird swooped down and bounced on the man's lip. "Bilo, bilo, bilo, lá... tetéia!" it sang, before flying back up into the trees. The man looked up, following the flight of the hummingbird.

"Move the branch, you ox!" the hummingbird jeered. Then, with a little snicker it slipped away.

The man saw in the branches a green, golden-beaked parrot spying on him. "Get lost, parrot," he said.

The parrot flew down and landed on the man's head, and the two kept each other company. The bird started talking in a gentle voice – unlike anything the man had heard before! – that was melodic and smooth like cachiri with wild honey, but which also evoked the danger of strange fruits from the forest.

The tribe had ceased to exist, the brothers had turned into shadows, the longhouse had collapsed, having been undermined by saúvas, and Macunaíma had ascended to the sky. But this aruaí from the entourage of that earlier time, when the hero was the great emperor, had remained.[1] And only this parrot kept the stories and lost language from being forgotten in the silence of the Uraricoera. Only the parrot preserved the words and the deeds of the hero.

He told the man everything, then spread his wings on a course for Lisbon. And the man is I, dear reader, and I'm here to tell you the story. That's why I came. It's the

---

[1] An aruaí is a species of parakeet known for its ability to imitate human speech.

reason that I perched upon this leafy riverbank, plucked the ticks from my body, strummed my violin, and sang to the world these obscene lyrics about the wisdom and deeds of Macunaíma, the hero of our people.

There is nothing more.

Macunaíma

ABOUT THE AUTHORS

The Pemón People

The Pemón people are an ethnolinguistic group who are indigenous to the area of the Amazon Rainforest at the triple border of Guyana, Venezuela, and Brazil. They are members of the Cariban language community, which is comprised of an estimated 60,000 to 100,000 people, speaking forty different languages, throughout northern South America and the Lesser Antilles. The word "pemón" means "person" in several of these languages. The Pemón are divided into four tribes: the Arekuna, Kamarakoto, Taurepang, and Macuxi. As of the publication of this translation, their population is approximately 35,000, with the vast majority living in Venezuela.

Theodor Koch-Grünberg

Theodor Koch-Grünberg was born on April 9, 1872, in the small town of Grünberg in Hesse, which at that time was a state within the German Reich and is now a part of Germany. As a young man, he studied philology at the University of Giessen, also in Hesse, and worked as a schoolteacher after graduation.

In 1898, Koch-Grünberg first traveled to Brazil, where he participated in an expedition to locate the source of the Rio Xingú, which winds through central Brazil until it flows into the Amazon River near the Atlantic Ocean. Upon his return to Germany, he took a position at the Ethnologische Museum Berlin ("Berlin Ethnology Museum"), but soon departed on a second expedition in 1903, to explore the Rio Japurá and the Rio Negro which flow into the Amazon River from Colombia to the north. There, he lived among the Baniwa people, which he wrote about in the book *Zwei Jahre unter den Indianern. Reisen in Nord West Brasilien, 1903-1905* ("Two Years among the Indians: Travels in Northwest Brazil, 1903-1905"), which was published in two volumes between 1910 and 1911.

In 1909, Koch-Grünberg began to lecture at the University of Freiburg, where he was promoted to professor in 1913. In 1911, he began a third expedition, traveling up the Rio Branco from Manaus to Mount Roraima at the triple border of Brazil, Venezuela, and Guyana. There, he lived among the Pemón people. He recorded their myths and legends, documented their customs, and took photographs. All of these papers he published in 1917 in the book *Vom Roraima zum Orinoco: Ergebnisse einer Reise in Nordbrasilien und Venezuela in den Jahren 1911-1913* ("From Roraima to Orinoco: Findings from a Journey in North Brazil and Venezuela in the Years 1911-1913").

In 1924, he departed on a third expedition, to the upper reaches of the Rio Branco, which was led by American explorer, Alexander Hamilton Rice, Jr., and a

Brazilian filmmaker named Silvino Santos. Koch-Grünberg died of malaria along the way at a settlement called Vila de Vista Alegre, a mile downriver from the town of Caracaraí. His final days were captured in the documentary *No Rastro do Eldorado: Expedição do Dr. Hamilton Rice ao Rio Branco em 1924-1925* ("On the Trail to El Dorado: The Expedition of Dr. Hamilton Rice to the Rio Branco in 1924-1925").[1]

Mário de Andrade

Mário de Andrade was born on October 9, 1893, to Carlos and Maria Luísa de Andrade in São Paulo, Brazil. As a young boy, he was a gifted pianist, and in 1911, he enrolled in the Conservatório Dramático e Musical de São Paulo ("Musical and Dramatic Conservatory of São Paulo"). In 1914, his fourteen-year-old brother died from a head injury during a soccer game, and Mário took a break from his studies to be with his family. When he returned to the conservatory, he stopped performing to focus instead on music theory, with the intent of becoming a teacher. He graduated in 1917.

That same year, he published his first book of poems, *Há uma Gota de Sangue em Cada Poema* ("There's a Drop of Blood in Every Poem"), under the pseudonym Mário Sobral. He then set out to explore the Brazilian countryside, documenting the culture, folklore, and music of the interior. In 1923, he began studying German under the tutelage of Frau Else Schöler Eggbert and Fräulein Käthe Meiche-Blosen. This experience would inspire his first novel, *Amor, Verbo Intransitivo* ("Love, Intransitive Verb"), about a teenage boy whose father hires a German

---

[1] This film is available on YouTube as of the date of publication, at https://youtu.be/9N54ktqGoLE.

tutor to teach him how to have sex. (Notwithstanding his having published this erotic heterosexual fantasy, Andrade's sexuality remains the subject of speculation, as he never married nor had any public relationships.) Published in 1927, the book was commercially and critically unsuccessful, and later regarded by Andrade as an experiment.

In 1926, Andrade read *Vom Roraima zum Orinoco* by Theodor Koch-Grünberg. In a letter to his friend, Alceu Amoroso Lima, sent May 19, 1928, Andrade wrote:

> I decided to write because I was desperate from lyrical disquiet when, reading Koch-Grünberg, I understood that Macunaíma was a hero without any character, neither moral nor psychological. I found this enormously moving, I don't know why, certainly because of the originality of the fact, or because I agree a bit with our time, I don't know…

Two months later, on July 26, 1928, Andrade published *Macunaíma, o herói sem nenhum caráter* ("Macunaíma: The Hero Without Any Character"). He did not provide attribution to the Pemón for creating the myths and legends of Makunaima, nor to Koch-Grünberg for first recording them for publication.

Rumors that Andrade had plagiarized much of *Macunaíma* soon began to percolate, and in 1931 they bubbled into public view. That year, Amazonian folklorist Raimundo de Moraes published his *Dicionário de Cousas da Amazônia* ("Dictionary of Amazonian Things"), in which he made an entry alluding to rumors that Andrade had plagiarized *Macunaíma*. Moraes wrote:

> Critics allege that the book *Macunaíma* by the

celebrated author Mário de Andrade is based entirely on *Vom Roraima zum Orinoco* by learned Koch-Grünberg. Being unfamiliar with the book of the German naturalist, I did not create this rumor, for the patrician novelist, whose work I perused in Manaus, possesses talent and imagination which don't require strange inspirations.

On September 20, 1931, Andrade responded to Moraes in an open letter in a São Paulo newspaper called *Diário Nacional* ("National Daily"). Although he confessed to copying Koch-Grünberg, he ridiculed his critics for suggesting that he meant to deceive anyone, and claimed that he'd believed that his references would be obvious to readers. He wrote:

> Yes, I copied, my dear defender. What amazes me and I find a sublime kindness, is that my critics forgot everything they know, restricting themselves to my copying of Koch-Grünberg, when I copied everything. Even Senhor [de Moraes] in the Boiúna scene. I confess that I copied; I copied verbatim at times. Really want to know? I not only copied the ethnographies and amerindian texts, but further, in the Letter to the Icamiabas, I took entire sentences from Rui Barbosa, Mário Barreto, and the Portuguese colonial chroniclers, and destroyed the precious and solemn language of the collaborators of the *Revista de Língua Portuguesa* ["Journal of the Portuguese Language"].
> ...
> In the end, I am obliged to confess once and for

all: I copied Brazil, at least in the parts in which I was interested in satirizing Brazil through itself. But not even the idea of satire is mine because it's already been done since Gregório de Matos, my goodness! The only thing left to me then is the luck of Cabral, who likely had the luck of discovering Brazil in the first place, and Brazil is still associated with Portugal. My name is on the cover of Macunaíma and nobody can take it off.

Macunaíma was the last novel that Andrade ever wrote, although he continued to publish poetry and essays until the end of his life. In 1935, Andrade was named the founding director of the São Paulo Department of Culture, which oversaw park construction and public events. After two years, his position was terminated and he took a job with the Federal University of Rio de Janiero, where he taught folklore and folk music. He returned to São Paulo in 1941, where he began to compile an anthology of his poetry.

Andrade died of a heart attack on February 25, 1945, at his house in São Paulo. He was fifty-one years old. His poetry collection, *Poemas Completas*, was published in 1955. On February 15, 1960, the city of São Paulo renamed its municipal library "Biblioteca de Mário de Andrade."

ABOUT THE TRANSLATOR

Carl L. Engel was born in 1985 in Tokyo, Japan, to American parents. He moved to the United States as an infant, where he grew up in a suburb of Philadelphia, Pennsylvania. Although he was a voracious reader throughout childhood, his passion for language, literature, and translation was first cultivated at his Jesuit high school, where he studied Latin, German, and English. In 2008, he received a bachelor's degree from Columbia University, having studied economics, political science, and more German, and in 2013, he received his juris doctor from Temple University School of Law. He made his publishing debut in 2021 with a translation of Professor Dowell's Head by Alexander Belyaev (USSR, 1925). He lives with his wife and dog in Philadelphia, where he is a practicing trial attorney and translates literature.

ACKNOWLEDGMENTS

As always, my gratitude belongs foremost to my wife, Mandy, whose enormous support and encouragement make all of my books possible, and who, as my first reader, is confronted with all of my typos and errors. Further thanks are owed to my good friends Adriel Garcia, Esquire, and Jennifer Waggenspack, both of whom read the manuscript and provided feedback and encouragement before publication. Acknowledgment is also due to Alejandro B. for designing a beautiful cover. Finally, while I have never been formally trained in Portuguese, I owe a debt to my high-school Latin teachers who introduced me to the Romance world. They are Meredith Morgan, Michael Dougherty, and Christie McGuire Villarreal. Thank you all.

Macunaíma

REFERENCES

The reader likely will notice that most of the works cited are from Portuguese-language publications. The primary reason for this is simple: Academics and students in Brazil are in closer proximity to the flora, fauna, history, and people referenced in the footnotes and, therefore, are much more likely to have published articles on these topics. There is, however, a noxious secondary reason: The paywalls that restrict access to English-language academic publications have become far too expensive for a scholar without access to a university library. Indeed, access to many articles requires either a subscription to a publication service that costs hundreds of dollars annually, or a single payment of more than a hundred dollars. To find an English-language article for less than thirty dollars is rare.

Perhaps this is by design, and American universities shield their work behind expensive paywalls so their professors do not have to compete in the marketplace of ideas with outsider scholars. American academia has come under fire for becoming a shelter for children of the rich, whose parents can support them for a decade of lean years until they complete their PhDs and obtain positions as tenure-track professors. Whether intended or not, these paywalls are certainly an effective way to keep this privileged class from having to compete with anyone outside the gates of their club.

The reader should know that this is not normal outside the Anglosphere. It was rare that I encountered a paywall when searching through Portuguese-language sources, and even when I did, the article was usually available for free on another website. Likewise, Spanish-language academic articles generally were free and easy to access. An argument can be made that, because the Portuguese- and Spanish-language articles come mostly from federally funded publications and universities, access should be freely given to the public, as the taxpayer ultimately has funded the research behind the articles. But that is true in the United States as well. American universities are awash in taxpayer cash harvested during the years leading up to the student-loan crisis, yet still charge the public an outrageous amount to access the articles published using these tax dollars. Americans have every right to, and should, demand that their government require articles regarding research funded by the public to be made available at no additional cost. Because such articles are not freely available and I self-fund my projects, I generally have left American academics out of this book.

Introduction

Braga-Pinto, César. *A Sexualidade de Mário de Andrade "Ninguém o Saberá Jamais."* Santa Barbara Portuguese Studies. 2nd Ser., Vol. 10, 2022.

Carvalho, Fábio Almeida de. *Makunaima/Makunaíma, antes de Macunaíma*. Revista Crioula, No. 5, May 2009.

Koch-Grünberg, Theodor. *Vom Roroima zum Orinoco*. Vol. II. Verlag Strecker und Schröder, 1924.

Lopez, Telê Ancona. *O Macunaíma de Mário de Andrade nas páginas de Koch-Grünberg*. Manuscrítica: Revista de Crítica Genética. No. 24, 2013.

Mesquita, Clélio Kramer de. *Tradução dos Capítulos da Obra, Vom Roroima zum Orinoco, de Theodor Koch-Grünberg (1924), em que são narradas lendas do mito indígena Makunaima*. Rónai: Revista de Estudos Clássicos e Tradutórios, Vol. 6, No. 2, 2018.

Schmitt, Maria Aparecida Nogueira. *Mário de Andrade: Incorporação das Cosmogonias Ameríndias em Macunaíma*. Juiz de Fora, Vol. 10, No. 18, Jul./Dez. 2010.

Chapter I

1. Google Maps, www.maps.google.com, *Uraricoera River*, accessed Feb. 22, 2023. Góes Neves, Eduardo. "Archeological Cultures and Past Identities in the Pre-colonial Central Amazon." *Ethnicity in Ancient Amazonia: Reconstructing Past Identities from Archeology, Linguistics, and Ethnohistory*, edited by Alf Hornborg and Jonathan D. Hill, University Press of Colorado, 2011, pp. 31-56 [Tupi tribes]. Rose, Françoise. "Borrowing of a Cariban Number Marker into Three Tupi-Guarani Languages." *Morphologies in Contact*, Akademie Verlag, 2012 [Tupi-Caribe relationship].

2. Dicio: Dicionário Online de Português, https://www.dicio.com.br/paxiuba, accessed Feb. 22, 2023.

3. Vieira Neto, Ernane Henrique Monteiro, *Influência do habitat e da disponibilidade de substrato vegetal na sobrevivência, crescimento e densidade de colônias da saúva* Atta laevigata *(Fr. Smith) em uma área de cerrado*. Universidade Federal de Uberlândia, master's dissertation, 2008.

4. Moraes-Costa, Denise, and Ralf Schwamborn, *Site fidelity and population structure of blue land crabs (*Cardisoma guanhumi *Latreille, 1825) in a restricted-access mangrove area, analyzed using PIT tags*, Helgoland Marine Research, Jan. 2018.

5. Prandi, Reginaldo. *Religião e sincretismo em Jorge Amado*. Caderno de leituras: O universo de Jorge Amado, São Paulo: Companhia das letras, 2009.

6. Domingues, Heloisa Maria Bertol. *Tastevin: uma história da etnografia indígena*. Boletim do Museu Paraense Emílio Goeldi. Ciências Humanas, Vol. 4, No. 1, 2009.

7. Cruz Pantoja, Magdiel, *Potencial do Guarumã como Biossorvente para Remoção de Íons Cobalto de Solução Aquosa*. Universidade Federal do Sul e Sudeste do Pará, student essay, 2016.

8. Amarante, Cristine Bastos do, Adolfo H. Müller, Marinete M. Póvoa, and Maria Fâni Dolabela, *Estudo fitoquímico biomonitorado pelos ensaios de toxicidade frente à* Artemia salina *e de atividade antiplasmódica do caule de aninga (*Montrichardia linifera*)*, Acta Amazonica, Vol. 41(3), 2011.

9. Dicio: Dicionário Online de Português, https://www.dicio.com.br/javari, accessed Feb. 22, 2023.

10. Dicio: Dicionário Online de Português, https://www.dicio.com.br/biguá, accessed Feb. 22, 2023. Dicio: Dicionário Online de Português, https://www.dicio.com.br/biguatinga, accessed Feb. 22, 2023.

11. Andrade, Mário de, *Macunaíma: O Herói sem nenhum Caráter*, edited by Luís Augusto Fischer, L&PM Pocket, 2017.

12. Mothé, Cheila G., and Carla R. de Araujo, *Caracterização Térmica e Mecânica de Compósitos de Poliuretano com Fibras de Curauá*, Polímeros: Ciência e Tecnologia, Vol. 14, 2004.

13. Dicio: Dicionário Online de Português, https://www.dicio.com.br/anta, accessed Feb. 28, 2023

14. La Barre, Weston, *Native American Beers*, American Ethnologist, Vol. 40, 1938.

15. Dicio: Dicionário Online de Português, https://www.dicio.com.br/caruru, accessed Feb. 22, 2023. Oliveira, Andréia Barroncas de, et al. *Morfoanatomia de semente de sororoca (*Phenakospermum guyannense*).* Revista Brasileira de Sementes, Vol. 34, 2012 [sororoca].

16. Rigamonte-Azevedo, Onofra Cleuza, et al.. *Copaíba: ecologia e produção de óleo-resina*. Rio Branco: Embrapa Acre, Documentos, Vol. 91, Oct. 2004 [copaíba]. Jeffreys, Manoel Feitosa, and Cecilia Veronica Nunez. *Triterpenos das folhas de* Piranhea trifoliata *(Picrodendraceae)*. Acta Amazonica, Vol. 46(2), 2016 [piranheiras].

17. Koch-Grünberg, Theodor. *Vom Roroima zum Orinoco*. Vol. II. Verlag Strecker und Schröder, 1924, 13 [pupaí]. Souza, Natália Oliveira de Souza. *Os Conhecimentos Indígenas Interligados aos Conhecimentos da Física: O Caso das Fases da Lua*. Instituto Federal de Pernambuco - Campus Pesqueira - Curso de Licenciatura em Física, Dec. 2021 [Guaraci and Jaci].

18. Montello, Josué. *O Polemista do Conto*. Ciência & Trópico, Recife, Vol. 9(2), Jul./Dec. 1981.

19. Silva, João Henrique Constantino Sales, et al. *Water restriction in seeds of* Cereus jamacaru *DC*. Revista Brasileira de Ciências Agrárias, Vol 16, No. 2, 2021.

20. Koch-Grünberg, Theodor. *Vom Roroima zum Orinoco*. Vol. II. Verlag Strecker und Schröder, 1924, 42-45.

Chapter II

1. Dicio: Dicionário Online de Português, https://www.dicio.com.br/aruraúba, accessed Feb. 22, 2023. Renhe, Isis Rodrigues Toledo. *Obtenção de corante natural azul extraído de frutos de jenipapo*. Pesquisa Agropecuária Brasileira, Vol. 44, No. 6, Jun. 2009 [jenipapo].

2. Ribeiro, Wellington Souto, et al. *Caracterização Pós-Colheita do Limão Cayne (*Averrhoa bilimbi *L.), Armazenado em Atmosfera Modificada*. Revista Brasileira de Produtos Agroindustriais, Campina Grande, Vol. 12, No. 2, 2010.

3. Carvalho, Paulo Ernani Ramalho. *Tatajuba: Bagassa guianensis*. Espécies Arbóreas Brasileiras, Vol. 4, Embrapa, 2010 [tatajubas]. Pinto, Gerson Pereira. *O Óleo de Uchí: Seu*

Esudo Químico. Boletim Técnico do Instituto Agronômico do Norte, No. 31, Jun. 1956 [umiri].

4.   Franzo, Vanessa Sobue, et al. *Estudo do Fórmula Vertebral do Tatu-Galinha.* Revista Científica Eletrônica de Medicina Veterinária, Vol. 9, No. 17, July 2011.

5.   Karadimas, Dimitri. *The Miraña Deer Skull: Mythological and Cognitive Implications of a Miraña Communication Instrument (Colombian Amazon).* Artifacts and Society in Amazonia, Bonn Americanist Studies, Vol. 36, 2004 [cunauru]. Ferreira, Cristina, and Thiago Lenz. *Duas Narrativas para o Lugar dos Indígenas nas Origens da Nação: A História Ficcional de Magalhães e Alencar.* Almanack, Vol. 23, Sep.-Dec. 2019 [maraguigana]. Nascimento, Lídio França do, et al. *Descrição do Comportamento de Superfície do Boto Cinza,* Sotalia guianensis, *na Praia de Pipa - RN.* Psicologia: Reflexão e Crítica, Vol. 21(3), 2008 [botos].

6.   Dávila, Carmen Garcia, et al. *Peces de Consumo de la Amazonía Peruana.* Instituto de Investigaciones de la Amazonía Peruana, 2018 [kinds of fish]. Txicão, Kavisgo, and Marcelo Franco Leão. *A Pesca Coletiva com Timbó Practicada pelos Ikpeng: Ensinamentos Dessa Relação Respeitosa com a Natureza.* Ambiente & Educação, Vol. 24, No. 1, 2019 [timbó].

7.   Pantoja, Gracilene Ferreira. *Uso e Aplições medicinais da mamorana (*Pachira aquatica Aublet*) pelos ribeirinhos de São Lourenço, Igarapé-Miri, estado do Pará, Amazônia.* Interações, Vol. 21, No. 3, Jul./Sep. 2020.

8.   Bauer, Irmgard L. *Candiru - A Little Fish with Bad Habits: Need Travel Health Professionals Worry? A Review.* Journal of Travel Medicine, Vol. 20, No. 2, 2013.

9. Zavaglia, Adriana. *Lingüística, Tradução e Literatura: Observando a Transformação pela Arte*. Alfa: Revista de Linguística, Vol. 48, No. 1, 2004.

10. Dicio: Dicionário Online de Português, https://www.dicio.com.br/maromba, accessed Feb. 22, 2023. Marins, Luciene Gomes Freitas. *O léxico rural no Brasil Central: designações para "bruaca."* Estudos Linguísticos, Vol. 43(1), Jan./Apr. 2014 [picuás and sapicuás]. Dicio: Dicionário Online de Português, https://www.dicio.com.br/urupema, accessed Feb. 22, 2023.

11. Koch-Grünberg, Theodor. *Vom Roroima zum Orinoco*. Vol. II. Verlag Strecker und Schröder, 1924, 42-45.

12. Xatara, Claudia, and Mariele Seco. *Culturemas em contraste: idiomatismos do português brasileiro e europeu*. Domínios de Linguagem, Vol. 8, No. 1, Jan./Jun. 2014.

13. Duca, Charles, and Miguel Ângelo Marini. *Breeding success of* Cacicus haemorrhous *(Linnaeus) (Aves: Icteridae) in different environments in an Atlantic Forest reserve in Southeast Brazil*. Ravista Brasileira de Zoologia, Vol. 25, Jun. 2008.

14. Moraes, Walmir Nogueira. *O Mito do Curupira: Vozes e Letras, Diálogos e Narrativas no Imaginário Tembé*. Master's dissertation, Universidade da Amazônia, Pró-Reitoria de Pesquisa, Pós-Graduação e Extensão, Curso de Comunicação, Linguagens e Cultura, 2016 [curupira]. Souza, Marcos Vinícius de, et al. *Tratamento Endodôntico em Irara (*Eira barbara *Linnaeus, 1758) - Relato de Caso*. Pensar Acadêmico, Vol. 19, No. 2, May-Sep. 2021 [papa-mel].

15. Portela, Adriana Soares. *Desenvolvimento e caracterização físico-química de iogurte batido adicionado de calda*

*do fruto do tucunzeiro (*astrocaryum vulgare mart*).* Brazilian Journal of Development, Vol. 8, No. 2, Feb. 2022.

16. Alves, Jose Jackson Amancio, et al. *Degredação de Caatinga: Uma Investigação Ecogeográfica.* Revista Caatinga, Vol. 22, No. 3, Jul.-Sep. 2009.

17. Quintairos-Soliño, Alba. *"Que 'di' o raposo?" A raposa enmascarada: como o folclore afecta ás unidades fraseolóxicas.* Cadernos de Fraseoloxía Galega, Vo. 22, 2020 ["fox's wedding"]. Koch-Grünberg, Theodor. *Vom Roroima zum Orinoco.* Vol. II. Verlag Strecker und Schröder, 1924, 52 [Vei].

18. Neto, Adony Querubino de Andrade, et al. *Intoxicação Natural por* Amaranthus spinosus *(*Amaranthaceae*) em Bovinos no Agreste do Estado de Pernambuco.* Ciência Veterinária nos Trópicos, Vol. 19, No. 1, Jan.-Apr. 2016.

19. Oliveira, Stefan Vilges de. *Albinismo parcial em cutia* Dasyprocta azarae *(Lichtenstein 1823) (Rodentia, Dasyproctidae), no sul do Brasil.* Biotemas, Vol. 22, No. 4, Dec. 2009.

20. Dicio: Dicionário Online de Português, https://www.dicio.com.br/tipiti, accessed Feb. 22, 2023.

21. Noelli, Francisco Silva, and José Proenza Brochado. *O Cauim as Beberagens dos Guarani e Tupinambá: Equipamentos, Técnicas de Preparação e Consumo.* Revista do Museu de Arqueologia e Etnologia, Vol. 8, 1998.

22. Dáttilo, Wesley, et al. *Primeiro Registro da Quenquém Cisco-da-Amazônia* Acromyrmex hystrix *(Latreille) (Formicidae: Myrmicinae) para o Estado do Maranhão, Brasil.* EntomoBrasilis, Vol. 3, No. 3, 2010.

23.   Falesi, Italo Claudio, and Osvaldo Ryohei Kato. *A Cultura do Urucu no Norte do Brasil*. EMBRAPA-CPATU, Belém, 1992.

24.   Dicio: Dicionário Online de Português, https://www.dicio.com.br/pacova, accessed Feb. 22, 2023. Dicio: Dicionário Online de Português, https://www.dicio.com.br/aluá, accessed Feb. 22, 2023. Dicio: Dicionário Online de Português, https://www.dicio.com.br/mapará, accessed Feb. 22, 2023. Dicio: Dicionário Online de Português, https://www.dicio.com.br/ata, accessed Feb. 22, 2023. Dicio: Dicionário Online de Português, https://www.dicio.com.br/abio, accessed Feb. 22, 2023. Dicio: Dicionário Online de Português, https://www.dicio.com.br/sapote, accessed Feb. 22, 2023. Dicio: Dicionário Online de Português, https://www.dicio.com.br/sapotilha, accessed Feb. 22, 2023. Dicio: Dicionário Online de Português, https://www.dicio.com.br/paçoca, accessed Feb. 22, 2023.

25.   Google Maps, www.maps.google.com, *Pernambuco*, accessed Feb. 22, 2023. Carvalho, Solange Peixe Pinheiro de. *As Memórias da Pedra do Reino*. III Simpósio Nacional Discurso, Identidade e Sociedade (III SIDIS), Dilemas e Desafios na Contemporaneidade, 2012 [Pedro Bonita].

26.   Google Maps, www.maps.google.com, *Santarém*, accessed Feb. 22, 2023.

27.   Pereira, Andreza Stephanie de Souza, et al. *Taxonomy of* Aspidosperma *Mart. (Apocynaceae, Rauvolfioideae) in the State of Pará, Northern Brazil*. Biota Neotropica, Vol. 16(2), 2016.

28. Filho, Paulo Edson Alves, and John Milton. *The Mixed Identity of the Catholic Religion in the Texts Translated by the Jesuit Priest Jose de Anchieta in 16th Century Brazil.* TRANS. Revista de Traductología, No. 12, 2008.

29. Silva, Jaqueline Mara. *Preparação e Caracterização de Nanofibras de Celulose de Jacitara (*Desmoncus polyacanthos Mart.*) para Obtenção de Compósitos Poliméricos.* Universidade Federal do Paraná, Programa de Pós-Graduação Engenharia e Ciência dos Materiais, Dissertação, 2018 [jacitara]. Silva, Leirson Rodrigues da, and Ricardo Elesbão Alves. *Caracterização Físico-Química de Frutos de "Mandacaru."* Rev. Acad., Ciênc. Agrár. Ambient., Curitiba, Vol. 7, No. 2, Apr.-Jun. 2009 [manducaru].

30. Silva, Renata Bortoletto. *Oloniti e o Castigo da Festa Errada: Relações entre Mito e Ritual entre os Paresi.* Cadernos de Campo, No. 13, 2005.

31. Koch-Grünberg, Theodor. *Vom Roroima zum Orinoco.* Vol. II. Verlag Strecker und Schröder, 1924, 20 [pódole]. Métraux, Alfred. "Boys' Initiation Rites." *Handbook of South American Indians*, edited by Julian H. Seward, Smithsonian Institution Bureau of American Ethnology, 1949 [tocandeira].

32. Koch-Grünberg, Theodor. *Vom Roroima zum Orinoco.* Vol. III. Verlag Strecker und Schröder, 1924.

Chapter III

1. Dicio: Dicionário Online de Português, https://www.dicio.com.br/igapó, accessed Feb. 22, 2023.

2. Costa, Fabiane Rabelo da, et al. *Análise Biométrica de Frutos de Umbuzeiro do Semiárido Brasileiro.* Uberlândia, Vol. 31, No. 3, May-Jun. 2015.

3. Sousa, Marcílio Pereira, et al. *Influência da Temperatura na Germinação de Sementes de Sumaúma.* Revista Brasileira de Sementes, Vol. 22, No. 1, 2000.

4. Souza, Natália Oliveira de Souza. *Os Conhecimentos Indígenas Interligados aos Conhecimentos da Física: O Caso das Fases da Lua.* Instituto Federal de Pernambuco - Campus Pesqueira - Curso de Licenciatura em Física, Dec. 2021.

5. Bruce, Maria Valcirlene de Souza, Iraildes Caldas Torres. *A Lua cheia protagonizando as lendas e mitos Amazônicos.* III Seminário Internacional em Sociedade e Cultura na Pan-Amazônia, Universidade Federal do Amazonas - UFAM Manaus, Nov. 2018.

6. Dicio: Dicionário Online de Português, https://www.dicio.com.br/pajeú, accessed Feb. 22, 2023.

7. Sá, Alexandre Lira. "Icamiabas - A Prole de Pentesileia." *Anais da II Jordana de Estudos Clássicos e Humanísticos de Parintins.* Universidade do Estado do Amazonas Centro de Estudos Superiores de Parintins, Mar. 2018.

8. Dicio: Dicionário Online de Português, https://www.dicio.com.br/mucuru, accessed Feb. 22, 2023.

9. Bindandi, Welliton Martins, Taisi Mahmudo Karim. *"Nandaia, Nandaia, Vamos Nandaiar": Línguas e Colonização no Estado de Mato Grosso.* Revista Ecos: Estudos Linguísticos e Literários, Vol. 30, No. 1, 2021

[jandaya]. Dicio: Dicionário Online de Português, https://www.dicio.com.br/tuin, accessed Feb. 22, 2023. Dicio: Dicionário Online de Português, https://www.dicio.com.br/curicas, accessed Feb. 22, 2023.

10. Dicio: Dicionário Online de Português, https://www.dicio.com.br/pajuari, accessed Feb. 22, 2023.

11. Dicio: Dicionário Online de Português, https://www.dicio.com.br/cocho, accessed Feb. 22, 2023.

12. Chuí and nalachítchi are indigenous slang words for penis and vagina, respectively. Santos, Luzia A. Oliva dos. *Literatura Indigenista: Metamorfoses Ambivalentes.* Revista Ecos: Estudos Linguísticos e Literários, Vol. 1, No. 2, 2006.

13. Silva, Angela Leticia Nesso Ramos da. *Uma Leitura Antropológica do Auto de Natal O Menino Atrasado, de Cecília Meireles.* Universidade Tecnológica Federal do Paraná, Curitiba, 2014.

14. Reed, Richard K. *Birthing Fathers: The Transformation of Men in American Rites of Birth.* Rutgers University Press, 2005.

15. Carone, Edgard. *A evolução industrial de São Paulo (1889-1930).* Editora Senac São Paulo, 2019.

16. Mello, Felipe. *Brasilianas IV e V para piano de Radamés Gnattali: uma análise musical tipificada, interpretativa e comparativa.* VI Simpósio Brasileiro de Pós-Graduandos em Música, Universidade Federal do Estado do Rio de Janeiro, 2020 [tutu]. Dicio: Dicionário Online de

Português, https://www.dicio.com.br/marambaia, accessed Feb. 22, 2023.

17. Aguiar, Viviane. "O peru de Natal e a "felicidade gustativa" de Mário de Andrade." *Lembraria*, lembraria.com/2016/12/16/o-peru-de-natal-e-a-felicidade-gustativa-de-mario-de-andrade, accessed Aug. 22, 2022 [Dona Francisca]. Lindoso, Dirceu. *Interpretação da Província: Estudo da Cultura Alagoana*. 2nd ed., Universidade Federal de Alagoas, 2005, 121-122 [Dona Joaquina].

18. Maia, Gleidys Meyre da Silva. *Mário de Andrade: A Viagem e o Viajante*. Organon, Porto Alegre, Vol. 17, No. 34, Jun. 2003.

19. Silva, Maria José da. *Modernismo e Identidade Nacional em* Macunaíma *e* Retrato do Brasil. Universidade do Estado do Rio Grande do Norte, master's dissertation, 2017.

20. Flores, Maria Bernardete Ramos. *Pensar com os mitos. Sobre ecologia nos boitatás de Franklin Cascaes*. Tempo e Agumento, Vol. 14, No. 35, Jan.-Apr. 2022.

21. Costa, Marcondes Lima da, et al. *Muyrakytã ou Muiraquitã, um Talismã Arqueológico em Jade Procedente da Amazônia: uma Revisão Histórica e Considerações Antropogeológicas*. Acta Amazonica, Vol. 32, No. 3, Jul.-Sep. 2002.

22. Koch-Grünberg, Theodor. *Vom Roroima zum Orinoco*. Vol. II. Verlag Strecker und Schröder, 1924, 63.

23. Gonçalves, José Rubens Cordeiro. *A Cultura do Guaraná*. Série: Culturas da Amazônia, Vol. 2, No. 1,

Instituto de Pesquisas e Experimentação Agropecuárias do Norte, 1971.

Chapter IV

1.	Dicio: Dicionário Online de Português, https://www.dicio.com.br/tembetá, accessed Feb. 23, 2023.

2.	Barbosa, José Luciano Albino. *Engenho de cana-de-açúcar na Paraíba: por uma Sociologia da Cachaça.* Universidade Estadual da Paraíba, 2014, 9-10.

3.	Maciel, Anna Mara Ferreira. *As fases da lua e a mitologia tupi-guarani: um caminho entre a ciência e a cultura numa aula para o ensino fundamental.* Periódico Electrônico Fórum Ambiental da Alta Paulista, Vol. 14, No. 2, 2018.

4.	None. My research didn't uncover Andrade's inspiration for these gods; they seem to first appear in *Macunaíma*.

5.	None. My research didn't uncover Andrade's inspiration for these characters; they seem to first appear in *Macunaíma*.

6.	Carvalho, Paulo Ernani Ramalho. *Espécies Arbóreas Brasileiras: Embiruçu (Pseudobombax grandiflorum).* Embrapa, Vol. 2, 2006.

7.	Koch-Grünberg, Theodor. *Vom Roroima zum Orinoco.* Vol. II. Verlag Strecker und Schröder, 1924, 20 [Kapei]. Dicio: Dicionário Online de Português, https://www.dicio.com.br/capar, accessed Feb. 23, 2023.

8.   Maeda, Jocely Andreuccetti, Luiz Antonio Ferraz Matthes. *Conservação de Sementes de Ipê*. Bragantia, Vol. 43, No. 1, 1984.

9.   Ferreira, Sidney Alberto do Nascimento, Daniel Felipe de Oliveira Gentil. *Seed Germination at Different Stratification Temperatures and Development of* Phytelephas macrocarpa *Ruiz & Pavón seedlings*. Journal of Seed Science, Vol. 39, No. 1, 2017.

10.   None. My research didn't uncover Andrade's inspiration for this character; he seems to first appear in *Macunaíma*.

11.   Dicio: Dicionário Online de Português, https://www.dicio.com.br/igara, accessed Feb. 23, 2023.

12.   Proença, M. Cavalcanti. *Roteiro de Macunaíma*. 3rd ed., Instituto Nacional do Livro, Ministério da Educação e Cultura, 1974, 145.

13.   Dicio: Dicionário Online de Português, https://www.dicio.com.br/mururê, accessed Feb. 23, 2023.

14.   Dicio: Dicionário Online de Português, https://www.dicio.com.br/apiacás, accessed Feb. 23, 2023.

15.   Dicio: Dicionário Online de Português, https://www.dicio.com.br/tracuá, accessed Feb. 23, 2023.

16.   Dicio: Dicionário Online de Português, https://www.dicio.com.br/siriri, accessed Feb. 23, 2023.

17.   Dicio: Dicionário Online de Português, https://www.dicio.com.br/bacupari, accessed Feb. 23, 2023.

18. Google Maps, www.maps.google.com, *Cananéia*, accessed Feb. 23, 2023. Vainfas, Ronaldo. "A tessitura dos sincretismos: mediadores e mesclas culturais." *O Brasil colonial*, edited by João Fragoso and Maria de Fátima Gouvêa, Civilização Brasileira, 2014 [Bacharel de Cananéia].

19. Fish, Suzanne K., et al. *Eventos Incrementais na Construção de Sambaquis, Litoral Sul do Estado de Santa Catarina*. Revista do Museu Arqueologia e Etnologia, No. 10, 2000 [shell middens]. Google Maps, www.maps.google.com, *Caputera and Morrete*, accessed Feb. 23, 2023.

20. Castillo, Andrés del. "Los Misioneros Teatinos en Asia durante Los Siglos XVII y XVIII." *Ordenes Religosas entre América y Asia*, edited by Elisabetta Corsi, El Colegio de Mexico, 2008.

21. Lagrou, Els. *Arte Indígena no Brasil: Agência, Alteridade, e Relação*. C/Arte, 2009, p. 18.

22. Ejelonu, BC, et al. *The chemical constituents of calabash (*Crescentia cujete*)*. African Journal of Biotechnology, Vol. 10, Dec. 2011.

23. Koch-Grünberg, Theodor. *Vom Roroima zum Orinoco*. Vol. II. Verlag Strecker und Schröder, 1924, 53-54.

24. Dicio: Dicionário Online de Português, https://www.dicio.com.br/aperema, accessed Feb. 23, 2023. Dicio: Dicionário Online de Português, https://www.dicio.com.br/teiús, accessed Feb. 23, 2023. Dicio: Dicionário Online de Português, https://www.dicio.com.br/muçuãs, accessed Feb. 23, 2023. Dicio: Dicionário Online de Português,

https://www.dicio.com.br/tapiocabas, accessed Feb. 23, 2023. Dicio: Dicionário Online de Português, https://www.dicio.com.br/chabós, accessed Feb. 23, 2023. Ragusa-Netto, J. *Chaco Chachalaca (*Ortalis canicollis, *Wagler, 1830) Feeding Ecology in a Gallery Forest in the South Pantanal (Brazil).* Brazilian Journal of Biology, Vol. 75, No. 1, Jan.-Mar. 2015 [aracuãs]. Silva, Jr., Fernando Alves da. *O Mito da Matinta Perera de Taperaçu Campo e o Conceito de Dádiva: Aproximando-se de um Conceito Antropológico.* Amazônica-Revista de Antropologia, Vol. 6, 2014 [Matinta Perera].

25.   Dicio: Dicionário Online de Português, https://www.dicio.com.br/tambaquis, accessed Feb. 23, 2023. Dicio: Dicionário Online de Português, https://www.dicio.com.br/tucunarés, accessed Feb. 23, 2023. Dicio: Dicionário Online de Português, https://www.dicio.com.br/pirarucu, accessed Feb. 23, 2023. Dicio: Dicionário Online de Português, https://www.dicio.com.br/curimatás, accessed Feb. 23, 2023. Dicio: Dicionário Online de Português, https://www.dicio.com.br/tapicuru, accessed Feb. 23, 2023. Dicio: Dicionário Online de Português, https://www.dicio.com.br/irerês, accessed Feb. 23, 2023.

26.   Tambara, Elomar. *A leitura escolar como construção ideológica: o caso na lenda do Negrinho do Pastoreio (1857-1906).* Revista História da Educação, Vol. 9, No. 17, Jan.-Jun. 2005.

27.   Dicio: Dicionário Online de Português, https://www.dicio.com.br/uirapuru, accessed Feb. 23, 2023.

28.   None. My research didn't uncover Andrade's inspiration for this name; and it seems to first appear in *Macunaíma*.

29.   Dicio: Dicionário Online de Português, https://www.dicio.com.br/igarapé, accessed Feb. 23, 2023. Google Maps, www.maps.google.com, *Tietê River*, accessed Feb. 23, 2023.

30.   Abril, Vanessa Veltrini, et al. "Elucidating the evolution of the red brocket deer Mazama americana complex (Artiodactyla; Cervidae)." *Cytogenetic and Genome Research* 128.1-3 (2010): 177-187.

Chapter V

1.   Dicio: Dicionário Online de Português, https://www.dicio.com.br/ubá, accessed Feb. 23, 2023. Google Maps, www.maps.google.com, *Rio Negro*, accessed Feb. 23, 2023. Google Maps, www.maps.google.com, *Marapatá*, accessed Feb. 23, 2023.

2.   Google Maps, www.maps.google.com, *Rio Araguaia*, accessed Feb. 23, 2023.

3.   Dicio: Dicionário Online de Português, https://www.dicio.com.br/vintém, accessed Feb. 23, 2023. B., Rafael Carreño, and Francisco Blanco. *Notas Sobre la Exploración del Sistema Kárstico de Roraima Sur, Estado Bolívar*. Boletín de la Sociedad Venezolana de Espelogía, Vol. 38, No. 38, 2004 [Roraima].

4.   Dicio: Dicionário Online de Português, https://www.dicio.com.br/camuatás, accessed Feb. 23, 2023. Dicio: Dicionário Online de Português, https://www.dicio.com.br/pirapitingas, accessed Feb.

23, 2023. Dicio: Dicionário Online de Português, https://www.dicio.com.br/dourados, accessed Feb. 23, 2023. Dicio: Dicionário Online de Português, https://www.dicio.com.br/piracanjubas, accessed Feb. 23, 2023. Dicio: Dicionário Online de Português, https://www.dicio.com.br/uarus-uarás, accessed Feb. 23, 2023. Dicio: Dicionário Online de Português, https://www.dicio.com.br/bacus, accessed Feb. 23, 2023.

5. Combès, Isabelle. *Pai Sumé, el Rey Blanco y el Paititi.* Anthropos, Vol. 106, 2011.

6. *The New Testament.* Translated by David Bentley Hart, Yale University Press, 2017, 221.

7. Dicio: Dicionário Online de Português, https://www.dicio.com.br/jacarè, accessed Feb. 23, 2023.

8. Dicio: Dicionário Online de Português, https://www.dicio.com.br/ingàzeira, accessed Feb. 23, 2023. Dicio: Dicionário Online de Português, https://www.dicio.com.br/mamorana, accessed Feb. 23, 2023. Dicio: Dicionário Online de Português, https://www.dicio.com.br/embaúba, accessed Feb. 23, 2023. Dicio: Dicionário Online de Português, https://www.dicio.com.br/catauaris, accessed Feb. 23, 2023.

9. Dicio: Dicionário Online de Português, https://www.dicio.com.br/sabiá, accessed Feb. 23, 2023.

10. Dicio: Dicionário Online de Português, https://www.dicio.com.br, accessed Feb. 23, 2023.

11. Dicio: Dicionário Online de Português, https://www.dicio.com.br/aruá, accessed Feb. 23, 2023.

12. Bezerra, Valeria Saldanha. *O Inajá (*Maximiliana maripa *(Aubl.) Drude) como fonte alimentar e oleaginosa.* Embrapa Amapá, Comunicado Técnico, Vol. 129, Dec. 2011 [inajá]. Dicio: Dicionário Online de Português, https://www.dicio.com.br, accessed Feb. 23, 2023 [the other palms].

13. Gonçalves, Margarete Regina Freitas, et al. *Metodologia para a caracterização de estuque de parede existente em edificações do patrimônio da cidade de Pelotas, RS.* Acervos Culturais e Suportes de Memória, Vol. 1, 2016.

14. Dicio: Dicionário Online de Português, https://www.dicio.com.br/bagarote, accessed Feb. 23, 2023. Barman, Roderick J. *Citizen Emperor: Pedro II and the Making of Brazil, 1825-1891.* Stanford University Press, 1999 [milréis].

15. Dicio: Dicionário Online de Português, https://www.dicio.com.br/tamarim, accessed Mar. 5, 2023.

16. Dicio: Dicionário Online de Português, https://www.dicio.com.br/papão, accessed Feb. 23, 2023. Gil, Pamela Alves. *Medicina Tradicional Indígena na Amazônia Brasileira: Uma Intervenção em Saúde.* Revista Ensino de Ciências e Humanidades, Vol. 5, No. 2, Jul.-Dec. 2019 [mauaris]. Saake, Guilherme. "O Mito do Jurupari entre os Baníwa do Rio Içana." *Leituras Etnologia Brasileira*, edited by Egon Schaden, Companhia Editora Nacional, 1976 [jurupari]. Queiroz, Renato da Silva. *Migração e Metamorfose de um Mito Brasileiro: O Saci,* Trickster *da Cultura Caipira.* Revista do Instituto de Estudos Brasileiros, Vol. 38, 1995 [Saci].

17. Filho, Haroldo Nélio Peres Campelo, and Luciana de Oliveira Dias. *Mitos Indígenas no Ambiente Escolar: Uma Reflexão sobre o Universo Guarani a Partir da Análise da Obra Tupã Tenondé*. Anais do I Congresso de Ciência Tecnologia da PUC Goiás, 2015 [Tupã]. Gabriel, Maria Alice Ribeiro. *De Sirenis: Imagem e Mito na Literatura Moderna*. Navegações, Vol. 12, No. 1, Jan.-Jun. 2018 [Mãe-D'água]. Ribeiro, André Luiz Rosa, and Edilece Souza Couto. "Mãe d'Água: representações das devoções afro-brasileiras na imprensa soteropolitana e na literatura Jorge Amadiana." *História, Cultura e Religiosidades Afro-Brasileiras*, Vol. 3, edited by Artur César Isaia, Editora Unilasalle, 2020 [Mãe-D'água].

18. Casemiro, Sandra Ramos. *A lenda da Iara: nacionalismo literário e folclore*. Universidade de São Paulo, Departamento de Letras Clássicas e Vernáculas, Master's dissertation, 2012.

19. Pallamin, Vera, and Rebeca Scherer. *Convite para a Comemoração dos 100 Anos do Prédio, Vila Penteado e Seminário sobre as Novas Áreas de Concentração do Programa de Pós-Graduação da FAUUSP*. PósFAUUSP, Vol. 10, Dec. 2001 [Rua Maranhão]. Costa, Oswaldo Antônio Ferreira. *Presença e Permanência do Ideário da Cidade-Jardim em São Paulo: O Bairro do Pacaembu*. Universidade Presbiteriana Mackenzie, Faculdade de Arquitetura e Urbanismo, Master's dissertation, 2014 [Pacaembu].

20. Koch-Grünberg, Theodor. *Vom Roroima zum Orinoco*. Vol. II. Verlag Strecker und Schröder, 1924.

21. Koch-Grünberg, Theodor. *Vom Roroima zum Orinoco*. Vol. II. Verlag Strecker und Schröder, 1924, 48.

22. Dicio: Dicionário Online de Português, https://www.dicio.com.br, accessed Feb. 23, 2023.

23. Cunha, Jakeline Fernandes. *As Várias Faces do Brasil: a Imagem do Caju em* Macunaíma. Universidade de São Paulo, Departamento do Teoria Literária e Literatura Comparada, Master's dissertation, 2009.

24. Dicio: Dicionário Online de Português, https://www.dicio.com.br/macuco, accessed Feb. 23, 2023. Dicio: Dicionário Online de Português, https://www.dicio.com.br/mico, accessed Feb. 23, 2023. Dicio: Dicionário Online de Português, https://www.dicio.com.br/mutum, accessed Feb. 23, 2023. Dicio: Dicionário Online de Português, https://www.dicio.com.br/penelope, accessed Feb. 23, 2023. Dicio: Dicionário Online de Português, https://www.dicio.com.br/jaó, accessed Feb. 23, 2023.

25. Dicio: Dicionário Online de Português, https://www.dicio.com.br/uru, accessed Feb. 23, 2023.

26. Dicio: Dicionário Online de Português, https://www.dicio.com.br/jacutinga, accessed Feb. 23, 2023. Dicio: Dicionário Online de Português, https://www.dicio.com.br/picota, accessed Feb. 23, 2023. Dicio: Dicionário Online de Português, https://www.dicio.com.br/jacana, accessed Feb. 23, 2023.

27. Dicio: Dicionário Online de Português, https://www.dicio.com.br, accessed Feb. 23, 2023.

28. Santos-Pinheiro, Alexandre, and Alexandre de Pádua Carrieri. *O blefe na vida cotidiana: o jogo (de truco) enquanto mecanismo imaginário para evasão do real*. Organizações & Sociedade, Vol. 70, 2014.

29. Dicio: Dicionário Online de Português, https://www.dicio.com.br/sarara, accessed Feb. 23,

2023. Koch-Grünberg, Theodor. *Vom Roroima zum Orinoco*. Vol. II. Verlag Strecker und Schröder, 1924, 19 [Kambezike].

30. Dicio: Dicionário Online de Português, https://www.dicio.com.br/jutaí, accessed Feb. 23, 2023.

31. Koch-Grünberg, Theodor. *Vom Roroima zum Orinoco*. Vol. II. Verlag Strecker und Schröder, 1924, 49-50 [Seléseleg]. Leenapeasanunt, Issariya. *The Advertising Campaign for Yale Digital Door Lock*. Assumption University of Thailand, Department of Visual Communication Design, bachelor's thesis, 2016 [Yale Lock].

32. Langer, Johnni. *Mitologias celestes: fontes selecionadas para o ensino fundamental e médio*. Associação Paraíbana de Astronomia, 2015 [Ceiuci]. Koch-Grünberg, Theodor. *Vom Roroima zum Orinoco*. Vol. II. Verlag Strecker und Schröder, 1924, 65 [Kamaliua].

33. Google Maps, www.maps.google.com, *Acará*, accessed Feb. 23, 2023.

34. Koch-Grünberg, Theodor. *Vom Roroima zum Orinoco*. Vol. II. Verlag Strecker und Schröder, 1924, 48-50.

35. Jinks, Roy G., and Sandra C. Krein. *Smith & Wesson*. Arcadia Publishing, 2006, 7-8.

36. Koch-Grünberg, Theodor. *Vom Roroima zum Orinoco*. Vol. II. Verlag Strecker und Schröder, 1924, 149-50.

Chapter VI

1. Dicio: Dicionário Online de Português, https://www.dicio.com.br/francesa, accessed Feb. 24, 2023.

2. Dicio: Dicionário Online de Português, https://www.dicio.com.br/taturana, accessed Feb. 24, 2023.

3. Dicio: Dicionário Online de Português, https://www.dicio.com.br/içás, accessed Feb. 24, 2023.

4. Google Maps, www.maps.google.com, *Campinas*, accessed Feb. 24, 2023.

5. Koch-Grünberg, Theodor. *Vom Roroima zum Orinoco*. Vol. II. Verlag Strecker und Schröder, 1924, 45-46.

6. Dicio: Dicionário Online de Português, https://www.dicio.com.br/membi, accessed Feb. 24, 2023.

7. Dicio: Dicionário Online de Português, https://www.dicio.com.br/campeche, accessed Feb. 24, 2023.

8. Palitot, Estêvão, and Rodrigo de Azeredo Grünewald. *O país da jurema: Revistando as fontes históricas a partir do ritual atikum.* Acervo, Vol. 34, No. 2, May-Aug. 2021.

9. Dicio: Dicionário Online de Português, https://www.dicio.com.br/acaricuara, accessed Feb. 24, 2023. Dicio: Dicionário Online de Português, https://www.dicio.com.br/itaúbas, accessed Feb. 24, 2023.

10. Dicio: Dicionário Online de Português, https://www.dicio.com.br/muirapiranga, accessed Feb.

24, 2023. Google Maps, www.maps.google.com, *Maranhão*, accessed Feb. 24, 2023.

11. Google Maps, www.maps.google.com, *Breves and Belém*, accessed Feb. 24, 2023.

12. Coirolo, Alícia Durán. *Homenagem a Emílio Augusto Goeldi no Centenário do Descobrimento do Sítio Arqueológico do Rio Cunani.* Boletim do Museu Paraense Emílio Goeldi, série Antropologia, Vol. 13, No. 1, 1997 [Rio Cunani]. Dicio: Dicionário Online de Português, https://www.dicio.com.br/tacacá, accessed Feb. 24, 2023. Dicio: Dicionário Online de Português, https://www.dicio.com.br/tucupi, accessed Feb. 24, 2023. Silva, José de Souza. *Aridez mental, problema maior: Contextualizer a educação para construir o 'dia depois do desenvolvimento' no Semi-Árido Brasileiro.* EMBRAPA Algodão, May 2010 [jacarezada].

13. Orellana, Juan Eduardo Morón. *La vid en el Perú y la elaboracion del pisco en Ica. Cultura,* Ciencia y Tecnología, No. 11, Jan.-Jun. 2017 [Puro de Ica]. Google Maps, www.maps.google.com, *Iquitos*, accessed Feb. 24, 2023. Google Maps, www.maps.google.com, *Minas Gerais*, accessed Feb. 24, 2023. Dicio: Dicionário Online de Português, https://www.dicio.com.br/caiçuma, accessed Feb. 24, 2023.

14. Honório, Rosely Marchetti. *Contribuição da História Oral.* IX Encontro Regional Sudeste de História Oral, Diversidade e Diálogo, Universidade de São Paulo, Aug. 2011 [Falchi brothers]. Dicio: Dicionário Online de Português, https://www.dicio.com.br/cumati, accessed Feb. 24, 2023. Moraes, Claide de Paula, and Edithe da Silva Pereira. *A cronologia das pinturas rupestres da Caverna da Pedra Pintada, Monte Alegre, Pará: revisão histórica e novos*

dados. Boletim do Museu Paraense Emílio Goeldi - Ciências Naturais, Vol. 14, No. 2, May-Aug. 2019 [Monte Alegre].

15.   Dicio: Dicionário Online de Português, https://www.dicio.com.br/embira, accessed Feb. 24, 2023.

16.   Dicio: Dicionário Online de Português, https://www.dicio.com.br/grigri, accessed Feb. 24, 2023. Silva, Islana de Oliveira. *Cultura escolar em Santiago do Iguape: ressonâncias, tensões e possibilidades*. Universidade Federal da Bahia, Faculdade de Educação, master's dissertation, 2008 [iguape]. Google Maps, www.maps.google.com, *Rio Gurupi*, accessed Feb. 24, 2023. Google Maps, www.maps.google.com, *Rio das Garças*, accessed Feb. 24, 2023. Dicio: Dicionário Online de Português, https://www.dicio.com.br/itacolumite, accessed Feb. 24, 2023. Dicio: Dicionário Online de Português, https://www.dicio.com.br/tourmalines, accessed Feb. 24, 2023. Miglio, Íris Soriano Nunes. *A saga dos primeiros aventureiros*. Revista do Instituto Histórico e Geográfico do Mucuri, Vol. 1, No. 1, 2010 [Vupabuçu]. Google Maps, www.maps.google.com, *Rio Piriá*, accessed Feb. 24, 2023. Google Maps, www.maps.google.com, *Macaco Creek*, accessed Feb. 24, 2023. Socorro, Orangel Aguilera, and Eduardo Tavares Páes. *A Formação Pirabas do Brasil (Mioceno inferior) e a subprovíncia tropical do Atlântico Noroeste Central*. Boletim do Museu Paraense Emílio Goeldi - Ciências Naturais, Vol. 7, No. 1, Jan.-Apr. 2012 [Pirabas Formation]. Google Maps, www.maps.google.com, *Cametá*, accessed Feb. 24, 2023. Rodrigueiro, Jane. *Tensão e redução na várzea: as relações de contato entre os cocama e Jesuítas na Amazônia do século XVII 1644-1680*. Pontifícia Universidade Católica,

São Paulo, master's dissertation, 2007 [Oaque]. Costa, Angyone. *Migrações e Cultura Indigena: ensaios de arqueologia e etnologia do Brasil.* Brasiliana Biblioteca Pedagogica Brasileira, Series 5, Vol. 139, 1939 [Calamare].

17.   Guilherme, Willian Douglas, and Wenceslau Gonçalves Neto. *Contrato Social de Constituição da Sociedade Anonyma Progresso de Uberabinha: Fundadora do Gymnásio de Uberabinha-MG-1919.* Revista Brasileira de História & Ciências Sociais, Vol. 2, No. 3, 2010 [conto]. Macedo, Limo de. *Amazonia: repositorio alphabetico de termos.* Adolpho Mendonça, Lisbon, 1906, 9 [Lake Jaciuruá].

18.   Dicio: Dicionário Online de Português, https://www.dicio.com.br/caterina, accessed Feb. 24, 2023.

19.   Dicio: Dicionário Online de Português, https://www.dicio.com.br/carnaúba, accessed Feb. 24, 2023.

20.   Koch-Grünberg, Theodor. *Vom Roroima zum Orinoco.* Vol. II. Verlag Strecker und Schröder, 1924, 47-48. Russell, Heaven. *The Tales of Black Children: The Evolution of Self Image and Cultural Value.* University of Chicago, master's thesis, 2022 [Uncle Remus].

21.   Dicio: Dicionário Online de Português, https://www.dicio.com.br/cumacaá, accessed Feb. 24, 2023.

22.   Dicio: Dicionário Online de Português, https://www.dicio.com.br/xaréu, accessed Feb. 24, 2023.

23.   Guedes, Angela Cardoso. *Museu Histórico Nacional.* Comunicação & Educação, Vol. 15, No. 3, Sep.-Dec. 2010 [Ponta do Calabouço]. Google Maps,

www.maps.google.com, *Guajará Mirim*, accessed Feb. 24, 2023.

24.   Google Maps, www.maps.google.com, *Itamaracá*, accessed Feb. 24, 2023. Fernandez, Sonia Inez G. *Do leitor configurado ou um leitura ficcional da obra* Macunaíma *de Mário de Andrade*. Literatura em Debate, Vol. 11, No. 21, Jul.-Dec. 2017 [Dona Sancha].

25.   Google Maps, www.maps.google.com, *Barbacena*, accessed Feb. 24, 2023.

26.   Dicio: Dicionário Online de Português, https://www.dicio.com.br/guzerá, accessed Feb. 24, 2023.

27.   Oliveira, Pedro. *A poesia popular*. NovaÉpoca, https://www.jornalnovaepoca.com/artigo/a-poesia-popular, Apr. 24, 2020, accessed Oct. 1, 2022.

28.   Google Maps, www.maps.google.com, *Paraná*, accessed Feb. 24, 2023.

29.   Dicio: Dicionário Online de Português, https://www.dicio.com.br/cambuí, accessed Feb. 24, 2023. Google Maps, www.maps.google.com, *Serra*, accessed Feb. 24, 2023.

30.   Gusmão, Ana, et al. *Determinação do saldo radiativo na Ilha do Bananal, TO, com imagens orbitais*. Revista Brasileira de Engenharia Agrícola e Ambiental, Vol. 16, No. 10, 2012.

31.   Dicio: Dicionário Online de Português, https://www.dicio.com.br/maripa, accessed Feb. 24, 2023.

32. Dicio: Dicionário Online de Português, https://www.dicio.com.br/jararaca, accessed Feb. 24, 2023.

33. Dicio: Dicionário Online de Português, https://www.dicio.com.br/mororó, accessed Feb. 24, 2023. Koch-Grünberg, Theodor. *Vom Roroima zum Orinoco*. Vol. II. Verlag Strecker und Schröder, 1924, 48.

34. Google Maps, www.maps.google.com, *Maceió and Marajó*, accessed Feb. 24, 2023. Dicio: Dicionário Online de Português, https://www.dicio.com.br/mocororó, accessed Feb. 24, 2023.

Chapter VII

1. Dicio: Dicionário Online de Português, https://www.dicio.com.br/peroba, accessed Feb. 24, 2023.

2. Dicio: Dicionário Online de Português, https://www.dicio.com.br/sapopema, accessed Feb. 24, 2023.

3. Andrade, Mário de. *Macunaíma: O herói sem nenhum caráter*. Edited by Telê Porto Ancona Lopez, CNPq, 1988, 444.

4. Prandi, Reginaldo. *Exu, de mensageiro a diabo: Sincretismo católico e demonização do orixá Exu*. Revista USP, São Paulo, No. 50, Jun.-Aug. 2001 [Exu]. Mendonça, Renato. *A influência africana no português do Brasil*. Fundação Alexandre de Gusmão, Brasília, 2012, 91 ["macumba"]. Prandi, Reginaldo. *Religião e sincretismo em Jorge Amado*. Caderno de leituras: O universo de Jorge Amado, São Paulo: Companhia das letras, 2009 [trance ritual].

5.	Soares, Layza Rocha. *Entrevista com Mãe Meninazinha de Oxum*. Fim do Mundo, No. 4, Jan.-Apr. 2021 [Aunt Ciata]. Dicio: Dicionário Online de Português, https://www.dicio.com.br/zungu, accessed Feb. 24, 2023. Google Maps, www.maps.google.com, *Mangue*, accessed Feb. 24, 2023

6.	Tozi, Desirée Ramos. *A agência política do candomblé: caminhos de mediação entre o terreiro e o estado (2010-2020)*. Universidade Federal da Bahia, Faculdade de Filosofia e Ciências Humanas, doctoral dissertation, 2022 [milonga]. Dicio: Dicionário Online de Português, https://www.dicio.com.br/cabatatu, accessed Feb. 24, 2023. Dicio: Dicionário Online de Português, https://www.dicio.com.br/açacu, accessed Feb. 24, 2023.

7.	Dicio: Dicionário Online de Português, https://www.dicio.com.br/candomblèzeira, accessed Feb. 24, 2023.

8.	Prandi, Reginaldo. *Religião e sincretismo em Jorge Amado*. Caderno de leituras: O universo de Jorge Amado, São Paulo: Companhia das letras, 2009.

9.	Sampaio, Yasmin Estrela, and Edgar Monteiro Chagas, Jr. *"Xirê orixá": a produção do espaço sagrado nas formas musicais e sons de atabaques em um terreiro de Candomblé em Belém do Pará*. Geograficidade, Vol. 8, Spring 2018.

10.	Prandi, Reginaldo. *Religião e sincretismo em Jorge Amado*. Caderno de leituras: O universo de Jorge Amado, São Paulo: Companhia das letras, 2009.

11.	Prandi, Reginaldo. *Religião e sincretismo em Jorge Amado*. Caderno de leituras: O universo de Jorge Amado, São Paulo: Companhia das letras, 2009 [Ogum]. Slenes,

Robert W. *O que Rui Barbosa não Queimou: Novas Fontes para o Estudo da Escravidão no Século XIX*. Estudos Econômicos, Vol. 13, No. 1, Jan.-Apr. 1983 [Rui Barbosa]. Camara, Andréa Albuquerque Adour da. *Africanias na obra de canto e piano de Luciano Gallet*. Brasiliera de Música, Vol. 31, No. 1, Jan.-Jun. 2018 ["Olelê"].

12. Prandi, Reginaldo. *Religião e sincretismo em Jorge Amado*. Caderno de leituras: O universo de Jorge Amado, São Paulo: Companhia das letras, 2009.

13. Carvalho, Leonam Maxney. *Trabalho, tradição e família nas Culturas Jurídico-Penais consuetudinárias de escravos africanos, Minas Gerais,1840-1860*. Temporalidades: Revista de História, Vol. 8, No. 1, Jan.-May 2016.

14. Carrasco, Iván Renato Zúñiga. *Interculturización de la Santería en el México de Hoy*. Revista Destiémpos, Vol 7, No. 36, Jul. 2019 [Yemaya]. Marques, Francisco Cláudio Alves. *Algumas considerães sobre umbanda e Candomblé no Brasil*. Revista Contemplação, Vol. 15, 2017 [Nana Buruku].

15. Prandi, Reginaldo, and Armando Vallado. Xangô, rei de Oió. Prandi, Reginaldo, and Armando Vallado. "Xangô, rei de Oió." *Dos yorùbá ao candomblé Kétu: origens, tradições e continuidade*. São Paulo: EDUSP, 2010, 141-60.

16. Maldonado, Tomaz Mota. *O Diabo na rua, no meio do redemoinho: uma análise do papel diabólico em* Grande Sertão: Veredas. Universidade de Brasília, Faculdade de Comunicação, bachelor's thesis, Jun. 2019.

17. Prandi, Reginaldo. *Religião e sincretismo em Jorge Amado*. Caderno de leituras: O universo de Jorge Amado, São Paulo: Companhia das letras, 2009.

18. Marmontel, Miriam. *Mamíferos aquáticos.* Nascimento, Sociobiodiversidade da Amanã, 2019 [Boto Branco]. Prandi, Reginaldo. *Religião e sincretismo em Jorge Amado.* Caderno de leituras: O universo de Jorge Amado, São Paulo: Companhia das letras, 2009 [Xangô, Omulu, Iroco, Oxóssi, and Obatalá].

19. Cachaça is a spirit distilled from molasses. [Dicio].

20. Farias, João Pedro. *As contribuições dos itan da nação Ketu-Nagô para o ensino formal e o empoderamento das crianças de candomblé.* Opará: Etnicidades, Movimentos Sociais e Educação, Vol. 6, No. 9, 2018.

21. Salum, Marta Heloisa Leuba. *O homem e sua obra, e, os objetos e os homens: da relação homem-matéria.* Revista do Museu de Arqueologia e Etnologia, Suplemento 7, 2008.

22. Paiva, Marilza Maia de Souza de. *Iconicidade lexical na representação musical da língua dos Brasis.* Universidade do Estado do Rio de Janeiro, master's dissertation, 2010 [Bambaquerê]. Wolff, Marcus Straubel. *Elementos não-europeus na brasilidade musical de Mário de Andrade e Camargo Guarnieri.* ANPPOM, Décimo Quinto Congresso, 2005 [Aruê]. Alves-Garbim, Juliana Franco. *Por uma estética da voz: o belo e poético em* histórias que a minha avó contava, *de Mãe Beata de Yemonjá.* Miscelânea: Revista de Literatura e Vida Social, Vol. 21, Jan.-Jun. 2017 [orobô]. Correia, Bruno Celso Vilela, Cristina Larrea Killinger, and Jesús Contreras Hernández. *A alimentação nas festas de candomblé da região da cidade do Recife já não possui o gosto dos orixás.* Revista de Alimentação e Cultura das Américas, Vol. 3, No. 1, Jan.-Jun. 2022 [mungunzá]. Eyn, Pai Cido de Oxum. *Acaçá, onde tudo começou.* Editora Arx, 2002 [acaçá]. De Oliveira, Luiz Henrique Silva. *O negrismo e suas*

configurações em romances brasileiros do século XX (1928-1984). Universidade Federal de Minas Gerais, postgraduate dissertation, 2013 [African speech].

23.   Dicio: Dicionário Online de Português, https://www.dicio.com.br/polaca, accessed Feb. 24, 2023.

24.   Dicio: Dicionário Online de Português, https://www.dicio.com.br/mazomba, accessed Feb. 24, 2023.

25.   Capone, Stefania. *O pai-de-santo e o babalaô: interação religiosa e rearranjos rituais na religião dos orishas*. Revista Pós Ciências Sociais, Vol. 8, No. 16, Jul.-Dec. 2011.

26.   Natalino, Geraldo Jose. *Quem disse que Exu não monta? Abdias Nascimento, o cavalo do santo no terreiro da história*. Pontifícia Universidade Católica de São Paulo, doctoral dissertation, 2019.

27.   Dicio: Dicionário Online de Português, https://www.dicio.com.br/romãozinho, accessed Feb. 24, 2023.

28.   Dicio: Dicionário Online de Português, https://www.dicio.com.br/jongo, accessed Feb. 24, 2023.

29.   Angenot, Jean-Pierre, Catherine Barbara Kempf, and Vatomene Kukanda. Arte da Língua de Angola *de Pedro Dias (1697) sob o prisma da Dialetologia Kimbundu*. Papia, Vol. 21, No. 2, 2011.

30.   Salles-Bento, Oluwa Seyi. *Orixá e Literatura brasileira: a estetização da deusa afro-brasileira Oxum em narrativas de Conceição Evaristo*. Universidade de São Paulo, Departamento de Letras Clássicas e Vernáculas, master's dissertation, 2021.

31.   Dicio: Dicionário Online de Português, https://www.dicio.com.br/uamoti, accessed Feb. 24, 2023.

32.   Brotherston, Gordon, and Lúcia Sá. *Peixes, constelações e Jurupari: a pequena enciclopédia amazônica de Stradelli*. Revista do Museu de Arqueologia e Etnologia, No. 14, 2004.

33.   Fonseca Teixeira, Mariana Pereira da. *A respresentação de Exu em obras de Edison Carneiro*. Z Cultural: Revista do Programa Avançado de Cultura Contemporânea, 2017.

34.   Garcia, Luis Eduardo Veloso. *Candido, santiago e a macumba: possíveis leituras da "dialética da malandragem" e do "entre-lugar do discurso latino-americano" dentro do capítulo "macumba," de* Macunaíma. Revista de Letras, Vol. 15, No. 17, 2013 [Bandeira, Cendrars, Ferreira, Bopp, and Bento]. Santos Coelho, Eduardo dos. *Arqueologia da composição: Manuel Bandeira*. Universidade Federal do Rio de Janeiro, doctoral dissertation, 2009 [Dodô]. Dicio: Dicionário Online de Português, https://www.dicio.com.br/macumbeiro, accessed Feb. 24, 2023.

Chapter VIII

1.   Koch-Grünberg, Theodor. *Vom Roroima zum Orinoco*. Vol. II. Verlag Strecker und Schröder, 1924, 20.

2.   Dicio: Dicionário Online de Português, https://www.dicio.com.br/pitiguari, accessed Feb. 24, 2023.

3.   Dicio: Dicionário Online de Português, https://www.dicio.com.br, accessed Feb. 24, 2023.

4.	Koch-Grünberg, Theodor. *Vom Roroima zum Orinoco*. Vol. II. Verlag Strecker und Schröder, 1924, 34-35.

5.	Google Maps, www.maps.google.com, *Guanabara Bay*, accessed Feb. 24, 2023. Neves, Siméia de Castro Ferreira. *Zarpo Desvairado: A transgressão espaço-temporal em Macunaíma*. Universidade Federal da Paraíba, master's dissertation, 2016 [Ilha de Fernando de Noronha].

6.	Dicio: Dicionário Online de Português, https://www.dicio.com.br/guariroba, accessed Feb. 24, 2023.

7.	Dicio: Dicionário Online de Português, https://www.dicio.com.br/jiquitaia, accessed Feb. 24, 2023.

8.	Koch-Grünberg, Theodor. *Vom Roroima zum Orinoco*. Vol. II. Verlag Strecker und Schröder, 1924, 51.

9.	Google Maps, www.maps.google.com, *Rio Paraná*, accessed Feb. 24, 2023. Dicio: Dicionário Online de Português, https://www.dicio.com.br/guaçu, accessed Feb. 24, 2023.

10.	Saraiva, Gisele Reis Correa, and Tayomara Santos dos Santos. *Joias do Maracanã: Tingimento natural de sementes*. São Paulo: Blucher, 2018.

11.	Dicio: Dicionário Online de Português, https://www.dicio.com.br/urucungo, accessed Feb. 24, 2023.

12.	Paulilo, André Luiz, and José Cláudio Sooma Silva. *Urbanismo e educação na cidade do rio de janeiro dos anos 1920: aproximações*. Revista de Educação Pública, Vol. 21, No. 45, 2012.

13. Paulilo, André Luiz, and José Cláudio Sooma Silva. *Urbanismo e educação na cidade do rio de janeiro dos anos 1920: aproximações*. Revista de Educação Pública, Vol. 21, No. 45, 2012.

14. Google Maps, www.maps.google.com, *Bahia*, accessed Feb. 24, 2023.

15. Dicio: Dicionário Online de Português, https://www.dicio.com.br/cerrado, accessed Feb. 24, 2023.

16. Tovar Silva, Cesar Augusto. "Santo Antônio, herói militar do." *Rio 456 Anos: A Igreja na História*. Edited by Prof. Pe. Josafá Carlos de Siqueira SJ, Pontifícia Universidade Católica do Rio de Janeiro, 2021.

17. Dicio: Dicionário Online de Português, https://www.dicio.com.br/portuguesa, accessed Feb. 24, 2023.

18. Koch-Grünberg, Theodor. *Vom Roroima zum Orinoco*. Vol. II. Verlag Strecker und Schröder, 1924, 51-53.

19. Koch-Grünberg, Theodor. *Vom Roroima zum Orinoco*. Vol. II. Verlag Strecker und Schröder, 1924, 76.

20. Google Maps, www.maps.google.com, *Flamengo*, accessed Feb. 24, 2023.

21. Raleigh, Sir Walter. *The Discoverie of the Large, Rich and Bewtiful Empyre of Guiana*. Edited by Neil L. Whitehead, Manchester University Press, 1997, 5-6.

Chapter IX

1. Sandmann, Marcelo Corrêa. *Frei Luís de Sousa- um clássico romantico*. Revista Letras, No. 51, Jan.-Jun. 1999.

2. Dicio: Dicionário Online de Português, https://www.dicio.com.br/sauria, accessed Feb. 24, 2023. Freud, Sigmund. *Edição standard brasileira das obras psicológicas completas de Sigmund Freud*. Imago Editora, 2021 [Freud].

3. Gonçalves, Ronaldo Pereira. *Ordens religiosas e missões no vice-reino do Peru*. Revista Faz Ciência, Vol. 14, No. 20, 2000 [Viceroyalty of Peru]. Henrique Fontes Cadena, Paulo. *Ou há de ser Cavalcanti, ou há de ser cavalgado: trajetórias políticas dos Cavalcanti de Albuquerque (Pernambuco, 1801-1844)*. Universidade Federal de Pernambuco, master's dissertation, 2011 [Cavalcanti].

4. Fleck, Eliane Cristina Deckmann. *De Apóstolo do Brasil a santo: a consagração póstuma e a construção de uma memória sobre o padre jesuíta José de Anchieta (1534-1597)*. Locus: Revista de História, Vol. 21, No. 2, 2015.

5. Reglero, Elisa Ramiro. *La porcelana del siglo XVIII. El nacimiento de un nuevo arte*. Ge-conservacion, No. 8, 2015 [Sêvres]. Dicio: Dicionário Online de Português, https://www.dicio.com.br/trireme, accessed Feb. 24, 2023.

6. Valle, Fernando Keller do. *Sandman: o mito literário de Morfeu nas obras de Hoffmann, Andersen e Gaiman*. Universidade Federal de Santa Catarina, Programa de Pós-Graduação em Literatura, master's dissertation, 2016.

7. Silva, Filipe N., and Pedro Paulo A. Funari. *Adriano e masculinidade*. Revista Veredas da História, Vol. 10, No. 1, 2017.

8. Morais Soutelo, Raquel de. *As interpretações de Marte em Conimbriga*. Plêthos: Revista Discente de Estudos sobre a Antiguidade e o Medievo, 2012 [Mars]. Martins, Paulo. *Augusto como Mercúrio enfim*. Revista de História (São Paulo), No. 176, 2017 [Mercury].

9. Oliveira, Lucia Lippi. *Bandeirantes e pioneiros: as fronteiras no Brasil e Estado Unidos*. Revista Novos Estudos, No. 37, 1993.

10. Trindade, Luísa. *Corpo e água: os banhos públicos em Portugal na Idade Média*. digitAR: Revista Digital de Arqueologia, Arquitectura e Artes, No. 2, 2015.

11. Dicio: Dicionário Online de Português, https://www.dicio.com.br/mineiro, accessed Feb. 24, 2023.

12. Dicio: Dicionário Online de Português, https://www.dicio.com.br/bonde, accessed Feb. 24, 2023.

13. Rouchou, Joëlle. *Álvaro Moreyra: um arquivo delicado*. Juiz de Fora, Vol. 11, No. 19, Jan.-Jul. 2011.

14. Rebollo, Tomas André. *Urbanismo e mobilidade na metropóle paulistana: estudo de caso o Parque Dom Pedro II*. Universidade de São Paulo, Faculdade de Arquitetura e Urbanismo, master's dissertation, 2012 [Parque Dom Pedro]. Minoda, Thais Klarge. *Artefatos no Jardim da Luz: usos e funções sociais (1870-1930)*. Universidade de

São Paulo, Faculdade de Filosofia, Letras e Ciências Humanas, master's dissertation, 2017 [Jardim da Luz].

15.   Lobo, Luiza. *Juana Manso: uma exilada em três pátrias*. Revista Gênero, Vol. 9, No. 2, 2009. Dicio: Dicionário Online de Português, https://www.dicio.com.br/mazorqueiro, accessed Feb. 24, 2023.

16.   Dicio: Dicionário Online de Português, https://www.dicio.com.br/paraibano, accessed Feb. 24, 2023. Dicio: Dicionário Online de Português, https://www.dicio.com.br/biga, accessed Feb. 24, 2023. Dicio: Dicionário Online de Português, https://www.dicio.com.br/quadriga, accessed Feb. 24, 2023.

17.   Ibañez, Nelson, Fan Hui Wen, and Suzana CG Femandes. *Instituto Butantan: História Institucional-Desenho metodológico para uma periodização preliminar*. Cadernos de História da Ciência, Vol. 1, 2005.

18.   Lago, Luiz Aranha Corrêa do. *A moeda metálica em perspectiva histórica: notas em torno de uma exposição*. Pontifícia Universidade Católica do Rio de Janeiro, Departamento de Economia, Jan. 2004.

19.   Klemenc, Alexandre. *Expografia em palácios de governo: um estudo sobre o acervo artístico-cultural dos palácios do governo do estado de São Paulo*. Universidade de São Paulo, Museu de Arqueologia e Etnologia, master's dissertation, 2016 [Palácio do Governo]. Adams, W.H. Davenport. *Queen of the Adriatic; or, Venice Past and Present*. T. Nelson and Sons, London, 1869 [Venice].

20.   Silva, Irene Izilda da, and Marcio Jean Fialho de Sousa. *Novos caminhos e novos olhares para o ensino de literaturas africanas de língua portuguesa no ensino regular.* Ribanceira: Revista do Curso de Letras da UEPA, Vol. 1, No. 4, Jul.-Dec. 2015 [Linnaeus]. Trevizam, Matheus. *A eneida portuguesa de João Franco Barreto: Tributária de Camões e Virgílio.* PHAOS: Revista de Estudos Classicos, Vol. 7, 2007 [Virgil and Camões].

21.   Toro y Gisbert, Miguel de. *Pequeño Larousse Ilustrado.* Librería Larousse, Paris, 1912.

22.   Silva, Márcia Moura da. *Análise de termos indígenas nas traduções hispano-americana, inglesa e italiana de* Macunaíma*: estratégias de tradução do ponto de vista cultural.* Universidade Federal de Santa Catarina, Estudos da Tradução, doctoral dissertation, 2013.

23.   Dicio: Dicionário Online de Português, https://www.dicio.com.br/polonesa, accessed Feb. 24, 2023.

Chapter X

1.   Bilitário, Bruno Freitas. *"A imundícia tá de calcinha": linchamento de travesti Dandara na periferia de Fortaleza-CE, Brasil.* Opará: Etnicidades, Movimentos Sociais e Educação, Vol. 8, 2020 [Antônio Tamandaré]. Mostaço, Edélcio. *Agruras da Inconstância.* Revista Brasileira de Estudos da Presença, Vol. 9, No. 2, 2019 ["Mother of God"].

2.   Silva, Isabelle Braz Peixoto da. *A santidade de Jaguaripe: catolicismo popular ou religião indígena?.* Revista de Ciências Sociais, Vol. 26, No. 1/2, 1995.

3.	Scherer, Bruno Cortês. *Ações Sociais do Espiritismo: A Sociedade Espírita Feminina Estudo e Caridade, Santa Maria–RS (1932-1957)*. Universidade Federal de Santa Maria, bachelor's thesis, 2013.

4.	Maurity, Clóvis, et al. *Estudo das cavernas da província espeleológica arenítica de monte alegre - PA*. Cadernos de Geociências, No. 15, 1995.

5.	Google Maps, www.maps.google.com, São Bernardo, accessed Feb. 24, 2023. Braghittoni, Nelson Leopoldo. *Dialogo rua/cidade: o caso da Rua Direita em São Paulo (1765-1977)*. Universidade de São Paulo, doctoral dissertation, 2015 [Rua Direita]. Costa, Regina Barbosa da. *Terra papagalli e a nova história cultural*. Revista Talares, Vol. 5, Nov. 2019 [Master Cosme]. Google Maps, www.maps.google.com, Cananéia, accessed Feb. 24, 2023.

6.	Koch-Grünberg, Theodor. *Vom Roroima zum Orinoco*. Vol. II. Verlag Strecker und Schröder, 1924, 77-78.

7.	Google Maps, www.maps.google.com, *Mooca*, accessed Feb. 24, 2023. Leonardi, Paula. *Associações católicas como instâncias socializadoras e de controle do tempo: o caso do Liceu e do Santuário Sagrado Coração de Jesus*. Pro-Posições, Vol. 28, No. 3, Sep.-Dec. 2017 [Coração de Jesus]. Google Maps, www.maps.google.com, *Avenida Rangel Pestana*, accessed Feb. 24, 2023. Segawa, Hugo M. *Prelúdio da metrópole: arquitetura e urbanismo em São Paulo na passagem do século XIX ao XX*. Atelie Editorial, 2000 [Rua Quinze]. Simioni, Rafel Lazzarotto. *Chiasms of Power: Art, Law and Politics in the Coronation of Dom Pedro II by Manuel de Araújo Porto-Alegre*. Anamorphosis: Revista

Internacional de Direito e Literatura, Vol. 7, No. 2, Jul.-Dec. 2021 [Iparanga].

8.	Dicio: Dicionário Online de Português, https://www.dicio.com.br/tucumã, accessed Feb. 24, 2023.

9.	Fritzen, Vanessa. *Mitos indígenas em* Macunaíma*, de Mário de Andrade.* e-scrita: Revista do Curso de Letras da UNIABEU, Vol. 4, No. 3, May-Aug. 2013.

10.	Albuquerque, João. *Decolonizing Brazil: Minor Heroism in Mário de Andrade's* Macunaíma. Brasil/Brazil, Vol. 35, No. 68, 2022.

11.	Almeida Nascimento, Naira de. *As metamorfoses de Macunaíma e o perspectivismo ame-ríndio.* América Crítica, Vol. 6, No. 1, 2022.

12.	Dicio: Dicionário Online de Português, https://www.dicio.com.br/fulano, accessed Feb. 24, 2023.

13.	None. My research didn't uncover Andrade's inspiration for this character; he seems to first appear in *Macunaíma*.

14.	Koch-Grünberg, Theodor. *Vom Roroima zum Orinoco.* Vol. II. Verlag Strecker und Schröder, 1924, 13.

15.	Dicio: Dicionário Online de Português, https://www.dicio.com.br/paracuuba, accessed Feb. 24, 2023.

16.	Dicio: Dicionário Online de Português, https://www.dicio.com.br/carapicu, accessed Feb. 24, 2023.

17.	Junqueira, Carmen. *Pajés e feiticeiros.* Estudos Avançados, Vol 18, No. 52, 2004.

18. Koch-Grünberg, Theodor. *Vom Roroima zum Orinoco*. Vol. II. Verlag Strecker und Schröder, 1924, 63.

19. Koch-Grünberg, Theodor. *Vom Roroima zum Orinoco*. Vol. II. Verlag Strecker und Schröder, 1924, 63.

20. Koch-Grünberg, Theodor. *Vom Roroima zum Orinoco*. Vol. II. Verlag Strecker und Schröder, 1924, 62-63.

21. Cury, Maria Zilda Ferreira. *Arte e criação em Macunaíma*. Ensaios de Semiótica, No. 6, 1981.

Chapter XI

1. Dicio: Dicionário Online de Português, https://www.dicio.com.br/cruviana, accessed Feb. 24, 2023.

2. Dalben, André. *Notas sobre a cidade de São Paulo e a natureza de seus parques urbanos*. Urbana: Revista Eletrônica do Centro Interdisciplinar de Estudos sobre a Cidade, Vol. 8, No. 2, 2016.

3. Google Maps, www.maps.google.com, *Arouche*, accessed Feb. 24, 2023.

4. Dicio: Dicionário Online de Português, https://www.dicio.com.br/ganzá, accessed Feb. 24, 2023.

5. Soave, Guillermo E., et al. *Dieta del Pirincho (Guira guira) en el nordeste de la provincia de Buenos Aires, Argentina (Cuculiformes: Cuculidae)*. Revista de Biología Tropical, Vol. 56, No. 4, 2008 [guira]. Dicio: Dicionário Online de Português, https://www.dicio.com.br/maquira.

6. Dicio: Dicionário Online de Português, https://www.dicio.com.br/parica, accessed Feb. 24, 2023.

7. Koch-Grünberg, Theodor. *Vom Roroima zum Orinoco*. Vol. II. Verlag Strecker und Schröder, 1924, 149-51.

8. Google Maps, www.maps.google.com, *Rua Libero*, accessed Feb. 24, 2023.

9. Dicio: Dicionário Online de Português, https://www.dicio.com.br/chuvisco, accessed Feb. 24, 2023.

10. Dicio: Dicionário Online de Português, https://www.dicio.com.br/mandaguari, accessed Feb. 24, 2023. Dicio: Dicionário Online de Português, https://www.dicio.com.br/aimará, accessed Feb. 24, 2023.

11. Dicio: Dicionário Online de Português, https://www.dicio.com.br/lambari, accessed Feb. 24, 2023.

12. Okumura, Mercedes, and Astolfo GM Araujo. *Desconstruindo o que nunca foi construído: Pontas bifaciais 'Umbu' do Sul e Sudeste do Brasil*. Revista do Museu de Arqueologia e Etnologia, Vol. 20, 2015.

13. Dicio: Dicionário Online de Português, https://www.dicio.com.br, accessed Feb. 24, 2023.

14. Barros, Candida, and Ruth Maria Monserrat. *Fontes manuscritas sobre a língua geral da amazônia escritas por jesuítas "Tapuitinga"(século XVIII)*. Confluência, No. 49, 2015.

15. Koch-Grünberg, Theodor. *Vom Roroima zum Orinoco*. Vol. II. Verlag Strecker und Schröder, 1924, 40-42.

16. Carvalho, Paulo Ernaini Ramalho. *Guapuruvu*. Circular Técnica: 104, Embrapa, Dec. 2005.

17. Garcia, Giovanni. *Formiga de Novato em São Paulo*. Insetologia, https://www.insetologia.com.br/2019/01/formiga-de-novato-em-sao-paulo.html, visited Oct. 29, 2022.

18. Trevisan, Ricardo. *Introdução ao ideário cidade-jardim no Brasil*. Arquitetura, Estética e Urbanismo: questões da modernidade, Jan. 2014.

19. Duarte, Durango. *Manaus: entre o passado e o presente*. Vol. 1. Mídia Ponto Comm, 2009.

20. Haag, Carlos. *O sonho do Eldorado amazônico: A arqueologia brasileira e a eterna busca por civilizações ocultas na Floresta Amazônica*. Revista Pesquisa, No. 160, Jun. 2009.

21. Google Maps, www.maps.google.com, *Paraná*, accessed Feb. 24, 2023.

22. Google Maps, www.maps.google.com, *Ceará*, accessed Feb. 24, 2023. Google Maps, www.maps.google.com, *Aratanha*, accessed Feb. 24, 2023. Google Maps, www.maps.google.com, *Rio Grande do Norte*, accessed Feb. 24, 2023. Neto, Silvana Fernandes, et al. *Conflito de uso da terra - microbacia hidrográfica serrote do Cabelo não-tem*. Revista Educação Agrícola Superior, Vol. 23, No. 1, 2008 [Cabelo-não-Tem].

23. Google Maps, www.maps.google.com, *Paraíba*, accessed Feb. 24, 2023. Google Maps, www.maps.google.com, *Mamanguape and Bacamarte*,

accessed Feb. 24, 2023. Pedra Lavrada is a town in Paraíba, and home to the Pedra de Retumba (or "Retumba Rock"). Oliviera, Dennis, et al. *Salvamento arqueológico da pedra de retumba: A evidenciação de uma lenda.* Clio Arqueológica, Vol. 35, No. 1, 2020 [Pedra Lavrada].

24. Google Maps, www.maps.google.com, *Barras and Poti*, accessed Feb. 24, 2023. Google Maps, www.maps.google.com, *Pajeú*, accessed Feb. 24, 2023. Google Maps, www.maps.google.com, *Inhamum*, accessed Feb. 24, 2023.

25. Dicio: Dicionário Online de Português, https://www.dicio.com.br/surucucu, accessed Feb. 24, 2023.

26. Petri, Setembrino, and Vincente Jose Fulfaro. *Geologia da Chapada dos Parecis, Mato Grosso, Brasil.* Revista Brasileirade Oeocunctas, Vol. 11, No. 4, 1981 [Parecis Plateau]. Natal is a large city on the Atlantic coast, and is the capital of the state of Rio Grande do Norte. [GoogleMaps]. Nogueira, Ismael David, and Armando Honorio da Silva. *Termos e expressões do coloquial do cotidiano da zona rural no Brasil central no século XX.* Goiânia: Gráfica UFG, 2017 [Camutengo].

27. Gandara, Gercinair Silvério. *Rios nossos que estão no sertão! São Francisco e Parnaíba.* Revista franco-brasilera de geografia, No. 23, 2015.

28. Dicio: Dicionário Online de Português, https://www.dicio.com.br/catingueira, accessed Feb. 24, 2023.

29.   Sampaio, Theodoro. *O rio de S. Francisco: trechos de um diario de viagem*. Escolas Profissionais Salesianas, 1905, 14.

30.   Google Maps, www.maps.google.com, *Rio Chuí*, accessed Feb. 24, 2023. Dicio: Dicionário Online de Português, https://www.dicio.com.br/jabiru, accessed Feb. 24, 2023.

31.   Santos, Gisele Barbosa dos, et al. *Gleissolo em ambiente de vereda no chapadão do Urucuia, oeste da Bahia*. Georgraphia Meridionalis, Vol. 4, No. 1, Jan.-Jun. 2018 [Urucuia Plateau]. Google Maps, www.maps.google.com, *Rio Itapecerica*, accessed Feb. 24, 2023.

32.   Mossoró is a town on the Atlantic coast in Brazil's north, and is near the vast dunes at the estuary of the Rio Apodi-Mossoró. da Rocha, Alexsandra Bezerra, et al. *Geoambientes, uso e ocupação do espaço no estuário do Rio Apodi-Mossoró, Rio Grande do Norte, nordeste do Brasil*. Revista Eletrônica do Prodema, Vol. 7, No. 2, Nov. 2011. Visoni, Rodrigo Moura, and Jão Batista Garcia Canalle. *Bartolomeu Lourenço de Gusmão: o primeiro cientista brasileiro*. Revista Brasileira de Ensino de Física, Vol. 31, No. 3, 2009 [Fr. Gusmão].

33.   Google Maps, www.maps.google.com, *Santana do Livramento*, accessed Feb. 24, 2023. Johnson, Kofi, et al. *O Monoteísmo na Religião Tradicional Yorùbá*. Thinking About Religion, Vol. 3, 2004 [Telhado do Mundo]. Villavicencio, Lourdes Milagros Mendoza, et al. *Google Earth Engine: Mapeamento das Mudanças na Cordilheira Vilcanota-Peru*. Anuário do Instituto de Geociências, Vol. 41, 2018 [Vilcanota].

34.   Google Maps, www.maps.google.com, *Amargosa*, accessed Feb. 24, 2023. Google Maps,

www.maps.google.com, *Gurupá and Gurupi*, accessed Feb. 24, 2023.

Chapter XII

1. Couceiro, Sylvia Costa. *Médicos e charlatões: conflitos e convivências em torno do "poder de cura" no Recife dos anos 1920*. Mneme-Revista Virtual de Humanidades, Vol. 5, No. 10, Apr.-Jun. 2004.

2. Pizzolato, Pier Paolo Bertuzzi. *Questões sobre o plano diretor para o complexo hospitalar do Juquery*. Cadernos de História da Ciência, Vol. 6, No. 1, Jan.-Jul. 2010.

3. Silva Martins, Vicente de Paula da. "Hipóteses psicolinguísticas acerca do processamento fraseológico por falantes do português como segunda língua." *Fraseologia, texto e discurso em diferentes abordagens linguísticas*. Pedro & João, 2020.

4. Cavalcanti, Paulo. *Eça de Queiroz: agitador no Brasil*. Companhia Editora de Pernambuco, 2015.

5. Dicio: Dicionário Online de Português, https://www.dicio.com.br/sucupira, accessed Feb. 24, 2023. Dicio: Dicionário Online de Português, https://www.dicio.com.br/parinari, accessed Feb. 24, 2023. Dicio: Dicionário Online de Português, https://www.dicio.com.br/guaruba, accessed Feb. 24, 2023.

6. Koch-Grünberg, Theodor. *Vom Roroima zum Orinoco*. Vol. II. Verlag Strecker und Schröder, 1924, 140-49.

7. Costa, Ricardo Felipe Santos da. *A cidade, o progresso e o espelho quebrado de Narciso: São Paulo entre a*

compaixão e o amor de si próprio (1890 a 1927). Resgate: Revista Interdisciplinar de Cultura, Vol. 27, No. 1, 2019.

8.   Mendonça, Andreza P., and Isolde Dorothea Kossmann Ferraz. *Óleo de andiroba: processo tradicional da extração, uso e aspectos sociais no estado do Amazonas, Brasil*. Acta Amazonica, Vol. 37, No. 3, 2007.

9.   Lessa, Ana Luisa Dubra. *Edição da correspondência Mário de Andrade & Ascenso Ferreira e Stella Griz Ferreira - 1926-1944*. Universidade de São Paulo, Instituto de Estudos Brasileiros, master's dissertation, 2012.

10. Dórea, Tainã Antunes, and Fausto Henrique Nogueira. *A presença do negro no urbanismo paulistano*. REGRASP - Revista para Graduandos/IFSP-Câmpus São Paulo, Vol. 4, No. 1, 2019.

11. Silva e Silva, Bruna Kathlen da. *Avifauna da escola normal superior - ENS/UEA e do mini campus da UFAM em Manaus, Amazonas*. Universidade do Estado do Amazonas, Escola Normal Superior, 2021.

12. Liviz, Clever do Amaral Mafessoni, et al. "Frutos de babaçu: um referencial teórico sobre sua composição química e aplicações nos alimentos." *Tópicos em ciências dos alimentos*, edited by Wesclen Vilar Nogueira, Pantanal Editora, Vol. 3, 2021.

13. Giovenardi, Eugênio. *As pedras de Roma*. Mais Que Nada Administração Cultural, 2009.

14. Koch-Grünberg, Theodor. *Vom Roroima zum Orinoco*. Vol. II. Verlag Strecker und Schröder, 1924, 140-49.

15. Vieira, Rosemary Silva. *Efeito da fragmentação florestal sobre borboletas (lepidoptera, hesperiidae) associadas à formiga-de-correição* Eciton burchelli *(hymenoptera, formicidae,*

ecitoninae). Universidade Federal de São Carlos, Centro de Ciências Biológicas e da Saúde, 2004 [murupetecas]. Rodrigues, Carlos Eduardo, and Christian Fausto Moraes Santos. *A praga em migalhas: a classificação dos insetos no tratado descrivito do Brasil (1587)*. Anais do IV Fórum de Pesquisa e Pós-Graduação em História, 2008 [guajuguaju].

16.   Dicio: Dicionário Online de Português, https://www.dicio.com.br/chalet, accessed Feb. 24, 2023.

Chapter XIII

1.   Souza, Cacilda da Silva. *Infecções de tecidos moles: erisipela, celulite, síndromes infecciosas mediadas por toxinas.* Medicina (Ribeirão Preto), Vol. 36, 2003.

2.   Fidelis, Thiago. *Rumo aos Campos Elísios: as eleições de 1954 pelas páginas do Estado de São Paulo*. XXVII Simpósio Nacional de História, 2013.

3.   Narciso, Isabella G., et al. "O resgate do pedestre na apropriação do Vale do Anhangabaú." *XII Seminario Internacional de Investigación en Urbanismo, São Paulo-Lisboa, 2020*. Faculdade de Arquitetura da Universidade de Lisboa, 2020.

4.   Lopes, Fanny. *Dois Monumentos a Carlos Gomes na Primeira República*. Encontro de História da Arte, Vol. 14, 2019.

5.   Dicio: Dicionário Online de Português, https://www.dicio.com.br/vigilenga, accessed Feb. 24, 2023.

6. Dicio: Dicionário Online de Português, https://www.dicio.com.br/gaiola, accessed Feb. 24, 2023.

7. Dicio: Dicionário Online de Português, https://www.dicio.com.br/vaticano, accessed Feb. 24, 2023.

8. Dicio: Dicionário Online de Português, https://www.dicio.com.br/cururu, accessed Feb. 24, 2023.

9. Kothe, Mercedes Gassen. *Organizações ligadas à emigração alemã para o Brasil*. Revista de História, UnB. Brasília, 1993 [Lloyd and Hamburg]. Guilherme, Regina Zimmermann. *A cidade de pedra: Leone Lonardi e os marmoristas italianos em Porto Alegre*. Porto Alegre, EDIPUCRS, 2021 [Conte Verde].

10. A marimbondo is a generic name for several species of wasp. [Dicio]. A cabas is another generic name for social wasps. [Dicio]. A potó is a kind of flying stinging insect. [Dicio].

11. Fausto, Carlos. *Donos demais: maestra e domínio na amazônia*. Mana, Vol. 42, No. 2, 2008.

12. Andrade, Mario de. *Macunaíma: o hero sem nenhum caráter*. Edited by Luís Augusto Fischer, L&PM Pocket, 2017.

13. Dicio: Dicionário Online de Português, https://www.dicio.com.br/caboclo, accessed Feb. 24, 2023. Google Maps, www.maps.google.com, *Taubaté*, accessed Feb. 24, 2023. Dicio: Dicionário Online de Português, https://www.dicio.com.br/pangaré, accessed Feb. 24, 2023.

14. Dicio: Dicionário Online de Português, https://www.dicio.com.br/pitomba, accessed Feb. 24, 2023.

15. Proença, Manuel Cavalcanti. *Roteiro de Macunaíma*. Civilização Brasileira, 1974.

16. Dicio: Dicionário Online de Português, https://www.dicio.com.br/butiá, accessed Feb. 24, 2023.

17. Dicio: Dicionário Online de Português, https://www.dicio.com.br/paca, accessed Feb. 24, 2023.

18. Marques, Rodrigo de Albuquerque. *Os verdes mares bravios do Turista aprendiz*. Aletria, Belo Horizonte, Vol. 31, No. 3, 2021.

Chapter XIV

1. Dicio: Dicionário Online de Português, https://www.dicio.com.br/curió, accessed Feb. 24, 2023.

2. Koch-Grünberg, Theodor. *Vom Roroima zum Orinoco*. Vol. II. Verlag Strecker und Schröder, 1924, 62.

3. Dicio: Dicionário Online de Português, https://www.dicio.com.br/tatajuba, accessed Feb. 24, 2023.

4. Dicio: Dicionário Online de Português, https://www.dicio.com.br/igarité, accessed Feb. 24, 2023.

5. Carvalho, Victor Campos Mamede de. *Por que se diz 'fábula' e Sobre os diversos nomes dos deuses:tradução de duas narrativas programáticas do Segundo Mitógrafo do Vaticano*. A

Palo Seco - Escritos em Filosofia e Literatura, Vol. 11, No. 12, 2019.

6.   Biron, Berty. *Frei Antônio do Rosário (1647-1704)*. Convergência Lusíada, No. 28, Jul.-Dec. 2012. Dicio: Dicionário Online de Português, https://www.dicio.com.br/tauari, accessed Feb. 24, 2023.

7.   Skutch, Alexander F. *Life history of the Little Tinamou*. The Condor, Vol. 65, No. 3, 1963.

8.   Koch-Grünberg, Theodor. *Vom Roroima zum Orinoco*. Vol. II. Verlag Strecker und Schröder, 1924, 93.

9.   Koch-Grünberg, Theodor. *Vom Roroima zum Orinoco*. Vol. II. Verlag Strecker und Schröder, 1924, 132. Dicio: Dicionário Online de Português, https://www.dicio.com.br/traíra, accessed Feb. 24, 2023.

10.   Tomàs, Estanislau. *The Catalan process for the direct production of malleable iron and its spread to Europe and the Americas*. Contributions to Science, Vol. 1, No. 2, 2000.

11.   Moreira, Carlos Alberto Castro. *Seleção de Habitat Pelo Noitibó-de-Nuca-Vermelha (Caprimulgus Ruficollis) Numa Região do Sul de Portugal*. Universidade de Evora (Portugal), master's dissertation, 2012.

12.   Google Maps, www.maps.google.com, *Boipeda*, accessed Feb. 24, 2023. Andrade, Mario de. *Obra Escogida*. Edited by Laura de Campos Vergueiro, Biblioteca Ayacucho, 1979, 139 [Cuisarruim].

13.   "Systematisação das Lendas Potyguares." *O Estado do Paraná*. Anno II, No. 563, Nov. 4, 1926, 6.

14. Google Maps, www.maps.google.com, *Santos*, accessed Feb. 24, 2023.

15. Koch-Grünberg, Theodor. *Vom Roroima zum Orinoco*. Vol. II. Verlag Strecker und Schröder, 1924, 132-34.

16. Dicio: Dicionário Online de Português, https://www.dicio.com.br/acapu, accessed Feb. 24, 2023. Andreeva, Yana. *A Manaus dos imigrantes na ficção de Milton Hatoum*. Études Romanes de Brno, Vol. 37, 2016 [Manaus]. Dicio: Dicionário Online de Português, https://www.dicio.com.br/japecanga, accessed Feb. 24, 2023.

17. Koch-Grünberg, Theodor. *Vom Roroima zum Orinoco*. Vol. II. Verlag Strecker und Schröder, 1924, 78-81.

Chapter XV

1. Google Maps, www.maps.google.com, *Pico do Jaraguá*, accessed Feb. 24, 2023.

2. Brunner, Gisbert. *History: Patek Philippe*. WatchTime Spotlight, 2009.

3. Google Maps, www.maps.google.com, *Goiás*, accessed Feb. 24, 2023.

4. Dicio: Dicionário Online de Português, https://www.dicio.com.br/ipueira, accessed Feb. 24, 2023.

5. Dicio: Dicionário Online de Português, https://www.dicio.com.br/antianti, accessed Feb. 24, 2023. Dicio: Dicionário Online de Português, https://www.dicio.com.br/pirá, accessed Feb. 24, 2023.

Dicio: Dicionário Online de Português, https://www.dicio.com.br/ariramba, accessed Feb. 24, 2023.

6. Dicio: Dicionário Online de Português, https://www.dicio.com.br/bromelia, accessed Feb. 24, 2023. Dicio: Dicionário Online de Português, https://www.dicio.com.br/embolada, accessed Feb. 24, 2023.

7. Dicio: Dicionário Online de Português, https://www.dicio.com.br/caburé, accessed Feb. 24, 2023. Dicio: Dicionário Online de Português, https://www.dicio.com.br/paçoca, accessed Feb. 24, 2023. Dicio: Dicionário Online de Português, https://www.dicio.com.br/arapaçu, accessed Feb. 24, 2023.

8. Souza, Gilda de Mello de. *O Avô Presente.* Discurso, Vol. 11, 1979.

9. Dicio: Dicionário Online de Português, https://www.dicio.com.br, accessed Feb. 24, 2023.

10. Muraoka, Tânia Rumi. *Tráfico de fauna silvestre pelos correios no Brasil: uma análise quantitativa e qualitativa.* Universidade Federal de Santa Catarina, Centro de Ciências Biológicas, master's dissertation, 2019.

11. Dicio: Dicionário Online de Português, https://www.dicio.com.br/Marion, accessed Feb. 24, 2023. Dicio: Dicionário Online de Português, https://www.dicio.com.br/piun, accessed Feb. 24, 2023. Dicio: Dicionário Online de Português, https://www.dicio.com.br/muriçoca, accessed Feb. 24, 2023.

12.   Freitas Santos, Aline de, et al. *A (des)construção da cultura Brasileira e sua ressignificação na tradução de* Casa Grande e Senzala *(1933) e* Macunaíma *(1978): vias para a decolonialidade na América Latina*. Revista Entreletras (Araguaína), Vol. 12, No. 3, Sep.-Dec. 2021 [Jucurutu do Solimões]. Melatti, Julio Cezar. *Notas para um história dos brancos no Solimões*. Rio de Janeiro: Paz e Terra, 1974 [Solimões].

13.   Albuquerque, Severino João. *Construction and Destruction in* Macunaíma. Hispania, Vol. 70, No. 1, Mar. 1987.

14.   Velden, Felipe Ferreira Vander. *Realidade, ciência e fantasia nas controvérsias sobre o Mapinguari no sudoeste amazônico*. Boletim do Museu Paraense Emílio Goeldi. Ciências Humanas, Vol. 11, No. 1, Jan.-Apr. 2016.

15.   Andrade, Mário de, *Macunaíma: O Herói sem nenhum Caráter*, edited by Noemi Jaffe, FTD, 2016, 161.

16.   Dicio: Dicionário Online de Português, https://www.dicio.com.br/cumaru, accessed Feb. 24, 2023.

17.   Martins, Daiana Bragueto. *As Representações do Mito do Minhocão: uma análise das narrativas orais pantaneiras*. Revista Eletrônica História em Reflexão, Vol. 1, No. 2, 2007 [Minhocão]. Barbosa, Roberta Tiburcio. *Brincando com as Palavras: Construção da Identidade Brasileira em Macunaíma*. Revista Interfaces, Vol. 13, No. 1 2022 [Oibê].

18.   Oliveira, Felipe Souza Leão de. *As cronotopias natalenses: Tempo e Espaço nas imagens de Natal na crônica de Luís da Câmara Cascudo da década de 1910*. V Encontro Estadual de História, 2012, Caicó. Anais Eletrônicos.

Natal: EDUFRN, 2012 [Morro do Estrondo]. Google Maps, www.maps.google.com, *Sergipe*, accessed Feb. 24, 2023.

19.   Castro, Janio Roque Barros de. *Os elementos da natureza e as dimensões sagradas e míticas das grutas e do morro da cidade-Santuário de Bom Jesus da Lapa*. Anais Dos Simpósios Da ABHR, Vol. 13, 2012.

20.   Florence, Arnaldo Machado. *Hercules Florence-O Pioneiro Da Fotografia-A Descoberta Da Fotografia No Brasil Em 1832*. Foto-Cine Clube Bandeirante, Boletim Vol. 3, No. 28, Aug. 1948.

21.   de Aquino, Patricia. *Corpo fechado: Frontières des corps afro-brésiliens (capoeira et candomblé)*. Sigila, No. 34, Feb. 2014.

22.   Google Maps, www.maps.google.com, *Santo Antônio*, accessed Feb. 24, 2023.

23.   Castro, Yêda de. *Notícia de uma pesquisa em África*. Afro-Ásia, Vol. 1, 1965 [Carrapatu]. Google Maps, www.maps.google.com, *Iporanga*, accessed Feb. 24, 2023.

24.   Melo, Érico. *As estrelas estando: astronomia cenográfica em* Corpo de baile. Aletria, Vol. 25, No. 1, 2015.

Chapter XVI

1.   Dicio: Dicionário Online de Português, https://www.dicio.com.br/monguba, accessed Feb. 24, 2023.

2.   Vieira, Jaci Guilherme, and Gregorio F. Gomes Filho. *Forte São Joaquim: de marco da ocupação Portuguesa do vale do Rio Branco às batalhas da memória - século XVIII ao XX*. Textos e Debates, No. 28, Jul.-Dec. 2015.

3. Toledo, Roberto Pompeu de. *Conheça a história de João Ramalho e Tibiriçá: Português tomou como esposa uma filha do cacique e formou-se entre eles uma aliança de sangue.* Veja São Paulo, Oct. 2010.

4. Dicio: Dicionário Online de Português, https://www.dicio.com.br/montaria, accessed Feb. 24, 2023. Google Maps, www.maps.google.com, *Marapatá Island*, accessed Feb. 24, 2023.

5. Dicio: Dicionário Online de Português, https://www.dicio.com.br/jaraquis, accessed Feb. 24, 2023.

6. Google Maps, www.maps.google.com, *Óbidos*, accessed Feb. 24, 2023.

7. Dicio: Dicionário Online de Português, https://www.dicio.com.br, accessed Feb. 24, 2023.

8. Dicio: Dicionário Online de Português, https://www.dicio.com.br, accessed Feb. 24, 2023.

9. Koch-Grünberg, Theodor. *Vom Roroima zum Orinoco.* Vol. II. Verlag Strecker und Schröder, 1924, 92-98.

10. None. My research didn't uncover Andrade's inspiration for this character; he seems to first appear in *Macunaíma*.

11. Dicio: Dicionário Online de Português, https://www.dicio.com.br/peccary, accessed Feb. 24, 2023. Tortato, Marcos A., and T. G. Oliveira. *Ecology of the oncilla (Leopardus tigrinus) at Serra do Tabuleiro State Park, Southern Brazil.* Cat News, Vol 42, Spring 2005 [oncilla].

12.	Dicio: Dicionário Online de Português, https://www.dicio.com.br/Tegu, accessed Feb. 24, 2023. Dicio: Dicionário Online de Português, https://www.dicio.com.br/jaguarundi, accessed Feb. 24, 2023. González, Clementina, et al. *Selection and geographic isolation influence hummingbird speciation: genetic, acoustic and morphological divergence in the wedge-tailed sabrewing (*Campylopterus curvipennis*)*. BMC Evolutionary Biology, Vol. 11, No. 1, 2011 [pampa]. Dicio: Dicionário Online de Português, https://www.dicio.com.br/margay, accessed Feb. 24, 2023.

13.	Freitas, J. F., and J. Mendonça. *Novo tricostrongilideo parasito de Chauna torquata (Oken)(Nematoda)*. Memórias do Instituto Oswaldo Cruz, Vol. 47, 1949.

14.	None. My research didn't uncover Andrade's inspiration for this insect; it seems to first appear in *Macunaíma*.

15.	Oliveira, Mikail Olinda de, et al. *Practical meliponiculture: use of trap boxes to control Tracuá Carpenter ants (*Camponotus atriceps *Smith, 1858), an important natural enemy*. Acta Scientiarum: Animal Sciences, Vol. 44, 2022 [tracuá]. Dicio: Dicionário Online de Português, https://www.dicio.com.br/mumbuca, accessed Feb. 24, 2023.

16.	Camargo, Luis Marcelo Aranha, and Marcello André Barcinski. *Leishmanioses, feridas bravas e kalazar*. Ciência e Cultura, Vol. 55, No. 1, 2003.

17.	Corney, B. Glanvill. *Some Oddities in Nomenclature*. Proceedings of the Royal Society of Medicine: Section of the History of Medicine, 1913.

18.   Dicio: Dicionário Online de Português, https://www.dicio.com.br/canjerana, accessed Feb. 24, 2023.

19.   Dicio: Dicionário Online de Português, https://www.dicio.com.br/uxi, accessed Feb. 24, 2023. Silva, Jonismar Souza da. *Formação de mudas de Ingá-cipó (Inga edulis) e Mulungu (Erythrina fusca) em argissolo vermelho amarelo com omissão de macronutrientes*. Instituto Nacional de Pesquisas da Amazônia, Programa de Pós-graduação em Agricultura no Trópico Úmido, doctoral dissertation, 2014 [guama beans]. Homma, Alfredo, et al. *Bacuri: fruta amazônica em ascensão*. Embrapa Amazônia Oriental-Artigo em periódico indexado, Jun. 2010 [bacuri]. Dicio: Dicionário Online de Português, https://www.dicio.com.br/cupuaçu, accessed Feb. 24, 2023. Ramos, Ana Luiza Coeli Cruz, et al. *Chemical profile of Eugenia brasiliensis (Grumixama) pulp by PS/MS paper spray and SPME-GC/MS solid-phase microextraction*. Research, Society and Development, Vol. 9, No. 7, 2020 [grumixama].

20.   Massapust, Shirlei. *A Lenda dos Tatus Brancos*. Academia.edu, https://www.academia.edu/52317151/A_Lenda_dos_Tatus_Brancos, 2021.

21.   Dario Filho, Luiz Pedro. *Segurança jurídica no ultramar: Domingos Jorge Velho, Conselho Ultramarino e o contrato de guerra aos Palmares*. História Unicap, Vol. 6, No. 12, 2019 [Jorge Velho]. Caruso, Carla. *Zumbi: O último herói dos Palmares*. Callis Editora, 2011 [Zumbi].

22.   Assis Fernandes, Girles de. *O umbuzeiro: descrição, usos e conservação*. Instituto Federal de Educação, Ciência e Tecnologia da Paraíba, post-graduate dissertation, 2021.

23. Brito Mendes, Julia de. *Canções populares do Brazil.* J. Ribeiro dos Santos, 1911 [O Bumba Meu Boi]. Dicio: Dicionário Online de Português, https://www.dicio.com.br/malabar, accessed Feb. 24, 2023.

24. Smyth, W. *Narrative of a Journey from Lima to Para, Across the Andes and Down the Amazon.* John Murray, London, 1836.

25. Brito Mendes, Julia de. *Canções populares do Brazil.* J. Ribeiro dos Santos, 1911.

26. Google Maps, www.maps.google.com, *Guarapes*, accessed Feb. 24, 2023.

27. Bourscheidt, Alvaro A., et al. *Estância Velha/RS - Análise das Cadeias Produtivas e Quocientes Locacionais.* Faculdades Integradas de Taquara, master's dissertation, 2018.

28. Pádua, Vilani Maria de. *Mário de Andrade e a estética do bumba-meu-boi.* Universidade de São Paulo, doctoral dissertation, 2010.

29. Google Maps, www.maps.google.com, *Açu*, accessed Feb. 24, 2023. Pádua, Vilani Maria de. *Mário de Andrade e a estética do bumba-meu-boi.* Universidade de São Paulo, doctoral dissertation, 2010 [original toada].

30. Pádua, Vilani Maria de. *Mário de Andrade e a estética do bumba-meu-boi.* Universidade de São Paulo, doctoral dissertation, 2010.

31. Lima, Carlos de. "Universo do Bumba-meu-boi do Maranhão." *Olhar, memória e reflexões sobre a gente do Maranhão.* Edited by Izaurina Maria de Azevedo Nunes, Comissão Maranhense de Folclore, 2003.

32. Koch-Grünberg, Theodor. *Vom Roroima zum Orinoco.* Vol. II. Verlag Strecker und Schröder, 1924, 92-98.

Chapter XVII

1. Dicio: Dicionário Online de Português, https://www.dicio.com.br/catolé, accessed Feb. 24, 2023.

2. Dicio: Dicionário Online de Português, https://www.dicio.com.br/papiri, accessed Feb. 24, 2023.

3. Cianci, Fernando C., et al. *Clarificação e concentração de suco de caju por processos com membranas.* Ciência e Tecnologia de Alimentos, Vol. 25, 2005.

4. Rocha, Liana Vidigal, et al. *Liga do Cerrado: identificação de elementos da cultura regionalista presentes na HQ tocantinense.* Apresentação de Trabalho/Comunicação, academia.edu, 2010.

5. Mota, Jacyra. *Estrela cadente nos atlas reginais brasileiros.* Revista do GELNE, Vol. 1, No. 2, 1999.

6. Viana, Maria. *Asa da palavra: Literatura oral em verso e prosa.* Editora Melhoramentos, 2016 [Tahina-Can and Imaherô]. Nunes, Eduardo Soares. *A cultura dos mitos: do regime de historicidade Karajá e sua potência "fria".* Revista Antropologia, Vol. 65, No. 1, 2022 [Karajá].

7. None. My research didn't uncover Andrade's inspiration for this character; he seems to first appear in *Macunaíma*.

8. Dicio: Dicionário Online de Português, https://www.dicio.com.br/piroga, accessed Feb. 24, 2023.

9. Viana, Maria. *Asa da palavra: Literatura oral em verso e prosa*. Editora Melhoramentos, 2016.

10. Viana, Maria. *Asa da palavra: Literatura oral em verso e prosa*. Editora Melhoramentos, 2016.

11. Dicio: Dicionário Online de Português, https://www.dicio.com.br/achiote, accessed Feb. 24, 2023.

12. Dicio: Dicionário Online de Português, https://www.dicio.com.br/araponga, accessed Feb. 24, 2023.

13. Teixeira, Dante Martins, et al. *As aves do Pará segundo as" memórias" de Dom Lourenço Álvares Roxo de Potflis (1752)*. Arquivos de Zoologia, Vol. 41, No. 2, 2010.

14. Dicio: Dicionário Online de Português, https://www.dicio.com.br/repiquete, accessed Feb. 24, 2023.

15. Silva, R. Fernandes. *Rotenona, sua extracção e importancia como inseticida*. Revista de Agricultura, Vol. 10, No. 11-12, 1935.

16. The term "nuquiiri" appears only in *Macunaíma*, but Andrade refers to the same body part as "coconuts" earlier in the chapter.

17. Espindola, Haruf Salmen. *Vale do Rio Doce: Fronteira, industrialização e colapso socioambiental*. Fronteiras: Journal of Social, Technological and Environmental Science, Vol. 4, No. 1, 2015.

18. Google Maps, www.maps.google.com, *Minas Gerais*, accessed Feb. 24, 2023.

19. Maynard, Dilton Cândido Santos. *O senhor da pedra: os usos da memória de Delmiro Gouveia (1940-1980)*. Universidade Federal de Pernambuco, Departamento de História, doctoral dissertation, 2008.

20. Dicio: Dicionário Online de Português, https://www.dicio.com.br/caipora, accessed Feb. 25, 2023.

21. Bignotto, Cilza. *Acusado de racismo, Lobato transformou o Saci no primeiro herói negro para crianças no Brasil*. Folha de S. Paulo, Vol. 17, No. 2, 2021.

22. Koch-Grünberg, Theodor. *Vom Roroima zum Orinoco*. Vol. II. Verlag Strecker und Schröder, 1924, 54-55.

Epilogue

1. Pizarro, Jerónimo. *La "Carta pras icamiabas": o la falta de carácter de un héroe imperial*. Revista do Instituto de Estudos Brasileiros, No. 46, Feb. 2008.

About the Authors

Braga-Pinto, César. *A Sexualidade de Mário de Andrade "Ninguém o Saberá Jamais."* Santa Barbara Portuguese Studies. 2nd Ser., Vol. 10, 2022.

Campos, Sheila Praxedes Pereira. *Ainda a Propósito de* Macunaíma*: Leitura Crítica da Correspondência de Mário de Andrade e de seus Amigos a Respeito da Concepção de sua Rapsódia*. Anais do VI Seminário dos Alunos dos Programas de Pós-Graduação do Instituto de Letras da UFF Estudos de Literatura, No. 1, 2015.

Carvalho, Fábio Almeida de. *Makunaima/Makunaíma, antes de Macunaíma*. Revista Crioula, No. 5, May 2009.

Koch-Grünberg, Theodor. *Vom Roroima zum Orinoco*. Vol. II. Verlag Strecker und Schröder, 1924.

Sá, Lucia. *Macunaíma and the Native Trickster*. Brazil Institute Special Report, Nov. 2008.

Silva, Francisco Bento da. *Naturezas e Culturas Amazônicas no Olhar de Mário de Andrade: O Turista Aprendiz Navegando nas Subjetividades e no Surreal*. Jamaxi, Vol. 4, No. 2, Jul.-Dec. 2021.

Professor Dowell's Head
by Alexander Belyaev

It is Paris in the 1920s, that frothy heyday between the World Wars. Hidden among the opulent cabarets, cafes, and theaters, a mad scientist toils away in his own private hospital, illegally performing grotesque experimental head transplants and reanimations on bodies stolen from the morgue. Under the tutelage of the disembodied head of a former colleague, the madman is well on his way to presenting the first-ever human head transplant to the scientific community, thereby achieving professional glory and securing his legacy as the greatest scientific mind of his generation. However, when one of his test subjects escapes, he risks being exposed to the authorities as a deranged criminal before he has a chance to prove that he is exceptional and above the law. Can he find her before she alerts the police? Can he replicate the experiment before his illegal laboratory of living heads is discovered? Will his staff remain loyal as the pressure to save themselves builds? For nearly a century, the answers to these questions have captured the imaginations of countless readers in author Alexander Belyaev's native Russia, where this bestselling novel has sold millions of copies, has been adapted into film, and has influenced a generation of science-fiction writers. This captivating story is now brought to readers of English in this smart translation of Professor Dowell's Head from writer Carl Engel.

Alexander Belyaev (1884-1942), known in his native country as "the Russian Jules Verne," stands as one of the giants of horror and science-fiction literature of the early Soviet era. He is the author of seventeen novels, of which Professor Dowell's Head is both his first and most famous, as well as scores of short stories.

Printed in Great Britain
by Amazon